Deadly Ruse

TINA SAXON

Deadly Ruse

Copyright © 2024 by Tina Saxon

ISBN Special Edition Print: 978-1-7353272-8-0
ISBN eBook: 978-1-7353272-6-6

Cover design by: Hang Le
Alternate Cover design by: Y'all That Graphic
Photographer: Wander Aguiar
Model: Andrew Biernat
Edited by: My Brother's Editor, Making Manuscripts
Proofread by: From Beginning to The End

Prologue

KALI

THIS IS NOT A NIGHTMARE.

Nightmares you can escape.

Thump.

Thump.

Thump.

They always seem to come in three.

I scream and pound on the splintered wood. I know he can hear the fear coiled around my vocal cords. My screams. And each three thumps of dirt are a sign he doesn't give a fuck. He doesn't have any compassion for life.

Especially this one.

Except for one sliver of light between two warped boards near my stomach, I'm engulfed in darkness. In the little room I have to move, I focus my punches there, hoping it's a weak spot and will give before it's too late. The makeshift coffin creaks under pressure as I fall further away from the living and closer to the dead.

My chest heaves as I panic, depleting all the air surrounding me. I'm suffocating. My insides are screaming, my soul on the verge of separating from my body.

Thump.

Thump.

Thump.

"Bastard!" I scream. "Is this how you get off? Burying women alive?"

His labored breaths sound further and further away as he jams the shovel into the earth, and I pray that's not the last human sound I hear. "Please don't do this! I have money! I'll give you all of it!"

I'm only twenty-two, and I have so much life to live. Nothing stops him until he's finished. Until he's satisfied with his job. *Making me disappear.* With a heaving chest and a tear-soaked face, I listen to the only person who can save me drive away.

And then the noisy world I've taken for granted disappears. Silence. I've been swallowed up by the earth. Literally.

Wetness coats my cheeks. Splintered wood mixes with blood on my hands.

My life ends tonight.

Seven days ago, I thought my life was about to begin.

I had a bucket list.

I pull in the deepest breath I can muster and scream the loudest I've ever screamed. *But no one is out there.*

No one is going to save me.

Or even miss me.

It's ironic. I thought winning the lottery would change my life.

I didn't know it would end it.

CHAPTER 1

Kali

One month before I was taken…

"Excuse me, miss, can I get a refill?"

I nod as I pass a table, balancing a tray stacked with dirty dishes. Where the heck is Pearl? That isn't even my table.

"I need my check!" another table yells at me.

My backside meets the swinging door, and I drop the tray on the counter, blowing the loose tendrils of hair out of my face, taking a quick breath. People are out for blood today.

"Has anyone seen Pearl?"

The cooks all shake their heads. *Seriously?* Couldn't she have picked a better time to disappear? We're right in the middle of the lunch rush. I pop my head out the back door, checking to see if she's smoking. She never would at this time, but where did she go? I groan in frustration when I hear the voices growing louder in the dining area.

As I'm about to push back through the swinging doors,

Roberto stops me. I open my mouth to tell the owner of the Wall-flower Diner that now isn't the time. But he beats me to the punch.

"Hey, Pearl's in the backroom, feeling woozy. I'm sending her home. Susie's coming in an hour early, but I'll come out and help clean off tables and run the tabs until she gets here."

I stare at him, needing more information. Pearl never takes off work. She'd come in medicated before she would call in sick. "Is she okay? What's wrong with her?"

He shrugs. "I'm not a doctor. She's really pale and says she feels like she's about to pass out." His nonchalant attitude toward her annoys me.

"Did she eat something bad? Her blood sugar could be low. Do you think she'll be okay going home by herself? Can she even drive?"

"Kali," he says in a firm tone, interrupting my rambling. "I. Don't. Know. And I don't care. She said she'll be fine. She just needs to go home and lie down. And I have a room full of people looking for their server." He points out the door. "Get out there."

Frustrated, I shoot him a narrowed glare, and he responds with a lifted brow, telling me to get moving. I huff, still worried about Pearl, but know he's right. People will only get worse if they have to wait much longer. Within fifteen minutes, we've caught back up, and the crowd thins to just a few tables. I take a peek at the tip tally I keep track of during the day, and despite the exhaustion, I can't help but smile at the better-than-normal numbers.

Making lemonade out of lemons.

"Oh my gosh, please tell me you haven't been sitting here very long," I say, stopping at a booth with a man sitting by himself, looking at his phone. He's in Pearl's section. No drink. No food. Who knows how long he's been here. The stranger looks up from under the brim of his burnt-orange baseball hat and offers a charming smile.

Hello, Mr. Gorgeous. You're not from around here, but will you marry me?

Dark curls peek out from the back of his hat, green eyes and perfectly straight white teeth greet me. Our town sits between two large universities, so college kids pass through frequently, especially during game weekends. This guy...totally fits the part. I imagine he's in one of those fraternities, with girls throwing themselves at him at the incessant parties they have—the ones I overhear the college guys talk about. *Yeah, I'm nosey like that.* I've always wondered when they squeeze in their studies. But this guy, I bet he uses his handsome, boyish good looks to ace his classes.

"Not too long," he responds.

Oh. He has a nice deep voice, too.

"Sorry. We're a little understaffed today."

"No worries. I'm not in any hurry. I've enjoyed watching you."

My eyes widen, and I stand up a little straighter. *Watching me?* He's out of my league, so my internal bullshit meter just popped up. I'm not horrendous. I'd rate myself a solid five. Long, thick, but mousy-brown hair with dull blue eyes, small boobs on a slender frame—*average*. This guy, however, doesn't strike me as someone who settles for average. Not when he can get a *ten*, easy.

"That sounded creepy," he adds, holding up his hand. "What I meant was, you've been working your ass off, so I didn't want to add any more work when everyone seemed to be in a rush to get out of here."

See, he's just a nice guy, it wasn't about me at all. "It's too bad people couldn't be more understanding like you." His boyish charm contrasts sharply with his muscular physique, his shirt stretched tight around his biceps. "Headed back to school?"

"Yep. Went down south to see the family for the weekend."

"Aw, that's sweet. You're a good son."

"I try to be," he says, his words carrying a trace of melancholy. I wonder about the story behind those words. The sadness behind them. But he shakes out of it, and he's back to his boyish grin.

"So, what'll be? It'll be on the house for being so understanding." Translated, I'll be paying for it because Roberto doesn't part with food without a transaction.

"I've heard about the famous cherry pie here. I'll just have a piece of that."

"Um..." I tug on my ear. I've already told at least five people we're sold out for the day. Yet, there is one slice left—the one I put aside for *me*. I deserve it after today's hustle. But you can count on me as one of the people who can be swayed with just a charming smile. I glance around the room and try to recall who ordered a piece. Most people have cleared out. "It's your lucky day. There is one piece left," I say in a hushed tone.

He glances to his left, around me, undoubtedly curious why I'm whispering, then he leans forward. "Is it a secret?"

Think of something witty.

"I guess you haven't heard," I whisper back, leaning forward. "The town has this thing where if an out-of-towner eats the last slice of cherry pie." I cringe, exaggerating by glancing around. "They'll put you in jail."

Really? That's what you thought of? Arrested? Kill me now.

He surprisingly plays along. "What's the charge?"

Shit. Now what do I say?

"Illegally hypnotizing a server because that is the only way you'd get the last piece of pie."

You should've stopped while you were ahead. Horrible, Kali.

He playfully acts serious, narrowing his eyes, then winks. *Yes, he winked at me.*

"Sounds like it's worth the risk," he says.

Okay...the morbidly embarrassing banter was worth the wink.

"Don't say I didn't warn you."

His laughter follows me as I walk away, laughing softly to myself.

Susie catches me exhaling through puffed-out cheeks. "Sweetie, you've got yourself a looker," she says, trailing behind me into the back.

"That he is, but there's only window shopping for this girl," I mutter to myself as I grab my piece of pie from the fridge, placing it on a plate and topping it with whipped cream.

Joe's brows furrow. "I thought you said if anyone touched that, you'd bite their fingers off."

I shrug. "Customers first, right?"

"More like a hot college kid first," Susie adds.

Joe tosses out kissy noises when I walk past him, making the other guys chuckle. *Juveniles.* Before pushing through the doors, I flip them off, causing them to howl in laughter. A flutter of anticipation swirls in my belly, and an unfamiliar giddiness takes me by surprise. I've served countless people before, and I've never been this excited to deliver food to someone. It's sad, but this is the highlight of my mundane week. Possibly a month.

I slide the plate on the table and say, "You better love this. It's about to cost you your freedom."

He looks at it and hums.

It does look amazing, doesn't it? The amount of cherry filling that fills the middle makes this pie amazing—not too sweet, not too tart. And it has the perfect golden crust…

"Wanna sit and share it?"

Yes.

But that would be weird.

I let out an awkward laugh. I can't remember the last time I was this flustered as I look down and straighten my name tag, even though I know it's straight because every morning I pin it at least five times until it's perfect. "That piece of pie is all yours."

He tilts his head, as if he's trying to decipher my thoughts, then he surprises me when he asks, "This was your piece, wasn't it?"

My cheeks flush. "You caught me. It was. But you look like you needed it more than me."

He puts the fork down and nods. "I look desperate, don't I?"

"No, I didn't mean it that way." Way to offend him.

Susie passes me, and we make eye contact. She wags her brows with a smirk while looking at the stranger and me. Thankfully, his back is to her, so he can't see her ogling over him.

"You had heard about our famous pie, and I didn't want you to leave with a poor opinion of the place because then you'd leave a scathing review. Then it'd be all my fault people would stop coming because of one horrible review."

He slowly nods his head. "So, you did it for the restaurant?"

"Exactly."

A few tables over, someone waves at me, forcing me back to reality. I have a job to do. And this poor guy probably wants to eat and leave. By the time I return, after taking care of a couple tables, he's left. I try to hide my disappointment, the silly thoughts flicker —he was flirting or sticking around trying to figure out how to ask me out. But reality sets in—I'm just a small-town waitress with average looks who's stuck in the town you drive through to get somewhere else.

At least he ate all the pie.

When I grab his cash, I spot a handwritten note on the back of the bill.

Thanks, Kali, for a memorable meal. I'd give the meal a four-star, service five-star plus. Hope to see you next time I stop in.

Despite the bitter tinge of disappointment, his words made my day.

See you later, Mr. Gorgeous. Next time, I'll join you.

"KALI," Pearl calls from the dining area, drawing my attention from the cook's window. After the chaos of yesterday, I was relieved to see her walking through the front doors this morning, looking like her crazy normal self. When I called her last night to check on her and tell her about the day, she called it a twelve-hour bug, but I suspected it was her body's way of telling her she needed a break—she's here six days a week, some seven.

I spot her holding a pink box. "Something came for you," she squeals.

When was the last time I received something nice? I know it's been a really long time. Was it the cupcakes my mom made me in third grade? I think it was. In an effort to combat the mean girls at school, Mom thought the sweet treat would help. It didn't. They were just mean girls on a sugar high afterward. Because, sadly, mean girls are always just that. Mean. She used to say, "kill 'em with kindness." Ironic really. She was dead two months later.

I shake the memory from my head. With no family left and the closest friend I have staring at me, the list of people who could have given me this is short.

"What is it?"

"It says it's from West Side Pies," she replies.

I tilt my head. Someone sent me a pie?

I grab the pink box, stamped with huge red letters on top, and unwrap the cellophane. When I lift the top, there's a pie inside. I glance around at the staff, wondering if someone is playing a trick on me because of the guy from yesterday. They would totally do this.

"Okay, who did this?" I chuckle. Everyone shrugs and shakes their heads. I stare at Joe. Him and his kissy-noises ass would do this. "You?"

He barks out a laugh, holding two spatulas in the air. "I wish I would've thought of it. But not me."

"Are you sure this is for me?" I ask Pearl. There's not even a card.

She nods. "That's what the delivery guy said. And he had a West Side Pie shirt on." She pulls out her phone she just bought. I'm still jealous of her new toy. Before, we shared the bond of being the only two people on earth who didn't own a cell phone. It's a luxury item I can't afford at the moment. "I don't know them. Let's look them up."

While she searches, I pull out the pie and find a bifold piece of paper taped to the bottom.

"They're an Austin pie maker. Ohhh…they have over five thousand five-star reviews. They must be good," she says as I detach the letter and open it.

Sorry to duck out so fast. I had to make a quick escape as the local police were closing in on me. Thanks for giving me your last piece of pie. But THIS is the best cherry pie I've ever had. You have to try it. And I promise, you won't go to jail eating the last piece.

A giggle escapes from nowhere. The slightest hint of attention turns me into a human jack-in-the-box. It doesn't take much to wind me up. But I can't help it, the charming stranger from yesterday surprised me with a pie.

A cherry pie.

My favorite.

This is better than flowers.

"It doesn't say who it's from," Pearl says, reading the letter over my shoulder.

He didn't leave his name. Again.

"Remember, I told you about that college guy? It's from him."

"Mm-hmm." She bumps me on the hip with hers. "Susie told me he was super cute. He must've liked you, hon."

I roll my eyes and grab a knife. I'm not holding my breath. "Who wants a piece?"

CHAPTER 2

Kali

Seven days before I was taken…

DO YOU EVER FEEL STUCK?

Where your mind moves on to better, grander, and exciting places, but the body is left behind? Where your feet are stuck in quicksand, and reality slowly swallows those dreams? That's my life. Every day. If only I could escape to the place where my mind wanders off to as soon as my head sinks into the pillow. A place where I have a loving mom and dad. A place where love isn't only a shadow in the past.

The only thing I feel here is stranded. Trapped.

Some people say it's strengthened me, and some people say I was the lucky one. But at the heart of reality, I was alone. I let out a deep sigh and push aside the self-loathing. I try not to pity myself. After all, everyone else in this town has that covered.

"Is everything okay?" Chip asks as I pour his coffee, his eyes narrowing as he studies me, and I force a smile at our breakfast regular and offer a feeble nod. It's nice he cares enough to ask. It makes my shitty day a little less shitty. I'm invisible to most people in this town, an insignificant moment while they catch a quick bite or a coffee during their busy day, so his concern is a welcome change.

I blow my side bangs out of my face, the ones I thought would look cute because it's the trend. However, seventy-year-old Margo doesn't quite grasp the art of trendy cuts. Most days, I end up looking like a mushroom head with my hair pulled back in a ponytail and the side bangs puffing out.

This happens after a cute guy sends you a pie.

A new haircut, painted nails, and an attempt at whitening your teeth with the cheap stuff found at the corner drugstore. But after the hair massacre, I'm glad he hasn't returned. All he'd find now is a mushroom head, half-chipped nails, and forget the white teeth—those strips had me cursing in shooting pain.

"It's been one of those mornings," I groan.

Chip's radio chatters next to his ear, and he tilts his head to the side to listen. I can't imagine being a cop, witnessing the worst of the world and then trying to see the good in people because you can't live thinking everyone is bad. That's a quick way to drown in misery. That's why I make it my mission to make Chip laugh every morning.

But not today. Today, I wish I could crawl back in bed and have a do-over.

"What did the zero say to the eight?" he asks, turning his attention back to me. I twist my lips and hum. I've got nothing. "That belt looks good on you."

"Pretty funny, Chip," I say over my shoulder, pouring coffee for another customer down the bar and chuckling at the total dad joke.

He claps his hands. "I made you laugh," he says from across the room. "It was my turn."

That you did. If only everyone knew how a simple act of kindness can flip a person's bad day with one gesture. Moments later, he drops cash on the counter and waves at me right before he leaves for work.

God, watch over him, I say to myself, looking up. Despite living in a small town where crime rarely happens, *it occasionally does*. You can ask anyone about our town, Blackburn, within a hundred miles in all directions, and the first thing they ask about is the Harpers.

Eighteen years ago, Elizabeth Harper walked in on her husband in bed with their neighbor. She went into a rage, grabbing a chainsaw. I was four, so I only heard the horror stories years after it happened. Gossip says you couldn't tell whose parts were whose by the time she finished. Here's the kicker: the jury found her not guilty for reasons I can't even understand. I want her lawyer if something ever happens to me. She's supposedly living across the country, living her life like she didn't slaughter two people. But yeah, other than that and my parents' accident, our small, sleepy town doesn't see much excitement.

"Looks like you got a little action last night." Pearl wags her pencil-drawn-in brows, wrapping her apron around her narrow hips. "Did a certain college kid find his way back here and have some pie?"

I groan as I pass her, stopping at the drink station to refill some sodas. It's been three weeks, and they're still at it. "You guys will never let me forget him, will you?" She shakes her head. "Sorry to disappoint, but no action here, just the typical curling iron excuse."

That's how my day started—burning the shit out of my neck.

Then, I spilled a full bowl of cereal all over my shirt and tripped on a rock while walking to work, cutting open my knee. I stare down at my worn-out canvas tennis shoes, each scuff and worn thread telling a story of the miles they've covered, my left one now adorned with a new embellishment of dried blood on it. Let's hope bleach will get that out.

The day drags on, and when I think it can't get worse, someone says, "Kali?"

I glance at the table it came from, and there's a stunning platinum-blonde woman sitting alone, waving. I stare at the stranger for a beat. As I approach her table, she leaps up and envelops me in a tight hug. The hug is stiff and awkward.

More like, I'm stiff and awkward.

"Kali, oh my gosh, it's been forever." All I can think is she smells like vanilla, her shirt is soft, and she reminds me of a Barbie doll. If she didn't know my name, I'd say she had the wrong person.

"Hi," I say.

She pulls back and lets out a short, humorous laugh. "You don't recognize me, do you? I mean, it hasn't been that long." I gaze into her bright blue eyes, detecting a glimmer of familiarity, but I'm still having trouble placing her. She dips her chin as if coaxing recognition from me. After a few awkward moments, throwing her arms out, she says "It's Ruth Ann."

My eyes widen in disbelief as they scan up and down her slender frame. Where did the rest of her go? "Wow." Nobody could blame me for not recognizing her. Who would? The last time I saw her, she was heavyset, had messy dark brown hair, and braces. Everyone teased her. *Except me.* I befriended her because I felt bad people treated her worse than they treated me. She left in the middle of our junior year. I hadn't seen her since. "You look… stunning."

"Thanks! I can't believe you're still here," she says, casting a disdainful look around. By around here, she means Blackburn, and her passive-aggressive comment lands with a sting, coming from the one person who I thought would never act superior to me.

Her life growing up wasn't much better than mine. Whispers hinted her mom was a prostitute where she spent most of her weekends in Austin. No one knew for sure, though. Her mom was high most of the time we hung out, and she rarely wore enough clothes to cover her boobs and ass, so it wouldn't have surprised me if it were true. They lived in a double-wide trailer on the outskirts of town, and Ruth Ann's lunch consisted of one peanut butter sandwich and one apple every day. She would always say her mom put her on a diet, but I wondered if it was because they couldn't afford anything else.

She slides back into the booth. "So, who else got stuck here?" I blink at her backhanded slap in the face. "Oh, I didn't mean to sound so rude." *Really? You could've fooled me.* "But you're still here cause you love it."

Now I know she's being condescending.

There are plenty of people who have deep-seated roots here and would never move. I am not one of those people, and every single person within the city limits knows that. *She knows that.* But she ignores my irritation as she launches into a ten-minute monologue about how great her life has been since she left here. Her mom did, in fact, go to jail for prostitution, and that's why she had to move her junior year. She moved in with an aunt she didn't know she had, who ended up being a wealthy purse designer, providing her a life of privilege. Lucky for her. She went to a private school and later to college. Now, she's in law school and only came back to this lousy town—*her words*—to take care of some of her mom's legal matters.

With every passing moment, jealousy coils around me like a suffocating vine. I can't help the twinge of bitterness, not only because of her condescending attitude but also because she escaped this place.

I thought I would too.

Once.

There was one time a family wanted me. My ninth birthday. Peggy Sue, the caretaker of the group home, bought me a light blue dress from the second-hand store that had white lace around the neck, and she did my hair in two braids the day they were coming to meet me. I sat on the bench in the entryway, with perfect posture, my legs crossed like a little lady, and my hands folded in my lap. I waited. And waited. Even with a sore butt from the wooden bench, I didn't move a muscle, afraid they would walk through the doors at any second.

They never came.

They had changed their minds, decided it wasn't a good fit. My already scarred heart was crushed. My nine-year-old self couldn't understand. I was a well-behaved kid, had a kind heart, and I wanted a family so badly it hurt. But in the end, no one gave me a chance to live a decent life like Ruth Ann.

Nothing like the past coming back to shove your misfortunes in your face.

I swallow my contentment and force a grin. "Ruth Ann, I'm—"

"It's just Ann now," she says, interrupting me, still with the plastic smile on her face that has yet to go away. It's like she's auditioning for a teeth-whitening commercial.

"Oh. Well, *Ann*," I reply, overemphasizing her name. "I'm thrilled for you. I always wondered how you were doing after you left." Total lie, but what else do I say? I'm trying to not sound bitter. Even though I am.

Especially today.

Pearl—my hero—notices how uncomfortable I am and makes up an excuse about how I'm needed in the kitchen. Once away from *just* Ann, Pearl asks, "Who's Miss America?"

I let out a bitter moan. "Another example that life gets better for everyone except me."

She looks into my eyes with fierce intensity as she grips both my shoulders. "You listen here, missy," she clips, her words cutting through the noise in the diner. "You are a beautiful, determined young woman who has years left before you reach your peak. This phase in your life, no matter how challenging, is only a stepping stone. It might be a bigger stone than what others face, but you'll climb it, and when you come out on the other side, you'll be better for it."

I take a deep breath, releasing it into a small, appreciative grin. She always knows what to say. "Thanks. Sometimes it's hard for me to see past this point in my life. I feel stuck. And then *just* Ann comes in, flashing her success, throwing in my face what I don't have."

"Hon, don't let someone else's success dampen your journey. Life has twists and turns, and right now you're navigating through a tough stretch. But remember, storms pass, and the sun will shine again on you. And like Dolly Parton said, 'If you *want the rainbow, you gotta put up with the rain.*'"

She's right. I need to snap out of this wave of self-pity. It's not like me to dwell on what I don't have. It's just been one of those days. And as I walk back out, a sense of relief washes over me spotting the empty seat where Ann had sat. I'll take the small wins.

THE SECOND FIVE o'clock rolls around, I'm out of here. I notice Pearl by the front window, staring out. I walk up behind her. "Whatcha looking at?" She jumps, startled. "Sorry, I didn't mean to scare you." I laugh.

"I was watching the storm off in the distance," she says, turning, and we both walk toward the back. "I'm not going to bingo tonight. The last thing I wanna do is hunker down with the town people while a tornado rips through."

I grab my purse from under the counter. "Is it supposed to get bad tonight?"

She nods, grabbing some plates to deliver.

And is it already Friday? My life has become such a routine that days aren't different anymore—a monotonous blur between days and nights. The only exception is Friday nights when I play bingo with the forty-plus crowd. Everyone else my age hangs out at On the Rocks bar. I bet Ann will be there, flaunting that she has morphed from an ugly duckling into a beautiful, successful swan. I'd kind of enjoy seeing the spectacle with all the has-beens still living here. Since she left the diner, and after I got over the initial envy, I realized I was actually happy for her. However, tonight, with a storm brewing, I'd rather stay home, too.

As I walk through the gloomy night, ominous clouds threaten rain during the wettest April we've had in years. My mind drifts to the plans I once had when I left the Stonemeyers' house and the idealistic notion of going to college so my mom would've been proud of me and then getting a career as a flight attendant.

This orphaned little girl wanted to see the world.

And not be trapped in the very town that took my parents. I hate this place. I hate the memories. Every day, I walk three extra blocks to avoid the stoplight the drunk asshole ran when he collided with my parents' car head-on. To see the exact spot where they suffered while they hung from their seat belts in their upside-down car, bleeding from their fatal injuries, makes me want to vomit each time I pass it.

If only I had a car to escape this stifling town. Instead, I'm stuck waitressing at the local diner, making enough to scrape by, never enough to move forward. For four years, I've saved every extra penny I've made in the hope of leaving this town. It isn't much, but soon I might have enough to buy a used car that probably has a million miles on it. Most people who work corporate jobs commute to Austin. My options in town for jobs were limited.

On my way home, I notice the gas station's G in their large GAS sign flickering above the store. I pause, debating if I could splurge a little tonight. A pint of ice cream won't put a huge dent in my budget, and of course, it'll make me feel a lot better. Since I'm not going to bingo, it'll be a wash. *Decision made.*

The door's bell jingles, and Henry, the owner's son, peeks his head around an aisle and grins. "Hey Kali. Surprised to see you here tonight." When I say we live in a small town, I wasn't kidding. Everyone knows what everyone does.

I point outside. "A storm and a crappy day makes Kali a boring girl. Nothing ice cream won't help."

"I get off in an hour. Want some company?"

Occasionally, we hang out, but lately I'm worried his feelings have changed toward me. I like us being friends, and that's it. "Not tonight, I've had the worst day and want to go to bed early," I murmur as I stroll toward the freezer section. He's a cute guy, in a big bear kind of way. He was once the town's prized high school linebacker, who unfortunately had to have reconstructive knee surgery during his senior year, and he decided to stay to help his parents with their business after high school. With the sweetest demeanor, it's hard not to like Henry. But that we've known each other since childhood makes it awkward. He knows my entire life history, and his mom still sees me as the homeless child from fourteen years ago—the town's charity case. I'm hoping his interest will fade and we can go back to being buddies.

He's already waiting for me behind the counter when I plop down the pint of cherry ice cream. He scans it and puts it in a plastic bag. "That'll be three forty-four." I dig out my five-dollar bill, and when I lift my eyes, they land on a bright lottery ticket ad. For a brief second, I think, *what if?*

What are the chances? One in five million? There's still one, right? How about it, God? Maybe do me this one solid?

"Kali?"

I shake out of my plea with God and find Henry holding his hand out for my money. Not giving it another thought, I blurt out, "I'll take a lottery ticket, too."

It's only a dollar. I spend five of them every week at Bingo, and I've never won there, but I keep doing it. His brow shoots up. "I have a better shot at taking you on a date than you winning. You know that, right?"

I laugh. "I won't hold my breath if you don't hold yours."

He snorts, and his cheeks burn red, making me chuckle. "I swear you would've grown out of that." He curses under his breath once and hands me my change and lottery ticket. "It's still cute, though."

He wags his bushy brows. "You think I'm cute?"

"Good night, Henry."

With only two blocks to home, I speed walk, both to prevent the ice cream from melting and to escape the looming rain shower threatening to drench me. I cross the train tracks, hoping the lightning stays distant. Heavy brush lines both sides of the street, and with my luck today, a bolt would strike a tree and land on my head. The pressure in the air gives me a headache, or maybe it's thinking about Pearl's words from earlier.

"It might be a bigger stone than what others face, but you'll climb it, and when you come out on the other side, you'll be better for it." Am I better for it, though? When I think about the successful escapees of Blackburn, it's hard not to succumb to the pangs of failure I feel regularly. *"But remember, storms pass, and the sun will shine on you."*

How I wish the sun would shine on *me* tomorrow.

THE FRESH SCENT of rain from last night and the gentle, cool breeze tousles my hair as I stroll through the apartment parking lot. Today is already better. I can feel it. I draw in a deep inhale, letting Mother Nature wash away any lingering bad vibes. I kick my foot up and smile at my bleaching skills.

Blood is gone, and they live another day.

As I turn the corner, the normally empty gas station parking lot is filled to the max with commotion. A crowd gathers in front of the store, with the only two squad cars in town parked to the right. I squint my eyes to read the side of one van. Channel Eight News. *Oh, my god. Henry.* What if someone robbed him? Or worse, shot him because he tried to fight them off? *He would do that.* But then he walks out the front door of the store with excitement on his face, alongside his family. Cheers erupt, and I let out a breath.

What the heck is going on?

I peek down at my watch and groan. I can't be late two days in a row. What am I worried about? I'll get the scoop the second I enter the diner. Sure enough, the restaurant buzzes with excitement.

"What's happening?" I ask Steve, the line cook today, as I tie an apron around my waist.

He flips a few eggs and shrugs. "Something about the lottery. Didn't pay too much attention as I don't play." He points out to the diner. "It's too early for this much activity. It's like our sleepy town woke up for the first time. It's weird."

"Did someone from Blackburn win the lottery?"

He shrugs again. "I guess."

I dart out of the kitchen, searching for Pearl, and the swinging wooden doors swoosh closed behind me. If there's anyone that knows town gossip, it's her.

"Pearl," I say, rushing toward her. "Did someone win the lottery here?"

"Yes, ma'am," she squeals, grabbing my arm. "This is exciting as a pig in mud!"

"Do we know who won?"

"Not yet. Word is, someone claimed it, but they haven't made it public. Can you believe it? Someone from here could be a millionaire! They better leave us a damn good tip."

The buzz of excitement permeates the diner. Conversations grow louder as people talk to their neighboring tables. Everyone is smiling, which is actually nice to see. Many in Blackburn struggle with the sameness of their lives, so no doubt this will bring some excitement to the community. I think about the lonely ticket on my dresser. Too bad it wasn't me.

MY VOICE IS HOARSE, and a splitting headache pulses at my temples by the end of the day. The incessant chatter about the lottery has filled every corner of the diner. How much the person was going to end up getting after taxes—*four million* dollars—and what said person should do with it.

"I hope to never hear the word lottery again," sighs Pearl. We both lean against the back station, arms crossed, observing the jam-packed restaurant. We've given up trying to keep everyone's cup filled. This unofficially became the hot spot of the day after people left the gas station. Everyone in this freaking town must've taken the day off as if they marked today a holiday. If someone wasn't here, wild speculation was that they were the winner. Nobody wanted to leave, afraid if they did, they'd miss something.

But the missing person would walk in, and the pendulum of speculation would swing to a new guess. The cycle persisted all day. Back and forth, it swung. Roberto issued warnings about loitering, but everyone started ordering drinks so they could stay.

"I hope it'll be back to normal tomorrow," I say, relieved to see our replacements walk through the doors.

"It better. My tips sucked today."

I nod. "Same." When I counted my tips earlier, a pit of panic surged in my stomach. Saturdays are our best tip days. I have rent due next week, and if I have another day like today, I won't be able to cover it. It'll piss me off if I have to dip into some of my savings.

"Bunch of cheapskate busybodies, if you ask me," Pearl barks as we push past the swinging doors.

That's for damn sure.

CHAPTER 3

Kali

AFTER THE DAY I HAD, I wished for nothing more than silence, but there's a tinge of curiosity brewing in my chest. I click on the TV and press zero-zero-eight on the remote. Maybe they'll announce the person who won. It's likely a commuter. With a TV dinner in hand, I settle on the couch to watch the six o'clock news.

I smile to myself when a picture of our small-town gas station pops up. It's the top story. The camera focuses on Henry and his family. They must've been filming when I walked by. He looks great on TV. He's a natural with his charismatic personality. Why he likes me, I have no idea.

I twirl spaghetti around my fork as I listen to him talk about what the store plans on doing with the one percent bonus they get for selling the winning ticket. When the story pans back to the news anchors in the studio, they add, "No one has come forward to claim the money yet, so if you have a ticket, double-check it. Here are the numbers again."

Wait? What?

The screen flashes blue with six white numbers on them. My heart quickens its pace.

Oh, shit. *Slow down!*

I toss aside my TV dinner and rush to find a pen and paper in my junk drawer. Frustrated, I can't find something within reach to write on, I resort to scribbling the numbers on the palm of my hand before they disappear from the screen.

"No way," I whisper to myself, walking back to the bedroom, staring at the numbers on my hand. I draw a deep breath, swiping the ticket off the table. With the ticket in my right hand, I uncurl my left hand and start comparing the numbers.

03

"Yes!" I made five dollars! At least it paid for my ticket.

10

"Ha! Two numbers!" I'm a millionaire. Not.

25

Three numbers! This is going to be a horrible letdown.

40

"Oh my god." My voice escalates with four numbers.

55

"Holy hell."

29

I freeze. I can't breathe. All six numbers. That perfectly match.

Panic and excitement collide, sending me into a frenzy. My hyperventilating turns into screaming and jumping around my tiny apartment, my shouts filling every corner, "Oh my god. Oh my god! *Oh. My. God!*"

A firm knock at the door snaps me out of my hysteria. I swing it open, looking crazed, with a grin plastered across my sweaty face. I attempt to contain it. "Hey, Murphy."

He peers at me, his brows knitted and his glasses perched low on his nose. He leans over to look past me. "You're not supposed to be having a party after nine." Even his typical squeaky voice doesn't bug me. Lucky me having the manager of the apartment building be my neighbor. "The rules were very specific when you moved in here."

I blow out my bangs hanging in my face. "Sorry. I just…got

some good news." His gaze darts to my hand where I'm holding the lottery ticket. I yank it behind me, hoping he couldn't tell what it was. "I'll keep the noise down."

"Yeah, you do that," he grunts, already turning to leave.

"Wait, Murphy, can I borrow your phone for a sec?"

"When are you going to get your own phone?" He sighs, yet he fishes it out of his pocket. Real soon. I promise you.

I hold up a finger and shut my front door. He grumbles on the other side about taking his phone. "I'll be just a minute." I can't help but let the corners of my mouth twitch upward, barely containing my excitement. Leaning against the door, my heart pounds against my chest as I dial Pearl's number.

She answers on the second ring. "Murphy, what in the world are you doin' calling me this late?"

Does she have everyone's number on her phone? "Pearl, it's Kali. I need you to come over. Like right now."

"GIRL, WHAT IS BURNIN'" in your britches that you made me put on a bra again and come all the way over here? You know how much I hate this thing," Pearl says, strolling in. She startles when I let out a loud squeal. I throw a hand over my mouth to stop myself, imagining Murphy's ear glued to the other side of the door, knowing Pearl is here. "Girl, what has gotten into you? I haven't seen you this happy since…well, ever.

"Promise me you won't scream. Murphy's probably listening."

She waves her finger in front of my face. "I'm not the one having a problem holdin' screams in," she teases.

I blow out a breath and shake out my hands, trying to control the frenzy inside me. "I won," I whisper-yell. She blinks, confused. I still keep my voice low when I say, "I won the lottery."

"Say what, sugar? I don't think I heard you right."

I pull out my lottery ticket from my back pocket and show her the numbers written on my palm. Her eyes jump from my hand to the ticket, then she looks up. Her eyes are the size of saucers.

"It was you," she quips, but then she repeats it with higher octaves in excitement. "It was you!" We both jump up and down, screaming. The adrenaline pumping through my veins is a rush I've never felt before.

Pearl knocks over a lamp, and it shatters on the vinyl floor. "Oh my! My tush did a little more push than I thought!"

"It's okay." I laugh, grabbing her hands and pulling her back into my celebration, bouncing up and down. "I'll buy another one!" *Because I can freaking afford it.*

I'm not surprised at the pounding on my door. Pearl rolls her eyes, and we simultaneously scream, "Go away, Murphy!" We hold our breath, listening for a few moments, expecting more pounding, but to our surprise, it stops.

We both fall back onto the couch, sweaty and giddy. Shock slams into me, quick and fast. She's still squealing as my rush comes to a complete stop. She rolls her head toward me, her laughter fading. "You didn't have a heart attack on me, did ya?"

I stare ahead at nothing in particular. "I won. Me, the unluck-iest person ever, won."

"Honey, you deserve this." She grabs my hand and squeezes. "Like I said yesterday, you had to wait out your storm. It's your time to shine." My thoughts jump to *just* Ann. How I wish I could thank her for adding to my horrible day, enough to push me to buy a lottery ticket. "Have you thought about what you're going to do with it? What are your dreams?"

"I haven't gotten past the part that this small piece of paper"—I hold up the ticket—"is worth four million dollars." We lean our heads against each other's and stare at it in silence. My mind slows, and everything I've ever wanted comes within reach. I exhale and tilt my head toward her. "I'm going to college."

She jerks back, and her lips pucker like she popped a lemon in her mouth. "College? Sugar, you should be dreaming about what beach you're goin' to be on, drinking one of those fancy cocktails out of a pineapple, and lookin' for a sexy man with a fancy yacht."

I laugh, shaking my head, not surprised at all that her dream includes a man. "I'll travel someday. Not now. I'm going to move to Austin and go to college. Buy a new car. I want to experience the life I missed out on. Traveling the world will come after."

She rolls her eyes. "I guess if that's what will make you happy," she says in a breezy tone. "So, Austin, huh? You goin' to look for Mr. Pie Guy?"

"Not him again," I say, elbowing her in the side. "Austin is a big city. I doubt I'll ever see him again."

"If it's meant to be, it'll be," she singsongs.

It's my turn to roll my eyes. Despite all her failed marriages, she still loves love. I'd expect her to be bitter, warn me to stay away from the heartbreak, but she's a romantic at heart.

I jump up, running to the kitchen, watching my steps, so I miss the broken ceramic pieces from the lamp. I'll clean it up later. There's no better reason to pop open, or rather, twist open, a bottle of wine. I giggle when I grab two red solo cups—a millionaire at her finest—and pour a heavy amount into each cup, taking a heavy whiff of one while walking back to the living room. I swirl it around, practicing the movement for the future. I'm almost certain all millionaires drink wine like this.

"Cheers, friend," I say, handing her a cup.

"Cheers to a new journey," she replies, tapping my cup. We both take a long drink. The wine's warmth spreads through me. *A new journey.* Suddenly, nerves tickle my tummy. The idea that everyone will find out about my winnings makes me finish the wine and pour another cup. I down that one too.

"Whoa there, Nelly." She laughs, taking the bottle from my hand and filling her cup up. She places the bottle on the side table. "This is a celebration. Not a race to see who can throw up first."

I freak out and pace the room. "I don't want anyone to know."

"Why not? You need to be more like *just* Ann." I chuckle when she refers to her like I do. "Go rub your fortune in their stuck-up noses."

I shake my head. "I just want to leave town without all the hoopla. I don't want to be the center of their gossip. They'll all act like my friends, making up stories about knowing me, or worse yet, start telling the world about my parents dying and the road I had to take to get here. I am not giving people a chance for their five minutes of fame." People I looked at for help at my lowest—who looked the other way—don't deserve to have a part of me at my highest.

Or richest.

She sighs but then nods. "Can I at least watch you quit? Tell Roberto to shove the job up his ass?"

"You're horrible. Roberto is not that bad." Roberto could be a stuffy jerk, but mostly, he's been a decent boss. After all, he hired me when most of the town looked the other way when I was searching for a job. The five-thousand-dollar insurance policy my parents left me when I turned eighteen didn't stretch too far, but it allowed me to find a place of my own. "I'll give my two weeks. My story is going to be that I've saved up enough to move."

"You're a much better person than me," she teases. "I'd be shakin' my hiney while I was wavin' around hundred-dollar bills and high-tailing it out of this crappy judgmental town. Peace out, bishes." I laugh, imagining Pearl doing just that.

Her questions about dreams stir up a memory. *"Ladybug, you can be anything you want if you follow your dreams."* My mom's words come back to me, and there's a warmth inside me. It's been a long time since I've remembered her words. We were lying on a pool float, staring up at the sky, when a plane flew right over us. I told her I wanted to live on a plane and fly all over the world. *"That sounds amazing. Just make sure to go to college first."*

Mom, that's exactly what I'm going to do.

CHAPTER 4

Kali

Four days before I was taken…

Do you know how hard it is to keep a million-dollar secret?

A million times hard.

Sleep became a distant memory. Nothing could silence the relentless churning of my brain. Counting sheep turned into a bizarre dance of dollar bills with arms and legs, illuminated by disco lights and the song "She Works Hard For the Money" by Donna Summer playing in the background. Basically, I hosted a rave in my head all night. I should be a zombie this morning after a night of insomnia, but the adrenaline coursing through my veins is like an IV drip of caffeine.

Yesterday started out with a bad wine hangover, then I ended up spending the afternoon at our small local library searching the internet. From searching how to claim the prize to colleges in the area to compiling lists of the top ten things lottery winners buy, my notes filled page after page. By the time I finished, I was in a mountain of debt.

Might have to cross some things off.

As directed by the back of the ticket, I signed it, putting more effort into writing my name than I've ever done before and hiding it in my bra. Nestled in the pocket with the padding. Since no one, other than myself, has even seen my bra in years, it's safe to say no one will find it. I don't think I'll ever again wear a bra in my life that will be worth four million dollars.

At least it's what I overheard Sam estimate the other day in the diner, after taxes that's the cash payout for eight million. He's an accountant, so he must know what he's talking about. Of course, I'm taking the cash payout.

The morning sun inches above the diner, and I stop and stare from across the street at the bright red roof and turquoise sign. The charming diner with a fifties flare looks different today. Everything feels different. Maybe because I'm not here to work since I have the night shift, but I'm putting in my notice. Or maybe anticipating the money, not yet in my bank account, has given me a fresh pair of eyes.

The promise of opportunities to come.

With a bounce in my step and giddiness, I skip into the diner.

Okay, Kali, chill.

I inhale and exhale slowly to calm the rush of nerves. I've rehearsed my story all morning. It's a plausible story. Everyone knows I can't wait to leave this place.

Pearl bites down on her growing excitement when she sees me walking through the front door. "Honey, you here to do the *thing*?" She does a little dance in place, more excited I'm quitting than anything.

"I'll miss you the most," I say, putting my head on her shoulder.

"Well, I won't miss you at all," she quips, her southern drawl heavier than normal. Which either means she's drunk or lying. She playfully pushes me toward Roberto's office. "You have some business to take care of. And I'm not ready to cry yet, so get your hiney movin'."

Yep, I'll miss her the most.

Roberto took my resignation letter with zero questions and little emotion. "Good luck," he says before turning back to his computer. When I stare at him, expecting more, he adds, "Do you need anything else?"

Yeah, how about a "I hate to see you leave. You're one of my best employees."

I hold up a finger. "Actually, my last day will be Friday." If he's going to act like I meant nothing, then he won't mind if I leave early. I gave him two weeks to find someone to replace me because I've always heard that is what you're supposed to do.

He shrugs without looking up.

This played out differently in my head. He begged me to stay. Offered to give me a raise. Of course, neither would've made me change my mind, but at least I'd have felt validated. I've worked here for five years. That's half a freaking decade longer than most people have worked here, and I got a casual *"don't let the door hit ya on the way out."*

Whatever. His cold shoulder can't spoil my high.

I turn to leave. "It's not like I need the money anymore," I mumble under my breath as I leave his office. Good riddance.

I pull out my short list of things I need to do before I move, which is sooner than I originally had planned. No reason for me to stay two more weeks now. First thing is to open a PO Box. I can't list a forwarding address because I don't know where I'll end up. The uncertainty adds a layer of anxiety and excitement.

As I pass the neighborhood boutique store, I stop and stare in. Trendy clothes, hats, and cute knickknacks for the kitchen. I've been here a million times, looking through the window, but this time I pull the door open. A gust of cold, sweet-scented air greets me. It smells like flowers mixed with something else I can't place.

It smells expensive.

A soft threaded red blouse glides through my fingers, and the price tag of fifty dollars dangles off the armhole. I saw this shirt on a mannequin last week, and I made a mental note to look for it at the second-hand store later in the year. Plenty of times I've found clothes from this place that, a year later, pop up on the racks there.

I pass by this place twice a day, to and from work, and I've only ever been in here once. Not as a customer—because I could never afford to shop here—but to hand the owner mail delivered to the diner by mistake.

A palpable unease settles over me the more I look around, aware of the judgmental stares from the sales associate. Ignoring her fixated gaze, I walk back to the silky top. It's calling my name.

"That would look amazing on you."

I just threw up in my mouth.

My eyes lift to Hobie Prackett. I resist the urge to roll my eyes as I respond, my tone devoid of any attempt at a polite smile. "Mayor Prackett. That's slightly inappropriate."

Considering he was my foster father at one point.

He shrugs dismissively. "You're an adult now." I shake my head in utter disgust. He takes two steps so he's inches away from me. "I just wish it would've been me sinking into your wet pussy that night." I gasp in horror, wanting to put distance between us, but I freeze from shock at his disgusting words.

"You sick, sick bastard," I whisper-hiss, not wanting to cause a scene. I know how this would turn out if I did. No one would believe their coveted town mayor could be so vile.

The warmth of his voice in my ear makes me flinch. "That's right, Kali. I am a sick bastard, but you're the town slut. And a beautiful one at that. You should come over later. I'll make it worth your while. You'd be able to buy that shirt." His gaze travels over me, leaving a trail of filth.

Tears form, and I blink them back. *Don't you dare cry for this man.* Why is he doing this? How can he be so hateful? The plastic hanger breaks in my palm. The snap is the jolt I needed. A jolt to wake the hell up and remember why I'm here, shopping.

Because I have money. And with money comes power.

God, I'd love to smear my winnings in his face.

"I suggest you take a step back, Mayor, or I'll be your worst nightmare. If you thought I dragged your good name in the dirt before, just wait. You have no idea how much power I have now. And I'll use every bit of it to take you down."

His face hardens with anger mixed with a layer of confusion. I lift a brow with a sense of confidence I've never had. *Where did this girl come from?* I haven't slept around since I was eighteen. Everyone knows I'm not the same wild child I used to be.

"And never talk to me like that again."

I spin around, not giving him a chance to respond. The sales associate probably saw the entire interaction, but from her point of view, with our backs to her, we were just talking. She lifts a brow with a questioning expression as I stride to the register and place the shirt on the counter.

She looks down and huffs. "You broke a hanger? Do you know how much those cost?" she says with a snide tone as she takes the shirt off the broken hanger and starts to hang it on another one.

"I'd like to buy that," I deadpan, stopping her in her tracks.

"Oh." Her cheeks blush as she slides the hanger back off. Her eyes dart past me for a beat before she rings me up. I glance over my shoulder, and Hobie stands at the door with a perplexed expression.

That's right, asshole, I can buy my own damn shirt.

Thankfully, by the time my new shirt is bagged, the mayor is gone. As I walk home with the bag in hand, I can't help but think back to my time with Hobie. He took me in when I was twelve. The year he became mayor. I was a pawn in his election, a way to show his constituents he cared about the residents and how he wanted to give an orphaned girl from this very town a privileged life. Young, attractive, single man taking in a child. To say women loved him was an understatement.

That was all part of his plan.

He hired a full-time nanny the second I dropped my black plastic bag of belongings on the bedroom floor, and the only time he showed me attention was when we were out in front of people. I hated him. I craved attention from the one man who took me in, who was supposed to be a father figure. Hobie didn't want to give me attention, so I found it in other places. He walked in on me having sex with an eighteen-year-old.

I shudder, thinking about his comment, *wishing it was him.*

I was fourteen.

Eventually, he said my extracurricular activities were affecting his career. In other words, he didn't want to deal with me anymore. He made it sound like he had no choice but to send me back to the group home. People didn't fault him because I was a troubled child, and no matter how stable a home he gave me, I needed help beyond his ability. I was painted as the town trash.

By the time I force the key into my apartment, I can't shake his words off. Hobie's breath is like a layer of ash from a fire on my skin. It burns. *"I just wish it would've been me sinking into your wet pussy that night."*

Fuck.

I always wondered how long he'd been watching us. He said he had just walked in, but he made no noise. By the time we saw him, we had finished. Steve rolled my naked body off his chest, and that's when we saw him standing in the doorway, arms crossed with a stoic expression. Steve jumped up and ran out. Hobie said nothing. Just turned around and left.

I retch, thinking about what he might have done after leaving the room. *Stop!* I yell at myself, not wanting to imagine him with a bottle of lotion and thoughts of a child.

Because that is what I was.

CHAPTER 5

Kali

WELP. My luck didn't change at bingo.

Typical Friday night.

Except tonight, I didn't mind dropping money for nothing in return. I even splurged for an extra card, drawing the skeptical gazes of those around me. A chorus of unspoken questions lingered in the air, as if my buying an extra card was noteworthy, and curiosity about the means of my departure. I shrugged off their questions and replied, "I'm feeling lucky." However, nobody questioned if I had won the lottery, as if the tragic girl could ever receive such luck. I don't blame them, though, since it's still hard for me to believe.

The slight sting of loss I felt leaving the old converted warehouse was surprising. My last Friday night here. *I can't possibly miss this. Can I?* I shake my head, determined not to admit that some of these people have wormed their way into my heart. A family I didn't choose and don't want, damn it. After the incident with the mayor, I didn't think I'd miss anything around here.

Well, besides Pearl. And making Chip smile.

She begged me to let her drive me to Austin, but I don't want to inconvenience her. Instead, I'm taking a bus to Austin, and I'm not taking anything with me. All my second-hand clothes were bagged up, except one tiny suitcase of necessities, and stuffed in the donation box in the grocery store parking lot on the way to bingo. This is the fresh start I've always wished for.

Tomorrow morning, my life starts over at ten when the bus leaves.

I push the melancholy thoughts from my head and replace them with excitement for Monday. The day I become a millionaire. A shot of energy rushes through me, and I shiver, dancing in the street.

I've lost count of the times I've checked the ticket, verifying the numbers, expecting to have transposed two digits, and this is all be a horrible mistake. Because that would be my non-luck. But every time is the same.

I won the lottery.

Of course, it'll be weeks until I see the money in my bank account, but between my credit card and the money I have saved up, there's enough to get me through the next few weeks.

As I pass the convenience store, I debate going and saying goodbye to Henry. There's no possible way he hasn't heard by now that I'm leaving. I've kept my distance from him this week, expecting he'd want to talk about the lottery. He knows nobody has come forward. He also knows I bought a ticket. I could try to lie, but with my runaway mouth, the moment he asked about my ticket, I'd spill the truth. So far, Pearl has kept her promise of secrecy, and I'd like to keep it to just her. I'll just send him a goodbye note instead.

My steps slow as the store's lights fade behind me, and the street in front of me darkens. I tilt my head, looking to my left and right. *Is it always this dark?* Just a block from my apartment, I wonder if the moon is hiding behind clouds. I'm close enough to my apartment building I can see a checkered pattern of lights from inside homes. But where I'm at right now, eerie blackness surrounds me. The tall trees don't help.

Focused on my building ahead, I quicken my pace, determined to shake off the odd sensation. I glance around. It's only ten o'clock at night, and off in the distance, there are a couple of car horns, probably coming from the On the Rocks bar. It's only a few blocks away from here, and some of the guys like to show off their new bullhorns. It's as if they're comparing the size of their dicks.

I keep my eyes wide open, and that's when I see it. A broken light at the tracks. *See. Nothing to worry about.* That's why it's dark. It must've burned out. I let out a sigh of relief and release the tension in my shoulders, slowing my pace.

I've never been scared of the night, but rather found peace in it. It's the time when all the judgmental townspeople are tucked away in their beds. It's also where I found trouble.

The fun kind. Boys, drinking, and parties.

My nights of wild parties are in the past and are now spent by myself on the roof of my building, sipping on a glass of wine from a box, but I still find peace when the moon is out. That's what I need tonight. A glass of wine and an eighties playlist.

Yep, it's the perfect going-away party.

I sing "Step by Step" by New Kids on the Block as I put one foot in front of the other, dancing in the street. I hop over the train tracks. I'm not an eighties baby, but there were sisters in the group home who had a crush on Joey McIntyre and would listen to them nonstop.

I feel the prick first.

My hand jerks to my neck. *What the hell stung me?*

A hand wraps around my mouth, and I'm forced back against a solid body. Panic claws up my throat as I scream into a gloved palm and writhe against his tight hold. His muscular arm holds my arms in place, so I kick back, hitting air at first but then connecting once to a shin. The man moans, but it doesn't deter him. Instead, his fingers curl tighter over my mouth, sending shooting pain down my jaw. Seconds pass, and my vision blurs. My legs feel like they are stuck in cement as I try to kick more. I focus on the lights in my building, determined to stay awake, but they slowly fade until my entire world goes black.

CHAPTER 6

Kali

Present day…

THE UNIVERSE HOLDS its breath as if time itself has frozen in this moment. There are no sounds. No lights. Nothing but black space surrounds me. Time has stopped between the space of heaven and hell. I'd say I was in hell, but you have to be dead to be in hell.

And I'm very much alive.

In the timeless void, there's nothing to do but think. My memories, still blurry, are likely due to whatever drug was jabbed into my neck. *I was walking home, and it was darker than normal. Did he shoot out the light? Where did he come from? Was he waiting for me? Why me? How long was I out?*

Question after question gnaws at my insanity, leaving me with an unsettling sense of unease. Again, I try kicking. Screaming. Punching. And then I scream some more until it feels like shards of glass are tearing through my throat.

"I'm sorry," I cry out, the words echoing into the emptiness. Not to him, he's not there. But I want to right all the wrongs I've ever done. The one time I stole a candy bar from Mr. Bane or the one time I told my mom that I didn't eat all the Pringles and blamed it on Dad. I'm even sorry for ruining Hobie's image by sleeping around, despite his awful words to me. I'm sorry to Henry. I should've given him a chance. We might have fallen in love and had a happy life. I'm sorry to Pearl for leaving her. And I'm sorry to God for asking for such a self-serving gift.

I close my eyes and concentrate on my breathing, allowing my body to drift into the void. The four walls around me blur as I send a silent prayer that I'll go fast. The realization that I'm going to die has killed the fight inside me. I'm already a corpse

waiting for the heart to give up. Numbness spreads through me, the tears have dried up, and the pain in my fingers and legs from trying to claw my way out throbs.

A song I haven't sung since my mom was alive pops into my head. The song she would sing to me at bedtime to put me to sleep.

She's calling me.

The words come out in a hum as I drift off to sleep.

I'm coming, Mom.

CHAPTER 7

Paxton

"Good job, Riggs," Lieutenant Cruz exclaims, bending over and giving him a hearty rub.

I shake my head in mock dismay. "How is it that whenever we take down a suspect, he's the one who always gets the praise? I had to sprint a fucking mile to catch the asshole."

"Turner, you want me to rub your head too?"

I lean my head to the side, grinning. "If that's the only way to get praise out of you, I'll take it," I say. He rolls his eyes and turns away. Riggs barks once, and I look down at him, shrugging. "He likes you better than me."

"Good job, Turner. Take the rest of the day off," Cruz yells over his shoulder before disappearing into his office. I laugh out loud. That's nice of him, considering today is supposed to be my day off. I should've been at the ranch already, but a five-in-the-morning phone call saying they had lost the suspect and needed me and Riggs stat, put a wedge in my plans. Usually, we're out the door by six in the morning, heading to the ranch to get an early start.

The pep in my step isn't the praise, it's because we took down one of the top-level sex traffickers in the area. He thought he was untouchable. He was touched today.

By Riggs's sharp teeth.

Rolling out behind a desk on his chair, my buddy Liam remarks as I pass him, "Damn, Pax, I saw a video of you jumping over a fence."

The fence was taller than I thought. I'll be rolling out my hamstrings tonight. Knowing there's a video, it's a good thing I cleared it. That's one meme that would've been stuck with me for decades.

"Track high jump king still has it," I reply, a grin spreading across my face as I pump my fist in the air. Riggs's gait is light as he trots next to me with his head held high. *Buddy, you're getting a steak tonight.* I find an empty communal desk and sink into the chair. Riggs takes his spot right beside me, and as I wait for the file online to load for the dreaded paperwork that comes with a day like today, I reward him with a rub behind his right ear, his favorite spot. His tongue rolls out in contentment.

"Hey, Paxton." A voice interrupts my post-operation duties. When I glance up, Lucy's leaning on the half wall of the cubicle. She's a relentless court clerk with a knack for pursuing officers. Unfortunately, she's set her sights on me.

A practiced smile masks my true thoughts. "Hey, Lucy."

"I'm glad you grew out your beard." I nod, keeping my focus on the computer. I had been hoping she preferred the clean-shaven men, considering that's when she seemed to notice me. "Where were you last night? I called you."

This conversation wouldn't be so awkward had I given her my number. But I didn't. It's clear she used the department system to find my information because I know there isn't a soul here who would have handed it over to her without being blackmailed.

I turn in my chair, dropping the smile. "I was busy with stuff."

"Too busy to answer your phone?" she presses. *What is with this woman?*

My brow raises at her persistence. "Look, Lucy, I'm not interested." I opt for direct. Riggs raises his head, watching her. As a fully trained K-9 for Austin PD, he's been my partner for three years. *Couldn't have been assigned a better one.* And today, he most definitely proved his worth.

Lucy's gaze shifts down to Riggs, and then her eyes bounce around the surrounding cubicles before returning to mine. Her cheeks redden, and she crosses her arms as if I offended her. "Is that what you think? I'm interested in you? I called to see if you could fill out some paperwork that was missed in the Olsen file."

At ten at night? Right. She's a court clerk, and her work ends the second she clocks out. At five. And every officer within earshot knows that as well.

"Well, I'm here now. I'd be happy to fill it out."

She huffs, frustrated she'd been caught, and I called her out on it. "It was an oversight on my end. I thought you missed something. But I was *not* calling because I like you." With that, she spins in place and storms down the hallway.

Detective Cates, who we helped this morning, takes her spot, shaking his head. "Remind me to stay away from that one," he comments.

I nod in agreement, aware that with Lucy you don't have to do anything to gain her attention.

"Anything exciting going on this weekend?"

"Just the ranch." Riggs's snout jerks in my direction. Yeah, buddy, I know. The ranch is his heaven. He can run with the cows, horses, and every other creature he can find, then cool off in the lake, acting like the wild and crazy dog that is trapped inside his rigid, demanding head.

I have to admit, it's mine too.

Someday, I'll retire there.

"Want any company? I could use a weekend of getting out of town."

I rub my beard. Any other weekend, I'd be game. "After the month we've had trying to get this guy, I just want to be alone. Decompress. Enjoy the outdoors. But next time, you're on."

Cates is good company, and I know he has his own reasons for wanting to escape the city—he's going through a nasty divorce—so I feel bad for declining. But for my own mental health, I need my own space this weekend.

"I get it. Enjoy the weekend. You've earned it."

"Same, man."

Forty minutes later, it's a definite sense of relief when I drop off the paperwork on Chief's desk. Riggs and I are off duty. I flick my wrist to see it's only eight o'clock in the morning. Only two hours late.

Fresh country air swirls around us as we speed down the winding road. Riggs, with his nose in the air, catches whiffs of various scents, and he can't contain his excitement, swinging from window to window. As we approach the ranch, Riggs's whines grow louder, telling me to speed up.

"Soon, bud, soon."

He barks, telling me it's not soon enough. I agree. Nothing beats days at the ranch.

My dad built the cabin back in the eighties, and I can still recall our summers here. The mornings were filled with boring chores, but Jack and I hurried through them to get to the fun stuff—shooting, fishing, swimming in the lake, and hunting for snakes and rabbits. Even with the seven-year age gap between us, we were best friends. We'd be out until we were called in for dinner. Then s'mores around the campfire, where Mom and Dad would dance around and we'd make disgusting noises at them when they'd kiss, but really, everything was perfect.

Until it wasn't.

Until...everything changed.

I was eleven.

Soon after, my mom lost her will to do anything. Dad and her divorced, the grief was too difficult on their marriage. And I moved between homes, living with a lifeless mother and a suffering father. It wasn't a year later, after their divorce was finalized, that he had an aneurysm and died. Apparently, it is a quick and painless way to die. *So I was told.*

For five years, the ranch stood abandoned, alone with his memories and empty rooms. I vividly remember my eighteenth birthday. *The day my life changed its course...again.* The vibrating phone in my back pocket, the weight of a gun in my hand, its barrel pointed at my stepfather's unconscious head. He was out cold, and I was about to destroy both our lives.

He didn't deserve to live.

But I couldn't ignore the buzzing. It would stop. And then start again. Frustrated and unable to ignore the persistent call any more, I slipped out of his room and took the call.

That day, my dad intervened from the grave and saved my life. He'd deeded the ranch to me. Unfortunately, it saved my stepfather's life too. He never knew how close to hell he was. It's where he belongs. I left my mom the next day and never turned back. We haven't talked since.

Don't care to start.

I shake off the unwelcome memories as I put the Jeep into park. Riggs seizes the opportunity, leaping out the back window and dashing toward the lake in hopes the ducks are there.

Crossing the threshold, I drop my bag, and a smirk of satisfaction plays on my lips. There's a surge of pride every time I walk into the house. I left the bones of the house my dad built, but the overhaul was all me. Five years of neglect turned into a complete renovation. I got a job in town with a construction crew when I was eighteen and learned every skill I needed to rebuild this place. It's been a slow grind, slowed even more by college, work, and a two-year flop of a relationship, but now I'm damn close to finishing.

I can't wait to fill the space with a family.

As if on cue, the bones of the house creak and I chuckle. "I'm working on it, Dad. You'd like this one."

There is a woman. It's too early to put a finger on how I feel about her when I know next to nothing about her. But there's an undeniable pull—an attraction—that's got me intrigued. Now, I need to find a way to get closer. Scratch that, I found a way. I just need to take it a little further.

A single whistle has Riggs charging toward me, dripping water with every shake. I cover my coffee cup to avoid a mix of lake water and dog. "Find you some ducks?" He hangs his head in disappointment.

The porch swing creaks as I sit on it. I lean back and attempt to relax. Other than the annoying mockingbird messing with Riggs, the morning spring air is still. Peaceful. Exactly what I need. I slip my hat over my face and close my eyes.

Really, Riggs?

"Stop whining," I say without moving a muscle. He does it again. Sometimes, I wonder who has who trained. "Dude. We'll go after my nap. Chill. She'll still be there."

CHAPTER 8

Kali

THE CONFINED space feels like a tomb. "I don't want to die," I cry out, continuing to pound my shredded knuckles into the hardwood. I turn over and try to push with my back against the top. It doesn't budge.

Where am I?

Who did this?

Why me?

I flip back over. The air is thick and wet, each breath a struggle. *How long have I been down here?* I was surprised to wake up, still alive. I lick my dry, chapped lips. The quiet, deathly silence amplifies the sound of my heart.

Someone has to find me. Right?

Does anyone even know I'm missing?

I freeze. What was that?

A sudden wave of terror grips me like a vise as a crawling sensation moves up my calf, like tiny little feet moving in unison. Eight of them, to be exact. My screams bounce off the closed-in walls as I thrash around, my bare legs colliding and scratching the wood to kill the supposed spider rather than just kick it off.

More tingles.

"I'm not dead! You can't eat me yet!" I scream, the words echoing with a mixture of defiance and desperation. Sweat or tears burn my cheeks. It's hard to separate them at this point.

Calm down, Kali. It's all in your head. There's nothing in here with you. If I say it enough, I'll believe it, right? With heaving breaths, I squeeze my eyes shut, repeating the reassuring words aloud. The tingles fade, leaving behind a cocktail of emotions—anger and, now, embarrassment.

"Noooo!" I exclaim, my hand reaching for the middle of my shorts at the apex of my legs. I'm met with wetness. Urine soaks my panties and shorts. The acrid scent mingles with the already foul odor of dirt and blood. "Don't throw up," I whisper, swallowing back the sour taste rising in the back of my throat.

How much longer can I take this? Minutes? An hour?

Everything is so...dark. *Cold.*

"Please, God. Send someone to save me."

"Just count," a sweet, haunting female voice urges, not my own.

My head jerks from side to side. *Mom?* Her voice, long absent from my life, resonates in my mind.

"Who said that?" I ask, but the void offers no response. "Count what?"

I'm losing my mind.

Taking a deep, steadying breath, I comply with the mysterious voice. Hearing her voice after each number, I focus on a happy memory with my parents. I have four years of memories that I've not thought about in a long time. It hurt my heart to let my mind go there. I had to suppress those feelings to move on, and before I knew it, they were nothing but a distant memory. I regret having to do that, but I was a kid, left behind in a messed-up world with no direction. But now, in this desperate moment, I want nothing more than to let their memories wash over me like a bittersweet tide.

"Four."

I chuckle through the fear, reliving one of the memories.

"Dad! Why are you dressed like a dinosaur?" My face heats with embarrassment as I hide in my hands, trying to escape the laughter and claps. *The last day of third grade, and this is how he picks me up? Is he trying to kill me?*

We both knew my embarrassment wouldn't last long. He was always goofy like that. Everyone wished they had a dad like mine. That was the last memory I had of my dad before their car accident the next day. I jump to the next number so I don't get stuck on that day. I've spent countless hours in therapy reliving it. That is not happening today.

Good thoughts only, Kali.

One after another, memories flood my mind. I keep my focus on the next number, the next memory, never giving myself time to be pulled back into the darkness.

"Twenty. Oh my gosh. I forgot about this day," I say to no one. Or maybe to my mom, who's obviously listening.

"Jimmy, what does that mean?" I hold on tighter to the merry-go-round as he spins it faster, then jumps back on. *My dad says I'm too young to be hanging around a ten-year-old. I'm not that young. I'm six.*

His grin grows as he does it again. "This?"

"Yeah."

"It means I love you. My mom taught it to me. Told me it's Hawaiian or something."

I copy his gesture, excited to learn something new. He cheers me on. "You got it!"

Later that night, my mom was putting me to bed, and I was ready. She gives me a hug and a kiss on the check and says, "I love you."

I flip my middle finger up, smiling wide.

"Kali!" she exclaims, forcing my finger down. "Why would you do that?"

With wide eyes, surprised at her reaction, I whisper, "It means I love you in Hawaiian."

Her laughter erupts around the room, and she falls back on the bed in hysterics. "Who told you that?"

"Jimmy."

She shakes her head, cheeks red from laughter. "Sweetheart, that does not mean I love you. It's more like I hate you."

I gasp. Jimmy lied to me.

I can't believe I'm smiling. *Keep going.* I channel all my energy into staying in the past, my eyes growing heavy by the time I hit thirty. With a sense of resignation, I allow myself to drift asleep.

CHAPTER 9

Paxton

THE SWING GROANS with each sway, its mournful echoing piercing my eardrums, distracting me from anything but the whereabouts of the damn WD-40. I'd bet it's still in the garage next to the four-wheeler. That's the last place I remember using it.

I drag my foot to halt the painful squeal and slide my hat back on.

"Does that grate on your nerves as much as mine?" I ask Riggs, lounging on the porch, before I push off to fetch the spray. When I return, he's sprawled on his back, undisturbed, and blissfully showing off his manly parts.

I fiddle with the chains, lubricating and adjusting the swing until its high-pitched screech dissolves into silence. *Well, now that I'm up, what else is squeaking?* I open the screen door, and a tiny noise slips out, so I spray it. On a mission now, I go through the house and test every door.

A tap on the screen door interrupts me as I've moved on to caulking around the new cabinets. *So much for a relaxing weekend.* I peek my head out from the kitchen, knowing it's one of the neighbors. If it was someone unfamiliar, Riggs would've let me know.

Mrs. Dayton waves excitedly. She owns the ten acres adjacent to mine and lost her husband recently, so I've lent a hand around the place. She reminds me so much of Grams.

"Come on in, Mrs. Dayton," I call out.

She comes in holding a cake, Riggs trailing close behind. It's an odd shape that I can't make out. I set down the caulking gun and rinse my hands. She slides it on the counter and claps once. "It's Riggs's birthday, and I wanted to make him something special."

It is?

I tilt my head, staring at the bone-shaped cake. Do *I* even know when his birthday is? She's old, but every time I've been around her, she's sharp as a tack, so I don't think she's confusing him with another dog. But it's possible.

"Well, not his actual birthday. But his gotcha day birthday. It was three years ago this weekend," she adds.

How does she remember that?

Riggs sniffs the cake. *Yeah, buddy, someone remembers important dates. Your partner sucks, I guess.*

"Did you forget?" she asks with a hint of disappointment, sensing my confusion.

I rub my beard. Were all my exes right? Is this why they called me a self-absorbed asshole? I think back to when I got him. I remember the day. It was in April. We had been working together for months, training. Graduation was one of the most important days of my life. I put more effort into this dog than I ever did in college.

Fuck. And I forgot it was this weekend.

The first weekend I had him, I brought him here to work more with him. *Amanda was so mad.* My girlfriend, at the time, didn't understand the time and commitment it took to be a K-9 officer. She thought after graduation, we'd have more time together. I never promised her that. Secretly, I enjoyed my time with Riggs more than I did with her. I wasn't sad when she left. But that weekend, Riggs met Mr. and Mrs. Dayton. It feels a lot longer than three years.

"Thank goodness you have me." She rubs Riggs's head, then walks into my kitchen to grab a plate. "This was made just for him. I found the recipe on Pinterest. I took a taste. You definitely don't want any." Her face contorts in disgust as she cuts a piece. Riggs sits, his tail sweeping the floor. He knows it's his.

He can smell it.

We watch him devour the piece of cake until he licks the plate clean, which takes all of two minutes. It smells like peanut butter.

"Thanks for doing this. After his morning, he deserves the whole damn cake."

"Oh, don't do that. He might have some unfortunate *runs*," she warns with a chuckle.

Noted.

"You mentioned this morning. I thought y'all got in last night."

"Nope." I flick my wrist to glance at the time. "We got here about an hour ago."

Her brows furrow. "Well, I thought I saw some car lights in your driveway during the night. It wasn't you?"

I shake my head. "Nope, I was home in Austin." There was a bit more to my night, but she doesn't need details. All that matters is I wasn't here.

"It was probably someone lost."

"Probably." I pick up the plate and place it in the sink, then stash the cake in the fridge just in case Riggs decides on a midnight snack. "You have anything you need done this weekend, let me know. We head back to town tomorrow night."

"No. You boys just enjoy your time off. I know how hard y'all work." I walk with her to her bright red golf cart she rode over. She gives me a hug, and off she goes.

I look down at Riggs, and I swear he's giving me the worst judgment expression a dog can muster. I bend at the knees and rub behind his ears. "Yeah, yeah. Happy gotcha day, buddy. Three years is a long time in dog years. I hope you still love me."

He licks my face, pushing his way on top of me. I have to roll out from under him. He bows and barks once, ready to play.

"All right, buddy, you ready to play your favorite game?"

He perks right up.

"Hold on," I say, running inside to grab my side piece from the dining table, double-checking it's snug in the holster, and finish off the last of my cold coffee. He positions himself at my side when I walk back out, ready for my signal.

Let's play seek.

"Ready?" His eyes lock on mine, and he lets out a bark. "Three...two...one...find her."

CHAPTER 10

Kali

"Hey, Mom, you there?" My voice cracks as I lay perfectly still, my body giving up the fight.

"*Ladybug. I'm here.*"

"Will you be waiting for me?"

"*With open arms.*"

"Will Dad be there, too? Or will I be interrupting his golf game? Wait. Is there golf up there?"

She softly chuckles. "He wouldn't miss this. And yes, there's golf. What do you think hail is? It's the guys playing tournaments."

Even my laugh cracks. I cough and then wince. Coughing hurts my headache.

Drifting in and out of consciousness, I close my eyes and dream about playing a round of golf with my dad.

I JOLT AWAKE, eyes wide open, wondering what woke me. Was that a sound? I take slow, deliberate breaths, honing in on every sense, focused on listening as if I'm taking a hearing exam. I let out a few curse words when all I hear is my own heart, hope quickly dying. But then I hear it.

A bark.

The hairs on my arms tingle as I listen again. It's faint, very distant, but unmistakably a bark. Hope surges through me, filling my lungs.

"HELP! HELP ME!" I scream until my throat burns, my voice on the verge of giving up. But I keep screaming. Within minutes, emotion overcomes me. He's here. There's digging. He found me. He's digging me out. Paws, fueled by determination above me, keep digging.

"Keep going. I'm down here," I weep, pounding on the unforgiving wood, hoping without the weight of the dirt, it'll give.

"What the hell?" I hear a man's voice. "Is someone down there?"

"Yes!"

"Damn it, I don't have a shovel."

"Please, please don't leave me," I plead, a surge of fear gripping me at the thought of being abandoned. What if I'm buried in a forest where every tree looks the same?

"Jesus fucking Christ," he mutters. "I'm not. I promise."

Clawing sounds reverberate on the wooden surface, then a slice of sunlight pierces through the suffocating darkness. *Please. Keep digging. I'm down here. Please find me.* Hysterical sobs erupt from my chest, a symphony of relief, disbelief, and overwhelming emotions.

"It's okay," the man reassures me, still pushing the earth away. "I'm going to get you out of there. Can you tell me your name?"

In between sobs, I manage to convey, "Kali Stevens."

"Kali, my name is Paxton Turner, and I'm a police officer. You're safe now. I promise."

The knot of relief in my throat stifles any words. Tremors course through me, a mixture of fear and relief shocks me to my core.

"Close your eyes so you don't get dirt in them. I'm going to pry it open."

Eyes shut, I press my hand over my mouth, tears streaming

down my face uncontrollably. The box creaks in resistance, giving the man a fight. But the moment the sun's warmth caresses my skin, I struggle to escape, needing to flee the stench of my coffin.

"Hold on. Let me help you." A dark silhouette against the shining sun, the man grabs under my arms, lifting my weakened body. He carries me a few feet away, placing me on the ground beneath the shade of a tree.

As fresh air fills my lungs, my head hangs low, tears still flowing unabated. I cough, feeling dizzy. My real hero, a German shepherd, sits beside me as if sensing the lingering threat.

"This is Officer Paxton Turner, Austin PD. I just found a woman buried alive. I'm going to need EMS, stat."

I glance up to the man, his gaze pinned on me, and he offers a pinched smile as I squint, the sun still too bright even in the shade. He takes his aviators off and slides them over my eyes.

"Yes, she's breathing." He stands and scans the area, running his hand through his hair, says yes a couple more times and describes what he's wearing, along with the fact that he's armed. When he states the location, I lift my gaze.

Where are we? I've never heard of this town.

He looks down at me. "How long were you down there?"

"I don't know," I whisper, still in shock. *I don't even know what day it is.* It felt like forever.

His expression hardens. "Copy that," he replies to the person on the phone. "Help is on their way. I'm sorry I don't have any water."

I nod, grateful for the air he gave me. The dog inches closer to me, his hair tickles my bare thigh. I rest my dirty, bloodied, and raw hand on his head and lean on him, struggling to stay upright.

"Thank you," I whisper.

CHAPTER 11

Paxton

"How did you find her all the way out here if your ranch is a few miles down the road?" I know the drill. I was expecting it. It's protocol. The first on the scene is always suspect number one.

I point to Riggs. "He did what he was trained to do. He must've heard her screams, but I didn't until I cleared those trees." I point to the clearing. "We were out searching for a doe who Riggs has become fond of. He barked when he found the doe, then he took off running in this direction."

"A doe?"

I shrug. "She's always out here. And I don't have a say in who he can make friends with."

The young officer's lips quirk up as he writes his notes. This is probably a first for him. Hell, I've from the city and have seen a lot of shit, and it's a first for me. I can't imagine they see too much action out here in the country. Unlike the city, where shootings and murders feel like a daily occurrence. "Did you notice anything when you got here? Anyone hanging around?"

"No. Riggs was already digging when I got here, and had there been someone around, he would've warned me."

"Have you ever seen this woman before?"

I shake my head. "Never."

CHAPTER 12

Kali

NOISE.

Something easily taken for granted.

Sometimes even irritated by it.

When that sense has been forcibly stripped away from you, the yearning for it becomes insatiable. You crave it. It drowns out the nightmare threatening to put me back in the box. Each time I shut my eyes, the boxed darkness seeps into my veins, and spiders crawl over me, making every breath a struggle. The adjacent room complained the TV was too loud. Instead of telling me to turn it down, they were moved to a room further away. The night nurse encouraged me to blast it as loud as I'd like. And to my credit, I've been hooked to a machine to pull the carbon dioxide from my system, which isn't exactly quiet.

A psychiatrist and a therapist—Dr. Betty—visited me yesterday and prescribed medicine to help me sleep, but I looked at them like they were crazy.

Did they expect me to sleep?

But my restless mind battled my anxious thoughts, and I gave in, taking the pill to quiet my mind. Moments of blankness followed. However, when I awoke this morning, I wished for more of the pills to take away the haunted memories, because they forged themselves front and center with the dawn of the day.

I lift my bandaged fingers up in the air. All ten digits required dressing, and I want to be thankful I survived, but the man who put me down there is still out there. Is he waiting for another opportunity to put me back? Did I escape death, and he'll make sure next time there will be nowhere for me to escape? How can I live knowing he's still out there?

The fear is a death sentence in itself.

Everyone knocks before they enter. Even the nurses don't come in unannounced. So, when a knock comes, I stare at the door.

Dr. Betty enters with a warm smile, pulling up the rolling chair. Her gray hair cascades long and thick at the sides of her face, giving her a youthful appearance. "How'd we sleep last night?" Her voice carries a soothing tone, reminding me of my mom's, which has a natural calming effect.

"No nightmares, no spiders, so I guess okay."

"How do you feel this morning?"

"Like there's a man out there who wants me dead."

She lays her hand on my arm and gives it a comforting squeeze. We talked last night about who she could call for me, and when I mentioned there wasn't anyone, she discreetly masked her concern. Yet, I caught a glimpse of sadness in her eyes—much like now. I've spent my entire life being pitied, and the shame, as if it's my fault, never goes away. But I don't need people's sympathy. I'm not a broken girl.

Well, I might be now.

I could have given her Pearl's number, but since finding out I'm two hours away, she'd have to take time off, and she can't afford that. Besides, I'm not her responsibility. I can't bring this burden to her front door. I'm on my own.

"The Texas Rangers were called in to help. They're here and would like to talk to you, but I wanted to come in here first to check if you're ready."

I take a deep inhale and blow it out with puffed-out cheeks. *Ready?* No. There will never be a time I'm ready to relive that nightmare. But I nod because I want them to catch him. There's not much for me to tell them, and the little I remember will not help find the guy. I never saw his face, his car, nothing.

Moments later, two Rangers walk in with serious expressions, both wearing khaki slacks, white button-up shirts, and ties. They have guns on their hips and the Ranger five-pointed star badge on their chest, and white cowboy hats on top of their heads.

They really look like that.

I've heard about them, but I've never seen them in person. The short, stalky one, who looks old enough to be close to retirement, comes over and extends his hand. When I lift my bandaged hands up from under the covers, he just nods and drops the gesture. "Ms. Stevens, I'm Major Martinez. This is Ranger Clark. We're with the Texas Rangers." Clark tips his hat in a sharp nod as he stands across the room, accessing me from a distance. Martinez sits down in the chair next to the bed, taking out a tiny notepad from his front pocket. *Glad it's small since I have very little to fill it with.* "Because you were taken across county lines and found in a rural county, they've asked for our assistance in the case." I nod, relieved they've called in the big guns. "Now, let's find the bastard who did this to you."

I like this guy already.

"Let's start with if there was any reason someone would want to hurt you—an ex, stalker, money, enemy—"

Oh no. His words fall off when I shoot up out of bed, my socked feet hitting the linoleum floor, and I search the small room. *Where are they?* They helped me into a hospital gown as soon as I got here, so what did they do with my clothes?

"What's wrong, Ms. Stevens?" the taller guy asks. I already forgot his name.

"Where are my clothes?" My head jerks left and right, searching the room.

"They're being processed. They might have some clues on them," he replies.

A tiny whimper escapes the lodged panic in my throat. My stomach bottoms out. Martinez stands aside with furrowed brows.

"We found nothing in the pockets." He guesses the reason I'm two seconds from a full-blown panic attack.

They didn't look in the right pocket.

At least I hope it's still there.

Dr. Betty comes over, puts her hand on my back, trying to diffuse the panic attack. "Kali, breathe."

"My bra," I say, finding my voice. "Did they look in my bra?"

The two Rangers exchange discerning glances. "What was in your bra?" one asks.

I collapse onto the bed, my body heavy with defeat. He didn't want the money because he already had it. How did he know where to look? Tears stream down my face. I can almost hear his mocking laughter when I offered him money.

I'm broken *and* broke.

"Kali," Dr. Betty softly interjects, redirecting my focus to her. "What was in your bra?" she repeats the question.

"Four million dollars," I deadpan.

"What was that?" Martinez asks, and I lift my gaze. *Yep. It's hard for me to believe, too.* "What *exactly* do you mean?"

"I won the lottery last weekend. The winning ticket was in my bra." My voice lacks any emotion. The excitement drained out of my soul, left back on the curb in Blackburn.

The tall Ranger pushes off the table and leaves the room, the other scoots his chair closer. "Ms. Stevens, who knew about the money?"

"Just Pearl Livingston." He notes her name on the pad. "But she had nothing to do with this. She's my best friend," I plead. I don't like that he doesn't say anything. She's going to hate me. She'll think *I* sent the cops to question her.

I glance at what he writes, but his handwriting is terrible.

He flips back a page and lifts his head. "Let's go back to Friday night. You left the bingo hall and walked home alone. That was about ten?"

I nod.

"Other than it being darker than normal, you didn't notice anything out of place?" He repeats what I already told him.

I shake my head.

He taps his pen against his pad, studying me for a beat. "Based on your carbon dioxide levels, the doctors estimate you were down there for around four or five hours. Silverwood to Blackburn is a two-hour drive."

He's getting to the part I've questioned since the doctor told me the same thing. *What did he do with me during those five unaccountable hours?*

Were they spent digging the grave? Did he take me somewhere else first? He didn't rape me. *Thank God.* One of the first things they did when I got here was do a rape kit. I didn't feel anything down there, but I was still in shock, so I agreed to one. Just in case.

"Whoever did this to you didn't want you to die quickly. The setup was meticulous. There was an air pump at the end of the box, supplying air."

My eyes widen as a chill runs down my spine. He purposely kept me alive. Why?

"So, either they intended for you to suffer or just wanted to terrify you for a short while. Because the air supply wasn't enough to deplete the carbon dioxide, you wouldn't have lasted forever."

My gaze flits around the room, my mind struggling to grasp the cruelty. The sick bastard intentionally wanted me to go insane before I died.

Mission *almost* accomplished.

"Tell me about your life in Blackburn," he asks.

I delve into my entire history in Blackburn. That includes the mayor and his recent pedophile dreams. Martinez writes everything down and puts a star next to the mayor's name.

Please. Dig deep on that one.

My voice croaks as I keep talking. I clear my throat but wince at the pain.

Dr. Betty looks at the Ranger. "She needs to take a break."

He nods in agreement and stands, sliding his notepad into his shirt pocket.

"You've been through so much, Kali," Dr. Betty murmurs, the hum of the hospital's air conditioning blending with her comforting voice as she sits next to me. *That's putting it lightly.* She grabs my water bottle and hands it to me. Drinking hurts the same as talking, but I take a sip to coat the dryness and hand it back to her.

The door swings open with a soft creak, and all eyes shift to the Ranger who left earlier. He flashes a crooked grin as he walks up toward me. "Good news, kid. You're still a millionaire."

Without a second thought, I push off the bed, run, and throw myself into his arms. He's my life raft in this sinking ship. My head tells me to let go of the stranger, but my emotions get the best of me, and I hold on tighter, crying into his chest. "Thank you," I murmur, my gratitude echoing in the sterile hospital room.

His emotional sigh reverberates through me as his hand pats my back. "You're welcome, Ms. Stevens. It's in a lockbox now, safe and sound."

OH MY GOD.

My mouth hangs open as I stare at the six o'clock news from my hospital bed in disbelief. It's about me. A picture of my grave site flashes on the screen, surrounded with yellow tape. I hold my breath, praying they don't reveal my name. When the next segment comes on without hearing my name, the tension in my shoulders releases. It'll come out soon enough.

I jump at the sound of a soft knock. When the nurse comes in, her eyes flash from me to the TV. She bites her lip, hesitant about what to do. We stay silent. *Is there anything to say?*

I swallow back my emotions. "It's okay. I just didn't expect to be on the news. Is it time for my vitals again?"

She shakes her head and jerks her thumb over her shoulder. "There's an Officer Turner here to see you?"

How could I say no to the man who saved me?

"Do you mind muting the TV for me?" It sucks a million times over not being able to use my hands.

When she leaves, I overhear him talking to the officer stationed outside my room, and I quickly adjust my flimsy gown to cover everything.

The officer walks in, his dog trotting faithfully by his side.

"Hey," he says, sounding unsure about being here.

"Hi." My voice comes out just as awkward.

The only thing I remember about the duo is the dog. He comes over and sniffs me, laying his head on the bed near my hands. *Hey there, hero.* The bandages make it an awkward rub, but he doesn't seem to care.

I think I need one of you.

"I hope it was okay to come check on you?"

"Of course. You're the reason I'm here."

His eyes widen, and I grimace. That came out wrong.

"I mean the reason I'm alive. Not that you..." I stop talking as my cheeks flush, and I focus back on the dog. The buzzing of anxiety in my chest calms. I let out a deep exhale and relax for the first time today. I gesture toward the TV. "Did you know it's on the news?"

He lets out an irritated sigh. "Yeah. The news has been calling me all day for a statement or interview." He sits down on the blue cushioned armchair beside the bed, his hands clasped in his lap. Tall, slim, athletic build, dark-brown hair that looks soft to the touch, and a neatly trimmed beard. Wait, I remember his light-brown eyes now. How intense they were when they stared at me. Like they're trying to reach into my soul. *I feel them right now.*

"The nurse said you haven't had any visitors."

That's embarrassing. I don't want to admit I'm alone in this world. As if it defines the person I am. Unlovable. "I don't have any family," I whisper.

Is that why it was me? How much did my kidnapper know about me? Was that the plan all along? Choose someone no one would miss?

Ugh, Kali! Stop with the questions you don't have answers to.

"I hear you're breaking free in a couple days." He winces at his choice of words and drops his head. "Sorry, I usually don't have a problem thinking before I speak."

"It's okay. But that's what I'm told."

"I'd be surprised if they didn't assign you police protection, but do you need a ride to your house?"

It didn't occur to me how embarrassing this sounds until now. "I don't have one."

"Kali, are you homeless? I didn't see it in the report, but if you are, it's an important detail to tell the Rangers because the suspect might be targeting homeless women. It's nothing to be embarrassed about."

"No and yes."

His thick brows furrow, confused with my answer.

"Saturday…" I tilt my head, and it takes me a moment to remember what day it is. The past few days have been a blur. "Or yesterday was supposed to be my last day in Blackburn. I was moving to Austin this weekend."

"Oh," he says, surprised. "Do you have a place in Austin?"

"No," I reply, sliding my bandages against the edge of the blanket. This made sense on Friday. For the first time in my life, I was being spontaneous. "I was going to stay in a hotel until I found an apartment."

He nods in response but doesn't say anything for a minute. I can see more questions swirling in his eyes, but without telling him about the money—and that won't happen—it doesn't make much sense, anyway.

Riggs barks once, and the man holds his hands up in the air. "Okay. I'm done. I didn't mean to sound like a detective."

Riggs settles back, laying his head down.

"You have a new fan."

"It's the other way around. You have a great dog. Smart."

"More like a smart-ass," he retorts, narrowing his eyes at him.

I shimmy the blankets up higher on my chest. "I'm sorry I have to ask this, but can you tell me your name again?"

"Shit," he murmurs, running his hand through his hair again, swooshing the loose piece back. It's definitely soft. "Sorry. I should've re-introduced us as we came in. This is Riggs, and I'm Paxton."

That's it. I remember him saying it when he found me. "Well, Paxton, thank you. Thank you for finding me."

His intense expression softens. "Listen, you don't know me, but…" He stands up and pulls his wallet out of his front pocket, grabbing a white business card. He slides it onto my bedside table and taps it a few times before removing his finger. "If you need anything, call me. I live in Austin, so if there's anything I can do to help you…" His voice trails off, and I offer a ghost of a smile. He's done more than enough to help me.

I'm here because of him. Alive.

With a swipe of his hand on his leg, Riggs lifts his head off the bed and moves to sit at attention to the left of Paxton, staring up at him.

My eyes widen in surprise. "Wow. You did that with just a swipe?"

He chuckles. "He's just trying to impress you. It takes me slapping my leg a few times to get him to listen."

I know that's a lie. But it makes me laugh.

He points at his card and says, "Anything." Without waiting for a response, he strolls out, Riggs glued to his side.

The spot where Riggs's head was turns cold and is a cruel reminder of how alone I am when I miss the comfort of a dog. I stare at the business card. What am I going to do next? I don't have a phone, a license, or money. Nothing. I can't even claim the lottery money until I get a new license. I thought I had the strength to start over. Now, I'm not even sure where to start.

CHAPTER 13

Kali

EARLY THE NEXT MORNING, Martinez strides into my room without a courtesy knock, followed by Dr. Betty, irritation written all over her face at his brusque entrance. I sit up, a sense of anticipation hanging in the air.

Maybe they found who did this to me.

He positions himself at the foot of the bed, his hands shoved deep into his pockets. "Dr. Betty filled me in on your situation."

My brows furrow. He's fully aware of my situation.

"We wanted to station an officer at your home, but considering you don't have one, we've come up with an alternative."

Oh. That situation.

Dr. Betty steps forward, casting a sidelong glance at the guy. "I work with an incredible facility that specializes in helping people who have been through severe trauma. I highly recommend you stay there to receive the help you need. It's located just outside Austin, so not far," she explains.

Panic sets in as my gaze darts between her and Martinez. "Will I still have protection?"

"The owner's husband is a retired police officer, and there will be another officer assigned to you at all times," he assures me.

A fear I've never known creeps up. "Will I be safe?" Given the circumstances, it's not an unreasonable question.

"Yes," he states with certainty, but it doesn't quell the fear clenching my chest. He reaches into his jacket pocket and presents a brand-new phone. "It has a tracker in it," he informs me as he sets it on the table, next to my breakfast plates. "And you have a new number." More like the *only* number I've ever had.

"Thank you for everything." With a tight nod, he then turns to leave. I wait until he's gone before asking Dr. Betty to help me set it up, as it's the first phone I've ever had. It's the same one Pearl has, so at least I'm a little familiar with it.

"How do the clothes fit?" she asks, picking up the phone. She brought a bag of clothes for me yesterday.

"They feel like butter against my skin. You didn't have to get such nice stuff."

She waves me off with a slight huff. "You needed something that was light, so it didn't rub against your healing skin." She skips the part about it needing to be easy to pull down for whoever is helping me go to the bathroom.

"That's very sweet of you. I really appreciate it." As she sets up my phone, I ask, "Do you really think this place will help me?"

She glances up, and her lips curve. "I do. It's a wonderful place. They incorporate animals into your therapy." *Animals? Can I request Riggs?* "And I'll be with you throughout your healing. You'll also have a nurse to help you with anything you need."

"I'm scared," I admit. I wanted to live. I wished for it. I begged for it. But how? How will I ever heal from this nightmare?

"It's completely normal to feel scared. Healing alone can be a difficult journey. We'll take it one day at a time. Remember, it's okay to feel vulnerable. That's part of the process and a sign of your strength and courage to face it."

She thinks I have strength and courage left.

I'm not so sure.

WHEN I SAID I would go to the rehab place, no one prepared me for a ranch in the heart of nowhere. A heads-up would've been nice— a chance to brace myself. One open field looks just like another one. Specifically, the one that imprisoned me. The weight on my chest gets heavier with each passing sight of yellow cornfields.

The officer seated next to me senses my rising panic. "These are good people," he offers in a calming tone. I turn my head toward him. "They won't let anything happen to you. I shouldn't tell you this, but they are part of the FBI family. Their daughter and son-in-law are both in law enforcement. They understand the importance of keeping you safe."

I nod, hearing his words, but they provide little solace against the storm of anxiety raging within me. Resigned to the fact my inner demons will follow me wherever I go, I fix my gaze back out the passenger window.

Smells I once loved twist my insides the moment the door opens for me. Fresh country air, wild grass, and dirt. Mother Earth's stench forces itself to the back of my throat, and it takes a concerted effort to remember to breathe.

Smells like death now.

My death.

Taking quick, shallow breaths to avoid passing out, I follow the officer up the dirt driveway toward the ranch-style house. A man in a cowboy hat and boots stands beside a woman with the sweetest, most sincere smile. She descends the three steps to meet us.

"Hi, Kali, I'm Amy," she greets me and points over her shoulder with her thumb. "And that's my husband, Ted."

"Hi," I choke out with a small wave, then cover my mouth and nose with my hand, pulling in the scent of the sterile bandages. "Do you mind if we go inside?"

Without hesitation, Amy replies with a wave, "C'mon, I'll show you to your room."

As I follow her through the farmhouse, I steal glances at collections of family pictures along the way. She has a large family. I stop and stare at one that was taken right on her porch. Everyone is making a funny face. Except Amy. You can see the adoration on her face as she looks at her crazy family.

"They're all nuts," she jokes, looking over my shoulder at the picture.

I would do anything to belong to a large, loving, crazy family like that. We continue down a lengthy hallway. "Here you are," she says, gesturing to the room. We walk into a bright yellow room, and she places my bag on the quilt with sunflowers all over. "The bathroom is fully stocked with whatever you need," she adds, pointing to an open door. "Do you need anything right now? Something to eat or drink?"

I shake my head. "No, thank you. I'm kind of tired. Is it ok if I just hang out in here?"

Her eyes fill with concern and empathy. "Of course. Just know we're here if you need us. Dr. Betty will be out in the morning. She wanted to give you a little time to get settled."

That would imply I'm going to get settled. In a place that reeks like death. *Not likely*.

Amy shuts the door behind her. The hum of the air conditioner brings a welcome coolness to my overheated skin until a shiver runs down my sweat ridden back. Uncomfortable with the silence, I grab my phone. I wiggle my free thumbs. Before leaving the hospital, they were able to wrap each finger individually on my left hand and keep my thumb out with just a Band-Aid around my knuckle. Still not easy, but usable. Very mummy-like. Enough to be able to hold things and use my phone. The right is still wrapped like a mitten. I open Spotify, turning on a random playlist. The nurses helped me set up the music app on my phone. I don't remember most of the things they told me the phone could do, but I paid extra attention to this one.

A wooden rocking chair by the window reminds me of the ones

Blackburn's gossip crew would sit on, whispering away as people walked by. I can imagine that I'm the current topic. I turn it to face outside and sink into it, pushing off with my foot for a soft rock. As I look out the window to a field of horses eating, a specific one grabs my attention.

"What do they feed that monster?" I whisper to myself, staring at a larger-than-life red horse. He and a white and black sheep dog play with a big blue exercise ball. Entranced by the two oddly paired friends and a best of the eighties country playlist, I lose track of time until a gentle knock at the door pulls me away.

Wrapped in a blanket, feeling at ease in the warm glow of the evening sun, rather than get up, I say, "Come in."

The wooden door creaks open, and Amy peeks inside. When she spots me settled in the rocking chair, she walks in and slides a tray full of food on the dresser. "Thought you might be hungry. We'd love to have you join us at the dinner table, but we understand if you'd like to be alone right now."

Do I want to be alone? No, I don't. But I don't want to be around a table of strangers either. I glance back out the window. "They make an odd couple," I remark, pointing.

Amy laughs over my shoulder when she gets a glimpse of the peculiar duo. "They are inseparable. The dog is Charlie, and that's Rusty, a.k.a. Ketchup."

I pull my gaze from the window and look up. "Ketchup?"

Her smile reaches her eyes, settling on the edge of the bed. "My granddaughter's nickname is Tater Tot, and she thinks Rusty is hers. In her words, tater tots always go with ketchup."

"That's adorable."

"You'll partner with Rusty." *Partner?* What does that mean? As my eyes widen in surprise, she reassures me, "He's a gentle giant. Don't worry, you'll fall in love with him."

Still confused as to my role in partnering with that towering creature, my gaze flickers to him, now munching on some hay. Returning my gaze to Amy, I bite my lip, hesitating to express my lack of enthusiasm. "I've only ridden a horse once, when I was like five. It didn't go so well. My feet do better on the ground."

Amy's lips twist, and she asks, "Did Dr. Betty talk to you about equine therapy?"

"She mentioned that I'd be working with animals. I guess I thought she meant like dogs and cats."

She bobs her head. "Close." In what world is that animal close to a cat? "What we do here is use horses as emotional support, helping guide you through recovery. I know it sounds weird, but horses have this unique sensitivity to how we are feeling."

I sigh, my eyes swelling again as memories of where I was four days ago flood my mind. "I don't think I want him burdened with my fears."

She attempts to hold back her emotions, but they get lodged in her throat. She clears it. "You won't, I promise."

How can a horse help me? Unless he can find the man who put me in a grave and stomp on his head until he's dead—which I'd be on board with—it seems like a lost cause.

"Kali, I can't sit here and say I understand how you're feeling because I can't. I can't even imagine the horror you went through. But with your strength and will, and by the grace of God that led that dog to you, you're here today. What I can tell you is that Rusty has magical healing powers." That sounds fishy. "You laugh, but I know firsthand. My daughter was his first partner. She also went through a horrible, horrible ordeal. I thought she'd never be the same snarky, bad-ass woman she once was. But she found her way back. And I believe you will too."

I feel like shit for laughing now. But her daughter's ordeal couldn't have been as bad as mine. *What could be worse than being buried alive?* A heavy sigh escapes me as the full weight of my situation settles in.

"Thank you for the food," I say, noticing the finger food, easy enough for me to pick up with my left hand.

"Of course," she replies, not making a fuss about the shift in conversation. She pushes off the bed and walks to the door. "Again, you're always welcome out with us. And if you need my help with anything because of your bandages, please let me know. I'm here to help you."

I nod, and watch as she disappears, closing the door behind her.

CHAPTER 14

Kali

IT WAS FIVE HOURS.

197,100 hours. That is how many hours I've been alive. I stare at the clock on the dresser until the second hand hits the top of the hour and then roll back over to stare at the yellow wall. 197,101.

Thousands of hours lived, yet my brain is chained to those five. I tried to push past it, to think about the money and the dreams that were so close to coming true, searching for that high. But all I find is darkness and pain.

Dr. Betty explained those five hours are like the wounds on my hands and legs. *Wounds on my brain.* It'll take time for them to scab over and turn into scars. A reminder. A memory. But like the scars on our body, they'll fade—not disappear—and become a faint memory.

That's when I started wondering if I needed a new doctor. Faint memory, my ass. There will never be a night when I lie in the darkness and not hear those thumps.

Thump.

Thump.

Thump.

I've been here for four days. Yesterday was a week since I was found. On top of living in this nightmare, I feel like a burden. I'm sure Amy didn't sign up to be a nurse, caregiver, cook, and therapist when Dr. Betty and the nurse aren't around. I'm an adult, yet I can't even shower on my own because of the bandages. It's humiliating.

Dr. Betty thinks talking to a friend might cheer me up. *Like Pearl.* But that takes energy. Energy that I can't find. Just the thought of talking to Pearl and the questions she'll have makes my chest tighten.

The door creaks open, and I already know it's Amy. I glance over my shoulder, and she greets me with that small, unwavering smile. It's mentally hard for me to get out of bed these days.

"Ready for your shower?"

I shake my head and roll back toward the wall. "I'm not ready to get out of bed yet." Despite it being eleven in the morning.

"How about I make you a deal? I'll give you another half hour, but I need you to give me something."

Bartering? Really? This is *my* life. I don't owe her anything.

"What do you want?" I mutter, already feeling the defeat because I need her help.

"I want you to meet Rusty."

I whip my head around, a surge of energy in the form of panic bubbling out. "I already told you, I'm not going to ride that beast." I've watched him from my window. He towers over Ted, and Ted is not a small man.

She chuckles. "Just meet him." I narrow my eyes, and she holds up her hands. "That's it. It'll do you good to get some fresh air, too."

Fresh air that smells like death.

I exhale, the weight of despair pressing down on me. And then force the answer out of my lips. "Fine."

I hate this person living inside me. The real me, the one that isn't unappreciative or rude, is being swallowed by the darkness. I can't find the light. Amy has been nothing but kind and encouraging, but I can't help but be insolent.

An hour later, Amy and I step out the front door. It's the first time I've been outside since I got here. The breeze caresses my face, and as much as I hate to admit it, it feels invigorating. I stop on the top stair, close my eyes, and focus on the sun's warmth and the cooler breeze swirling around me. If I listen closely, I can hear cows in the distance and birds flying overhead. It's actually peaceful out here.

I can do this. One step at a time. I open my eyes, catching Amy staring at me, a triumphant smile playing on her lips as if she had won a silent battle.

"Ready?" she asks softly.

I nod and take the three steps down. *I only have to meet him,* I keep reminding myself as we approach the bright red barn standing out against the green grass surrounding it.

With hay crunching underfoot, we step through the large door. I've been in a barn once. Devon Michaels was a farmer's kid, and one night after a party, we found a quiet spot in one stall. The smell of horse manure takes me back. One of the many regretful nights I had been searching for the male attention missing in my life.

Shaking off the memory, I follow Amy. I recognize Rusty the second I see him. His powerful red head sticks out of his stall, eyes full of curiosity.

"Hey big guy," Amy says, producing a carrot out of her overalls and feeding it to him. I stand back in awe of the magnificent creature. He's larger in person, which I didn't think could happen. "Rusty," she says, petting his muzzle, "this is Kali." She nudges his head in my direction. "Kali, this is Rusty." She gestures for me to come closer.

It takes me a beat to work up the nerve to move. Not wanting to scare the animal, I take slow, hesitant steps until I'm standing beside her. I hold up my bandaged hands, a silent reminder. Again,

I don't want to scare the beast who could kill me with one stomp. She shakes her head gently and takes my left hand, guiding it to his nose. My heart races triple time.

"Hi," I whisper, wishing I could feel his coat.

"I'll be right back," Amy says. I jerk my head toward her, panic rising. She can't leave me alone with this giant. "It'll be okay. I just need to take Cash out to the runner."

I watch her lead another horse from the barn, leaving me alone with Rusty. A warm puff of air hits my face as his velvety nose nuzzles my cheek, surprising me. I jump back, my speeding heart jumping into my throat.

I am not a carrot, dude.

He lowers his head and then bobs it up and down, as if encouraging me to come closer. *That's what it means, right?* I take a hesitant step forward, and he nuzzles my face again. This time I laugh—a sound I haven't heard in days. His nostrils flare as he takes in my scent.

I lift my left hand and run it over his nose. "I hear you're supposed to help me," I say, my voice trembling. He responds by stroking his muzzle against my cheek again. I press my forehead against the bridge of his nose, placing both of my hands on his powerful jaws, and close my eyes. I listen to his breathing, noting how still he's keeping. *For me.*

An intense wave of emotion crashes over me, breaking through the numbness I've built around my heart. *I can't live in this darkness anymore.* My hands shake, but Rusty doesn't move away. *I don't think I'm strong enough to get through this alone.* Tears stream down my face, and I hiccup as I plead, "Please, please help me."

CHAPTER 15

Kali

"I'M EXHAUSTED, and it's not even noon yet," I say to Dr. Betty, walking out of the barn, dusting off my jeans. Therapy helps, I think. Sometimes, I wonder if it just mentally occupies my mind so the fears don't have a chance to surface. Dr. Betty doesn't agree and promises me she can see me slowly healing. I stop walking when I see an unfamiliar pickup truck in the driveway.

Usually, they warn me when expecting anyone.

The front door opens, and Martinez walks out. His eyes meet mine, and he tips his hat. I haven't seen him since I left the hospital two weeks ago. I try to read his expression from this distance, but his steely expression gives nothing away.

Please be here with good news.

We reach the stairs, and Dr. Betty pats me on the shoulder. "I'm going to go in and talk with Amy for a little bit before I head out. You okay?"

"I'm all right," I say, leaning against the stair railing.

Martinez leans against the other side and waits for Dr. Betty to go inside.

"I just wanted to touch base with you about the investigation," he starts, and I nod in anticipation. "This is going to sound frustrating because we're still in the stages of collecting and analyzing everything, so we don't have a lot to tell you. But a few things have come up I wanted to run by you."

I sigh. Not what I wanted to hear.

"Okay."

"We've interviewed a lot of people in Blackburn. We had two different people talk about a car they saw off Main they had never seen before." Main was where I was taken. A rush of hope stirs. It's something, right? "It was a dark four door, late model sedan. Nobody could give us any more description. Does that ring any bells? Can you think back to when you were walking down the road?"

I take my thoughts back to that night. I was singing. Excited. It was dark. The light at the train track was out. I squeeze my eyes shut. *Focus, Kali.* I glanced around. Saw the lights on the apartments ahead. The trees were still. So dark. No one drove by. Nothing seemed different. I let out a frustrated groan and drop my head. "I don't remember seeing it."

"It's all right. As your brain begins to heal, something might come to you, so keep trying." *God, I hope.* "We also talked with Pearl Livingston. She really wanted your phone number to check on you. We, of course, didn't provide that info to her, but I told her I would pass along that she's worried about you."

Oh, Pearl. I miss you. I just need a little more time.

Martinez studies me as the conflict inside me plays out. I shouldn't be afraid to call my best friend, but something is stopping me. Embarrassment? Fear that she'd want to smother me? Ask all the wrong questions that I can't handle yet? *Or maybe I'm not ready to look back.* "I'll call her. I'm just not ready to talk to anyone."

"She also has a solid alibi." What? Why would they question her? I told them she didn't do it. Why are they wasting their time on her? "Everyone we interview, we ask what they were doing that night," he adds, reading my irritation.

"Does the mayor have an alibi?" I ask sarcastically. They probably didn't ask *him* because he's the mayor.

His lips press into a tight line, and the hairs on the back of my neck tingle. "Did Mayor Prackett know you won the lottery?"

Shit. I swallow hard, my fingers pinching the bridge of my nose as the memory of my threat surfaces. "I didn't tell him I had won. *But* I did tell him I had power now." I cringe inwardly, realizing how dumb that was. Why did I think provoking him was a good idea? "Did he say he knew?"

It had to be him. He did this to me!

"He didn't say anything to us about knowing. But when we interviewed Henry Walton, he recalled the mayor asking about you buying a lottery ticket. He's fairly certain it was the day before you were kidnapped."

I push off the rail, my hands balling into fists. "He doesn't have an alibi, does he?"

He lets out a sharp sigh. "He does." Sensing my frustration, he quickly adds, "He's not off our radar, just yet. But there are other concerns we have. We can't really discuss the details though. How well do you know the mayor?"

He's right, this conversation is frustrating.

"Other than what I told you about his sick obsession of *wanting to have sex with a fourteen-year-old...*" I feel it's necessary to repeat that so he understands how horrible he is. "He never let me get close to him. I was with the nanny more than anything." He asks me her name, and it takes me a moment to remember. It's been a long time since then. A lot of emotional baggage to dig through.

He closes his notepad, sticks it in his pocket, and pauses. "Kali, we're going to find who did this to you."

My eyes water, and I stare up at the sky. A tear falls over my cheek, and I wipe it away.

"I can't heal knowing he's out there." My voice trembles. "Every noise I hear at night, I'm afraid he's trying to finish the job.

He wanted me down there for a reason, and I don't think it was to be found."

The front door creaks open, and Dr. Betty steps out.

"Major Martinez, I think we're done for the day," she says, sternly.

"Yes, ma'am." He takes the two steps down and looks back up at me. "Kali, don't lose hope. And don't give him control. Fight and take it back," he says.

I'm trying. But how do you fight a ghost?

"RUSTY, THAT'S NOT COOL," I snap at the heathen animal, hurling the brush into the bucket. He rolls around in the grass and dirt. *Right after his bath.* Ever tried bathing an enormous horse? It takes a long time, and then for him to get his ass dirty right after, it's frustrating. He's frustrating.

But then he flips over and trots over to me, flashing me all his teeth, reminding me of Ann when she showed up to the diner. I can't help but laugh at the goon, instantly forgetting how exasperating he can be. And how much I've grown to love him.

It's been a long month of facing my fears. After Martinez left, I wrote down his words, *don't give him control,* on a small piece of paper and have it stuffed in my pocket every day. It's become my daily pledge. I often run my fingers along the paper when bad thoughts creep up.

While the claustrophobic fear might never disappear, I can finally sleep at night without dreaming of dying. Time has helped calm my memories, and being on the ranch, surrounded by a million spiders, I've become more numb to those as well. Not saying the first two weeks weren't torture whenever I'd see one, screaming they wanted to eat me.

Ted is my arachnid-slaying hero.

Dr. Betty has transitioned me to the next phase: self-defense.

Work on rebuilding my confidence, a step toward reclaiming my life. Martinez gave me the horrible news a couple days ago that I was losing my officer detail. I bawled like my death was imminent.

They don't care about my safety anymore.

Ted reminded me that I don't need them. If I was really worried about it, I could hire my own security. I've yet to adventure outside the gates of the property, but I'm thinking he's right. I have the money. Well, *almost.* Until I gather up the courage to leave, the lottery ticket is safe and sound in a deposit box.

This might be the push I need.

After a hearty protein-filled breakfast Ted insisted I would need, I meet the man who represents my next phase. A short, muscular man with a buzz cut and tattoos peeking out under his T-shirt up his neck stares at me.

"Kali, I'm Zander." He makes a calculated effort to not squeeze when we shake hands.

Since I've started physical therapy on my hands, they're starting to feel normal, so I wish he didn't hold back. *They still don't look normal.* Martinez told me Zander works with Austin PD, teaching police self-defense. When he learned about what happened, he personally volunteered to help me.

"Nice to meet you. So, you're here to help me kick ass."

He chuckles, but not in a funny way. More sarcastic. "I'm here to teach you to defend yourself. But the first thing you need to learn is to read the room."

I raise a brow, placing a hand on my hip. "I have no problem reading rooms."

Like right now, you're being an asshole.

"The night you were kidnapped, did you notice the strange car that had never been parked there before? Or that the streetlight was out?"

Way to shoot straight for the jugular.

I cross my arms, feeling attacked.

"Don't get all defensive," he remarks, a hint of amusement in his voice. I find none of this amusing. "You did what most people would do. You knew the area well and were complacent. I bet half the time you walked home, you didn't remember getting there."

Now, I feel exposed.

"I felt something was off, but then I saw the light was broken. What am I supposed to do? Live a life questioning everything?"

"No," he responds. "I'm just saying to pay more attention. If something seems out of place, question it. You were on a dark street, alone, with no protection. Why did you keep going?"

Because I was complacent.

I nod in resignation because, he's right, I didn't see the car. I'll be living in a big city soon, so I should listen to the guy and be more vigilant. Yet, for the time being, he doesn't have to worry about me not looking over my shoulder and questioning everything.

"I'll be better at that," I murmur, a silent promise to myself.

His militant eyes bore into mine for a beat, as if he's attempting to install the sixth sense into my brain. His loud clap makes me jump. "Ok. Now, let's learn how to kick ass."

"WAIT, I CAN'T BREATHE," I say, doubled over, holding my chest with one hand as my heart tries to implode. When he doesn't respond, I lift my head, and he stands there with a heavy brow lifted high.

He glances at his watch. "We've been running for five minutes." No way. It had to be longer than that. "You better hope you don't have to run from someone," he deadpans.

This guy is not a motivational speaker.

"I have a good five minutes of running to get away," I retort, standing with a smug yet breathy smile. I wipe off the bead of sweat running down my temple.

"You call that *good*?"

Wow! He is not a nice person. My middle finger jumps up on

its own and flips him off. He deserves it. It's the first time I've heard his laugh. It's loud and bold, a lot like his personality. "I thought everyone here was supposed to help me, not demean me and make me feel like shit."

"I'm sorry, I didn't take you for a princess."

"I'm not," I spit back. I've always been a fighter.

Just not a runner.

He exhales a long, measured breath. "I know you're not. I've read your file. I want you to reach deep inside and pull out the anger you have simmering in your veins for all the people who have screwed you over in your life and channel that rage to energize yourself." His finger taps my chest over my heart. "It's in there. Put all that focus on the motherfucking asshole who's still walking the streets that put you in a grave."

A surge of adrenaline courses through my veins.

While the wounds of my past lie buried within, the mention of the grave unleashes a fierce, burning intensity on the surface. Without waiting for him, I spin around and sprint as fast as my legs will carry me down the narrow dirt path alongside the barbed fence. I round the large oak tree where Rusty and I grab apples. Despite the ache in my hips, I press through the pain until I can't run any further. Collapsing under the shade of a tree, I catch my breath. Zander jogs up, not even breaking a sweat. Despite the burn in my lungs and the spots dancing in my vision, I manage to muster a smile.

"Better?" I mutter, swiping the beads of sweat off my forehead.

He nods. "It's a start."

My smile falls, and I huff. "I don't think I like you very much."

He offers me his hand, pulling me up in one swift motion. "Not here to be your friend."

"Do you have any friends?" I ask, dusting the dirt off my butt.

He bursts into genuine laughter. "Ready to run back?"

"You are definitely my enemy," I murmur, jogging at a sluggish pace this time toward the house, with him laughing behind me, strolling along like he's on a leisurely walk.

Later that night, as I lie in a hot saltwater bath, my muscles protesting every move, I think about Zander's words.

"I want you to reach deep inside and pull out the anger you have simmering in your veins for all the people who have screwed you over and channel that rage to energize yourself."

For the last month, I've been urged to be calm. Spend time with Rusty and let his strength become my own. But I need to find my own inner strength.

Dr. Betty told me part of the healing process will also involve confronting my fear head-on. But how do I do that? What does that even look like? Does she expect me to get back into a confined box? Because I struggle being in the bathroom with the door closed. Even when I die, I want to be cremated. The idea of lying there for eternity, even after death, is not an option.

Not anymore.

Strangely, my thoughts drift to Officer Paxton Turner. Does he have nightmares about finding me? Thoughts of *what if* he hadn't found me. Does the profound impact of finding me resonate as strongly with him as it does with me? Then I remind myself he saves people every day. It's his job. But the urge to reach out and tell him I'm doing better is constantly on my mind. I need to thank him for everything.

Emerging from the water, I reach for my phone, resting on the tub's edge, playing music. I saved his number in my phone. Mainly to add more contacts than just two—*Dr. Betty and Martinez.* I'll text him. This way it doesn't have to be awkward if he doesn't want to talk to me.

> Me: Hi Paxton

I pause before continuing. Are we on a first-name basis? I shake my head and hit delete and try again.

> Me: Hi, Officer Turner. This is Kali Stevens. I just wanted to tell you and Riggs that I'm doing good, thanks to you.

I hit send before I can talk myself out of it. He won't text back, but I already feel better thanking him. After all, he likely shares his number with all the victims he deals with.

My phone dings, and I jump so fast for it that it tips, falling toward the hot water. I catch it right before it submerges. *Nice save.*

> Officer Turner: Kali, that is great news. Please, call me Paxton. I've been thinking of you.

I stare at his response until the water turns cold. For a moment, I let his response be what it isn't. I imagine a man telling me he misses me and can't wait till the next time we see each other. The fantasy unfolds further to the day we meet again, and he pulls me in for a tight embrace, his hard body pressed against mine as he passionately kisses me.

Another ding brings me back to reality, and I chuckle at my momentary lapse into a fantasy world. Paxton probably has a wife and kids. Still holding my phone, I almost forget another text came in. When I look down, I can't help the warm glow flowing through me.

> Officer Turner: If you need any help moving into a new place, let me know.

CHAPTER 16

Kali

> Me: I have a question.

> Me: Feel free to say no.

THIS HAS to be the dumbest idea I've ever had.

> Paxton: Yes.

I can't help but laugh. I wonder if he's this funny in real life. For a few weeks, we've been texting back and forth. I feel normal when we text, not the broken girl, even though he was the one who rescued me. It's like my brain has separated the two.

> Me: Okay. You said yes. Meet me here on Saturday.

> Paxton: Time?

Oh, shit. This is really happening.

> Me: Um...three?

Paxton: See you at three.

AT EXACTLY THREE O'CLOCK, Paxton stands at the front door. My belly aches from nerves as I open the door and our eyes meet. I might not have thought this through. It's been two months since we saw each other in the hospital. Talking through texts has been easy.

This isn't easy.

"Hi," I say, trying to act normal. Trying to breathe normally.

His smile, softened by the rough stubble and intense eyes, surprisingly steadies me. "Hey," he says, breaking the awkward tension. "I brought a friend."

"Riggs!" I exclaim, beaming as I notice the dog I'd missed in my focus on Paxton. I kneel to give him some deep rubs behind his ears before standing back up when I hear Ted behind me.

Ted insisted on meeting him before we left. It felt weird and wonderful having a father figure worry about me. Having both Amy and Ted so invested in my healing has helped me become a stronger version of myself. Zander may be the one who is equipping me physically, but dinnertime conversations around the dining table, movies on the couch, and laughter with Ted and Amy have made me feel so much stronger emotionally.

I've never felt this cared for—loved—since I lost my parents.

Introductions are made quickly, and we're out the door. I needed to rush things along because the longer I stood there, the more second thoughts crept in.

Paxton opens the door for me and asks where we're headed. I bite my lip, hesitating as he stares at me with a lifted brow. "We're going back to the spot."

He does a hard nod and shuts my door without a word. He probably thinks I'm crazy. When he gets in, I wait for him to say something—anything—but he stays silent, putting the Jeep in drive and heading down the dirt drive.

Minutes pass before he finally asks, "You sure about this?" His focus is on me as the wind swirls around us in the open Jeep.

Stray hairs dance in the gusts, and I all but give up keeping them in check. I try to control the jittery nerves, my leg bouncing with pent-up energy. As I chew my inner cheek, my eyes fix on Paxton, still surprised he's here.

I fidget in my seat. "This is stupid, isn't it?" Please say it is.

"This is your thing. Personally, I'd rather never see that place again, but if it's something you need to do, I'm happy you called me." Riggs barks in the back seat, and Paxton gives him a side eye over his shoulder. "Okay, us. Called us. Better?" Riggs barks again, making me laugh. He can't be that smart, can he?

Paxton's crooked smile sends a subtle thrill in places it shouldn't. *He's so good-looking.* I avert my eyes forward and focus on the monotonous stretch of road ahead, rather than on the muscles in his arms or the way his sturdy fingers grip the wheel. Or how sexy he looks with his baseball cap backward. There's something familiar about him with his cap on, but I can't place it. He looks younger. But my thoughts, at the moment, are a chaotic mess when all I can focus on is my next phase: confronting my chamber of horror.

What is wrong with me? Dr. Betty mentioned alternative approaches to confront my trauma, but I must do this on my own. A way to prove to myself that he didn't win. I think of the worn paper in my pocket. *Don't give him control.*

Needing a distraction, and clearly Paxton is a distraction, I shift in my seat.

"Are you married? Or have a girlfriend?" Brown eyes turn toward me with a hint of amusement. I wave him off as if I'm not asking for a personal inquiry. Maybe I'm asking for a friend. "If a lady calls me upset about her husband spending time with me, I want to be prepared. I should've asked this before."

His laugh catches in the wind. I love his laugh. It's carefree and infectious and what I need right now. "If some woman calls you saying she's my wife, I'm gonna need a heads-up so I can get a restraining order in place."

"Girlfriend?" I press, because there's no way this guy is unattached. Not looking like that. He loves his dog, and he's a live-action hero. Saving people every day, myself included.

He shakes his head, and I remain still, shooting him an incredulous glare because it's difficult to believe. He shrugs. "I date. I haven't found the woman I want to spend the rest of my life with yet."

Riggs sticks his head between the two of us and I scratch it. *You need to approve of her too, huh?*

But any fluttering butterflies in my chest die a swift death the second the Jeep veers off the main road. Even though I don't know our location, an eerie sense of closeness fills the air. The stench is already clogging up my throat. I'm thrown back in time. My hands grip the bar in front of me, and I squeeze my eyes shut in sheer terror.

The truck comes to an abrupt stop. "That's it. We're turning around."

My eyes fly open, and a wave of blistering heat hits me, intensifying the moment. "No." I take quick breaths and plead with my eyes. "I can do it. I need to do it."

He lifts his ball cap off and runs his hands through his hair before putting it back on. "I don't know if I can stomach watching you torment yourself."

I shake out the tenseness in my arms and sit up taller. He's right. I'm here to prove this place doesn't control me, but now the invisible leash tightens, proving the opposite.

"Please," I beg, desperation lacing my plea.

He shakes his head in disapproval but puts the Jeep back in drive.

We stop, the empty grave to the right of us. I unfasten my seat belt, not allowing myself any time to reconsider. Both my feet hit dirt, and my mouth feels like a desert, making it impossible to swallow. This is where he stood, reveling in my terror, listening to my desperate pleas for life as I fought like a rabid animal, caged.

Paxton walks around to the front of the Jeep and waits for me, an unspoken understanding lingering in his eyes. Paxton directs Riggs to stay.

"When you get there, Kali, remember that you survived. As you confront that faceless, cowardly demon, you remind yourself that you survived. He didn't win. You survived." Dr. Betty's words swirl through my mind as I sense the evil around me.

With each step, I whisper, "I survived" to myself. The earth shifts with each footfall, the weight causing a slight earthquake underneath me. I pause for a moment, glancing at the tree Paxton placed me under, giving me a moment to regain my senses. I exhale with puffed-out cheeks, shaking out my hands. Fresh scars line the tops of my hands, serving as a visceral reminder of the ferocious struggle. My nails, though still horrendous, are growing back. "I survived."

I continue, nearing the edge of the hole, and Paxton matches my steps, a silent pillar of support at my side. The closer I get, the harder it is to breathe. Yellow tape still surrounds the hole, a stark reminder to the world that the girl buried alive suffered right here. As we approach, Paxton tears off one side of the tape, letting it fall to the ground. It dances like a serpent in the breeze before getting wrapped around the wooden stake.

I gaze down and swallow hard. They removed the box, leaving behind a random hole in the ground. I thought it would be deeper. In the suffocating darkness, it felt as if there was a mountain above me.

Squatting down to a sitting position, I sit at the edge before pushing off and jumping into the hole. It's only about four feet deep. Being free, it's surreal to think this was the exact spot that held me captive.

A hawk soars overhead, casting a fleeting shadow, circling in search of death.

Not going to find it here. Not today.

Paxton watches me from above as I lie down. His crossed arms are tense, but he remains quiet. There's a single cloud above, shielding me from the intense afternoon sun. Off in the distance, a clap of thunder warns of impending rain.

My fingers dig into the bed of the grave, and I take a deep whiff of the surrounding earth. *This is not the devil's playground.* The dirt is as innocent as me. *I am not afraid of you.* For the first time, my stomach doesn't twist. "I am free. This hole can't hurt me anymore. It's not the villain."

A sense of calmness envelops me, and my lips curve up. Even though Dr. Betty told me I had made great improvements, I questioned if I really had. I was in a controlled arena, and I wondered if I would crumble the second I got within five feet of this place. But I didn't. I did it. "I beat you, asshole. You didn't kill me. You didn't break me. I. Beat. You."

That same surge of energy propels me upward. Paxton extends his hand to help me up from the shallow hole, but my uncontrollable excitement sends me right into his arms. He catches me effortlessly, my feet dangling above the ground. In that perfect moment of a million milliseconds, everything around us disappears. His eyes fill with longing as they drop to my wet lips. My heart moves faster than my brain, like lightning chasing thunder, and before I can stop myself, I lean in to kiss him.

And then it ends before it begins.

He sets me down and twists away from me, his shoulders tense as he silently fights with himself.

Oh my gosh. Why did I do that? "I'm sorry. I didn't mean—"

He whips back around, shaking his head and running his hand over his stubbled beard. "Kali, there's nothing to be sorry about." He sighs, shoving his hands into his short pockets. "You're the one dealing with all these emotions. I'm supposed to be the one in control."

Right," I say, relieved he's offering me an out to one of the most embarrassing moments of my life. "Because if I was in control, we'd probably both be dodging emotional landmines like it's a game of Twister."

His laugh lightens the moment. "You would totally win because I'd trip on the first one."

"Oh, whatever, sly. I saw the video of you jumping some fence." Of course, I googled him and that was the first thing that popped up.

He rolls his eyes, biting his bottom lip. "I can't believe you saw that."

"It was the comments from the women that did it for me. I've never seen women act that desperate. I was a slightly afraid for your safety," I tease, happy to have moved on from the awkward kissing attempt.

"Freaking man-eaters," he says, laughing out loud as we start heading back to the Jeep.

I stop before getting in, turning to face him, a weight of gratitude filling my chest. "I just…can't thank you enough."

"Stop. You don't have to thank me for anything," he insists. I have everything to thank him for. He has to see that. I don't imagine this area gets a lot of traffic. If not for him and Riggs, we'd be standing at my gravesite. A flash of lightning brightens the sky behind him. The storm is getting closer. "Was that your stomach?"

"No, it was thunder," I lie, a blush coloring my cheeks as I glance down. Dirt covers my brand-new white shoes. "I should've eaten lunch." Glancing at my watch, I realize it's already four. I had too much anxiety to eat before I left, but now my stomach is revolting.

"I have stuff to cook at my cabin," he offers, but sensing my hesitation, he quickly suggests, "Or, I can take you to dinner? Either way, you're getting something to eat."

It's not about the food, it's him taking me to his house. I practically just threw myself at him. But he's right, that was a momentary lapse of judgement caused by an emotional heart attack. This is silly, I can control myself around him. I'm not one of those man-eating women. With my clothes covered in dirt and having already fished rocks and sticks from my hair, I'd rather not embarrass him in public.

I brush my palm against my dirty shorts. "The cabin sounds great, if that's all right. I'm a bit of a mess right now."

"No, it's perfect," he says, reassuring me. "I just stocked up on groceries. Hope you like steak and potatoes."

I stare at him for a few seconds, biting my lip. "I'm a vegetarian," I deadpan.

His face contorts as if he ate a lemon before he manages to plaster a forged smile on his face. "Okay. I, ah, think I have stuff to make a salad."

He shifts from foot to foot, and my laughter bubbles up. "I'm kidding. Texas girl here, through and through. Medium rare, and I'll eat any type of potato that's put in front of me."

"Kalico, you are my type of person."

Did he just give me a nickname? "Kalico?"

"It's fitting. You're cute and have nine lives."

Cute? Like little sister cute? Friend cute? Cute is not the word for a girl you like, right? I tamper down the flutters in my belly. *Don't misread him, Kali.* He just made it clear he wasn't into you five minutes ago. He's just being a nice guy. A friend.

He walks around the Jeep. "I've got pie too," he says over his shoulder, and I freeze, wondering why his words give me pause. I blink as memories of the college guy who sent me a pie flood my mind. "Kali, what's wrong?"

Light-brown eyes meet mine, and I draw comparisons between the two guys. No. It's not him. *There is no way.* That guy had green eyes, was clean shaven, and he was a student—definitely younger.

They both have a sexy smile. But that doesn't make them the same person.

"Nothing... I just got lost in thought." I wave him off. "What kind of pie?"

"Pecan, of course. Is there any other?"

I can think of at least five that's better than pecan.

I playfully sigh as I shake my head. "Nobody can be perfect."

CHAPTER 17
Kali

HE DIDN'T CAPTURE my breath; he breathed life back into me.

And now, my heart is confused.

Leaning against the counter, I let my gaze wander up and down his silhouette while he peels potatoes. Though I offered to help, he insisted I sit back and relax. He glances over his broad shoulder, catching me staring, and responds with a curious lift of his dark brow.

"You're going to spoil me," I remark, never having had a man cook for me.

He shrugs and turns back around, replying, "You deserve to be spoiled."

That's incredibly sexy, adding another layer of confusion. My heart thuds against my ribs, shouting at me to take notice. *I see, heart, I see.*

But a guy like him, one who could have any woman, doesn't want a small-town girl like me with a brand-new set of emotional baggage that weighs two tons. If he knew the real me, the one before he became my hero, I'd never be on his radar. Maybe if I told him I was a millionaire, he'd change his mind. I inwardly groan, dropping my head. Manipulation isn't my style, and I'm not that person.

"Hey, where'd you go?"

I glance up to find him leaning against the counter, arms crossed, his eyes fixed on me. Self-doubt is another unattractive trait I know he wouldn't appreciate in a woman, so I ease into a smile and shake my head. "Just a lot to think about."

Rather than probing further, he grins and suggests, "I have the perfect place for that."

He grabs a candle, bug spray, and a blanket, holding the door open for me. The screen door slams behind us, and I turn back to see Riggs sitting at the door, whining. I shoot him a sympathetic look. *I'd bring you if I could, buddy.* Paxton ignores him and leads me down a set of stairs to a lower deck, steps from the water.

The scene unfolds in pure tranquility, with the water laying still like a reflective mirror beneath the fallen clouds. The storm shifted directions and seems this round will miss us.

"How can you ever leave this place?" I marvel.

"If it wasn't for work, I'd never leave. But it's also why I spend most of my free time out here," he shares.

I settle into one of the Adirondack chairs. He places the bug spray and candle on the table beside me and retrieves a lighter, lighting the candle.

"The damn mosquitoes are vampires. This'll help." The scent of citronella wafts through the air as the candle flickers.

"This is amazing," I reply.

He tilts his head, gesturing that he's going back up, and waits for me to nod before leaving. *His momma raised him well.* I bet he's a big momma's boy.

After he's out of sight, I spot a red canoe at the water's edge, tempting me. Would it be rude? He offered this space for me to think...and the water looks so inviting.

I forget the phrase Pearl always used—something about asking for forgiveness later. He won't mind. I've never been in a canoe. It can't be hard, right? I pick up an oar and slide into the single seat. Now what? The canoe stays wedged between the water and the shore, half in and half out. To free it, I sway back and forth, using the oar to push off the ground. I groan at the stuck canoe.

What was I thinking?

I know how to canoe like I know how to surf—clueless and likely to end up drowning.

"Need some help?"

I yelp at the voice, twisting around. Paxton stands there with an amused expression.

Good, he's smiling.

"Naw. I'm trying to see how a beached whale feels," I joke.

His laugh echoes over the lake. "In that case, it's my job to keep you wet." Cold water splashes on me, running down my skin.

"Paxton!" I half yell, half laugh as I wipe my arms off. "You are mean, sir."

"Kali, you have no idea." He laughs.

He surprises me again with a quick shove. The ground releases me, and I'm floating atop the water. My fingers have a death grip around the sides of the canoe. The slightest movement makes the canoe tilt.

"What are the odds of this thing turning over if I move?" I inquire, frozen in place, afraid to even look back at Paxton.

A brief hum makes me regret taking it out. "You should be all right."

"That doesn't sound reassuring." I chuckle nervously. I'm glad he finds this whole thing entertaining. I don't. The water beneath me is murky, and I'd rather not find out what's waiting for me below the surface or how deep it is.

"You can swim, right?"

"You're not helping," I quip, but thankfully the answer is yes. Yes, I can.

"Keep it steady, no sudden movements," he says. *I figured that much out myself.* "Put the oar in the water to one side and glide it through the water." I follow his instructions with minimal motion, but the canoe turns rather than goes forward.

"Shouldn't I have two oars?" I ask as the canoe pivots, now facing Paxton. I lift the oar, hoping that will make it stop turning.

"You alternate sides," he explains, gesturing the movement. Sounds simple enough. But it'd be easier with two oars, though. I try it out and move in a straight line. "I'm going to go finish dinner. Think you can stay out of the water?"

Switching between smiling and wincing and then smiling again, I nod, excited I'm getting the hang of it, but still afraid to move. I hadn't noticed Riggs on the beach until he laid down, keeping his eyes trained on me. As I glide closer to the middle of the lake, I slow my strokes, letting the warmth of the sun blanket me. This is how I imagined it would be out here: quiet. Not dead quiet like my box, but a peaceful quiet. It's freeing. Now and then, a cicada sends out its battle cry, but in between is where the magic happens.

I lie back—carefully—and watch the fluffy clouds morph into shapes above me, throwing me back in time. Summer days with my mom, a time when nothing was more important than our trips to the public pool and what friends were going to meet us there. I was naïve to the evils of the world. They hadn't invaded my life. Yet.

But right here, right now, this is…

Crack.

Shuffling sounds follow what seemed like someone stepping on a branch coming from the shoreline. The opposite shoreline. I jerk up, staring, gripping both sides of the canoe. Searching. Glancing back to Paxton's side, Riggs is standing alert, staring at the same spot where the noise came from. Chills run up my back, and my arms and legs break out in goose bumps. I remember Zander's words, *"Question things that seem out of place."*

Riggs barks, and it's not a friendly bark. It's a warning.

A warning for me to get the hell out of here.

With hurried, careful strokes, I navigate the canoe back toward Riggs, stealing glances over my shoulder every few seconds. Nothing like freaking out in the middle of a lake. Paxton is already at the shoreline when the canoe slices up the bank, pulling me in further and helping me out. My chest heaves with panic.

"What happened?"

"I think…" I turn, my gaze fixed on the spot, still seeing nothing but the dense cover of trees. I clear the panic from my throat. "I think someone was there. What if it's…" My voice trails off. It doesn't need to be said. He understands.

He looks down at Riggs, still barking, and then stares across the lake for a few moments. Riggs settles and sits. "It was probably a deer. He always goes crazy when he sees one."

That makes sense. Of course, there's wildlife all around here.

"Now I feel silly," I say, shaking out my trembling hands.

He takes my hands in his. "I promise, you're safe here."

I'd like to believe that, but a madman is out there, and Paxton isn't invincible. But I sigh and nod.

"I need to throw the steaks on the grill for a few minutes to finish dinner. Still hungry?"

More so now that I spent all my energy between fear and rowing like my life depended on it. "Before we eat, do you mind if I take a shower?" There's a layer of wet dirt caked on my skin, a combination of dust and sweat. The thought of him being close, watching me, makes me feel violated.

"Not at all. Second door on the right is the guest bathroom. There's shampoo and soap. Let me know if you need anything else."

"That's great. Thanks."

The renovated bathroom gleams in sparkling white with clean lines, more of a modern flare. I'm certain it's a stark contrast to the original design. I turn the faucet on, shedding my shirt, and cringe at the line of dirt where my shirt used to be. Gross. Despite knowing my clothes will still be dirty when I put them on, I won't be. My eyes shift to the empty towel rack. Great. I check all the cabinets, finding no towels. Typical man. Not one towel in the guest bathroom. I hate bothering him, but there's not even a rag I could use to dry myself off. Grabbing my shirt off the floor, I slip it back over my head and turn off the shower. As I'm about to round the corner, I overhear Paxton talking.

"If you could check it out for me."

I peek around and see he's on the phone, so I decide to wait for him to finish.

"There's no way I'm leaving her, or I'd do it myself," he murmurs into the phone.

My shoulders tense. Screw privacy. He's talking about me. Leaning my ear forward, I shamelessly eavesdrop.

"Riggs doesn't bark like that with other animals. He saw someone."

I suck in a quick breath and yank my hand over my mouth to stifle the noise. He lied. There's a long pause while I assume the other person talks, or he heard me gasp.

"No. She's taking a shower right now." Another pause. "Shut it. Nothing is going on. I'm helping her out. I'm taking her back after dinner."

I sigh, unsure if the dispelled air is because he lied to me or that he's not into me. It shouldn't be the latter, because what would I even do with a relationship right now? I don't know what tomorrow looks like. Still, there's a lingering sting of rejection.

Not caring anymore if he sees me, I step into the living area where he's standing, staring out the window. Riggs glances up from his bed, causing Paxton to shift his attention to me. He plays it off.

"Okay, cool. Thanks for your help." I wrap my arms around my waist, staring at him. "That was a quick shower."

"Couldn't find a towel." I can't hide the irritation.

He arches an eyebrow. "You heard." It's not a question. A low growl emerges from the back of his throat as he tucks his phone into his pocket. "I didn't want to scare you. Well, more than you already were."

A sarcastic laugh escapes my lips. He didn't know my insides were exploding like the finale of a fireworks show. "That wasn't possible."

"Truthfully, I doubt it was him. Sometimes, people hike over there. There's no way he would find you here. You have a new phone, so he can't be tracking you."

"Unless…"

There was a movie I watched with Ted. *Divergent. That was fiction.* My subconscious tries to reason with me. But *what if* it can be done?

The idea detonates into panic and erases any shred of sanity. I tear off my top and drop my shorts and stand nearly naked in front of his surprised expression. "Search me."

CHAPTER 18

Paxton

DON'T LOOK.

I try not to. I *really* do.

But she's almost naked, begging me to search her, and that's like asking a dog not to eat a steak that's laid down in front of them. *Impossible.*

My immediate response should've been professional. I should've kept my gaze locked on hers, resisting the urge to let them wander. Matching light pink lace bra and panties. *Pull your shit together, Pax. Treat her like any other victim in panic mode. She's not stripping for me.* Pulling away when she tried to kiss me took inner strength I didn't know I was capable of.

It was too soon. When she's with me—and she will be—it won't be under duress.

"What am I searching for?" I swallow hard.

Panic flickers in her eyes as she frantically examines herself, twisting her arms and legs, searching for something. "He drugged me, and since I was buried for only five hours means he had hours to do whatever he wanted with me. What if he implanted a tracking device somewhere?" She motions with her hands down her body.

It's possible but not likely. I've read about things like that in sci-fi books, but I've never come across it in real life.

"You probably would've noticed a lesion."

She looks up and blinks. "I had a million cuts all over."

Fuck, I'm stupid.

I tug on my ear. "Just double-checking, would you rather have a female look you over to make you feel more comfortable. I can call a female officer."

"Paxton. I don't care who looks me over. You're here. So, please, look." Her blue eyes plead with me.

"If I find a lump, we are *not* digging it out," I state firmly, staring at her until she agrees. I don't need her freaking out and cutting holes in her body. "I'll call a doctor friend if we find something."

She draws in a long breath and blows it out slowly, nodding.

I start with one wrist, since she's already holding them out, and run my thumbs over the veins. She flinches at my touch, and I glance up.

"Sorry. It tickled."

Tell me to stop.

"Keep going."

I nod and continue up her forearm, searching for any marks or lumps. Inch by inch, the struggle intensifies as temptation tightens its grip. This is torture, and I just started. Truthfully, I don't know what it would look like, but I'm assuming there'll be a mark. If it makes her relax, I'll do whatever she asks. I pay extra attention to her upper arms, starting with the left and moving to the right. It's where I would plant one on someone. Easy access. She has a scar on her upper right shoulder, but it's not a new one.

"Did you know your scar looks like Florida?"

She shifts her shoulder forward, scrutinizing the scar with a thoughtful expression, and tilts her head. "Huh. I never noticed."

"What's it from?" I ask, needing her to keep talking to drown out my heavy breaths.

"When I was a kid, I fell out of a tree." She chuckles with a small shake of her head. "My dad was so mad at me. He always told me to stay off this specific branch. He warned me it was dead and wouldn't be able to hold my weight." As she gets lost in her story, I keep searching, grateful for the distraction. "I was more mad at him, saying he was calling me fat, and I wanted to prove him wrong. That didn't go well." She laughs.

"Sounds like my dad," I remark, scanning each leg. "The first time I shot a shotgun, he told me how to hold it, but I didn't listen to him. I was a stubborn kid. By then, I'd shot a gun plenty of times and knew what I was doing. So I thought. Let's just say the recoil was more than I was expecting. Walked around with two black eyes for a week."

"Ouch," she empathizes.

I grab her clothes off the floor after finishing checking her over. Other than the fresh scars on her knuckles, knees, and elbows, I found nothing else.

"It hurt my ego more," I confess, standing in front of her. My laugh dies down as the naked space between us fills with a charged silence. My grip tightens around her clothes.

"Thank you," she whispers.

"You're welcome."

Her eyes fill with need. Every part of me screams to reach for her. But I can't. I don't want a quick fling, and if we take it there tonight, that's all it'll be. She'll leave here with regret and never call me again. When I don't move, her cheeks redden, and she reaches for her clothes. Fuck. I'd be an asshole if I pulled her into my bedroom. A satisfied asshole, but a major asshole, nonetheless.

"Ahh... I'm going to go take that shower," she murmurs.

Our fingers brush against each other, and I swallow back the temptation.

"Oh, wait," I say, my brain finally working as I jog to the hallway linen closet. I pull out a towel and walk over to her. "You might need this."

"Thanks." She grabs it and turns, heading to the bathroom.

My eyes linger on her heart-shaped ass. "Kali, will you go out on a date with me?"

She glances over her shoulder and scrunches her nose adorably while nodding.

"That a yes?"

She chuckles. It's such a welcome sound. I thought I messed everything up when she overheard me on the phone with Pete earlier. Could there have been someone over there? *Possibly*. People hike all around these parts.

"It's a yes. Thanks for not letting me think it was just me. You like me, Officer Turner," she says as if there were ever a question. She walks into the bathroom, shutting the door behind her.

A half-strangled laugh comes out because my desire for her has been a relentless force since I laid eyes on her. She's defiant. I like it. She's determined to prove to the world that she's fine. Even lying in the empty grave that threatened to take her life was an act of defiance, a statement to herself that it wouldn't. She probably hated showing her vulnerability earlier. I'm glad she did it with me. *Me.* I was the one person she shared that moment with. When I got her call, I canceled meeting up with Liam at the gym and canceled my dinner plans with a few buddies. I would've canceled dinner with the president for her.

Of course, I like her.

I mean, finders keepers, right?

And I found you.

CHAPTER 19

Paxton

"HOW'S THE KID?" Liam asks the moment he catches sight of Riggs and me walking into the training center. Liam is close to joining the K-9 unit with Bear, the largest bloodhound I've ever seen.

"Shaken, but alive. Learned a valuable lesson. Fuck around and find out. He won't ever run away again." Some tween—a term for a preteen I hadn't heard before—was pissed at his parents for taking away his Xbox for grades, so he ran away. Dumbass should've gone to a friend's house, but instead took a walk through hill country and got lost.

"You ready to get some training on?" I ask Riggs, walking over to sign us in at the front desk.

"You rappelling today?"

"Heck yeah," I say, pumped and ready to rappel off a thirty-foot building, Riggs strapped to my back. I'm not certain what Riggs will think about it, but we're about to find out.

"I'm going to stick around and watch."

As we walk out to the training area, I can't shake the thoughts of my date with Kali this weekend.

"Have you thought about what I should do with Kali?" I ask.

"What is it about this girl?" he responds.

Isn't that the question of the hour? I've asked myself the same thing. There's a connection, a pull, that I've felt from day one. I need to see where this goes.

"You think this is a good idea?"

He acts as if I'm committing a crime. I'm not. Sure, Internal Affairs might have a few questions, but there are key points that are important here. First, it's been a couple months since her incident, and second, she contacted me. That's not to say I wouldn't have contacted her, but they don't need to know that tidbit because she beat me to it. *She feels our connection, too.* After our dinner last week, I took her home right after. The day's adrenaline hit her like a wall, and she could barely keep her eyes open. But I left her with a promise that I was taking her on a proper date.

"I'm not doing anything wrong." I shrug. "So, help me figure this shit out."

For the first time, well, ever, I don't have any idea where to take Kali on a date. The pressure to find the perfect first date setting shouldn't be this hard. I have this fear that I have one shot. Dinner at a restaurant feels too impersonal. It sounds ridiculous, since that's where I typically take a woman on a first date.

But Kali isn't typical. I want a more intimate setting. Where it's just us, no distractions.

"Take her out on the boat for dinner under the stars. Women eat that shit up," he says.

I lift a brow, surprised at his suggestion. I never would've pegged the man as a romantic, but it makes sense if he is chasing tail. Romance isn't his end goal. It's a means to an end for him. But in my case, where I want her to myself, it's a damn good idea. Plus, she likes it out on the water.

"You won't mind?" It's his boat, after all.

He shakes his head. "Hell no. You can always take it out. Mom needs help with moving some stuff this weekend, so I won't be using it."

His mom rocks. Especially when she sends us sweet treats.

She's retired and has become our personal department's pastry chef. Everyone loves Momma Rose.

He veers off to watch from the side, and I hear him say, "Maybe now you'll get some work done and stop fretting about this damn woman."

"I'm great at multitasking. I was even thinking about where I should take her when I was kicking your ass at the gym last night," I yell back, and he continues rumbling with excuses about how his hip was still hurting from tackling some guy during a robbery as I pull out my phone. I'd rather call her, hear her voice, but considering I'm about to jump off a building in five minutes, texting will have to do for now.

> Me: Is four on Saturday good? Pack a swimsuit.

I slide the phone in my side pocket, not expecting her to reply. She's probably out with Rusty and having a session with Zander. But when I feel it vibrate, I can't help the shit-eating grin.

> Kalico: Yes! Can't wait! Where are we going?

> Me: It's a surprise.

> Kalico: If you don't answer me, I'm not bringing a swimsuit.

> Me: Fine with me. It's been a while since I've been skinny-dipping.

> Kalico: I'll bring a suit

"I'M NOT SURE ABOUT THIS." My grams's voice echoes in the Jeep as I drive to pick Kali up.

Why is everyone giving me their opinion that this is a bad idea? Kali is the best idea I've ever had. I've gone through a lot of trouble to get to this point, and I'm not backing away now.

"Why's that?" I prompt, even though I know what's coming.

"That girl's been through so much already."

I stare at my dashboard with my mouth hanging open. And here I assumed I was her favorite. Dating me will not add to Kali's troubles. I'm a damn good catch.

"It might be too soon. And they're going to find out," she adds, her voice lowering.

It's been two months, and they haven't yet.

We'll cross that bridge if we get there.

I let out a sigh, hating that I'm worrying her. "Grams, I'm not pushing her to do anything. I'll go as slow as she needs. But I'm telling you now, I'm marrying this woman."

"Pax! You barely know her."

She's right. I could be wrong about Kali, but I don't believe so. I laugh, already knowing the answer, but I ask to make a point. "How long did you and Pops date before getting engaged?"

"It was a different time," she snaps back.

Well, as much as Grams can snap at me. She and Pops have been my rock through the years. I wouldn't have survived losing Jack and Dad if it hadn't been for them. And even though Mom made it almost impossible for them to get in touch with me after Dad died, whenever they got a chance, they were quick to remind me that they were always on my side.

"Mm-hmm," I murmur, pulling up to a red stoplight hanging from a wire above as I drive into town. A sheriff hangs out in the gas station parking lot, waiting for an out-of-towner to miss the drop in speed. Man, I'd hate to work in a small town. I bet he's there often during the week. "Well, I'm almost here, so I gotta go. Tell Pops hi and love you both."

"Love you too. Be careful, Paxton."

"Always, Grams."

CHAPTER 20
Paxton

"I COULD'VE MET you somewhere. This place is so out of the way for you," Kali says as she settles into the Jeep, tossing her bag into the back seat.

I shut her door and circle around to the driver's side. The moment she stepped into the living room and smiled, the way her eyes lit up— damn, I knew this wasn't a mistake. I want to get to know this woman more. The light missing from her eyes the day I saved her is returning to its vibrant, natural state.

Before reversing, I twist in my seat and stare for a moment longer than necessary. Her cheeks flush pink, and she shifts in her seat. "It's our first date. I am not making you meet me somewhere. Grams would kill me if I did that."

Her face lights up. "Tell me about your grams."

I put the Jeep in drive. "Her and Pops live in Michigan. She's the glue of our family. Without her, I'd have been in jail right now."

Her eyebrows shoot up in surprise. "For what?"

I smirk. "Murder."

"Is this when I should be concerned?" Her voice dances with

amusement. She thinks I'm joking. I'm not. But discussing my stepfather wasn't how I wanted to kick off our date.

As we merge onto the main road, I'm careful with my speed, aware of who's waiting ahead. "Let's say...she was the light at the end of my tunnel. Pushed me toward the badge and all."

"Aw, the classic transformation of bad boy to hero," she quips playfully.

I give her a sideways glance. "Do I look like a bad boy?" I'm curious about her impression. After all, she's only been around me twice. Her laughter fills the Jeep, and I find myself drawn to it.

She shakes her head. "Nah. The badge kinda ruins the rebellious image," she teases, glancing over with a grin. "You have the mysterious vibe, sure, but you're too...what's the word? Sweet? Yeah, too sweet to be a bad boy."

"Sweet?" I arch an eyebrow, taken aback. Being called sweet is a first for me. "That sounds close to soft." And I am not fucking soft.

"No, not soft. Sweet as in respectable. In a good way," she clarifies. I suppose with her, sweet isn't a stretch. She brings out this protective instinct in me I've never had for a woman. Usually, they're storming out, hurling insults like self-serving, narcissist, and arrogant. Those are the words I'm used to. Not sweet.

"We'll see if your opinion stays the same after a couple of months."

"Really? How can a man who loves his grams be anything but?" She pokes me in the shoulder. "You're trying to seem like a badass. But I see the real you."

That's my biggest fear.

"All right. All right. We're done talking about me. Let's talk about you. What was life like in Blackburn? And what brought you here to Austin?" The night at my cabin, she kept our conversation light, focusing on the cabin and its renovations. Oh, and the horse. She talked a lot about him. The way he made her smile, it made me a little jealous. I want that smile when my name comes out of her mouth.

Tonight, I want her to open up to me.

"I was born and raised in Blackburn. I was a waitress at the lovely Wallflower Diner." She pauses, her attention drifting out the window. There's a moment of hesitation, as if she's carefully choosing her words. She continues without meeting my eyes. "My dream was always to leave town and go to college, so I saved until I could make that happen." She lets out a sigh and twists in her seat toward me. "And then everything changed."

She's holding back. There's more, something she's not telling me. But I don't want her to focus on the night everything changed, so I ask, "What colleges are you considering?"

Her lips curve up, and I can tell she's excited. "The University of Texas." She beams.

"Good thing you'll look cute in burnt orange," I tease, throwing up the Hook 'em Horns hand signal. "I wore it non-stop for four years."

"Did you go there?"

I confirm with a nod. "Yep."

She dives headfirst into a barrage of questions about my time there. As I'm telling her about my fraternity days, I sense a shift in her energy. Her body tenses. We're almost to Austin, and as expected, there is heavier traffic. I glance over, and she's sitting on her hands, biting her bottom lip.

"You okay over there?" I ask, curious about the sudden mood swing.

"It's like everyone goes out driving at exactly the same time," she exclaims. City driving can be a nightmare, even for seasoned drivers. "And you drive with such ease, I'm jealous. When I'm behind the wheel, I'm gripping it for dear life, my foot hovering over the brake, swearing up a storm that everyone is out to get me." I chuckle, picturing her. "They are!"

I guess she didn't come to the city very often. "You get used to it," I assure her as Luke Combs's "Fast Car" plays in the background.

She tries to relax and taps her thumb against her bare thigh to the beat, and I find myself distracted by the sight of her long, tan legs. For someone so short, she's all legs. I force my eyes back to the road.

"I hope so. So, are you gonna tell me where we're going?"

"Not big on surprises, are you?"

Brake lights flash in front of us, and she slams her foot against the floorboard. I press my lips together to hold back my chuckle, easing the Jeep to a gentle stop. She exhales sharply, as though we narrowly avoided an accident. It wasn't even close. "Do I need to install a brake pedal over there for you?"

"Only if you're aiming for a case of whiplash," she jokes and cranes her neck to look at the small fender bender wreck that was causing the slowdown. "Do you report that?"

The people gather behind their cars, exchanging information. "Looks like they have it under control. They'll call it in if they need to." As traffic clears and I hit the gas, her shoulders relax.

We drive by a billboard advertisement for a restaurant on Lake Travis, and she asks, "Are we going to the lake?" Her question hangs in the air, and I respond with a grin. She lets out a playful huff that I won't tell her. She'll figure it out soon enough.

Not long after, off to the left, through the tall trees, glimpses of the lake come into view but are then hidden again as the road snakes along hilly terrain. There's a comfortable lull in the Jeep as music continues to play in the background.

As we reach the marina, her voice lifts an octave when she asks, "You have a boat?"

I park and turn off the engine. "I wish. It's a buddy of mine's. He lets me use it, and I let him hunt at the ranch in the winter."

Her head whips around, and her bottom lip sticks out as she pushes my bicep. "He better not kill Riggs's girlfriend."

I turn in my seat. How should I say this without offending her? Women seem to have bleeding hearts when it comes to hunting. "But that boy is a player. He has a lot of girlfriends. He can't have them all."

She drops her head with a silent laugh, and I'm relieved to see it. "I can totally see him as the Casanova of dogs."

"Ha! He likes to think so."

TOGETHER, we unload the Jeep and make our way down the dock to the boat. Despite the sun hanging low in the sky, it's still blazing hot, so as soon as we're on the boat, I yank my shirt over my head, toss it aside, slide my hat on backward, and fire up the boat. I catch a quiet hum of approval from her direction and can't help but smirk.

"Is there anything I can do to help?" she offers, watching me untie the line and bringing it into the boat.

"Nope. Sit back and relax that foot," I jest, flicking water on her as I pass.

"There's no need for war," she replies with a light laugh, setting her bag on the back bench.

I open the canopy to give her a bit of shade, but she stops me, wanting some sun. When she takes off her dress, I bite my lip, not able to turn away from her bikini-clad body. The rays of the setting sun dance across her skin, casting a golden hue over her curves.

She holds her arms out. "You told me to bring a swimsuit."

Stop staring, dipshit. Except, I can't.

"I had to get a new bathing suit since I didn't have one."

"Wait…" Her confession breaks my trance. "You didn't own a swimsuit? You live in Texas."

She shrugs, laying out a towel across the bench seat in the front left of the boat. "I mean, I had a swimsuit. But when I was getting ready to move, I donated all my clothes to charity. I hadn't gotten one since I left."

"You were really starting over, huh?"

She nods. "I was ready for a change," she says, sitting down and stretching out her legs. I understand that more than most, having done it myself at eighteen—I left and never turned back. "Turned out not to be quite the change I was looking for, but..." Her voice fades away.

I focus on steering the boat from the slip, giving her a moment without me staring at her.

Why? Why did I do this to myself on our first date?

I glance over. "But you're doing it. I'm in awe of how strong you are."

She peers over at me with a lopsided grin. "You're giving me too much credit. He still lives in my head. His voice—even though I never heard him—is always there, threatening me. Which is weird, right? How in the world do I know what he sounds like?"

"A lot of times, our brains project what we think we heard or saw. It's the same with witnesses. Often, it's hard to take witness accounts as facts unless we get multiple sources saying they saw the same thing. But we could have five witnesses who all say the person was wearing five different color shirts."

She stares out at the water. "Yeah. That must be it."

As we pick up speed, the wind drowns out our words, so she settles across the cushions, taking in the sun while it's still out. The boat glides over smooth waters, the surface sparkling like a thousand diamonds as we make our way farther out. I've spent countless weekends on this lake, so I know the entire layout—where to avoid and where the best places are.

When I make it to my favorite spot by the dam, I kill the engine and let the boat drift. Walking over to the cooler, I grab a couple Coronas and hand her one. Then I pull out the picnic basket from the cooler.

"Wow. You thought of everything," she says as I unpack a board of cheese and meat and remove the plastic wrap.

I will never remember what the hell women call these things. When Joy, our nosy admin, overheard Liam and me talking about my date, she suggested ordering one of these trays. I thought she was talking Spanish when she called it by its name.

"Aww. I love this charcuterie board. You didn't make this, did you?"

There's that dumb name. Who would name something so difficult to remember and say?

"Would you believe me if I said yes?"

She stares at me, contemplating. "You're pretty talented with your hands." I fight the wicked grin growing on my face by coughing once and pulling out the plates. She has no idea, but I'd love to show her how skilled they can be. "So, maybe."

My ego grows a little larger that she thinks I can do anything. Could I have made this? Heck yeah, it doesn't take a sous chef to make one of these. It's cubed cheese, sliced meats, throw in some nuts and fruit, and you have a fancy board. Mine wouldn't look this decorated—still not sure why the same kind of nuts are in three different spots—but who cares? It's here to eat, not to be admired. But I didn't have time to do it myself.

"I'd like to say it was me to impress you, but sorry, I don't make shark cuties."

She burst out laughing. "What was that?"

I chuckle with embarrassment, but it's so worth it to witness her deep belly laugh. "Whatever the hell you called it. I don't do those."

She's laughing so hard, tears well up in her eyes. She pats them away, sniffs, and says, "They'll always be shark cuties to me now." I cock my head to the side and stare at her while she composes herself. Kali is the only woman that can get away with making me the butt end of a joke. "Don't be mad. It's…adorable." I lift a brow as she pops a grape into her mouth.

Sweet. Adorable. Who the fuck am I turning into?

I point a toothpick at her. "If you ever tell a soul, expect your steak to come out charred from now on."

She gasps, edging closer to me. "Now, sir, we do not joke about overcooking meat around these parts." She's so close, I can smell her suntan lotion.

She leans over and cuts a piece of cheese and brings it to my mouth. Calling me sir and having her feed me has caught the attention of my dick. Poor guy, it's been six months since he's seen any action...other than my hand. I fight to think with the rational head.

I pick up a grape and act like I'm going to feed it to her and then pop it in my mouth. She laughs, picking up her own grape. "You're stunning, especially when you laugh," I say. Her cheeks flush as she turns away and sits on the bench that wraps around the table. She scoots to the middle part of the U shape. I follow her lead and sit to the left of her, wondering what turned on the shyness. Surely I'm not the first to tell her she's beautiful.

She fills a plate and glances at me. "Tell me more about your family. You've mentioned Grams, and I know your dad passed away."

Nice deflection.

I scratch my head and stare out at the water, my turn to feel uneasy. There are a few boats off in the distance, and I focus on them. This is not a favorite topic of mine. In fact, it's a topic I never talk about with anyone. "My mom isn't part of my life. I'll leave it at that." My gaze jumps back to her and there are questions on the tip of her tongue, so I keep going, not giving her a chance to ask them. "However, my grams and pops are the two most important people in my life."

Her expression softens. "I love when you mention your grams."

Note taken—talk more about my grams.

"I met none of my grandparents. My mom and her parents had a falling out when she married my dad, and they disowned her. I never found out why, but they weren't happy about it. They could still be alive, but they've never contacted me. My dad's parents passed away in a house fire when he was in his early twenties."

"Wow."

She shivers. "Right? That's a horrible way to die."

About as bad as being buried alive.

"Any brothers or sisters?" she continues.

These questions are getting worse. When can we move on to wondering what each other's favorite movie is or which side of the bed we sleep on? I swallow back the discomfort, reminding myself this is a normal conversation between two people on a first date. Maybe I should've picked a less intimate setting if this shit is going to get to me.

I push off the seat and stick my hand in the ice to grab another beer, hoping the cold will numb not just my hand but this conversation. "Want another one?"

"Sure," she murmurs. Fuck. I'm messing everything up because I can't handle a simple conversation with a woman.

I twist the top off and hand it to her. "Sorry." I wring my neck with my icy hand. "I had a brother. Jack. He was older than me, but he died when I was eleven. A couple of years before my dad passed away. He was my best friend." I sigh, falling back on the bench beside her, stretching my legs out. Jack's smirking face pops into my mind. Man, I miss that guy. "It's another thing that's hard for me to talk about."

"It's okay. I get it…" Her voice trails off as she picks at the beer label. "More than you know."

I need to steer this conversation in a different direction. "Damn. Enough of the sad talk. Tell me what your favorite movie is."

Her lips curl up. "That's easy. *Dirty Dancing*."

"Is that right?"

I pull out my phone and open a music app, pressing Play when I find the song. This is the perfect segue. I hold my hand out as "Hungry Eyes" by Eric Carmen floats around us.

"Dance with me?"

She shakes her head in amusement as she puts her hand in mine, and I pull her up into my chest, swaying to the beat of the song. Lights strung overhead sparkle as the sky fades to a deeper blue, and the gentle sway of the boat under our feet matches us in a rhythmic dance.

"You're smooth, Officer Turner."

I wink at her. "As butter."

"And so not lacking in confidence," she teases. I wrap my arm around her waist, tighter, as we spin in a circle. There is nothing wrong with a healthy ego.

As the song fades, our bodies have molded together, and the air grows heavy. We stop moving, and I stare down into her blue eyes. Her breath hitches. I lick my lips, staring at hers, and then lean down. Her hands tighten around me in anticipation. I stop, barely touching her lips, and draw in a breath.

"Do you want this?" I whisper, the warmth of my breath grazing her lips. I need to ensure there's no room for regrets. She needs to think she's in total control.

Even though she's not.

"Yes," she answers breathlessly.

I cup her neck and press my mouth against the corner of her soft, plump lips, kissing my way over. She hums right before she parts her lips and lets me deepen the kiss. I keep it soft and tender, afraid I'll devour her if I let go. I want to savor her taste, revel in the feel of her body's warmth against me and take my time with her. There is no rush.

Suddenly, Kali breaks the kiss and jumps back as if something bit her. I can promise you it wasn't me, despite wanting to.

"What was that?" she blurts out.

I furrow my brows, confused. "What was what?"

"Something flew by me and squeaked. It was inches away from our heads. I felt it. You didn't?"

I shake my head, scanning the empty boat. Her lips and her soft sighs were consuming my attention. "It was probably a bird."

"Oh my god!" she shrieks, pointing to the edge of the boat. "That is not a bird."

I walk over and staring up at me are two little beady eyes, a little snout, and tiny ears twitching. "Hey, buddy. You take a wrong turn?" I say to the unexpected visitor.

Kali stands right next to me, straining her neck forward. "Is that a bat? He's kind of cute." It wasn't so cute when he interrupted us.

"It is. Every night, thousands take flight from under the Congress Avenue Bridge searching for food. It's like a monumental event every night for people around here."

"Thousands?" Her eyes widen in amazement as she stares at the creature. "I think I found our next date."

A smile tugs at the corner of my mouth. She's already thinking about date two. Well, damn, now I'm thankful for the interruption.

Not a couple minutes later, our new friend is back in flight, and the next song is already playing. "I hope you like the eighties." I chuckle hearing "I Want to Know What Love Is" by Foreigner.

"I love it," she says, walking back into my arms.

As we dance, she tells me about the classes she signed up for. I've never heard someone talk about college with that much excitement. While it was some of the best times of my life, it wasn't because of the classes. Partying and women. That is what I aced in college.

"So, what do you want to do when you grow up?"

"A flight attendant. I've dreamed of traveling the world." Her confidence about what she wants and her determination to make it happen are sexy. After what she's been through, most women would be afraid to live. Not Kali.

But after everything we've talked about, there's one thing she's yet to tell me—her rags-to-riches story. She's changed from before.

Before being buried.

How does a woman go from being a small-town waitress with tattered shoes to buying a brand-new car, an entire new wardrobe, and enrolling in college?

It seems we both have secrets.

CHAPTER 21

Kali

IN MY ROOM, where the sun seems to live twenty-four hours a day, I'm shocked I haven't gotten bored with the canary yellow walls. But it's grown on me. It makes me happy when I'm in here.

Amy sits on my bed, watching me get ready for my date. We've become close. She's even asked about my mom. *Nobody ever asks about her.* Which is why I think I bottled up their memories, too afraid to speak their name.

The other day, we made a recipe that my mom used to always bake—peanut butter cookies. Amy didn't care that it was the simplest cookie recipe ever, using only three ingredients. It was the story I shared with her while we cooked it that made it special.

If only I had them as foster parents.

And even though she knows what happened to my mom and dad, and of course the nightmare I went through, she and Ted never look at me with pity or judgment. I'm not ready to let her go yet. I hope she knows that I'll never forget her.

"You like him," she states matter-of-factly.

Very much.

"I enjoy being around him," I respond without lifting my gaze as I swipe my left lashes with mascara. Having a man call you daily, telling you that you're beautiful, is so heart-poundingly addictive, I don't know if I could stay away even if I wanted to. And I don't.

When she doesn't reply, I steal a glance up at her through the mirror. I've learned Amy is the master of thinking before she speaks. I squint my eyes and tilt my head. "What? You said you liked him?"

She bobs her head, hesitates a moment, and then takes two long strides to my chair, gently placing her hands on my shoulders. "We do. He seems to be a great guy." I sense a but in there as she twists her lips. "We just want you to be careful."

Careful? Where is this coming from? Paxton is the epitome of safe. The few times we've been together, he scans our current surroundings, searching for any hint of the unusual. I can relax around him and let go of the anxiety that clings to me when out in public because he takes on that burden for me.

"You don't have anything to worry about with Paxton," I assure her.

The sound of tires crunching on the pebbled driveway grabs my attention. I jump up to peek out the window, hoping it's not a delivery truck. I watch Paxton hop out of his Jeep, and he leans over, checking his reflection in the side mirror, messing with an errant piece of hair. When he straightens, his eyes dart to my window, and I jerk back out of sight. My cheeks burn with embarrassment at being caught, and Amy lets out a chuckle as I rush around the room to gather my stuff.

"He's taking me to look at apartments today," I say, double-checking that my driver's license is in my wallet.

"Are you looking at the ones right next to the college?" she asks.

Ted gave me an approved list of apartments. Not that I have to choose one of those, but they're ones he vetted.

Of course, I'll pick one of those.

I'd do anything to make them proud of me. In three short

months, they have helped me more than anyone has since my parents died. Amy guided me through the crazy process of obtaining a driver's license and indulged me in countless shopping sprees. My entire life, I've never had more than a week's worth of clothes, and I might have gotten a bit carried away. Then there's Ted, who helped me set up a trust so I could deposit the money, and no one could trace it back to me without a lot of research. I'm officially rich but each time I get my bank card out to pay for something, it feels as if I'm on the verge of waking up from a dream where I'll find myself back in my dingy studio apartment in Blackburn, swimming in a lot of debt.

I bought my first car—a brand-new cherry-red Mustang. Ted went with me, ensuring the predatory salesperson didn't take advantage of me. Those folks are vultures. *And I was fresh meat.* We were there less than a minute before a guy approached with a pasted-on grin and arms stretched out as if he were our long-lost friend.

Step by step of getting my life back, they've been by my side. Two months ago, I never would've imagined I'd be in a place without nightmares again. At least without the help of drugs. But I did. On my own. I've finished my therapy here, and despite Amy and Ted telling me I can stay as long as I need, there are other people out there who need their help more than I do now. Even though my assailant—the new word Martinez gave me—runs free, I'm not letting him take away anything else from me.

I'm ready to start my life.

Ted knocks once and peeks his head through the cracked door. "Paxton's in the living room." I nod, slinging the cross-body purse over my shoulder. "Remember what I said. Read the entire contract if you find a place. Or you can bring it home and we can sift through the details with you." He pauses, meeting Amy's adoring expression, and adds with a subtle smile, "If you want."

They are the best.

Insecurities are a bitch. It's the moments right before I see

Paxton that the gnawing fear creeps in—the kind that he'll realize I'm not worth the trouble and decide I'm not enough for him. The notion that I'm too scarred to live a normal life plays on a loop in my mind. He could find another woman who's not broken, because no matter what I tell myself, there will always be a nagging fear in the back of my mind that I'll end up back in a grave. But then I walk into the room, and he focuses intensely on me, staring at me like I'm the only woman in existence. All the self-doubt disappears.

"Ready, beautiful?" he says as he gathers me into a tight hug.

Sigh. Pick me up off the floor because this small-town girl is falling fast and hard. Amy winks at me as we pass them, and I smile back at her.

See, nothing to worry about.

As we're about to pull out onto the main road, Paxton looks over at me and stares. I catch him doing it often, making me blush and wiggle in my seat.

"Stop." I chuckle, covering his eyes, not used to this much attention. Men have never looked at me like Paxton does, and he's not bashful about it at all.

He pulls my hand away, kissing the palm. "I can't stop," he says. "Seeing you once a week isn't enough."

He's also not shy about saying what's on his mind, either. I like that. It won't be much longer that I'll be minutes away from him rather than an hour.

"After I move in, would you want to go to Blackburn with me one weekend? I want to see Pearl and Chip, and I'd love for you to meet them." I was putting important dates for college into my calendar the other day and remembered it was Pearl's birthday this month. I feel a little guilty that I haven't called her.

His lips curve. "I'd love to meet the people who are important to you."

I wonder what my monster would say if he found out he gave me the best gift ever—Paxton. He unwittingly created something beautiful amid the chaos. And that single thought makes me want to flip my middle finger up and say, "*Thanks.*"

THE FIRST SET of apartments we look at are farther from campus than I'd prefer, so I nix those immediately. I want to walk to class. The next ones, however, steal my heart. Brand new and opening for the fall semester, they are right across the street from the college. There's a catch, though—they only have a dozen rooms available, so if I want one, I have to sign a contract soon. They fill the apartments similar to dorms on campus. They call it individual leasing. I'd share an apartment with someone, but I'd have my own room and bathroom. They explained that they match room-mates with an app similar to a dating site. Of course, that meant nothing to me because I've never used or seen one. Paxton thought it was funny when he mentioned me swiping right, but I stared at him confused. *Swiping right? What does that even mean?* He explained it to me, and it sounds like a horrible way to find someone.

"Are you okay rooming with someone? Someone you don't know?" Paxton asks as we head toward his Jeep.

I don't answer immediately because I don't want to sound immature for wanting the full college experience, roommate and all, considering I'm twenty-two. But I've wanted this life since I graduated from high school.

"I'd rather have a roommate than be by myself," I admit. I've lived alone for years. It's lonely. I thought that I'd love it after living in a group home where personal space was nonexistent, but I ended up missing the friendships, having someone always there to talk to about everything. Or days you just needed someone *there*. Even though we fought like rabid cats sometimes, we also were each other's lifeline, our laughter echoing throughout the halls, our comfort in times of despair. Back when nobody wanted us, those connections meant everything. I wish we could've stayed in touch somehow. "And I can choose my roommate."

"Will you let me check into the person you choose?"

"Even if I said no, I doubt you'd listen," I tease, bumping him with my hip as we walk back toward the Jeep.

He squeezes my hand and raises it to his lips, kissing my hand again. "I only want to make sure you're safe."

"You're the best boyfriend ever," I reply. My cheeks heat when his eyes widen at my proclamation. We've never put our relationship into words, so his reaction has me regretting them. "I mean—"

He puts his finger over my mouth, pausing me and walking me backward until my back hits the passenger side door of his Jeep. "You know what?" he says, leaning down, getting a whispered length away from my lips.

"What?"

"I like the sound of that," he murmurs, tipping my head with a gentle nudge, his eyes bouncing back and forth between my eyes and lips.

My pulse quickens. With that, he presses his lips to mine. I love the way he kisses—gentle at first and then dominant and greedy. He groans into my mouth as our tongues tangle together.

When he pulls away, he presses his forehead against mine. Our eyes locked, our breaths heavy with need. "I like it a lot," he finally says.

CHAPTER 22

Kali

THERE ARE times Paxton is broody and so serious his tenseness hurts my forehead. Especially when he's talking about his job. Today is not one of those days. Today, he's like a kid in a candy store. And as sexy as his broody side is, this side of him is my favorite.

"I've never ridden a roller coaster before," I confess, staring up at the colossal green monster coaster, spiraling and flipping upside down. I'm certain if I wasn't here, Paxton would run to get in line with the group of boys that just passed us.

As soon as he asked me to go to Six Flags, my answer was a resounding *yes*. Growing up, kids were quick to brag about their Six Flags trips to San Antonio or Dallas. They raved about the rides they rode and how much fun they had. Most of the time, I figured they were exaggerating.

They were not.

"We could start smaller," he teases, a playful glint in his eyes. He points to a different ride. "Like that one?"

I stare at the ride. Cars in a circle on a spinning disk. I might as well throw up now. The only benefit of that ride is that it's on the ground. But my stomach squeezes at the dizzying sight. *No, thanks.*

I pucker my lips and shake my head. "I say we jump right in. I'm ready to ride that big boy."

"Is that right?" He wags his thick brows with a salacious grin. "I know a big—"

My skin warms as I cover his mouth with my hand. "Don't promise things you might not be able to deliver."

He draws me into his chest, tickling my side. "Oh, Kalico, just you wait."

This is the weekend—the *weekend*—when I get to rip his clothes off and make mad love to him. It's been a month of flirting, innuendos, passionate kisses, and a lot of heavy petting. But he's been the perfect gentleman, letting me take the lead on where this goes. My insecurities held me back. *Remember, I'm a five. He's not.*

He sent me flowers. I've never received flowers from a man before, not counting the ones that Chip would give me on my birthday. Those were like flowers from my dad. Sometimes, I have to sit back and remind myself that this is my life now. I have everything I've ever wanted at the moment.

And he's made it clear that he wants me.

One more week, and I move into my apartment. It's only fifteen minutes from Paxton's apartment, so it'll make it easier to see him more than once a week.

"I'm done waiting."

He stares down at me. "Like done, done? Like we need to leave right now, done?"

"We just got here. But tonight..." I lean into him and lift on my toes, giving him a sweet, chaste kiss on his lips before pulling back and whispering into his ear, "I might even let you use the handcuffs."

"Damn woman," he says, turning away to adjust himself. "This will be interesting." He snorts, pulling me behind the same group of boys that ran past us to get in line. He leans down and whispers so the little ears don't hear. "I've never had a boner while on a ride before. Either I'll never have kids again, or I'll need to change my underwear after this."

I smack my hand on my forehead. Leave it to a man to wonder how a roller coaster can get him off.

My heart picks up speed as we wait behind the yellow line. The car pulls up, and everyone exits to the other side. We're next. I crack my knuckles and shake out my hands. The group of boys are two rows ahead of us. They see me and joke about how nervous I am. I roll my eyes. Little jerks.

I settle into the seat and lower the harness, pulling it as tight as possible against my ribcage. A teenage kid pulls on my seat belt and harness. *Are you kidding me? Are you even old enough for this important job?* It seems this job is way above his pay grade. If it's not, it should be.

"Get ready, baby," Paxton says, winking at me as he turns his hat backward. "This ride is just a prelude to the actual ride tonight."

"There you go again. Promising things. I hope you're not setting yourself up for failure."

His laugh roars as the red light goes from yellow to green, and we shoot out and start moving up. Oh shit! My fingers grip the handles for dear life. I was not expecting the initial burst, and I think I peed myself a little.

I changed my mind.

Spinning on the ground sounds much safer.

I should've gone for safe.

Every click, click, click of the track underneath us vibrates in my chest. Holy shit. Will it ever stop climbing? I've decided I'm not a heights person. Wish I would've figured that out while on the ground. I exhale and stare at the blue skies, pretending I'm lying on the ground as we inch up—at an excruciatingly slow pace. This has to get better, right?

Little did I know that was the best part.

Because we stopped. "What…" Panic spikes as I look to my

left, then right at Paxton. "Why aren't we moving? Is this supposed to happen?"

"Uh…I don't believe so."

Right before it got to the top, it stopped. It was moving, *click, click, click,* and I cursed it was taking too long, and then nothing. We're at a steep angle, nothing to do but stare up at the clear blue skies and the glaring sun. This isn't happening. I jerk my hand around, searching for Paxton's hand. He finds me and squeezes.

"It's okay, Kali."

"Is it?" My voice cracks at such a high octave.

Voices grow louder, creating a cacophony of confusion and panic. The unforgiving sun beats down on our faces. Thankfully, we both have sunglasses on, so it's not miserable. Yet. I take that back. This is beyond miserable, but at least I'm not blind.

"Hey, look at me," Paxton says, leaning forward to see over his harness. I hesitate as if the mere movement of my head will tilt the train over and we'll fall to our deaths, but I glance over when I tell myself that I'm being ridiculous. "We're fine, and we can't fall out. We're safe right here."

"This can't be safe." My heart pounds in my ears, and despite the ample air and bright sun, I feel myself slipping back into the dark box. My breathing becomes loud and labored, sweat beads trail down my back and across my forehead. "That's it, no more big boys for me," I snap, squeezing my eyelids shut.

"Well, that's disappointing."

I jerk my head forward and turn in his direction, pursing my lips. Anger temporarily disables the fear. "I'm not in a kidding mood at the moment," I snap.

Minutes crawl by, and nothing. Some of the chatter has now turned into small cries. My fingers burn from gripping the harness. I release them, one at a time, to shake out the tension, only to clench back onto it, holding on for dear life.

"Close your eyes," he urges.

They already are, but now he has me questioning why he

wants them closed. What does he not want me to see? Unable to resist, I open them again. "Why? What's going on?"

"Everything is okay. Close your eyes and focus on my voice," he reassures.

Reluctantly, I do what he says, closing my eyes and trying to calm the racing thoughts. I lick my dry lips and try to slow my breaths. "They're closed."

"Tonight, we're going out. Think about what you're going to wear. Where we are going. What you are going to drink," he prompts.

I fight to transport myself to a bar setting. "Tequila. Lots of it," I declare, the first thing I wish I had right now. It might be the only thing that would make this situation more bearable.

He laughs. "Tequila it is. Now imagine yourself sitting there. I've left to go to the bar," he continues, and it's becoming easier to immerse myself as he keeps talking. "You wonder where I disappeared to because it's been a few minutes."

I play along, but I wonder where this is headed.

"And then you see me on stage, tapping the mic. Is this thing on?"

"What are you doing?" I say, leaning forward and looking at him again.

"Shhh. Close your eyes. Get back to the bar," he demands.

The panic subsides as I close my eyes again, intrigued to find out what he's up to.

"You there?"

"Yes."

I chuckle to myself as he hums a tune. It's familiar, but it's hard to place with only his hum. Then he starts singing. Right there in the midst of this mess we're in.

"Where it began…I can't begin to know when…"

My laugh, filled with equal parts terror and confusion, fills the air as he sings "Sweet Caroline" by Neil Diamond. He's not horrible, but he's not about to be the next winner of a singing show either. He builds up to the chorus, singing louder, and my fear morphs into worrying about the other passengers and what they're thinking. I half expect people to yell at him to stop, that it's not the time for karaoke. But to my surprise, a dad one row ahead of us chimes in. Then, one by one, they all join, a chorus of panicked people coming together to find something else to focus on.

"Sweet *Kalico*," he says, during the next round of chorus.

I'm past the point of shock, moving on to, again, finding him adorable. The tune is not as upbeat and fun as you'd find in an actual bar, this version has a more melancholy vibe. Many people clap with him at the iconic "bum, bum, bum" part.

I steal a glance at him with astonishment, and he responds with a humorous shrug as if he's as surprised as I am.

"Well, this is a first." A man appears at the side of the train, smiling and holding bottles of water. The song stops as everyone waits to hear what's going on. Another man joins behind him. They are both tethered to a bar on the side of the stairs. "Is everyone all right?" they ask as they pass out the water. They answer each of our questions thrown at them. "Yes, it's safe." "No, it can't roll backward." "They are working on it." And the most important: "We don't know how much longer."

Great.

After thirty minutes and the beginning of a sunburn that'll hurt later, we're told that we're going to walk down the stairs. All two hundred feet of them.

"The ride is broken," they said.

No shit.

I could've told them that thirty minutes ago. A group of fire-fighters appear in full gear and spread themselves out at our side. *Shit just got real.* They explain that they'll be releasing us by car. Thankfully, ours is last.

"We're next," Paxton says, squeezing my hand.

I exhale a heavy breath and nod. Though deep down, fear

courses through me like a chilling wind. Legs trembling, heart pounding. *I think I'd rather stay here.* But I don't want him to see me weak. He's already witnessed me shattered at my weakest, and I'm afraid if I keep showing him that fragile side, he'll grow tired of playing the hero.

And I'm not a weak person. I'm a survivor who keeps getting herself in tough situations.

When it's our turn, Paxton hops out of his seat like it's nothing, puts his harness on, and extends his hand to grasp my shaking fingers. "Look at me," he instructs as my eyes pop out of my head, seeing how far up we are. The sheer height takes my breath away. *Literally.*

I take a step over to his seat and plop down, needing to find the air in my lungs.

"Hold on," I murmur, resting my head against the seat in front of me. I fight the light-headedness. *Do not pass out.* I repeat the words over and over to myself, and I focus on my breathing. In and out.

"This is the worst part. Once you're out and standing on the stairs, it's much better," the firefighter reassures me.

I let out a sarcastic laugh. "Coming from a person who lives on ladders."

"Want me to sing again?" Paxton grins when I turn my head toward him.

"No." I snicker, gripping the chair in front of me as I pull myself up. Once again, he holds his hand out.

That single step is the most terrifying step I've ever taken. While it doesn't compare to the horror of being buried alive, it's not something I want to ever repeat. With both hands clutching the bar, they secure me to a harness, and while I feel better not being at an angle anymore, the stairway descent is still crazy scary. I blow out a breath through puffed-out cheeks and focus only on the metal stairs beneath me.

Paxton places a gentle kiss on my forehead, standing one step down from me. "You're doing great, Kalico."

No. No I'm not.

"I'm mad at you for making me use one of my nine lives," I nervously joke, but am thankful for his calm demeanor. "I don't have many left."

He shakes his head. "You have a million moments left in your lifetime. This will just be one we tell our grandkids, and they'll think we're the coolest."

Does he mean *our* grandkids?

Clearly, he didn't. *Way to jump ahead fifty years, Kali.* We've been dating for one month, I remind myself. I glance down, pretending to check the tightness of the harness, even though I know it's tight because I confirmed it as soon as they secured it.

"If everyone is ready, we're going to head down. We're taking one step at a time, slow and steady," the firefighter instructs.

"I'll be a bundle of stories," I mutter sarcastically, taking the first step down.

CHAPTER 23

Kali

ONE AND DONE FOR ME. Never again.

All that safety nonsense they kept spewing to us afterward was bullshit. That was not safe, and no one will ever be able to talk me into believing that. Paxton didn't argue when I told him I needed a break. When he mentioned maybe leaving the park to get lunch, that was all I needed to turn around and head for the exit.

Bye bitches, I hope to never see you again.

My insides are still buzzing. From the window of the restaurant, I can see the green tip of the roller coaster we were stuck on, peeking over the neighboring buildings. I can't believe that just happened. *What are the chances?* To make matters worse, I inhaled my hamburger and fries as if it were my last meal. Paxton still has half a burger left, and that's mainly because he likes to watch me eat. It's a little weird. Cute weird, but weird.

I glance at him. "Enjoying the show?" I tease, trying to shake off the lingering adrenaline.

He grins, not missing a beat. "I am. You eat like you're savoring every bite, and it's kind of adorable." I roll my eyes, but I can't help the smile tugging at my lips. He finally focuses on his own burger, only needing to take two more large bites before he's finished.

"Are you okay with me being with a cop?" he asks, leaning back against his chair.

If he knew that my dreams of him begin with him in uniform—*because holy hell, there's something about a man in uniform*—he'd know that I was okay with it. But I know being a cop is more than wearing a uniform and a badge. It's dangerous, so I get that.

"Of course. Why?"

He takes a long pull from his beer before replying, and worry creeps in. *Please don't be looking for an out.* "Women love the idea of being with a cop, a '*hot cop.*'" He rolls his eyes and makes air quotes, making me snort. Glad I didn't tell him about my dreams. "But then reality sets in and most women can't handle it. I've had plenty of relationships end because it's no longer sexy, it's too difficult."

I dip my fry into ketchup and think. There isn't a woman alive who wouldn't worry. But it's never made me question if I could be with him. Of course, I haven't been in the moment where I'm sitting at home worrying if my boyfriend is dead. I want to say I can handle that.

"Before we get further into this, it's best we find out now," he adds.

I pause, thinking about all the loss in my life. Would it break me to lose the man I loved, too? *Yes.* Do I fear the possibility of loss enough to make me back away?

"I didn't think you would hesitate," he says, worried. He's lost just as much as I have, and he's not backing away. Look at Pearl. She's never given up on love, despite her many attempts. The feeling of love alone is worth it.

He's worth it.

"Honestly, I like you more because you're a police officer. It speaks volumes about your character. You put your life on the line every day, and for what? To save people. That's pretty damn sexy."

His lips widen against his beer, and I wrinkle my nose. "And you're pretty awesome at saving people."

"You might be a little biased," he teases, setting his beer on the table.

Speaking of saving me, I've wondered if being with me has any repercussions at his job. Do they know that we're dating? Is it even allowed? He's never mentioned otherwise, but then again, I've yet to meet his friends.

"You're not going to get in trouble for dating me, are you?"

He shakes his head. "Anyone who has any problems with us being together can go take a hike." He reaches for my hand, interlocking our fingers. The fire in his eyes and the ruggedness of his voice light a spark of desire through me, right down to my core.

"We should go," I say.

There's a hint of amusement in his expression as he licks his bottom lip. "I agree," he says, reading me. He pulls out his wallet, dropping more than enough cash to cover the bill and tip. He shoots up and grabs my hand, not caring to wait for change. I chuckle to myself. At least he's more excited about this than the roller coaster. "What's so funny?"

"It's cute how excited you get for all your rides."

His laughter rings around the diner as we walk through it.

He holds the door open, and as I pass him, he murmurs, "Well, if this morning's ride was a prelude for what's coming, hold on tight, baby."

As we step into the elevator, the steamy elevator scenes from the romance novels I've devoured lately flood my thoughts. I've always wanted to make out in an elevator. And I was a mere second away from attacking him in the empty elevator before a hand appeared, halting the closing doors. Really?! The man nods at both of us as his family of seven piles in. He has no idea what he just interrupted.

Paxton squeezes my hand with a knowing smile. He winks down at me, and I stifle a giggle. Once behind the closed door of our hotel room, Paxton scoops me up in his arms, and I wrap my legs around his waist. He carries me to the bed and then gently lowers me and says, "I have something for you." He walks over to his luggage and grabs something. "I was going to give it to you at dinner, but we might not leave the hotel room the rest of the night." He stands between my legs and hands me a box. "Happy one-month anniversary." Panic bubbles up in my chest. Was I supposed to get something for him?

I take the box and look up at him. "I'm a horrible girlfriend. I didn't get you anything."

"Kalico. You being here means more to me than anything you could've given me."

He sounds genuine, but how can he be this perfect? "It's so pretty," I say, staring at the blue box.

"You haven't even opened it yet," he teases. "But I'm glad to learn that you like boxes."

"I'd like anything you gave me." I lift off the top, and there's a delicate gold necklace with a tiny bat wings pendant. "It's beautiful. I love it."

He helps me put it on. I never thought a man could be this attentive. Remembering little things that meant so much to me, but figuring they were inconsequential moments to them. I hold the wings in between my fingers, remembering our little buddy on our first date and wondering how I got so lucky with Paxton, and then I chuckle to myself—it wasn't luck at all.

It was fate.

"The necklace isn't what's beautiful. You are," he whispers, putting his knee on the bed, bending over to capture my lips, his hand gliding through my hair.

I realize in this moment how hard it is for me to let go and let him in completely, as the wall around my heart has been built by countless betrayals and silent scars of broken promises. There's fear he could wake up tomorrow and leave me like everyone else has in my life. It's not being alone that I fear, it's rejection.

But he's slowly breaking down that wall.

I want to let go.

To trust him.

When he stands up, our gaze holds for a silent beat. Mine is a silent plea for a promise. His desire and need. *He's here, Kali. Let him in.*

His fingers play with the edge of my shirt, brushing against my bare waist, and I lift my arms so he can pull it up over my head. After he tosses my shirt to the side, I undo his buckle and unbutton his shorts. In one tug, he yanks off his shirt and then grabs my hand, pulling me onto my feet.

He trails kisses up my neck. "Tell me you want this as much as I do," he says, a hint of desperation in his voice.

"I want this," I whisper, my voice trembling with emotion. "I want you."

He lowers, pressing his lips to mine in a kiss that's both tender and demanding. As his hands move to unclasp my bra, I shiver, not from the cold air blowing but from the anticipation and the raw, unfiltered need coursing through me. Biting his bottom lip, he watches as he slides the white lace bra off. A slow growl emits from the back of his throat, and he bends to take one of my boobs into his mouth.

"I've wanted to do this since the day you stripped in front of me at my cabin."

I playfully gasp. "I was in a vulnerable state." Did I really think I had a tracking device inserted somewhere? Fear made me do silly things.

He flashes a quick grin. "That's why I didn't. But I wanted to."

Next, he pulls my shorts off, dropping to his knees as he does it. I run my fingers through his curls, loving how they feel. "You are the most exquisite woman I've ever seen."

I don't believe him. I'm average. A five, at best. That doesn't equal exquisite.

"Why are you looking at me like that?" he asks.

I wrinkle my nose. "I'm just..." I've always been okay with being average until this moment where I have to explain how average I am. My cheeks heat from embarrassment.

"Do you trust me?"

"With my life," I respond.

"Then trust I know what I'm talking about." He kisses my belly, and then his tongue skims the top of my panties. Desire tingles around my spine, the air around us electrifies, the current lighting a fire to my insecurities. *Let go.* "Trust..." Fingers brush against my swollen center. "Me..." I gasp as he pushes aside my panties and runs his finger through my wetness.

"I do," I breathe out, panting and begging.

"Good girl," he says, slipping one finger inside me. He lets out a curse and slams his mouth onto my clit. "So fucking wet for me." He sucks and pumps his finger at the same time, and I grip his hair, needing something to hold on to. Frustrated that my panties are in the way, he shoves them down and pushes me onto the bed. I fall back, and he presses my legs wide open, jumping right back where he left off. His tongue drags to my center and then inside my wetness. My hips buck at the sensation of his tongue fucking me.

Never has a man made me orgasm with his mouth, let alone like this. *His tongue inside me.* The ache between my legs builds, every nerve ending ready to explode. The knot of heat in my lower belly grows, and I try to push away from his mouth because I don't know if that's what he wants.

Foreplay is new to me.

But he wraps his arms around my legs and keeps me pinned against his mouth. His tongue doesn't skip a beat and continues to push me toward the edge I'm teetering on.

The vibration of his hum pushes me over.

"Yes! Yes! Yes! Pax!" I scream, fisting the comforter as a gush of heat bursts out of me and he moans with me. My hips buck against his mouth, my eyes roll back, and I ride the wave of my orgasm. Stars fill my vision. My breaths shallow. *What just happened?* Does it always feel that way?

He stands with a wicked grin and drops his shorts and underwear together. His large cock springs loose, and my eyes widen. I'm not a virgin, but I have doubts that thing will fit.

He chuckles when he notices my expression. "I told you, this is one ride you'll never forget."

He grabs a condom out of his pocket and rips off the corner of the foil. I watch as he rolls it down his shaft. Watching him touch himself stirs the heat inside me. I lick my lips. I've never begged for sex, but at this moment, I think I'd do anything to feel him inside me. The bed shifts when he climbs on it, and I bend my knees so he's situated at my entrance. His fingers brush the inside of my thighs as he widens my legs, taking a heated look at my center.

He runs the head of his dick up and down my center, and I flinch when he rubs my oversensitive clit. "I'm afraid if I put it in right now, I'll come too fast. But…" He growls. "I want to be inside you."

The muscles in his biceps flex, and his chest rises and falls. It's empowering to see what I'm doing to him. Testing his control and watching it slip. *I'm doing that.*

With a surge of confidence, I lift my hips up, rubbing against him. "I want to feel you inside me. Fuck me."

"Damn," he moans and slides his cock inside me.

"Oh shit!" I scream, fisting the blanket again as he fills me entirely. He gives me a moment to adjust to his size, biting back his smile. I blink at the full sensation, a mixture of pain and pleasure.

"You good?" he teases, eyes bright.

Cocky bastard. "Just waiting at the top for the ride to start."

He throws his head up and stares at the ceiling for a moment. His Adam's apple bobs. When his eyes reach mine, there's a delicious wickedness in them that almost makes me have another orgasm.

Hands on my hips, gripping tight, he moves in and out. His eyes never waver from mine as if he's memorizing my every whimper and moan, adjusting his movement based on them. When he hits the spot—the one that makes me scream out—it's like he hit a bull's-eye. My core clenches and heat builds again.

"That's it, baby," he says, pressing his thumb on my enlarged clit and increasing his tempo, hitting his target every time until my moans are constant and I'm screaming his name again.

He bends over on top of me. It feels more intimate this close, his face an inch above mine. I don't know what's more intimate than having sex with someone, but this, it's raw and laced with possibilities. The unspoken promises that I needed before.

"I like hearing my name come out of your mouth when my dick is inside you." He grinds his hips into me, slow at first, but he picks up his pace, thrusting with urgency as he chases his orgasm over the edge. His body hardens, twitches, and my hair muffles his moans. Both of our chests heave against each other, and I wrap my arms around his back.

The air conditioner hums to life, sending a blissful chill over our sweaty bodies. We lie there, letting the cool air and passing seconds calm our racing hearts.

That was definitely a ride I won't ever forget.

He lifts his head, pressing his forehead against mine, and murmurs, "You fit me perfectly, Kalico."

I blink back a couple tears, not wanting him to see me get emotional. I've always heard that guys hate that. But I've never been a good fit for anyone, so I have to force those words to seep through my thick skin.

"I'm crazy about you," he whispers, and then kisses me gently on the lips. He lets them linger there a moment before he looks back up, winks, and rolls off me to head to the bathroom.

For the first time in my adult life, I feel treasured. The sex was incredible...as is the man I had sex with. I don't feel cheap but adored. *It's liberating.* For so long, I was afraid to get into a relationship because of my past. Afraid of being used.

Somehow, Paxton keeps setting me free.

"MY TURN FOR A QUESTION." I press my cheek against his warm, bare chest, his heartbeat a comforting steady rhythm as his thumb traces gentle circles on my back. Every sensation is heightened after our amazing sex. I might as well have been a virgin because my teenage sex was nothing like that. That was like an itch to scratch. This was an exploration of the body, sensual and emotional. Addicting.

"Okay," he says lazily.

"Are you okay with being with a woman who will never go on a roller coaster again?"

His stomach trembles with quiet laughter beneath my touch. I squeal as he rolls us over and hovers above me. "As long as you never stop riding this, I think I can handle it."

A pang of guilt surges through me. I'm irritated the thought pops up right now. It has to be because of how close we're getting or that I've been hiding something from him.

Trust goes both ways.

"Damn woman." He pushes up with a quizzical expression. "That was not the response I was expecting. Did you not enjoy yourself? By the sounds you made, you're either a fantastic actor or—"

"You were amazing," I interject, halting his words as I cup his worried face. "There's just...something I haven't told you." I attempt to squirm out from underneath him.

He shakes his head, pinning me in place. "What is it, Kali?"

I blow out a breath. "Right before I was kidnapped, like a week before..." I hesitate, nibbling on my lip as I focus on a single freckle on his neck. Why is this so difficult? It's not like it's a bad thing, and there's a chance he already knows. "I won the lottery," I blurt out and watch his reaction as he blinks, opens his mouth, and then shuts it again. Yeah, it was a surprise for me too.

"Did you tell Martinez?" he finally asks. There's no competition between the two, so why is he worried about that? When I give him a quizzical look, he adds, "This might have something to do with you getting kidnapped."

I totally misread that. "He knows. The lottery ticket was in my bra, buried with me, so I kind of freaked out when I couldn't find my clothes."

"That's why you were moving to Austin with nothing set up?"

I nod. "I don't understand. Why were you afraid to tell me?"

I let my hands fall to the sides and shrug. "It's still hard for me to believe, and most of the time, I don't even remember myself."

His brows perk up in surprise. "You don't remember being a millionaire?"

"With everything that has happened, and you and college coming up, it's there in the background, more of a safety net than a fixture. If that makes sense."

He kisses my forehead and rolls to my side. "It makes perfect sense. And I'm glad you weren't going to tell me you were moving or something like that."

I mirror his position, rolling to my side and propping my head up on my hand. "That would be rude. Here, let's have sex, but... bye."

He chuckles. "I would've hunted you down," he teases.

"Oh yeah?" I reply in amusement. "And then what?"

"I'd make love to you until you changed your mind."

"That sounds horrible." I lick my lips before saying, "Did I forget to tell you I'm moving to Florida?"

He falls on me, and I laugh out loud as he says, "The hell you are."

CHAPTER 24

Paxton

"LET ME OUT!" I scream, the sound reverberating around me as I pound on the splintered wood.

It's always night. Darkness swallows me as the fear of being down here forever takes hold. I lose track of time, worrying about the scurrying of mice and cockroaches in the shadows.

I pound again.

And again.

"Let me out!"

I jolt awake, grasping for breath. It takes a moment before the fog lifts, and I find myself surrounded by the four white walls of the hotel room. I yank the drenched shirt off and throw it on the floor. And then I notice Kali next to me. The reason for the nightmare. I hold my hand over my rapidly beating heart, grateful the echoes of my dream didn't wake her.

She would have questions.

How do I explain I know how she felt in that box?

Not that I was ever in a box, but our nightmares run parallel lines.

I shake off the lingering dream and scoot out of bed, careful not to wake her. With a soft close of the bedroom door, the bright morning sun in the living area greets me. I drop on to the stiff green couch, stretching out my legs, and stare up at the ceiling. Memories of last night, owning her in every way, wipe away any unwanted thoughts. The way she gave herself to me was surprising. She wasn't as innocent as I thought. I wondered who she'd been with, and that pissed me off. I've been with plenty of other women, and I've never once thought of their exes. What is going on with my head? She's got me having feelings I've never experienced.

The bedroom door opens, and Kali walks out with tired eyes and her hair thrown into a messy knot on top of her head, with only my white T-shirt on. She yawns. "You're up early," she remarks, padding over to me and then straddling my lap.

"Yeah, I can't turn off my internal alarm." I gently squeeze her thighs. "Sore?"

"Yes," she admits, her hands reaching for mine to move them. Being tense and walking down two hundred feet of stairs, it's not surprising. Even I'm sore, and I work out every day. She leans in, planting her lips on mine for a soft, quick kiss. "I had fun last night, Officer Turner."

Fun doesn't even cover it. Best night ever.

I pull our joined hands behind her back. The shirt tightens, accentuating her small, perky tits. They're perfect. Just like she is. Leaning over, I suck on her nipple through the shirt, and she lets out a soft moan. I switch sides, giving the other nipple equal attention, and sit back and revel in her hard nipples sticking out.

"There's no need for this," she says, slipping the T-shirt over her head and throwing it on the ground. My eyes drag down her nakedness as my dick presses into her, trying to free itself from my shorts. My stomach muscles flinch when she drags her nails over every inch of my abs. She lifts her head with amusement. "Ticklish?"

I palm her bare ass and pull her forward. Her arms wrap around my neck. A part of me was hoping she was horrible in bed

—something to help burn off this obsession I have with her. She deserves someone better than me. She told me her secrets, and I'm an asshole for keeping mine.

But if she finds out, I'll lose her.

My fingers travel lower to her center, finding her already hot and wet. She moans against my mouth when I slip one finger inside her. And then two. She rotates her hips for more friction, and I about lose it. I need to be inside her, so I flip her over on her back, my knees sinking into the couch cushions as I pull out my dick. There is nothing in this world more sexy than the way she smiles up at me in anticipation, greedy for my cock.

"So fucking perfect," I say as I sink into her. She arches her back and gasps as I fill her to the hilt. She begs me to move as she grinds against me.

This is music to my ears, and I could listen to this playlist every day.

<hr />

WITH OUR BAGS packed at the door, I draw her close and kiss the tip of her nose before we head out. I'm selfishly not ready to give her back to the world. "Thank you for telling me about the lottery." It wasn't a shock to learn she came into some money, that much was obvious. What caught me off guard was to hear it was in the millions. "But you know, it doesn't change anything. I'm still paying for everything."

She shrugs. "I'll just have to buy you a boat."

I stare, unsure if she's joking or serious. Because the hell she is. I don't need her to become my sugar momma. "Don't even think about it. The only thing I need from you…is you."

She nuzzles her head into my chest. "How are you still single?"

Because I've been waiting for you.

The coffee pit stop was supposed to be quick, but the line creeps forward. Kali's reading an email from one of her professors about an upcoming class while we wait. It's when she's not looking that I'm unable to stop studying her. She's wearing the necklace I gave her. The first piece of jewelry I've ever given a woman. I wasn't being shortsighted when I told Grams that I'd found the woman I'm going to marry. I've known from the moment I saw her.

I'm just waiting for Kali to catch up.

It's only been a month, but there's an insatiable desire to be with her all the time, and with each passing second spent with her, my obsession deepens. She must sense me staring because she glances up. Her expression remains neutral and relaxed.

I don't know why I didn't see it before. It's at that precise moment that I realize something.

She has her dad's eyes.

CHAPTER 25
Paxton

HERE WE GO.

This was not the way I wanted to start my Monday morning after the best weekend of my life. I mentally shake out my nerves as I stare at the Texas Ranger seated across the table. Martinez. He questioned me right after Kali was found.

"So, you got the girl?" he starts. I can appreciate the no-bullshit rhetoric even though my entire insides are on fire. It's weird being on this side. I wouldn't suggest it. "Was that your plan all along? What do they call it? The Hero Syndrome?"

"What are you talking about?" I respond, maintaining a neutral tone and holding his gaze. When the Texas Rangers called me this morning, needing to ask me a few questions, I knew it was about her. They're just doing their due diligence. However, when my captain joined us, I sensed this was more.

They know something.

I can feel it hanging over my head.

"C'mon," he says. "You're a cop. According to your record, a damn good one. So, you know this looks bad."

I sit forward, resting my arms on the cold metal table, and lock eyes with him. "I never planned on having a relationship with

Kali. It just happened. Internal Affairs didn't find a problem with it, and last I checked, it's not a crime. We didn't even talk until a couple months after it happened."

"You told the officer at the scene that was the first time you'd ever seen Kali."

I nod, but a shiver runs down my back. I told my grams I'd deal with this when it happened…and it's happening.

He sighs in disappointment, confirming my thoughts. Opening a folder, he pulls out a picture and slides it in front of me. I force my eyes to not look away, force my breathing to stay slow and steady.

Fuck. Fuck. Fuck.

"That would be a picture of my Jeep," I reply matter-of-factly. My insides twist as I notice where my Jeep is at. I was hoping this incident would've been forgotten, considering the officer had no reason to document our interaction. Especially after I showed him my badge. I was just parked in a parking lot.

"We also have a record of a phone call you received," he adds.

I know what call he's referring to. It was from the chief, wanting an update on the case. In hindsight, I wouldn't have answered it.

"When you were in the same restaurant where Kali worked."

My jaw clenches.

"Funny thing about small towns, people see everything. You can't wipe your ass without someone knowing you took a shit. You visited that town more than once. At least two other times. And you don't have an alibi for the night Kali disappeared."

He pulls out another photo and taps his finger against it. A sharp pain pinches in my chest. I haven't seen that picture in years, and I would be happy if I never saw it again.

He continues. "I could understand if you wanted revenge."

I swallow the lump in my throat, staring at the photo. He has no idea what I want.

"What I don't understand is what's your plan now that you're with her? Do you plan on finishing the job?"

What the actual fuck?

I shoot a hard stare at my boss, needing to get out of here and explain to Kali before she hears this from them and forms an opinion without knowing the other half of the story, if they haven't already. "Are you arresting me?"

Martinez replies, "Not yet. But we have a warrant to search your properties. I suggest you don't leave town."

"Paxton," my boss pleads. "I know you didn't do it. Help us help you."

What the hell is this cliché bullshit? I realize this looks bad, so I'm not saying anything. Not without my attorney.

When I don't respond, he follows up with a resigned sigh. "We're going to need your badge and gun while the investigation is ongoing."

"I didn't do it," I blurt out when I realize I'm up shit's creek. "There is no way I could've made it from my ranch and been to work by five thirty if Kali was buried around four in the morning. And I didn't lie. When the officer asked me, I didn't recognize her. It wasn't until I visited the hospital that I figured out who she was."

Total lie.

"Why didn't you say something?"

I throw my hands up. "'Cause of this, right here."

"Why did you go to Blackburn twice?"

Because one time wasn't enough. Yes, I searched for her. I needed to find the girl left behind. When the case I was working on landed me in the neighboring town, I couldn't help but stop in. Her life was simple. I imagined her paycheck was just enough to put food on the table and a roof over her head. The tattered tennis shoes had seen their day. Her natural dark lashes were exceptionally long, her face was without a trace of makeup, except for Chap-

Stick. I only knew that because I saw her put it on. I wondered if she tasted like strawberry or cherry.

That was the beginning of my obsession.

I shrug. "Curiosity." It's as simple as that.

My captain curses under his breath, irritated with my answer. "Goddammit, Paxton, you're not making this easy!" he yells, slamming his palms down on the table.

They just wouldn't understand.

"Search everything. You won't find anything because I didn't do it."

He stands tall, scrubbing his chin, his face a deep shade of red. I've never seen him this mad. "Until you're cleared, we're placing you on administrative leave. Riggs will be assigned to Liam for the time being."

"You're taking Riggs?" I roar. This is ridiculous. I saved a woman. Fueled by anger, I slam my gun and badge on the table, well aware they have me pinned in a corner. The chair scrapes against the cement floor as I push back to stand. I start to walk away, but then the anger stops me, and I whip back around. "You say that everyone knows everything that happens in Blackburn, so why haven't you found out who really buried Kali?"

His stare hardens, and his mouth thins with displeasure. "We're working on it."

No, they're wasting their time trying to pin this on me. Fuck this. I spin on my heels and take long strides to the door.

"Oh and, Officer Turner? Stay away from Kali Stevens."

Fuck you.

That will not happen.

"If you refuse," Martinez warns, stopping me as I grip the handle in my hand.

I clench my teeth and wait for his threat.

"Well, let's just say that Ms. Stevens might learn that it was her father that killed your brother."

CHAPTER 26

Kali

EACH STREET PASSES BY, and I slow down to read each sign, searching for Parker Road, even though the navigation system insists I still have half a mile to go. I've been racking my brain over why Paxton wanted to meet but told me not to tell anyone where I was going. *Make up an excuse to go to the store* were his exact words.

"*Make the next right. You've arrived at your destination.*"

Next question—why are we meeting in a deserted gas station that is surrounded by empty storefronts? The place is a ghost town.

I ease into the parking lot, spotting the back of Paxton's Jeep in the rear of the gas station, the only car in sight. An instinctual unease creeps over me, urging me to turn around. What if the guy who kidnapped me got to Paxton and is luring me here? Fear prickles my scalp as I slow my speed to a crawl, keeping my foot on the brake, debating what I should do.

I've seen all the scary movies, and I've seen this scene before. The one where it's so obvious that the girl is about to be killed, but she keeps going into the creepy shed. I exhale a sigh when I see Paxton alone. At least, I hope he is. I keep going even as Zander's voice echoes in my head about reading the room.

I'll just drive by and see if he's alone before parking. Paxton slides out of his Jeep and waits for me to park. His smile erases the tension in my shoulders. I still haven't been able to stop thinking about our weekend getaway. I rub the wings on my necklace. My life is finally moving forward, and for the first time ever, my future is defined. It's more than a dream. And I'm falling in love.

Paxton is so skilled at construction, maybe he bought one of these abandoned buildings to fix it up. It wouldn't surprise me. He's so talented.

"This isn't sus at all," I jest as soon as he opens my door for me. "You had me kind of freaked out."

His smile fades, and he runs his hand through his hair. "Sorry. I just…we need to talk. With no one around."

I stare at him as I step out of the car, confused.

"Can you take a ride with me?"

"Uh…" I pause. My brows pinch as I scan the deserted lot. Something about his tone has me shaking my head no. I grip my phone in my palm. "There's no one here, Paxton. Can we talk here?"

As if this is safer than his car.

His attention flickers around, searching the area, a panicked expression flittering across the handsome features I've fallen for. Part of me wants to reach out to him, reassure him, for what, I don't know. The other part feels like jumping back into my car and hauling ass out of here. I hate this. He's supposed to be my safe zone.

He paces, stops a few feet away, and then turns his body toward me. "Kali, don't hate me."

Never start a sentence off with that. It's the telltale sign that what comes next will not be good.

"What… what did you do?"

He swallows hard. I watch his Adam's apple bobble, but he can't spit it out.

"For what, Paxton?" I yell, tears threatening to fall as I fear the worst. The monster got to him. He told him how to find me.

"I didn't do it. I swear to you, I didn't do it. You have to believe me," he pleads.

I do a double take. Is he asking me... "Do what?" The two words come out slow.

"They think I'm the one who kidnapped you."

I jerk back, clearly having heard him wrong. Who would think that? "I've never thought you did." It's been three months, and never once have I questioned if he did it.

I could never fall in love with the man who tortured me.

Could I?

"Someone is trying to frame me," he says, almost frantically, as he paces again. What is he talking about? Who would frame him for this? He takes a deep inhale, blows it out, and drops his head. "The day I saved you wasn't the first time I had seen you," he admits. I try to snatch hold of his words and make sense of what he means because I'd never seen him before.

"When? When had you seen me before?" He mumbles and I catch a few words—something about his Jeep. "Dammit, Paxton. Tell me!"

Finally, he stops pacing and casts his eyes down. "I had a hat on and was wearing glasses. I didn't have a beard."

Our eyes meet, and I narrow mine. It was him. He's Mr. Pie Guy. "Your eyes were green?"

He slowly nods. "Contacts. Before I stopped in, I had been undercover for a nearby case. I forgot I had them on. The moment you said hello, I was drawn to you."

This just took an unfortunate turn off the what-if cliff. The idea has me backing up, wedging myself between the door and the car. He reads my fear, and like the gentleman he always is, he takes two large steps back, allowing me some distance between us. I'd thank him if I wasn't so mortified.

"I went back once, trying to find the courage to talk to you again, but when you left the restaurant in what looked like a bad mood, I chickened out."

My brows furrow, trying to figure out when that might have been.

"I was going to try again a different day but got busy with another case. And then just a few weeks later, I'm digging you out of a grave."

"I don't understand," I roar, anger overtaking the fear. "I slept with you. I'm falling in love with you, and you never mentioned any of this. Why, Paxton?"

He shoves his hands into his pockets. "Kali, please believe I would never hurt you," he pleads.

Liar! This fucking hurts.

It's difficult to imagine the man before me capable of such evil. But I never expected him to lie to me either. The possibility that he tried to kill me is out there in the world. The notion leaves my stomach feeling twisted. I squeeze the bridge of my nose, trying not to throw up. Why is everything so difficult in my life? Dating him was easy. He was the perfect guy. I imagined myself with him ten years from now.

"I'll take a lie detector test to prove to you I didn't do it."

"I've heard people can trick the system."

"That's pretty rare."

He didn't say impossible.

"I'm going to prove to you I didn't do it. I'll spend however long it takes to clear my name. They're searching both my properties, and I can promise you, they won't find anything because I. Didn't. Do. It."

Everything clicks. The meeting in the middle of nowhere, the not telling anyone that I'm meeting him, the confession. A headache threatens at the base of my neck, the tension knotting into a tight wad of *what is happening?*

"You're a suspect." It's not a question, but he nods. "Would you ever have told me? If you weren't a suspect?"

"Yes. I would have had to, eventually."

What the hell does that mean? People who skirt the truth rarely tell it if they never get caught. What am I missing? "Why?"

He runs his hand through his hair again, pulling it at its ends. His dark eyebrows pull together. "There's more…" He pauses and draws in a harsh breath. What more could there be? Isn't this enough? "The accident…where your parents died." My confusion grows tenfold. Where is he going with this, and what does this have to do with us? "My brother was in the other car."

His words steal my breath. Our meeting wasn't a coincidence. "You knew who I was?"

"I did," he whispers. "But it's not—"

"Not what I think, Paxton? Do you know how cliché that sounds? I don't know what to believe. You've been lying to me. About everything." I sit down in the car, unable to move. "Why did you look for me? Because you felt sorry for the girl left behind because your brother killed her parents?"

His mouth falls open before he snaps it back. "Is that what everyone told you?" He throws his head back, looking up at the sky, and squeezes his hands into fists before finding my gaze again. "Kali, that's not even what happened."

Excuse me? I can't get out of the car fast enough, the rage building. "That is what happened!" I storm over to him, getting in his face. "Your brother drank and drove that night. He took my parents away from me! He stole the only people on this earth who loved me unconditionally!" I scream.

"Kali." His emotions get clogged in his throat as his voice breaks. "I'm sorry your parents were taken from you that night. I am. If there's anything I wish, it'd be that night never happened. But it wasn't my brother who was drunk."

The earth shifts beneath me. "What are you saying?"

My mind jumps back to my eight-year-old self. The police coming to the babysitter's house. CPS taking me that night to a home. They told me there was an accident. I overheard one saying that alcohol caused the accident. My parents didn't drink. At least never around me. There wasn't even alcohol in our house.

I shake my head, backing up. "No. You're wrong."

"Kali, wait."

"No." I hold up my hand to stop him from getting closer. "We're done. I can't do this. You are a liar!"

I slide into my car, slamming the door, needing to get as far away from him as possible. I cover my sobs with my hand as I drive away.

Everything I thought was a lie.

CHAPTER 27

Kali

I TURN RIGHT INSTEAD of left when I hit the freeway.

There's no plan, just questions leading me in the wrong direction.

A small sign, one that you'd miss if you blinked, reads Blackburn 10 miles. Ten miles to the city that took everything from me. I was supposed to see this city in my rearview mirror, never to visit again, as I waved around four million dollars. But here I am, being pulled in, searching for answers. How could I live my entire life believing a drunk driver killed my parents and no one ever told me the truth?

Because he's wrong.

An hour passes, giving me time to calm down. But as soon as I hit Main Street, the hairs on my arms stand tall as I slow. The August heat, keeping everyone inside, makes it look as deserted as the place I just left. Even the town gossip crew's bench outside Jack's shop is empty, taking their daily meetups inside in the air conditioning. I come to a complete stop at the spot where I was taken. Given some kind of drug and tossed in the car like trash. I lean against the headrest, closing my eyes, letting my thoughts take me back to that night.

It was darker than normal. Didn't even notice the car parked on the side of the road. Where I'm parked right now. I fight the haze in my memories. I must've seen the car. How did I pass it without glancing at it, though? I would've walked by it. Right before someone slid out of the shadows.

Right before my world went black.

Knock. Knock. Knock.

A scream slips out of my lips as I'm yanked to the present. A pair of concerned brown eyes meet mine out the driver's side window. I hold a finger up, and he stands up, giving me a moment to catch my breath and open the door. The second my feet touch the ground, Henry pulls me into his chest.

"Kali! I didn't think I'd ever see you again. Everyone has been a mess since you…" His words trail off as his arms tighten around my chest, making it difficult to move my arms. Henry's a big teddy bear.

"Henry, I'm fine. But you're going to pop me like a balloon if you don't let me go." He pulls in a deep inhale and blows it out before releasing me. As our eyes meet, Henry blinks back tears, and I squeeze his bicep.

"Why are you right here?" He points to the ground where we stand. "This is where…" He shakes off the rest of the words as he looks up at the sky, fighting with his emotions.

"I was just trying to remember more about that night. Maybe if I was right here, something would come to me."

His brows shoot up. "And? Anything?"

I sigh. "No. At least not since you scared the shit out of me."

"Sorry." He shrugs unapologetically. "I saw a strange car pull up on the security monitor and figured I'd check it out."

"Security monitor?" That's new.

He nods. "They're all over town now. Between the Rangers being here forever, questioning everyone, and the fact they haven't caught the guy, people are scared."

Who could blame them?

Thanks to the Texas humidity, I wipe a bead of sweat off my forehead. "Can we go inside? It's a little warm out here." I lock the door and then follow him to the front of the store and then inside. The black-and-white monitor behind the register catches my eye. Sure enough, my car sits right in the middle of the screen.

"If only you would've let me walk you home." I jerk my head away from the screen to look at him. I've walked home by myself every Friday night for years. I never accepted his offer to walk me home because I never wanted to lead him on. Regardless, if someone wanted me, they could've found another moment in my monotonous life to take me. "Dammit, I should've kept you safe, Kali." The anger in his tone surprises me.

"Henry, this isn't your fault."

"I would do anything to keep you safe. Stay with me." Excuse me, what? "Don't look at me like that. You might be in danger," he growls, throwing his hands up. "They haven't caught the guy."

I shake my head. "I can't live in fear my whole life. It's been three months already. Who knows if they'll ever catch him?" His jaw tightens. "I need to start living. Put this all behind me. I've enrolled in college and start at the end of the month," I say in excitement. I want him to be happy for me. Despite his pining hopes we would one day be together, we've always been friends. Ever since we were five.

He rolls his eyes in resignation and walks behind the counter. The half door snaps shut behind him, and we stare at each other in silence for a few awkward beats. "I wish you would've never won the lottery."

My spine straightens, and I cross my arms. There is no way he found that out on his own. My attorney guaranteed it. "Who told you?"

"Pearl was talking to me one day, and it slipped. She was upset and made me swear to not tell anyone. But I already had my suspicions after Hobie came in and asked if you bought a lottery ticket."

"What did you tell him?"

"I lied. You know I hate that fucker, and I thought it was weird that he was asking. But then I started thinking about it and it made sense. You were suddenly moving, and you were avoiding me."

"I'm sorry. I wanted to say goodbye, but I was afraid of people finding out. But why would you say you wish I hadn't won? So I would've been stuck here the rest of my life?"

"No, Kali. Obviously, you getting kidnapped has something to do with that money. I don't know how, but it's a little too convenient to happen right after you win millions. I knew this town couldn't keep you. You deserved more than this town ever gave you. Even though I wished that I was your more, I'm not stupid."

"Henry, I've always lo—"

"Don't," he snaps, leaning forward on the counter. "Don't tell me you love me, just not *like that*. You'll break my heart." His lips quirk up, and I release the tension in my shoulders, realizing he's kidding. "If you ever change your mind, you know where I'll be." He winks. And just like that, we're back to our usual banter.

I grab a pen off the counter and a random receipt beside it. "If you're ever in Austin, call me." I write down my number. "I finally got a phone. This is my number."

He takes it and adds it to his phone's contacts. "Good luck, Special K."

I laugh at the childhood nickname as I wave and walk out the door.

Dozens of shoes have been worn down to holes walking these streets, and I've never once felt unsafe. Until now. I hate this town. Looking at my life, I'm certain it hates me, too.

With a quick glance in both directions to look for cars, I cross the street and head toward the Wallflower Diner. It's a heavy lunch crowd today. Not one empty parking spot in front of it. The door's bell jingles as I enter. Multiple gasps fill the air, and all heads turn toward me.

"Mommy, isn't that the girl who—"

"Shh!" a mother snaps, holding her hand over the little girl's mouth.

I'm not sure if I should laugh or cry. If I had a tagline for my life, that would be it.

Isn't that the girl who lost her parents?

Isn't that the girl who the mayor's fostering?

Isn't that the girl who lives with those mean people on the hill?

Isn't that the girl who was buried alive?

Yep, that's me. I am that girl.

"Well, thank the Lord, she's come back to us!" I smile at the crazy redhead making a beeline to me. "Y'all stop gawking!" Pearl barks at everyone staring. One by one, heads turn away, and a rolling thunder of quiet voices enfolds around me.

Holding my arms out to hug Pearl, I'm instead snapped with a hand towel. "Hey!" I say, grabbing the towel out of her hands so she'll stop hitting me. "Sheesh! What is that for?"

"I've been worried sick to death about you. You could've at least called and told me you were okay." Freckled arms wrap around me. Her musky perfume invades my nostrils, and I wonder why she's wearing it. She never wears perfume at work.

I hold on to her tight. "I'm sorry. It's taken me a little time to deal with what happened."

"Shh. I was joshing. You don't owe me an explanation. I'm just as happy as a goat jumping around a playground that you're here."

I can't help but laugh. Typical goofy Pearl. "I'm happy to see you, too."

"Come." She pulls me to the counter and guides me into the only barstool open. "Guess what kind of pie we've got?"

"Cherry?"

She nods, and my mind drifts to Paxton. I stare at the booth he sat in. Pearl would die if she found out that I was dating Mr. Pie Guy. *Dated.* Because as of right now, we are not together.

"Yours?" It has to be. The pie always sells out by now.

She wrinkles her nose. "Girl, I would give you anything right now. I'm just so excited," she squeals as she walks through the swinging doors, screaming at everyone in the kitchen that I'm here.

"A Mustang? Really?" I spin in my chair to the right at the familiar, deep voice and watch Chip slide next to me. He adjusts his gun belt so it's not hitting the side of the chair.

I flash a wide smile, happy he's not bringing up the elephant in the room. "What should I have bought instead?"

He hums and taps his finger against his lip. "A Ford F150 truck."

"Is that your joke of the day?" That makes him laugh.

"It's great to hear your laugh, dear." His voice turns serious. That didn't take long. But that's why I'm here. To ask questions. Not to shoot the shit. The faster I leave this town, the better.

I take a deep breath and let it out slowly. "I have questions. God, I have so many questions. But first, about the guy in the blue Jeep."

"You probably know more than I do," he deadpans with a lift of a brow.

"Do you know he's a cop?"

He nods.

"Do you know he's the one who found me?"

Again, he nods.

"Do you think he might have…done it?" I croak, hating how it sounds out loud.

He runs his hand up his other arm and shrugs. "I hate to think it's one of us. But I can't ignore the evidence."

"He says he didn't do it."

He gives me a sideways glance. "Don't they all?"

My mouth opens to defend him, but I can't form the words.

"Here you go, honeybun. Cherry pie and vanilla ice cream," Pearl cheers, interrupting us and setting a plate in front of me with a rolled-up napkin on the side. I take a large spoonful, getting a little ice cream with the pie, and shove it in my mouth. The tart cherries mixed with the sweet vanilla ice cream make me hum.

For the next half hour, I tell them about college and the classes I'm taking. How I'm excited to live on campus and start my communication degree. Between Chip's lit-up expressions and Pearl's cheering, I put aside my doubts and questions and enjoy the two people who have been like family to me.

"So, you find any cute boys yet?" Pearl says, wagging her brows.

Shaking my head, I reply, "That's the last thing I'm looking for right now."

Had I seen her yesterday, I would've told her about Paxton. How everything was going right in my life. I would've told her all about his ranch house and Riggs and how he makes my heart beat faster every time I see him.

But that was yesterday.

Her brows furrow as she puckers her red lips. "Honey, you should always be open to love." With her aroma, she's open for husband number five. She picks up a coffee pot and flitters away.

I turn to Chip, placing my spoon down on my empty plate. "You know about my parents' accident, right?" He didn't live here when it happened, but I have no doubt he knows all about it. His smile drops as he nods.

"Was my dad drunk? Was the accident his fault?"

Did my dad kill Paxton's brother? And my mom? My stomach clenches at the awful notion.

Chip lowers his coffee cup. "I don't know all the details. What were you told?"

"That's just it. I can't remember if I was told or if I just assumed. I was only eight. But all my life, I've thought the other guy was the reason for the accident."

"I can find out for you. If that's what you want, but there are some things better left buried." His eyes widen to saucers as soon as the words leave his mouth. "Shit. Talk about sticking my foot in my mouth. Sorry, kid."

I lay my head on his shoulder and sigh. "No worries."

We sit there, quiet for a few moments.

"I heard about the money," he murmurs, and I snap up. "I hope that when your life settles, you'll make the best of it."

Pearl walks back up to us, and I narrow my eyes.

"Lady, you have some loose lips."

She roars, laughing. "Hon, these lips have been married four times. They're looser than a sail flapping in the wind."

I try not to laugh. Those lips weren't the ones I was referring to. "You know what I mean," I say, half laughing, half trying to be serious. "How many people did you tell about the money?"

She looks at Chip and then back at me. "I'm sorry. I was so worried about you it might've slipped out a couple of times."

"A couple?"

"I swear. Just Chip and Henry." She winces at Henry's name.

"I already heard." I nod. "I saw him before I came here."

"I promise, that's it." She holds up two fingers. "Scout's honor."

"Pearl, put those fingers down. You wouldn't know honor if it hit you upside the head," Chip howls.

She swats him with a towel, laughing. "You be quiet."

I lift a brow, watching them tease each other. Something's different between the two of them. *They're flirty.*

"You miss this," she says, filling up Chip's coffee mug.

He winks at her. She blushes and my emotions go wild. I love this. It's like Mom and Dad are getting together.

"I do. I'll come back and see y'all." I'd say I'll come back for the wedding, but I don't want to jinx it.

She waves me off. "Don't you dare come back to this dump. We'll come and visit you in the city. Won't we, Chip?"

He grumbles something about hating big cities, making us chuckle.

My eyes scan the packed diner. These are people I've known my whole life—workers from the nearby warehouses, stay at home moms with their children—some I went to school with, neighboring shop owners, and the local church choir group. I've been gone three months, and I haven't thought of them once. The people that are important to me are the three I already talked to. Pearl's right, I don't need to come back here. This might be my home, but my heart isn't here.

I need to find a place for my heart to call home.

CHAPTER 28

Paxton

"Go away!" I scream at the incessant pounding on the front door, shoving a couch pillow over my face. It doesn't stop.

"Don't you talk to your grams that way," comes the stern voice from the other side of the door.

Fuck.

I lost my woman. Lost my dog. I'm afraid if I open that door, I'll lose my grams too. She doesn't deserve to be caught in the wreckage of my life. But she's a stubborn old lady who flew across country to be here. I jump when there's a knock on the window next to my head and come face-to-face with her.

"I see you, Paxton Reagan. Open the door now, or I'll break this window and crawl through. I didn't come all this way for you to tell me to go away!"

With a groan, I scrub my overgrown beard and swing my legs off the couch. This is why I should've answered her calls. I unlock the door, open it a crack, and shuffle back to the couch.

It's been a week since my life imploded. Breaking Kali's trust and seeing the pain in her eyes nearly destroyed me. But I swear I'll win her back. I know I lied. I messed everything up. There's no doubt about that. She just needs time, and I'll give her that.

"Jesus, have you eaten anything but pizza in the past week?" Grams asks, staring at the pile of boxes by the couch. *Be happy I was eating anything.* She walks to the kitchen, shaking out a large black garbage bag. The clinking of the beer bottles echoes through the room as she fills the bag. I close my eyes, not wanting to see her judgment in hers. It's bad enough she felt the need to come.

"They took away my dog," I snap, still angry about it. I know he's not mine, but he's a part of me. We have a connection no one will ever be able to replace, and they're punishing him for no reason.

I hear her sigh. I open my eyes, and she has her hands on her hips, giving me that look—the one filled with pity and disappointment that cuts deeper than any words. "Talk to me, Pax. They're going to clear you and give you Riggs back."

I can't sit up fast enough. "He probably thinks I deserted him. He doesn't understand that it's temporary." She lifts a brow at my sharp words. *Bring it down a notch, Pax. She's not the enemy.* "Fuck. I'm sorry, Grams." I blow out a harsh breath and stare up at the ceiling. "I'm just not in a good headspace."

"Have you tried to call Kali?"

I stare at my phone across the room on the floor. Where it fell after throwing it against the wall yesterday. Her eyes follow, and then she walks over to pick it up. She holds it up. "Cracked, but still works."

"Sounds like me," I say snidely.

Her eyes glance around the room. "I wouldn't call this working. Sweetheart, you need to pull yourself together. Because she will call you back. Eventually. And...how do I put this in words you'll understand?" She pauses, tapping her finger against her lips. "Get off your ass and grow a pair of balls."

My eyes bulge out of my face, staring at my sweet, innocent sixty-five-year-old grandma. *Did she just say that?*

The chuckle comes out on its own. "Wow, Grams."

She shrugs. "Do I have your attention now?"

How could she not?

"You screwed up. Not only did you lie to Kali, you dropped a bomb in her lap. She's going to need time. But this? This isn't fixing anything." She opens her arms out wide. It's the first time I've actually opened my eyes and seen how bad my place looks. Drawers are still wide open from when they searched the place, papers on the ground, trash dumped over. "Have you even taken a shower in a week? 'Cause it smells in here." Her nose wrinkles.

Just having to think about when the last time was means it's been too long.

"Don't lose yourself in this mess, Paxton. Kali needs to see you're worth fighting for."

I nod, letting her words sink in. She's right. If Kali were to come walking in right now, I'd be mortified. This isn't the man she was falling for. I roll my shoulders and stand up. All my senses are revving back to life.

I get a whiff of myself.

Yeah. Let's start with a shower.

CHAPTER 29

Kali

"Still haven't talked to him?" Amy asks, helping me put away some of my new dishes.

Today is move-in day. The apartment building is booming with laughter, excitement, and moving boxes lined up and down the hallways. Multiple people have peeked in as they passed my room and said a quick hi. I'm anxious about meeting my roommate. We've only talked through texts to tell each other what we're bringing to the apartment, so we don't have a lot of doubles.

I shake my head and sigh, irritated with myself that I'm letting a broken heart ruin the moment. I've wanted this for so long.

I'm going to college!

When I told her and Ted what happened when I got home that night, Ted told me he could help me find out what happened with my parents' accident. I didn't want to find out, but I needed to. I owed it to Paxton to learn the truth. We both lost a lot from that accident.

When I allowed myself to think about it, I already knew what the report was going to say. Why would he lie to me, knowing I could debunk his story? All it took was a simple request to see the accident report, and I had my answer. I've wanted to call him and tell him, but something deep down is stopping me. It's been two weeks since we talked.

"I think it's better that you don't," Ted says in his stern voice, dropping the last box on the kitchen table. "I don't like that he lied to you."

That makes two of us. At least about the lying part. The other part is where the lines blur. I'm mad at him for lying to me, but I also miss him—the way he touches my hair, his chaste kisses when I least expect it, and when he calls me Kalico. I won't believe that he's the person who hurt me, but until he's cleared, it's best that we take a break.

Two hours later, I can't stop staring at my room. *This is my freaking room!*

When Amy asked me what theme or colors I wanted for my room, I stared at her like she had two heads. It never occurred to me I should decorate my room, and even if I wanted to, I wouldn't know where to start. I'm used to ragged, mismatched old furniture. She told me to leave it up to her, asking me only for the colors that I liked. There was a bedspread that I found while out shopping that was turquoise, gray, and white, so she planned the entire room around that. I've never been a girly girl. In fact, I can count on my hands the number of times I wore a dress outside work, but this room makes me want to go put a dress on.

"I love it!" I wrap my arms around Amy's shoulders, staring at the room over her shoulders. There's a fuzzy white rug on the floor, with matching pillows on the bed. The artwork on the walls ties in all the colors of the room. "It's amazing," I whisper.

"I figured you didn't want a yellow room," she teases.

"I would've loved it too. And it would have reminded me of you."

Her eyes soften. "I expect you to keep in touch with us. Tell us how class is going. And you're welcome to the ranch anytime."

Ted comes over and wraps his arm around my shoulder. "And

if you ever feel in danger or need help, you call me immediately. I'll be here as fast as I can."

This. I'm going to miss this so much.

With a tearful goodbye, they wish me well on my exciting journey.

I'VE KEPT the front door open because I'm enjoying meeting my neighbors. And it seems to be the thing to do. Two girls from across the hallway brought me cookies already. In the five years I lived in my apartment, my neighbors kept to themselves, and no one ever made me food. *But this is college,* I keep telling myself. It's different. Being social is part of the deal. That's the part that might be the biggest change for me.

I just sat down with my new laptop when I hear a voice. "Please tell me you like pineapple on your pizza and Dr Pepper." A woman breezes into the apartment, balancing two boxes. One covers her face. She drops them in the entry and blows out a breath before I can offer to help. A petite platinum blonde with lively eyes greets me. She's wearing blue scrubs. "Also, I don't do messes or crying. Please don't be a crier. I get my fill of tears at work."

I stare at her, first wondering if she's my roommate, and then blink, thinking, am I a crier? Sure, I've cried a lot in the past three months, but I had a reason for every tear that fell from my eyes. When I conclude I am not a normal crier, I reply, "No, to the pineapple..." Because, gross. "Yes to the Dr Pepper, I'm a tidy person, and crying isn't my thing."

She claps her hands twice as if she just won a prize and then walks over to me, her hand stretched out. "That just means more pizza for me. I'm Zoe."

I stand and meet her handshake with a warm greeting. "Kali." Zoe exudes an energetic vibe. Totally opposite to me, which surprises me because, hello, we filled out a compatibility question-naire. I was expecting someone more grounded…not bouncy.

She buzzes around the apartment, looking at everything with so much energy I wonder how much caffeine she's had today. "Do you need help with more boxes? I'm all moved in, so I can help."

"Oh my gosh!" she exclaims when she gets to my room. "Your room is to die for. You need to help me decorate mine."

"Ahh…" I stare at my room, still not believing it's mine, and shake my head. "That is not my doing. A friend did that for me. Give me a blank room, and it'd be worse than it started."

"Oh well. I'll just spend all my time in your room." She laughs, but I have a feeling she's not kidding. "I saw that you're a fresh-man, but we're the same age, right?"

When I chose her, it was because we were the same age. I couldn't imagine living with an eighteen-year-old, and we have nothing in common. "Yep. I had to save up some money to come to school."

She hands me a box, grabs the other one, and I follow her to the kitchen to unload it. "Good for you! They say if you don't go right after high school, the odds are that you'll never go."

That's me. Breaking all the odds.

She's easy to talk to, given she likes to talk. After thirty minutes, I know her entire life story. All she knows about me is that I'm from Blackburn. Which is fine. There isn't much more that I'm comfortable disclosing, so I'm happy to let her do the talking.

She sets out two plastic cups and pulls out a bottle of red wine, showing it to me before pouring. Like I care what it is. After handing me a cup, she raises hers and says, "Here's to a new exciting year with a new friend."

"Cheers," I say, the excitement bubbling up inside me as this new adventure awaits. Dream number one is about to begin.

"Since we're getting to know each other, is there a man?" She wags her brows. "Not that I care, but I like to walk around in my panties and bra sometimes, and I'm certain you don't want your man seeing that."

I bob my head from side to side. "Yes. And no?"

"So, complicated?"

That about sums it up in one word. I nod. "We're taking a break. It might not work out."

She lifts a brow. "You sound like you miss him. Are you sure it's over?"

How do I tell her he's the prime suspect in my torture case? At least she'd understand the complicated part.

"That's a loaded question, Zoe," I say, wrinkling my nose, staring at my cup. I don't want to start off our first day together talking about all my drama. "We'll get to that another day. Tell me more about what you're studying." I swallow the rest of my wine as she easily jumps into telling me about her nursing degree.

CHAPTER 30

Kali

"Where are you hiding, woman?" Zoe's voice bounces into my room as she swings open the front door.

"In here," I reply from my bedroom, dropping the heavy world history book in my lap. She waltzes in, wearing lively pink scrubs with yellow ducks on them. "Cute," I say, pointing at her, and she does a little butt shake.

"The kids love them." She works in pediatrics at the university hospital while she's finishing her nursing degree. "Ugh. My least favorite subject," she groans with a scrunched-up nose, eyeing my book. School has been a lot tougher than I imagined it would be. The four-year gap hasn't done me any favors.

"Test tomorrow. Already." I sigh, holding up note cards. How can a professor assign a test when we've only been in school for two weeks?

"Have time for dinner? After the day I had, I can eat a whole damn pizza," she says, patting her stomach. I can't imagine working with sick kids. The stress, anxiety, and on top of that, seeing innocent children hurt and in pain. I shudder at the thought.

"Pizza sounds delicious. Not studying sounds better."

I SHOULD'VE HAD another beer. I'm making a new rule—study drunk, test sober. I groan, anticipating the mountain of study cards awaiting me as I stare up at our apartment building from Zoe's front seat. Can you tell how much I hate studying?

"What's that?" Zoe points at my car as we pass it, and I notice a small white paper under my windshield wiper. I shrug. It wasn't there when we left because I had to grab my sunglasses out of it, and I would've noticed. But now, with the sky a midnight blue, the white stands out from the lights overhead.

I walk around my car. "It's probably an advertisement to join some club." Flyers are a frequent occurrence on cars being so close to campus. When I pull it out and realize it's an envelope, I glance around at other cars and notice I'm the only one with one.

The hairs on the back of my neck tingle as I slide a paper out and read the words. The earth opens underneath me, swallowing me whole. I'm back there. Buried in darkness.

My knees buckle, and my bones go limp like Jell-O. Someone yells my name.

"Kali, wake up!"

My eyes flutter open and I'm flat on the ground. Zoe pulls on my shoulders, placing me in a seated position.

"Put your knees up and put your head between your knees."

I can barely follow her directions, but she helps.

"Take a deep breath. Now let it out."

Uncontrollable tears fall as I tremble with fear. Zoe wraps her arms around me.

"It's okay, babe. You passed out."

No. It's not okay.

He found me.

"I…I need to get inside," I mutter, pushing off the cement, the envelope clutched in my trembling hands. My eyes dart in every direction, searching. I gasp in horror when I find him. Anger is the only thing keeping me on my feet.

A man stands alone off in the distance, too far for me to get a good look, but close enough for me to see his silhouette. He's standing right outside the ring of light from the streetlight, wearing dark jeans and a black hoodie, his large, broad figure turned sideways with his face hidden in the shadow of his hood. "Hey!" I scream. My heart pounds against my chest. "You psychopath! If you want me, come and get me!"

I don't know what the hell I'm doing.

But I'm way past being rational.

"Kali, who are you yelling at?"

"Did you see that guy?" I ask, pointing in the direction he was standing, but he's no longer there. "The guy in the hoodie?"

She shakes her head. "I was picking up your purse. Sorry," she adds when I wince and drop my head. I didn't imagine him. He was there. "C'mon, let's get inside. You're freaking me out."

Once inside, behind locked doors, I curl up into a ball on the couch. Zoe lays a blanket over me. I've crumbled the note up in my fist, biting the urge to light it on fire.

"What happened out there? What did that note say?"

I toss it at her and draw in a shaky breath. She glances at the ball of paper for a moment and looks at me with uncertainty. I could tell her not to look, but that'll make her want to even more. She opens it.

"You don't belong here. You belong in a box. It comes in three." Her words are slow and steady, as if not wanting to read it wrong.

I flinch, hearing it out loud. As if the knives are sharper, going into my heart the second time.

"Who the hell is this from? And what does it mean?"

I fought to move past this, not live like a victim, and I haven't talked about it with anyone. Now I wonder if I put Zoe in danger.

"Did you hear about the girl buried alive? Almost five months ago?"

"That happened close by. Of course I heard about it. But what does that..." Her words trail off mid-sentence, putting two and two together. Her eyes widen as she gasps, slapping her hand to her chest. "That was you?" she whispers.

I can imagine she's trying to figure out how I survived, how long I was down there, and what it was like being trapped. She's the first person I've told. All I can do is nod.

"Oh, Kali." She runs over and wraps her arms around me. She pulls away, her eyes filled with concern. "We need to call the police."

A knot tightens in my stomach, and I brace myself for the painful journey back into the nightmare I thought I had escaped. Finding my voice, I point to my purse. "I have a Texas Ranger's number in my favorites."

Minutes later, my small apartment swarms with police officers, and not long after, Martinez storms in. They brought in a K-9 unit, hearing that there was a possibility he was close by. I can't help but think of Paxton and Riggs. We still haven't talked. He tried to call, but I wasn't ready. Our future is still questionable, but before we can find out, he needs to no longer be a suspect. The last time I talked with Martinez, they were still working on it. They had found nothing yet, but they were being thorough.

"Could this be someone trying to scare you?" Martinez asks. "Who knows about what happened to you?"

I shake my head hard. "It's him. He made sure I knew it was him."

"How?"

The air in the room tightens as I recall details only I know. "His words...it comes in three," I whisper.

His forehead crinkles, the information not making sense to him. Of course, it doesn't, it's new information. I didn't tell anyone.

"I didn't figure the detail was very useful." When he flashes a stern look, about to lecture me, I add, "It's not like knowing he has OCD will help find him."

"Tell me now," he says sharply. I really didn't think it was that important.

I drop my head and continue. "Every time he shoveled dirt, he did it three times and then took a break. Not a long one, but enough to notice. Thump. Thump. Thump. Then silence." A tear runs down my cheek as the memory strikes an emotional chord. "Why is he back for me?" My voice cracks, pleading for answers from Martinez. "This wasn't supposed to be about me."

Martinez exchanges a glance with one officer, his expression serious. Zoe clasps my hand and puts her head on my shoulder. Guilt rips through the center of my heart and intertwines with fear that I brought this terror to her.

"Will I ever be safe from this monster?" I overhear officers in the doorway, directing our neighbors to go back into their apartments.

This is great. Everyone will find out who I am now.

A bark and a streak of brown bursts through the open front door, weaving around officers. A dog darts directly at me and leaps onto the couch, finding the small space between Zoe and me.

"Whoa. Where did he come from?" Zoe says, shifting away from me as Riggs fixes his black orbs on her.

"Riggs?" I glance toward the door, half expecting Paxton.

"Where did this dog come from?" Martinez snaps, standing at attention with his chest puffed out. He also knows who the dog belongs to, and he's not happy.

Right on cue, Paxton runs in with a dangling leash in one hand. Martinez sends him an icy glare, and Paxton just shrugs, holding up the leash.

"Bullshit. He fucking let him loose," Martinez mumbles under his breath.

Paxton's wearing a black T-shirt with "security" written in large white letters on the front. He shoots me a quick apologetic glance, and my heart flutters. One officer gives him a nod and a pat on the back before Martinez confronts him, almost nose to nose.

"Why are you here?"

"I was working a security job when I got the call," he replies, unfazed. "Now, if you don't mind, I'd like to talk to Kali."

"I do mind." Martinez shifts to his right, stopping his advance. "You left your security job? Just like that?"

Paxton's expression hardens. "There were two of us working. I called the company and told them I had an emergency. I'd be happy to give you all the information."

"You do that," Martinez clips, standing firm in his position, making Paxton go around him. "And put that damn dog on his leash."

A weight lifts off my chest. It wasn't him. I try to stand, but somehow Riggs's solid head feels like a hundred-pound bowling ball in my lap.

Paxton comes and kneels in front of me. "Hey, you okay?"

I nod, even though inside, my nerves feel like they are on crack. "You got Riggs back. Does that mean you got your job back? You're cleared?"

"I did." He jerks his thumb over his shoulder. "Guess Martinez didn't tell you, huh?"

I sigh, shaking my head. Why can't they work together on this and stop butting heads?

"I tried to call you, but with everything...I figured you needed more time. I get it. A buddy of mine messaged me and told me what happened tonight. Nothing could've kept me from coming. Since I didn't know exactly where your room was, Riggs helped me find you." He winks, and Riggs moves in between our legs and sits, proud of himself.

I really like this dog.

"It was *him*. I saw him. He was here."

"What?" Paxton's jaw slams shut and he clenches his teeth together. "You saw him? Did he say anything?"

"He was standing pretty far away, probably watching for my reaction to the note." I hate that I passed out. He's getting a kick out of my fear, and I handed it to him on a silver platter. "I told him to come and get me, and then he disappeared."

He smacks his hand to his face, and Riggs's dark eyes stare at me. "Please tell me you didn't goad a psychopath?"

"It wasn't one of my finer moments. It all boiled over in a rash outburst." Let's hope he doesn't take me up on my offer.

"You can't play games with a guy like that. He's dangerous. Come stay with me for now," he says. "At least until you can get your security detail. Because you will get it now."

"Paxton, I don't know if now is a good time for us—" I begin, but he cuts me off, standing up and crossing his arms with a rigid posture.

"I'm not asking."

Well, then. Bossy Paxton is kind of sexy.

My instinct is to argue—I'm an independent woman who can take care of herself, and we're not in the best of places at the moment. But I remember how quickly it took for the guy to drug me and throw me in his car.

And now he knows where I live.

"I'll grab some of my stuff," I concede, a trace of defeat in my voice.

Paxton lifts one side of his lips, satisfied, and reaches down to scratch Riggs's head. "Riggs will sleep sounder knowing he's protecting you."

I know I will.

"Let me tell Martinez where I'll be."

"He'll love that," he quips, putting Riggs's leash on. "I'll wait for you outside."

First, I walk over to Zoe. She's texting someone. I'm sure her phone is blowing up as the news gets out. She glances up when she sees it's me. "Can you stay at your parents' house for a couple of nights? I don't want you here alone," I ask.

"I already called them, and they're coming to pick me up." She pulls me into a tight hug. "Are you going to be all right?"

That's the million-dollar question, and I'd pay that amount if it meant finding the bastard. My head is pounding from all the adrenaline.

"I don't know when I'll be back here." I sigh, uncertainty hanging over all my plans. "If you have a friend who wants to live with you rent-free for the semester, I'd be okay with that."

She nods and gives me another quick hug. This freaking sucks. He's forcing me into a state of isolation. I'm afraid to have friends. I'm afraid to live my life. What good was it I lived if I can't live?

I want to scream.

As I walk over to Martinez, he's talking to three officers, so I wait for him to finish. For a moment, I wonder if I'm making the right choice leaving with Paxton. There's so much we need to talk about, but is this the right time? While I'm staying at his home?

When Martinez notices me, he turns. "The dogs haven't picked up a scent. But we're getting access to every camera around that area."

I nod. Something tells me they won't find him. Which makes my decision to stay with Paxton final. "Why didn't you tell me that Paxton was no longer a suspect?"

He pulls in a harsh sigh, releasing an irritated exhale. He looks past me, over my shoulder, and back to me. "Because I feel there's still a connection."

"If there is," I say in his defense, "he doesn't know about it. I'm going to go stay with him. He'll keep me safe."

He puts his hand on my shoulder, and his eyes soften. It makes me wonder if he has kids. Do they cause him this much stress? "I hope you're right. Just be careful, Kali."

CHAPTER 31

Kali

KNOCK. *Knock.*

I turn to Paxton, trying to stop the panic rising in my chest at an alarming rate at the mere sound of a knock on the door. *Calm down, Kali, the bad guy won't knock on a cop's door.* "Expecting someone?"

He nods and pushes off the chair, offering no explanation. He's been giving me space, not sitting right beside me, not touching me, and keeping the conversation formal. The distance feels strange, but I appreciate it.

I curl up in the blanket, my nerves still raw. Riggs walks in sync with him and sits when Paxton opens the front door. My position on the couch hides the visitor from view, but when Paxton closes the door, he's holding a brown bag. I tilt my head, questioning, but he returns the gesture by holding a finger in the air. Riggs settles at my feet, my silent guardian.

"I'll be right back," he says with a devilish grin.

He disappears into the kitchen, and I listen as he opens cabinets, hearing the subtle clinks of silverware. The paper bag crumples, and I assume, by the sound, that he's taking out whatever was in the bag. I hope he didn't order dinner. I'm still stuffed from the pizza.

In the ten minutes we've been here, he showed me around his small two-bedroom apartment, and we only settled on the couch right before the knock. This is the first time I've been here. On one of our dates, I asked him if he was hiding away a wife, and that's why he never brought me here. Now, sitting here in the typical bachelor pad, devoid of any personal effects other than the one photograph of his grandparents, it tells me where his priorities are. The ranch and his work, not this small temporary space he stays at during the week.

"What are you doing in there?"

"Still not into surprises," he teases, sticking his head out from behind the kitchen wall. I wrinkle my nose at him. I'd be lying if I said I didn't miss this. He's still wearing his security shirt.

"Why were you working security if you got your job back?"

"A buddy of mine has a used car lot. He's been having his cars broken into at night, so he asked me if I could work a couple shifts off duty until he can get something permanent in place. So, Liam and I were working tonight," he explains from the kitchen.

"Sorry I took you away from your job."

He peeks out again. "Don't be. They knew we were there. They might be shitheads, but they aren't dumb shitheads. They weren't going to touch the cars tonight." His head disappears again.

"If I'm going to stay here, we need to talk about things." The panic from the night is settling, leaving behind a dust of unanswered questions and wondering if I made the right decision to stay here.

He comes strolling into the room holding a plate. Riggs's head lifts, his nose in the air. When Paxton settles next to me, I see what he's been up to, and my tension eases. He hands me a spoon, understanding my weaknesses too well. I stare at the cherry pie with a dollop of vanilla ice cream on top and glance up to him with a smile.

"A pie is not going to fix everything," I say.

"No, but it'll make you feel better."

It already does.

Only the people close to me know the key to my heart is cherry pie. I hold the spoon out to dive in, but then pause. "We need to talk," I repeat, making sure he heard me this time. No amount of pie will erase his lying. He has some explaining to do. He nods in agreement but still waits for me to grab a spoonful. When the warm pie hits my taste buds, my eyes close in bliss. Damn, that's good. So, so good.

"What was it you wanted to discuss?" he teases.

I shake my head, chewing. It can wait. He's not going anywhere. I take another generous bite, and he chuckles. "Are you not going to eat some?" I ask, gesturing to the pie that has more than enough for two people on the plate. If he doesn't, I'll eat the entire thing. And I'll have zero shame. So much for being stuffed from the pizza.

"I'm almost scared to take a bite," he confesses, watching me devour it. "You're like a bear eating to stock up for hibernation."

I roll my eyes, paying no attention to how I appear as a pig—or bear—and continue to take another bite. "You can't like pecan over this perfection," I mumble, covering my mouth with my hand since I forgot all my manners. Wait a minute. I point my spoon at him. "Admit you made that up because you didn't want me to figure out you were the pie guy."

He takes a hefty spoonful and puts it in his mouth, eating it with an exaggerated shrug.

"No, you don't get off that easy," I say, elbowing him in the side.

"Actually, with you, I do."

A thrill of arousal travels down my spine and settles between my legs as his words carry a hint of something more, throwing me back to a month ago—to the first time I experienced him losing control, when his eyes would squeeze shut and his jaw would tighten and he'd roar "fuck" as his orgasm ripped through his sweaty body. It was raw and real. It was exhilarating. Until everything changed. He lied.

I shake from the memory, and reality slams into me.

Dammit.

This is why I should've found somewhere else to go. "I need a drink," I blurt out, rushing to get up, not wanting him to see my flushed cheeks. I snatch a bottle of water from the fridge and press it against my cheeks before opening it and taking a long drink.

When I get back to the couch and plop down, he murmurs, "Sorry." He slides the plate on the table and sits back against the pillows, resting an ankle on the other knee and his arm draped over the back of the couch. I take another long sip of water to wash down the pie and lingering desire. "That was out of line. It's tough pretending there is nothing between us." He sighs. "Let's talk."

I had prepared a list of questions, but now, in this moment, with my head reeling from tonight's events, nothing is coming to mind except one thing. "I saw the police report." The words tumble out, dragging an icy chill over my skin. I pull the blanket around me, still not okay with finding out that my dad killed my mom and Paxton's brother. "I'm sorry."

"Kali, you were eight. What are you sorry for?"

"Not believing you."

"I wouldn't blame you if you hated me. I should've been honest with you from the start. I just…" Uncertainty creeps into his expression. "I didn't realize I'd fall for you so quickly."

"I could never hate you," I whisper, fiddling with the label on the bottle. As the silence stretches between us, my swirling thoughts settle. "You mentioned you came back to the diner but saw me come outside mad. When was that?" I've been racking my brain trying to pinpoint that day, wondering why I'd been so upset. Enough to make him not want to talk to me.

He hums. "It was a few weeks later, maybe. You burst outside, looked up at the sky, and started cursing." He snaps his fingers as if a lightbulb just turned on. "We were getting bad weather that night. I remember sitting in the car and the radio announced that there were possible tornadoes. But I was certain you weren't cussing at the sky."

I remember that day.

The day *just* Ann came in, and the night I bought the lottery ticket. "You were in the parking lot?"

He nods. It's crazy how a single decision in time could alter your entire life. If he had gotten out of his car and came up to me, I wouldn't have bought a lottery ticket.

"So why? Why search for me after all these years?"

He picks at a spot on his jeans for a moment and then lifts his gaze with an uneasy expression. "After the accident and the initial shock of my brother's death, my dad was worried about you. He kept in touch with child protective services to see what was going to happen. When he found out they put you in a group home, it gutted him."

I stare at him, blinking, unsure what to say to that. Why would his dad care about the child of the man who murdered his son?

"He talked my mom into adopting you. They always wanted a girl."

I gasp, recalling a family that wanted to adopt me. The family that never showed up. Were those his parents? "Were they the ones that said I wasn't a good fit?"

He reaches for my hand. "Kali, it wasn't because of you. My mom just couldn't…"

"Paxton," I say, stopping him. "I can't even imagine…" I pause, shaking my head, still in disbelief at our connection. "I understand. Your mom was still grieving the unimaginable loss of her child. I don't imagine anyone could ever get over that. Let alone expect her to stare at the same eyes as the man who took her child every day for the rest of her life."

"But you're not him."

"Still. That's a lot." I wouldn't want to grow up with that guilt. It makes me sad he doesn't talk to his mom. She's lost everything.

I feel as though a dump truck backed up and dropped its load on me. I might not be buried alive, but the weight of everything is suffocating. We almost became brother and sister. Nope, that is one idea that never needs to be mentioned. A shiver runs down my spine.

"You okay?" he asks, watching me with intense eyes.

I nod, remembering the broken-hearted little girl sitting on the hard wooden bench for hours. "Just thinking about unanswered prayers."

CHAPTER 32

Paxton

SURVIVING a week without touching Kali has been hell. The past couple days, though, there's been a shift. This morning, she gave me a hug goodbye, and she let it linger. The entire morning, her smell stayed with me. She wants this as much as I do. I can see it in her eyes. But for now, I'm giving her all the control. She's in the driver's seat, still using her brake pedal a little too much. I just have to trust that she knows we belong together.

"It's that time, huh?" I say to the ten-pound weight nestled in my lap. Riggs, with his dark eyes and furrowed brows, glances up as he keeps his head planted. "You'll have to move if you want me to get up."

He perks up and jumps back. *Let's get this done before our meeting.*

The scorching late September weather is confused, it thinks it's July, reaching a beating hundred degrees. He better not take forever to find a spot to piss. At least there's shade at the park across the street. When we get to the light, I notice a woman sitting alone on a park bench. I tilt my head forward, narrowing my eyes at the familiar face. Dammit to hell. *It can't be.* When the crosswalk flashes to go, Riggs stares up at my hesitation. *Let's get this over with.* As we draw closer and she comes into a better view, it's her—older and thinner, but sporting the same contrived smile she wore when anyone was looking.

I groan, not having enough time to get myself ready to deal with her. Riggs looks at me confused when I pause. "What the hell are you doing here?"

"Paxxy, that is not a nice way to greet your mom," she replies, standing. I cringe, her voice triggering a visceral reaction that I haven't had in a long time. "Come, give me a hug, sugar bear."

I hate her.

Ten years wasn't long enough to forget the hell she put me through or what she allowed that bastard to do to me. As she takes a step toward me, I retreat, pacing a few steps to our left so Riggs can find his spot on the grass. "Sorry, he has to piss." Right on cue, Riggs lifts a leg and does his business.

"You've grown into a man," she says, walking over.

Could it be because I am a man? I draw in a deep breath, hoping there's a shred of patience in the air that will fill my lungs. I don't want to be an asshole to the woman who bore me, but every feeling I have about her is her fault.

I exhale, not finding any. "Yep, that's what time does."

She huffs. "Stop being so stuffy. Come sit with me for a few minutes."

"Mom. I have to get back to work."

"A few minutes," she repeats with a slight pleading undertone. I nod once in resignation and gesture to the bench. She turns and I follow her until we're both seated, Riggs settling at my feet. "He's a handsome guy," she says, leaning over and scratching his head.

I catch the faint scent of her musky perfume and have to swallow back the revulsion. After all the years, she still wears the same perfume.

Her phone dings, and I glance down and read it. I shouldn't care, but her unexpected visit has me on edge. *Beth, where are you?*

She grabs it before I can see who it's from. Probably that asshole who keeps her on a tight chain.

The one I almost killed.

Almost.

I exhale. "You still with Ray?"

"Noooo," she says with disdain. She should be repulsed by how he treated the two of us. But I doubt I'll ever hear a sorry out of her. She waves me off. "I haven't seen him in years." That surprises me. I was certain that he'd kill her before letting her leave him. He was that much of a bastard he'd do it.

"Are you still living in Oklahoma?"

She bobs her head. "A little here and a little there. I've adopted the nomad lifestyle living in a trailer."

I turn toward her, gripping the leash in my hand. "Are you running from him?" Despite my resentment, she's here now, and there's a deep-rooted instinct to protect her if she's in trouble. It's who I am at my core.

No thanks to her.

"Sweetie, I'm fine," she says with a singsong voice, the same one she would use when talking to family and friends about how things were going after my dad passed away.

She wasn't fine. Anything but. I glance at my watch. I have a meeting in ten minutes, so I need to hurry this along. "Why are you here, then?" I wonder how long she had been waiting out here. Did she know I would come out, or was she sitting here debating about coming into the precinct?

"I'm headed out west. Going to give beach living a try," she says. "I got a job as a traveling nurse."

It's always baffled me how someone without compassion could be a nurse.

I've yet to hear how this concerns me. I didn't care where she was for the last ten years. Why does she think I'll care about the next ten? Is she wanting money? "Mom. Do you need something from me?"

"No, Paxxy. I just wanted to see if you were doing okay. It's been so long."

I bite my tongue to stop myself from reminding her why that was. She rubs Riggs on the head again and then looks over at me. "Are ya married?"

"Nope."

"Seeing anyone?"

Kali, of course, comes to mind, but I sure as hell don't want to tell her about her. She'll taint it somehow, or God forbid, start thinking she's a mom and ask to meet her.

"Nope," I say, shaking my head and staring ahead. I'll be damned if Kali meets her before Grams does. "It's just me and Riggs."

I feel her eyes on me for a moment, and then see out of the corner of my eye as she looks forward with a quick hum. *Hmm what?* "I hope you're not against love because of what happened to me."

I jerk my head toward her. "Ain't that a box of bullshit? You act like you didn't have a choice. It didn't happen to you, you let it happen." She opens her mouth, but I'm not done. "And no, you and your choices have no effect on my love life." Unlike her, I know who to fight for. I stand up, not wanting to stick around to hear her excuses. "I gotta get back to work. Hope you find some happiness wherever you end up."

Crossing her legs, she lets out a sigh. "Don't waste my gift to you."

I look up at the sky before turning back to her. She's even more batshit crazy than I remember. "And what gift would that be?"

"Love."

I blink hard once and then again. My eyebrows raise as a chill runs down my sweaty back. "I'm sorry. What did you say?"

"The ability to love deeply," she adds when I stand motionless. "My heart is bigger than my head. You got that from me." She places both hands on her heart.

As if she has one.

For a moment, the thought that she might have something to do with Kali flickers in my mind, but as soon as she spoke again, that thought vanished, replaced with a surge of anger. She is so delusional. Her heart must've not been big enough to care about her only kid.

Just the man she was fucking.

I'm at the point of mindlessly nodding, done with her. "Bye, Mom. Nice seeing you," I say, with zero authenticity. "Good luck on your adventure." I spin on my heels, and Riggs is right by my side. When we get to the front door of the precinct, I lean over and whisper to Riggs, "If you ever see her again, nip her in the ass."

He barks once as if understanding, and I laugh. He's too well-trained.

Unfortunately.

CHAPTER 33

Kali

"WOMAN, IT'S NOT A DIFFICULT QUESTION."

It is. It's like a multiple-choice question where the answer is all of the above. Settling on a single restaurant is impossible when everything sounds appetizing.

Today marks six months. It's been half a year since I thought I was going to take my last breath in a coffin. Paxton insists it calls for a celebration, a recognition of my strength and perseverance.

Unfortunately, like my investigation, the sighting of the man ended at a dead end. I'm at the point where I'm doubting the Texas Rangers. We live in a digital society. How has one camera not gotten his picture? Martinez said the guy knows what he's doing. He's precise in everything he's done, leaving no traceable evidence behind. They found the guy who put the note on my car through a chain of five others, each paid one hundred dollars to pass an envelope to another guy, which when opened was a hundred-dollar bill and another envelope with instructions to pass on. Then the final guy's note was to leave the envelope on my car. The first guy claimed he received it at an outdoor farmer's market, a place where there weren't any cameras. His description of the person was vague—middle-aged with a baseball hat on. That leaves half this freaking county as a suspect.

"I have to run to my apartment real fast first."

"Hold on, I'll go with you."

"Pax, it's five doors down. Finish your report, and I'll be right back."

After staying at Paxton's house for a couple weeks, we started to get close again. It's not that I didn't want that—I do, *more than anything*. But with everything that has happened, I need to have our relationship grow organically. I couldn't bear the thought that he might be doing it out of obligation just because I was staying with him.

So, I found a place.

I didn't go far. As a compromise, I moved into an apartment right down the hallway from Paxton. I gave up my apartment with Zoe because I didn't want to put her in danger. She understood and was probably relieved. Truthfully, I feel more at ease knowing Paxton and Riggs are close by.

And moving out is exactly what our relationship needed to progress. We found our way back to each other, but this time, it's stronger. The connection between us deepened, bonding us on an entirely new level. I love this man, and he loves me, even though he's yet to say it.

"Where's Stan?" he asks.

I stare at him incredulously. "I do not need someone to walk me twenty feet. I gave him the night off since I knew we were going to dinner." I hired a bodyguard for when I wasn't with Paxton. It's weird having someone tail you. On the third day, I almost panicked, ready to call Martinez about the suspicious guy following me. Paxton and I got a laugh out of it. "I'll be right back. If I don't get back in five minutes, send a search team."

"That's not even funny," he says, his tone serious.

I walk over to the kitchen table where he's set up his computer. Leaning against the arms of the chair, I give him a chaste kiss.

"Thank you for worrying about me. But seriously, I need you to dial it back."

It's been a month since *he* found me, and I'm trying to find the sweet spot between terror and moving on that will allow me to live. His overwhelming need to keep me safe isn't helping.

He sighs, running his hand through his hair. "Sorry. I just…"

I need to remind myself that he's doing it because he cares deeply for me. It's sweet, even though it's overbearing at times. "I'll take Riggs with me."

His smile grows and he immediately commands Riggs to stay with me. He winks. "Thank you."

Not three minutes later, we're walking back into the apartment.

"I got it!" I exclaim and snap my fingers. Paxton turns from his chair with a lifted brow. "Matt's El Rancho. Sitting on the patio with their famous Mexican martini." I hum, just the thought of the drink makes my mouth water. I glance outside the back door. The low-hanging clouds in the distance will create the perfect backdrop for a colorful Texas sunset. Amy introduced me to this place on one of our girls' shopping outings. It was delicious. I can't believe I forgot about it.

"We can't go there," he counters.

"Why?"

"Just kidding." He smirks, pushing off the couch. I shoot him a playful glare. "I mean, we might run into an ex-girlfriend there. So, I'm warning you now. That was her favorite restaurant."

Ex-girlfriend? He never talks about his exes. "Now I really want to go."

He rolls his eyes. "Only you would want to see my ex."

I wrinkle my nose. He doesn't understand that I want to know everything about him.

Riggs gives a dissatisfied huff when Paxton tells him he has to stay home, and he drops on his bed, pouting.

"Are you sure he has to stay here?" I ask, feeling sorry for the furry guy. Riggs's ears perk up. I'd bet the restaurant allows dogs on the patio.

Paxton wraps his arm around my waist, pulling me to his chest. "Nope. You're all mine tonight. He's the worst third wheel ever. Takes all your attention."

"Not all my attention," I whisper, running my hand up his white button-down shirt. "Last night, I remember my attention was entirely focused on making you come in my mouth."

He groans as he leans down and pulls my bottom lip into his mouth, biting it and then sucking the pain away. "Dinner can wait. I think I need some more attention," he murmurs against my lips. He walks me backward down the hallway until we hit the bedroom and then kicks the door shut behind him. He spins me around until my back is pressed against the wall.

"Tell me you'll never leave me," he whispers, kissing my shoulder and sliding his hand up my skirt.

I fist his hair and pull in a quick breath when his finger pushes aside my panties and slips inside me. It's hard to think about anything other than what his fingers are doing. Ever since we got back together, Paxton's insecurities creep up now and then, no matter how many times I promise him I'm his. My moans grow louder and louder as he alternates flicking my swollen clit and sliding two fingers inside me. The heat builds but right before I explode, he stops, the weight of his body pressed against mine, and he pins me with his eyes.

"Tell me."

I groan in frustration. "Don't stop," I whisper, trying to move my hips, desperate for the release.

His lips quirk up on one side. "That's not what I want to hear."

I chuckle. "I hate you."

"As long as you don't leave me, I'm fine with that."

He pulses his fingers against my G-spot, and my eyes roll back in my head at the delicious pleasure. I hum and moan at the same time.

"I'm yours," I say, heat spiraling down my spine as his fingers move quicker inside me. "Forever." My orgasm rips through me, leaving my legs wobbly and my breath quick and shallow.

I drop to my knees, undoing the buckle of his belt. "My turn," I say, gazing up at him.

It's not until I have his cock out in my hand that he lifts me up and spins me around. His hands caress my arms until our fingers intertwine. "No. I need to be inside you." He drags our hands against the wall until they're above our heads. "Keep them here," he whispers into my ear and then nibbles it as his hands move down to remove my skirt and panties. They fall to the floor, and I kick them back. "That's it. Spread those long legs for me." His fingers press into my inner thighs until my legs spread wide.

His dick springs loose against my back. He guides it down between my cheeks, and when it hits my center, I arch my back, begging for it. He hisses into my ear as he snakes his arm around to my boobs, pinching and pulling as I suck in a breath. I press my hands against the wall, wishing I had something to hold on to.

He pushes inside me, and I scream out his name as he thrusts in and out. Hard and fast. Possessive. One of his hands covers both of mine, our fingers intermingling. His other hand moves to my clit and circles it. I push back into him, making him go deeper and deeper until my body trembles, stars float in my vision, and I'm pulled under by my orgasm ripping through me, his moans and cursing follow.

"Fucking...mine," he roars, chasing his release. He buries his face into my hair. His heart pounds fast and heavy against my back, and we don't move until we find our breath again. He pushes my hair to the side and kisses down my shoulder. He pulls out and spins me around, his intense eyes pinning me in place. "I love you, Kalico."

My heart swells as everything falls into place. We belong together. "I love you, Paxton."

"OFFICER TURNER," the blond hostess bellows, her glossy pink lips almost touching her heavily eye-shadowed eyes as soon as we walk through the front door. She looks at me for a brief second with a confused expression before turning her attention back to him. How long ago was he here with his ex? "Does Jose know you're coming in?" she asks.

"He doesn't. Last-minute dinner plans," he replies.

"Let me go find him. He'll love to see you."

"You don't have to…" His words trail off as she darts away. "Do that."

I stare at him, wondering why he looks uncomfortable. Is this about to get awkward? Is Jose his ex-girlfriend's dad? After a quick sigh, he explains, "Last year, when I was having dinner here, a disgruntled employee came in swinging a gun around and threatened to shoot the owner. I neutralized the threat before he could do anything."

Is that when she became his ex?

"Did you have to shoot him?" I whisper, not able to imagine sitting in a restaurant, having a nice dinner, then having to jump up and stop a shooter. Is this one reason he asked if I could handle him being a police officer? I can see how that could scare off a potential partner. Even though I already told him I didn't care that he was a police officer, it's one thing to understand the risks in theory and another to have a front-row seat when he has to confront them head-on.

He shakes his head. "I talked him down, convinced him it wasn't worth going to jail the rest of his life." He reaches for my hand, searching my face for any apprehension. "It's a lot when your dinner date might have to turn into…well, something out of an action movie."

I squeeze his hand. "I already know that you're a hero, so it doesn't surprise me. If anything, it makes me feel safer with you, knowing you can handle these intense situations."

"Paxton!" The voice cuts through the busy restaurant, deep and resonating. Everyone's attention turns to him, then our way to see who he's yelling at. I watch as a stocky man with a bushy mustache and bright, flushed red cheeks, wearing a well-worn apron rushes toward us. His arms are flung open wide in anticipation, and when he reaches Paxton, he pulls him in for a robust hug. Paxton pats him on the back a couple times.

"Jose, it's great to see you."

"I can't believe you didn't tell me you were coming in. I would've saved the best table for you," he says in a heavy Mexican accent, mixed in with the kind of warmth that feels like home. "It's been far too long." He shifts his attention to me, his smile extending its warmth my way. His smile is infectious, and I find myself returning it. "And who is this lovely lady?"

Paxton introduces me, and when he refers to me as his girl-friend, butterflies flutter in my stomach.

As we follow Jose through the bustling restaurant, it's obvious he bumped us to the front of the waitlist. I understand why, but none of those people do. I push back the awkward feelings, instead taking in the vibrant colors and lively atmosphere. The chatter of diners, the clinking of glasses, and the occasional laughter create a symphony of sounds that make the place feel alive.

Jose leads us to a cozy table nestled in the corner where the lighting is softer and the noise muted. He pulls out a chair for me and then turns to Paxton with a conspiratorial wink. Paxton chuckles, shaking his head.

An apologetic smile plays on Paxton's lips after he strolls away. "He's a character."

"I can see how much he adores you."

Our server wanders up and places a bottle of Blue Moon in front of him, leaving me puzzled because we haven't ordered yet. Then she looks at me and asks if I'd like something to drink. I order my Mexican martini. When she walks away, I shoot Paxton a quizzical look.

"Regular here?" I inquire.

He gives a vague nod, taking a pull from his beer. He wasn't kidding when he said this was one of his ex's favorite restaurants. I can tell he doesn't want to talk about it. I don't know why, but I have so many questions about her. How long were they together? What was she like? What does she look like? All questions I shouldn't ask but want to. Thankfully, my drink arrives—a pleasant distraction to get my mind off his ex.

"Look at this email I received today." I pull out my phone and search for the message. "It's a producer interested in creating a documentary about me on Netflix. How one escapes six feet under, were his words." I pass the phone to him.

He reads it and then looks up from the phone. "Be careful. Most of these are scams," he remarks, echoing my initial thoughts, but I looked the guy up. He's a legit producer who has done other docuseries. But it doesn't matter how real he is, I don't want to be in the spotlight.

"I know," I reply, taking back my phone. "I wouldn't do it anyway. Not with him still out there."

Our conversation takes a pause when a server places a basket of chips in between us and two small bowls of salsa. I grab a chip and dip it before the guy can walk away. Yep, this was a damn good idea. We didn't have a Tex-Mex restaurant in Blackburn, and I was cheated out of something my entire life.

"How was school today?"

"School," I reply dryly, making him chuckle. "I didn't know it was going to be this hard. I barely scraped by passing my math test. It makes me wonder if college is for me."

"My motto was D is for degree," he quips.

Now, it's my turn to laugh.

"I hated school, so I feel you. But it'll be worth it in the long run. At least that's what my grams always told me."

His affection for his grandmother warms my heart. When he told me he hates his mom and won't talk about her, it raised some concerns. Who could hate their mom? I wish I had one more second with mine. But the love he shows for his grams settled those thoughts.

"Tell me about your ex," I say, taking a chip.

He rolls his eyes. "Really?"

I laugh. "Yes. How long did y'all date?"

"You're really not going to let this go, are you?" He's the one who brought her up first. I shake my head, smiling. "We dated a few months. Eight, maybe. She couldn't accept my life." When I lift a brow, he adds, "Being with a K-9 police officer is a lot. There's a lot of sacrifice. Time. We're always on call. And then this happened…" He gestures with his hand, the restaurant.

That was the tipping point. I can't say I don't understand. I don't agree with it. It's part of who Paxton is, and I love that part.

Paxton's phone rings on the table, and his chief's name flashes on the screen. He offers a quick apology before answering. Whatever. Less talking for me means more time to munch on chips.

After a brief exchange, he replies, "No." He listens, nodding. "How long has she been missing?"

My hand halts, a chip with salsa hanging in the air, as a shiver races across my skin. His words trigger a surge of panic through me. Paxton studies me as he talks, assessing me as if trying to gauge my reaction. Thoughts race through my mind, fragments of the conversation leaving me unsettled. Is his chief calling to tell him my monster kidnapped someone again? My appetite vanishes, and I drop the chip on the plate. I sit and wait. Questions and fear tighten around my throat as Paxton reaches across the table and squeezes my hand, as if reassuring me that everything is fine.

But is it?

After he hangs up, the first thing he says is, "People go missing all the time."

"Then why did he call you on your day off?"

A momentary look of discomfort crosses his features. "They want Riggs and I to be ready if they need us."

I rub my face, attempting to drown out the unease. Like he said, people go missing daily, and I can't let my emotions hijack me every time I hear about one. "You don't know her, do you?" The question slips out, regret flooding me.

His shoulders tense. But Martinez's voice repeats in my head. There could be a connection, even if it's not direct.

"Are you still having doubts about me?" He mutters curse words under his breath, his eyes darting around the room. "I thought we were past that?"

"We are. I'm not saying you did anything. But what if there is a connection? Somehow? You can't deny that it's a possibility considering how everything went down."

"Well, you'll be happy to learn I have no idea who she is." His voice carries an edge, and while, yes, I'm relieved, I feel bad at the same time.

I toy with a crumb of a chip that's fallen on the table, breaking it into tiny pieces with my nail. Our food comes, and I stare at the generous burrito, not hungry anymore. Between the inhaled chips and my talent for putting my foot in my mouth, I'm done.

"My boss had the same question."

I pick my head up, understanding his brash tone.

"That's one reason he called me. I think it just pisses me off that I'm being tossed into question because everyone thinks I have the answers. And I shouldn't get this mad because you're right, I would've asked the same question if I were in your shoes."

"Can we take this to-go?" I ask, and he nods.

He might not be so in agreement with my next request.

CHAPTER 34

Kali

"I KNOW MARTINEZ. He's thorough. He's already been out here," Paxton says as the Jeep's tires struggle to stay on the winding, wet dirt road. I don't care. I need to see for myself. My concern mounts with each second that she's not found. He can tell me all day this has nothing to do with me, but after seeing her picture on the way over here, I don't believe him.

Thick, mousy-brown hair. Pale-blue eyes with a slim build.

She could be my sister.

The possibility that she's buried and going insane right now is making me go crazy myself. He told me he would go for me, but there was no way he was leaving me home on my own with my thoughts, so here I am.

The Jeep comes to a stop, and my heart does the same as I stare ahead. A single yellow caution tape, long forgotten, whips through the air, clinging to a wooden stake to the right of the hole in the ground.

A ping of relief runs through me. She's not buried here. There is a chance that she is not buried at all. I'm jumping to the worst-case scenario.

"See, there are fresh tracks. There's no way they didn't search this area first," Paxton says, hopping out.

I glance at the fresh tire marks and nod. He's right. This is ridiculous.

"Stay here. I'll just check it out real quick."

You don't have to tell me twice.

Been here. Done this. Twice. I was hoping to never come here again.

Paxton's attention is stuck on the hole for a moment, and I watch him, expecting him to walk back. Instead, he starts cursing up a storm and takes his phone out of his pocket while he paces. My stomach sours, those chips working themselves back up my throat. I picture her body lying at the bottom of the hole. Dead. Paxton's sympathetic gaze finds mine, and he shakes his head as he talks into the phone. What the hell does that mean?

It's not what I think?

Don't come look?

Is it what I think?

What?!

The unanswered questions are killing me, and I can't wait anymore. I draw in a deep, confident breath and walk over, putting one foot in front of the other, wringing my hands in front of me until I freeze on the spot. Never mind, I can't do it. Why do I even want to see a dead body?

"She had to see for herself," Paxton explains into the phone. "Just get here and stop interrogating me. We'll wait for you."

Obviously he's talking with Martinez. He groans with an eye roll as he shoves the phone back into his pocket.

"Is she…" I pause, still at a distance where I'm not able to see the bottom of the hole.

"No."

My head jerks back in surprise. If she's not down there, what is? Curiosity takes hold, clouding the fear, and I close the short distance between me and the hole in two long strides.

Bad, bad idea.

My knees buckle as the bastard takes hold of me with his words, twisting and tormenting from the comfort of his own uncaged life. I stare at the bright pink spray paint.

It's your fault. You're next. 3x

I point at it, my finger shaking so hard I can't keep it straight. "Is that saying…she's missing because of me?" I stutter. What, I found him a new hobby? It takes a few moments for my body to catch up to my thoughts. I curl my fingers into my fists and tap my head with them. "You motherfucker!" I scream at the top of my lungs. The guilt will eat me alive. He knows that.

I'm still his prisoner.

Paxton wraps his arms around me, and I dig my head into his chest. "We'll get him."

How can he say that? They haven't yet. Even he knows that over fifty percent of violent crimes go unsolved. Those odds are not in her favor. Or mine.

Tires grinding over dirt pull our attention to the west. Two black SUVs in a line head in our direction, three local cop cars behind them. The black cars have a nice coat of brown mud halfway up their sides by the time they arrive.

Paxton doesn't waste any time giving our statements, trying to get me out of here as fast as possible. "I'm taking her home. If you need anything else from us, you know where we'll be."

My mind spirals out of control. The darkness pulls on a frayed string in my mind, one that hasn't mended yet, one that can unravel with just the right tug.

Tingles crawl up my leg.

"You need to stick around. Agent Martinez is on his way. He wants to talk to you both."

I fight to stay present. Focus on their words.

"Kali." I hear Paxton, but his voice is muffled.

"Keep digging! I'm down here!" I scream and claw at the air, pleading with him not to leave me.

Except it's not air.

It's a wooden box.

A GENTLE STREAM of light slips through my closed eyelids before I jerk awake, shooting straight up. Riggs barks from the foot of my bed, gazing at me. My T-shirt clings to my back, drenched in sweat. The door creaks open, and Paxton steps into the room.

"You okay?" he asks.

I rake my fingers through damp hair and free it from its ponytail. "Yeah. I had a horrible nightmare. I dreamed he did it again. Kidnapped someone and then I was back in another box. It felt so real."

"Kalico. You scared the shit out of me." He kisses my forehead and pulls me in for a hug.

My brain teeters between my nightmare and reality. *How did I scare him?*

"There's someone here to see you. I thought it would be helpful to call her."

I look at the door and notice Dr. Betty standing just inside the doorway. When I tilt my head at her gentle smile, they share a look of concern.

"Hello, Kali," she says.

"What's happening?" I question, pushing the covers off and scooting toward the end of the bed. Why did I wear jeans to bed? No wonder I'm sweating like I've been running in one-hundred-degree weather. Wait. What time is it? There's darkness behind the shades. My eyes dart to the clock. Eleven o'clock. Why is Dr. Betty here this late?

"It wasn't a dream," she says, her words blending between my dream and reality.

Considering I'm not in a box, I'm confused.

"There was another kidnapping."

Flashes of memories ignite, and everything comes rushing back. Driving to the hole, the paint, the fear.

"Being there triggered a flashback," she explains, taking a seat next to me.

I draw in a ragged breath, the cold sweat chilling my trembling body. "I can't do this. I can't do this anymore." Anger reverberates through my bones.

"Yes, you can," she insists, wrapping her arm around my shoulder.

My fight-or-flight kicks in, and an intense wave of leaving this place takes root. Putting distance between me and this nightmare is the only thing that makes sense right now. I have money. I can go anywhere. But then there's Paxton. Except our relationship can't move forward, not when I'm being held captive by a psychopath.

He will always be my hero.

I raise my eyes to meet Paxton, and the ache in my heart intensifies. "I think I have to leave."

His brows furrow as he stands taller in a defensive stance, crossing his arms over his chest. "Leave where?"

"Somewhere not in Texas."

"They're going to catch this guy," he argues. "Why leave everything?"

Why leave him, he's asking, and my heart cracks open.

"He's tormenting me," I murmur, standing and walking over to him. I place my hand on his chest. "I thought I could put what happened behind me and move on, but not now." I shake my head. "Not with what he's doing."

"Running won't stop him."

"I know that. But I don't need a front-row seat to it." My hands clench his shirt, a desperate plea for him to understand. I know what I'm about to ask is fueled by fear, but my breaking heart pushes the words out. "Take some time off. I have plenty of money for both of us. Run away with me."

He bows his head before locking eyes with me again. "I can't just up and leave my job. I worked years to get into the K-9 unit. And Riggs—I'd have to give him up. There has to be another answer." His eyes dart past me to Dr. Betty, pleading for help. She can't change my mind either. "You're letting him win," he asserts.

"I don't know what to do!" I throw my arms out in frustration. "I've tried continuing with my life here. We take one step forward, and he shows up, and we end up taking three steps back."

"Tell me you don't love me," he demands, his words intensifying.

"I do love you." I bite my lip. That's why this pain in my chest deepens by the second.

"I'm sure Amy would let you go back to the ranch," Dr. Betty adds, attempting to untangle the knot of our impasse.

"That's it. That's what you should do." Paxton pleads with his eyes, cupping my face with his hands.

It crossed my mind, but if I keep putting my life on hold because of this bastard, I'll have more regrets than leaving. *I want a life.* I just can't have one here. I shake my head again, and he drops his hands. His expression turns to stone.

"You just told me today that you'd never leave me. Remember?"

That was before. Everything has changed.

He growls in frustration. "If you leave, we're finished."

I jerk back in surprise. "Really? You're giving me an ultimatum right now?"

"You've left me twice. I love you and would do anything to keep you safe, but you keep leaving me!" he roars.

I glance at Dr. Betty for help, but she keeps quiet. Of all the times to keep quiet, it has to be now? I clear the emotions from my throat, trying to keep my tone neutral. "You have to understand this from my side."

"I don't!" he snaps back and then storms past me out of the bedroom.

Tears roll down my cheek. "Way to back me up," I mutter to Dr. Betty, falling back on the bed.

"He has a right to be upset. While I understand you feeling the need to put space between you and your captor, his feelings are justifiable as well. He'll come to an understanding. But it might not be the outcome that you want."

I sit up. "Am I wrong for ruining this?"

"I can't answer that." Her hands, though aged with spots and thinned by time, are loving and warm as she reaches for me. "Sometimes, people need more than love. Only you can answer that. But don't make a rash decision, Kali. Give it a day to sink in, and then make your decision."

Tomorrow won't make this pain go away. The woman's screams are living in my head. I feel the scratching and kicking in my hands and legs. Distance won't help this torture, but there's an irrational hope that if I wasn't around, he wouldn't be doing this. Maybe he'll let her go if he finds out that I'm gone. That he can't get to me.

He's doing this show for me, and if I don't attend, the show's over.

We walk into the living room, and Paxton's sitting on the couch, his ball cap lowered over his face. Dr. Betty reaches for my hand and gives it a small squeeze. "Call me and let me know your plans. I'm always here for you."

I nod. "I will. Thank you for coming."

Paxton stands, putting his cap back on his head. "Thanks, Dr. Betty."

She gives him a slight nod and then leaves. The air chills around us, mirroring the icy tension between us.

"I'm so sorry," I whisper, tears burning my eyes. The fear and anger that was weighing my emotions down dissipates, and I can't stop the torrent of tears. "I just can't breathe. How can you love me? This isn't me. I don't even recognize myself." I throw my arms out. "I've never been so flighty in my entire life. I've moved three times in the last couple months, college is so overwhelming, I'm not even sure it's for me, and then on top of all that, there's *him*. I just don't know which way is which anymore. He lets me become comfortable to just show back up and..." I hiccup through the tears. "It feels like he's wrapping his hands around my neck and squeezing. And now he has a plan. *I'm next. I. Can't. Breathe.*" He pulls me into his chest, wrapping his arms around me and squeezing as I cry. My body trembles against his solid frame.

"You'll be alone, though," he murmurs into my hair, his earlier harsh tone now softened.

If there's anything I know in this world, it's how to be alone.

We stand in each other's embrace for several minutes in silence. My head spins. Nothing is clear. It's hard for me to focus on anything except the way I feel in his arms.

"Where will you go?" he finally asks.

I sniff. "I think I'll drive west."

"You should have a plan." He pulls back and looks down. "The FBI can help you. They'll give you a new identity."

He's no longer my boyfriend, he's Officer Turner.

That sounds horrible and is not at all what I want. "I don't want a new identity. I just need to find my footing. I'll just find a place to hole up for a while."

"That sounds so much better than being with me," he quips with sad sarcasm.

The naked space between us fills with a storm of emotions. I wrap my arms around my waist, uncertain if I should bite back or just let it go. He's mad, and I'm scared. There are no winners in this fight.

He lets out a forceful sigh when I say nothing. "I love you, Kalico. I see you. *The real you.* I see your fear, and I feel it." He holds his hand to his heart. "I want to be by your side. Help you fight against this psychopath. But I get it. I know I can't force you to stay." He runs his hands through his hair. "Is this goodbye forever?" he asks quietly.

"I don't know. I hope not." It's the most honest truth I can give him.

I watch his eyes, the pain in them as they jump from my eyes to the door and back to me. He lets out a strangled breath. "If you need a hero, you know where to find me." With that, he spins in place and walks out, shutting the door behind him.

Riggs stands at my side and stares up at me, confused.

I rub his head, wiping tears off with my other hand. "Sorry, buddy." My heart feels like it's been torn from my chest, leaving a hollow ache.

The front door opens, and Paxton doesn't make eye contact with me, just calls for Riggs. Riggs goes to him but glances back once before he closes the door again.

And just like that, I'm alone. A lump forms in my throat as I swallow it back, wondering if I have the strength to do this alone. Leaving the only state I've ever known. *This is what you always wanted,* the small voice inside my head reminds me. Not like this. Not having to decide between love and fear.

With fear winning.

CHAPTER 35

Kali

I'VE REALIZED that life is predictable, no matter who you are or where you live. I've been in this vacation rental home for two weeks, hiding away. The first week, all I did was cry. The second week, everything inside became numb.

The house is in the middle of a suburban neighborhood in a small town, nestled between mountains and a river. My plan wasn't to stop until I hit California. I needed space between me and Texas. And him. It wasn't until I stopped for gas that the town's tranquility at sunset convinced me to stay. It was quiet here.

I could finally breathe.

Back to predictability. While I waste away here, I've memorized my neighbors' schedules by watching their lives through the lens of my front window. I glance at the time on my phone. Grace—her name isn't Grace, but she looks like a Grace—is about to run out on the heels of her daughter. I always want to walk over and hand her a glass of wine. Even though her day is just starting, she looks like she's been running hard and hung out to dry. Her daughter's in middle school, according to the sticker on the back of her SUV, and by the usual sound of screaming between the two of them, it's never a relaxing morning in that household.

I take a sip of my coffee and watch the morning unfold, watching everyone stick to their daily schedules.

"Right on time," I whisper to myself, watching the white Honda pull up to the curb.

Mark—yep, he looks like a Mark—gets out. Short black hair, chiseled face, tan skin, wearing his typical tank top stretched out over his bulky muscles, and short gym shorts. He grabs his bag from the back seat. Most people would think he's the wife's trainer. He shows up exactly an hour after the husband leaves for work, two days a week. Heck, I thought he was her trainer, too.

Until today.

Sun. I need some vitamin D. I frown thinking about the humidity being negative one hundred. Or close to it. *It doesn't matter. You need fresh air.* At least my subconscious is concerned about me.

"Hmm. What book should I read?" I walk to the small office. There's an entire wall with built-in bookshelves, filled to the max with books. I was reading a lot when I stayed at Amy's, but when school started, I didn't have time. But if there was ever a time for me to start reading again, it'd be now.

"Definitely a rom-com," I say to myself, running my fingers along the spines, reading the titles. I focus on the bright pinks and oranges. I don't need angst, horror, or sadness. I'm living that. I pull out *Worth It* by S.M. Shade and C.M. Owens. It looks like a fun book just by the cover.

I haven't flipped the first page, and I'm already deep-belly laughing. This is exactly what I needed. *Thanks subconscious.* I lift my head, irritated when I overhear the wife and Mark come out. She giggles. And then a splash. I imagine he dove in because women don't jump into pools, they walk in. I would jump, but I'm a rebel. There's no talking. After a few minutes, I wonder if they went back into the house, and I focus my attention back to my book.

"Does *he* make you feel this way?"

My eyes widen, and I fixate on the wooden fence between us, wondering if I just heard what I think I did because it wasn't loud, but then an unmistakable moan follows. I cover my mouth, afraid they'll hear me breathing as I continue to listen to them have sex. Not that I want to, but I'm afraid to move. I'm stuck listening to a live-action porn on the other side of my fence. *Doesn't she care that someone might hear them? Like me?*

I make the gag gesture when he says, "That was a great session."

Her response is equally nauseating. "We should add the pool more often."

Poor hubby. He's an attractive guy, if you like the nerdy type, who always leaves wearing a suit, has a friendly face, and you can tell he adores his wife. Just this past weekend, they were out for a walk, and he held her hand, his genuine smile shining at her as they strolled by my house. It'll crush him when he finds out his wife is a lying, cheating bitch.

I drop my book to my side and groan after I hear her tell him goodbye, followed by a car driving off. I can't even focus on my book now. This is the juicy gossip Pearl would've gotten a loud chuckle out of. *If only I could call her and tell her.*

Dammit. I need some friends. And I'm just getting antsy. I need to go somewhere. Do something. It's time to figure out what I'm going to do.

Because it can't be this.

I glance at a flyer laying on the counter that was stuck to the front door yesterday. It's for a new coffee shop that opened in the small strip center at the front of the community. Even though I had a cup of coffee already, a latte sounds better. And different scenery.

The dry air here is no joke. My skin acts like it's stranded in the Sahara Desert without a drop of moisture despite the bottle of Aquaphor that is almost gone. I even have to stick that shit up my nose so I don't have a bloody mess later. The sun perches high in the sky, and the slight breeze brushing against my face is a welcome reprieve from the stuffy indoors. Cacti line the sidewalk, and I wonder how many people have stumbled into one of them. Who thought this was a good idea? They're everywhere. I get to the coffee shop, free of cactus in my ass, ready to talk to an actual person. Besides a few brief conversations with Martinez over the phone, the only other person I've talked to is myself.

There's only one person at the counter ordering, so I stand back to read the handwritten menu hanging above the barista. When I decide on a latte, the guy is still ordering. I glance around the cozy little shop. It's warm and homey, but the TV hanging in the corner grabs my attention, and my heart stops. The sound isn't on, but I don't need it to know what's going on. A reporter stands in the middle of an empty field delivering the news, a hole in the ground behind her, delivering news. The words on the screen confirm my fears: Shanna Clark has been found. It feels like a hand has closed around my throat.

My worst nightmare comes in full force, slamming into me like a tornado. She was buried alive. I somehow force my feet to take me home, everything around me a blur as I struggle to keep my panic from erupting. Once I'm inside the confines of the four walls of my living room, I turn the TV on.

They found her in a makeshift coffin in a county an hour away from where I was found. A torturous death was the end of her story. Her desperate screams break open all the scars that had begun to heal. They're raw, and her torture is like pouring acid into the wounds. How can I be thankful for being alive with the guilt that my death might have prevented this?

Would he have found his release if I had died?

Tears stream down my face as I sit glued to the TV. Being a thousand miles away couldn't stop this pain. She's dead. Bile threatens when they refer to him as the Grave Killer. They gave him a name. Like his persona deserves a title. When my name and picture flash across the screen for the world to see, the lucky one, they say, I can't hold it back anymore and dart to the bathroom to throw up my breakfast.

Why did they have to show my picture?

Panic takes hold next, and I rush to the fridge. Please let me have enough food to last me a few days. I'll wait out the story, give it a week to die down. The picture is outdated. I don't even know where they found it, but it's an old one from when I lived in Blackburn, so I'm not too worried about someone noticing me. People here won't be on alert since this is happening states away.

They don't have to wonder if there's a box waiting for them.

My phone rings, startling me. I stare at my purse, dropped on the floor from when I first entered the house. It's probably Martinez telling me the news. *Too late.* I ignore the call, not having the energy to move. I need a minute to process this, anyway.

The phone rings again. Wiping the tears from my cheek, I push off the couch and grab my purse, figuring I should answer so he doesn't worry about me. He has other things to focus on. When I see the name lighting up on the screen, I squeeze the phone in my palm with conflicting emotions. I haven't talked to Paxton since I left. We agreed that if I was going into hiding we wouldn't talk. Since I've done nothing to fill my time here, the regret of leaving him has solidified. It weighs on my chest. But everything that has happened today strengthens my reason for leaving.

With a shaky breath, I slide across the bar to answer. "Hi."

"Shit. I can tell you already heard."

"It's all over the news here."

"I was hoping you weren't watching the news." I hadn't been. "I hate that you're there by yourself." He hesitates and then adds, "You are by yourself, right?"

I laugh once and realize it's the first time I've laughed in a month. "Yes."

"I wish I was with you."

"Me too," I whisper, a surge of emotions getting stuck in my throat. "How'd they find her?"

"Some people were out on a hike and saw a newly dug grave and called it in."

But it was too late.

The line is silent for a long minute. I don't know what to do. I didn't escape anything by being here. No, I did. I escaped his reach.

"Paxton, you guys have to find him. Before he does it again," I urge with desperation.

"I promise you, we're throwing everything we've got at this, working day and night. We have some new information we didn't have before. For instance, those tire tracks we saw? They didn't match any of our vehicles. It was a truck. I know it's not much, but each piece of evidence we gather gets us one step closer to him. Just don't..." He exhales into the phone, and I imagine him raking his hand through his curls. "Don't lose hope."

I've learned that hope is a fickle thing. It comes and goes in a blink of an eye. "I won't." I lie to make him think I'm okay. But I am anything but.

"So, where did you end up?"

"A small town in Arizona."

The line is quiet, and I peek at my phone to see if the call dropped.

"Kalico," he starts, breaking the silence, "I'm biting back a lot right now because this is already fucking hard, but damn it, I miss you." There's a shuffling noise like his phone rubbed against something, and then Paxton's light chuckle follows. "That was Riggs. He says he misses you."

A wave of longing washes over me. "I miss y'all, too." More than I'd care to admit since I'm the one who left.

We end the call on a sad note. I sit alone on my couch, staring out the window that has more life than I do. This sucks. And now, I'm stuck in this freaking house for a week. By myself. I flop across the couch, my limbs flailing in a fit of childish rage.

"FUCK my life!"

As EXPECTED, one week was all it took. The world has forgotten about Shanna Clark. The headlines have moved on. I click off the TV, tired of watching the news, when I hear the thrill of my phone ringing out from the bedroom. I debate letting it go to voice mail. It's probably Martinez with another update, of *no updates*. But I can't let it go.

One of these times, it will be good news.

I run back, catching it on the fourth ring.

"Hey, Martinez," I say, sitting on the unmade bed. I figured at some point I'd be crawling back into it today.

"Hi, Kali. Just wanted to give you an update." Yep. I should've let it go to voice mail. He wouldn't begin that way if they had found him. "We might be dealing with a copycat, or there's more than one person we're looking for." My ears perk up. What the hell? How many sick bastards get off on burying women?

"Why do you say that?"

"The only similar thing between the two cases is that you guys look alike. Everything about the boxes are different. Hers, there wasn't a chance of survival. The doctors say she only had minutes to live."

"How do you explain the note to me?"

He hums. "We're not sure. Maybe they're partners. Maybe perp B knows perp A?"

That doesn't help the sharp pain in my chest. I force my thoughts not to put myself in her place because I know how those last moments of her life were spent. I barely hear the rest of what he has to say as I stare down at my scarred fingers.

"You okay, Kali?"

"Yeah," I murmur, fisting my hand and pushing off the bed. *I will not go there.*

"Hang in there, Kali."

It's his typical response because there's nothing else to say. He can't give me what I want, so he tries to assure me each time, but his words mean less and less each time we talk. Just like the note I used carry. The words have faded, the paper has worn down.

I called Dr. Betty last night. She's the only one who helps me to see that my life isn't defined by what he did to me. Or Shanna Clark.

That defines him. He's the monster.

Or, in recent news, they are the monsters.

It's up to me to define my life.

And I'm doing a lousy job defining anything these days other than my neighbors' schedules and marital affairs.

This morning, I woke up determined to live my life. I'm young, healthy, and alive. I'm fortunate enough that I can do anything.

And I'm going to live for Shanna.

I peer out my front window and blow out a breath. *I'm done living through you.*

Facing my reflection after showering, I decide it's time for a change. I open Pinterest on my phone, searching for photos of haircuts. I wonder what I'd look like as a brunette? I look down at the photo and then back up, contemplating the leap. It'd be drastic, but drastic is what I need.

When I walked to the coffee shop, I spotted a salon situated in the corner of the shopping strip. I double-check I have enough cash in my purse, as that's the only way I've been paying before heading out. The receptionist, engrossed in her magazine, twirls a curl around her finger, lost in her own world. I clear my throat, and she looks up.

"Oh, hi. You snuck in here like a mouse," she says, smiling. "Do you have an appointment?"

I glance past her into the salon, regretting I didn't call first, but there are only a few chairs filled with customers. "I don't. Is that okay?"

"Absolutely. It's a slow day. What would you like done?"

Moments after sharing with her that I'd like a cut and color, I'm whisked away to a sink for the most incredible hair wash ever. The woman massages the shampoo in with magic fingers, and my eyes roll back into my head as she continues massaging.

When she finishes, I ask, "Can I hire you to wash my hair every day?"

Her laughter rings out. "I get that a lot."

I follow her to a chair and wait for another person, Lucy, to get there. I pull up my saved Pinterest pins to show her what I want. While waiting, I overhear the woman in the chair next to me talking. I can't help but listen when she mentions she's a flight attendant. She's not quiet, so I catch every word. She just got back from Paris a few days ago and is now recounting how her night in town ended in bed with a handsome French man.

A lady with bright pink hair and matching lips walks up behind me. I glance at her through the mirror. "Hi. I'm Lucy. I hear we're trying a darker color today." She picks up a section of my hair, inspecting it.

"Darker and shoulder-length. Maybe some layers?" I show her my saved pictures.

"Are you sure? That's a lot of hair coming off." I nod. Her lips twist as she plays with my hair. "Light brown, dark brown, or black?"

"Dark brown?" I didn't mean to make it sound uncertain, but there was a brief hesitation.

She eyes me, giving me a chance to back out. But I smile and nod again. "Dark brown and a lob coming up." There's excitement in her voice, which is reassuring. "This is going to look amazing. You have such thick hair."

She pulls out a swatch of hair colors. I stare at the multiple colors of brown. Why are there so many? I point to a chestnut brown. Lucy agrees the dark reddish brown will complement my complexion and blue eyes.

While she mixes the color, my attention drifts back to my neighbor. Her stylist asks her about her upcoming trips, and I can't help the envy creeping in. It all sounds like the perfect life. Jet setting, seeing the world, and getting paid to do it.

"How hard is it to become a flight attendant?" I blurt out, catching both of their attention. My cheeks burn in embarrassment as they both stare at me.

Her stylist chuckles before asking, "Where are you from? You've got the cutest accent."

"Texas. Never thought I had one until I moved here," I reply.

"Oh, you have one," the flight attendant adds. "There's a job fair at the beginning of next month for flight attendants in Phoenix. That'd be the time to apply."

I looked into the community college in town, but every brain cell I have was screaming at me not to do it. This sounds way more exciting. As soon as she tells me I don't need a degree to apply, I think about postponing going to school.

Sorry, Mom. It'll happen. Just not right now.

Instead, my focus shifts to planning a trip to Phoenix. We talk for the next hour about things I should say and what to expect. Excitement builds by the minute. The highs and lows of my life are that of a roller coaster. Right now, I'm stuck again, but I just need that little push to keep me going. *This is it.* This is what I needed. We're chatting so much, I haven't paid any attention to my hair until it's finished.

"Ready to see the new you?" Lucy asks, swiveling my chair around.

My eyes widen at the stunning woman reflected in the mirror. *There is no way that's me.*

"This is not my hair," I exclaim, running my fingers through the dark, silky locks, marveling at the luxurious, shiny brown. The stylish cut and waves meld into a sophisticated hairstyle.

I've never looked sophisticated.

Lucy claps her hands. "Girl, you are gorgeous. Ready for the next chapter."

She has no idea how right she is. I am ready. *It is time* for my next chapter to begin.

I can do this.

My cheeks hurt from smiling so big. "I hope so. Thank you for making the new me!" I say to both her and Sadie, the flight attendant. She passes me her number and tells me to call her with questions. The second I get home, the first thing I work on is my resume.

It's time to make my dreams come true.

Try hitting a moving target, Mr. Grave Killer.

CHAPTER 36
Paxton

Six months later…

"STILL AT IT, HUH?" The chief leans against the partition, eyeing me with a mixture of concern and curiosity.

I glance up from the files spread across the desk and shrug. "Somebody had to miss something." Desperation keeps me here. I need her back with me. I'm off duty, so he doesn't care.

Last month marked the one-year anniversary since I dug Kali out of her grave. Every Tuesday night before I go home I pore over the case files, reexamining every detail, statement, and suspect's interviews. Including mine. Each week, I wonder what's being missed. When I compare Kali's case to Shanna's, you'd think we had a copycat or we're dealing with two suspects.

Their cases are unique.

The makeshift coffins tell a twisted story. One meant for the person to survive, the other was not. Kali's box had air being pumped in, Shanna's did not. The construction of the coffins differed as well. Screws, wood, and the process, all different. But both cases were meticulous, not leaving any prints. Not even a partial.

Both were buried in remote spots, far from a lot of traffic and cameras. At least I know that Kali being buried close to me was just a coincidence. But why keep her alive and not Shanna?

I run my hands through my hair, a headache beginning to throb at the base of my skull. Are there two perps at play here or just one trying to throw us off? He said there'd be three, so why hasn't he done it again? Was he truly doing it to get Kali's attention? Was she right to leave?

There's always the one question I get stuck on that has nothing to do with the case; will Kali ever come back to me? We haven't talked since right after they found Shanna. I texted her Happy Birthday and got back a simple "thank you" in response. That pissed me off. I deserve more than a fucking thank you. I called Grams after that message, at a loss. Maybe her wise wisdom had some insight.

"Paxton, honey. You said she's your future wife. If that's true, why would you give up on her?"

"I fu…" I dial back my anger reminding myself who I'm talking to. *"I didn't give up on her. She. Left. Me."*

"You told me she asked you to go with her."

"That was an impossible request. I've dedicated my life to being a K-9 officer. I can't just get up and leave after working my ass off to get Riggs. If she loved me like she said she did, she would've found a way to be with me."

And all I got was radio silence and a thank you text.

"I love her, Grams, but I don't know if I can wait for her. It felt like Mom shutting down all over again. And then just…she just moved on."

"I'm sorry you had to experience that. But every woman is not like your mother."

"I can't walk around with this brokenness inside me every day, Grams. I need to move forward."

I need to move forward.

The throbbing in my head refuses to stop, so I lean back in the chair and close my eyes, pressing my fingers into my temples. Why am I putting my life on hold for someone who has moved on?

For someone who can't even live here.

I'm done trying. Six months, and I've memorized every word in that damn file. I'm no closer to solving the case than on day one. I slam the file shut and march it back to the records room. A sharp ache settles in my heart. One that has been threatening for months, but I've pushed it back with hope. Hope she would see being with me is better than running.

She chose to run.

And now the stabbing pain is the icing on the fucking migraine cake.

"You know what you need?" Liam says.

"Do not tell me pussy," I retort, throwing back another shot of tequila and slamming the empty glass on the table. "Because I might actually punch you in the nose."

After last night's decision to move on, I called Liam and told him I needed to get trashed. He's taking his job seriously, flagging down the bartender so she knows that my hand should never be without a drink. The only rule I had was that I was not looking for a hookup.

"That's not what I was going to say, jackass," he snaps back.

I stare at him, waiting for his bright idea.

"You need closure."

"I think not talking to her for six months is enough closure."

He shakes his head. "Make her tell you it's over because that screwed-up brain of yours won't let you get pussy until it knows it's over."

"It's over," I insist.

"Bullshit. It's in limbo. If it was over, you'd notice that table of women staring at us all night. Hell, you haven't even looked at them once. And they're all hot."

Zero part of me wants to look over and see who he's talking about. "The couple of times I've tried calling her, it always goes to voice mail. And if she wanted to talk, she would've called me back. I don't know what else to do."

"Listen, I'm not all about chasing women, but you seem to think this is the one for some weird reason." I let out a bitter laugh. I thought she was the one. "Take a few days off and go see her. Figure out your shit so you can put this to rest because, for the love of God, I'm speaking for everyone in the office, we're tired of you moping around the department."

Damn, he acts like I've been bawling my eyes out daily since Kali left. I haven't. Sure, I might be a bit more on edge, throwing myself into finishing the cabin renovations and looking at her case once a week, but I'm not moping.

But he has a point.

Ever since she left, I haven't felt like myself. It's that lingering hope that she's coming back. He's right, I need to end things officially. Before I can change my mind, I pull out my phone and hit Call when I find her number.

"I didn't fucking mean right now," Liam quips.

I shrug. No time like the present, but she doesn't pick up. I hang up, frustrated that she's ghosting me. How the hell am I supposed to cut the tie if she won't even talk to me?

"I have a friend. He can track anyone down," he offers, already calling a number. "Hey, Frank. I need a favor."

CHAPTER 37

Kali

"THAT WAS A FUN FLIGHT," Ari says with heavy sarcasm as we step into the transfer van headed to the employee hotel. The driver grabs our bags, offering a quick hello.

Screaming for a doctor.

Screaming at people to stop videoing.

Doing chest compressions, not on a dummy, for the first time.

Yeah. *Fun night.*

I sigh, collapsing into the seat. "I hope the guy is all right," I murmur. Dealing with someone going into cardiac arrest mid-flight in our first month on the job is scary. No matter how much training we had in emergency situations, nothing prepares you to deal with it firsthand. At least we're off tomorrow and can head home whenever.

"I need some hard liquor after that," she says, letting her head fall back and closing her eyes.

Shots. I need shots to drown out that experience. The van pulls up to the hotel shortly after, and we hand the driver a few bucks on our way out.

"What are we thinking for dinner? I'm starving," Ari asks.

"How about we just hang out in the hotel bar?" I suggest, my

voice tinged with exhaustion. "I need to wind down after tonight."
Bonus, we don't have to go out in the freezing cold.

"Sounds like a plan," she says, leading the way through the
double sliding doors into the brightly lit lobby. "Hold, please. My
plans could change for him. Lord, let him be single," she murmurs
as we stroll toward the front desk.

"Really?" I sigh, wrestling with my suitcase, whose stubborn
wheel keeps jamming. They sold me a lemon. It's only a couple
months old, and they've fixed it once already. I glance up at her.
"Geez, Ari, we haven't even made it past the lobby."

"Don't judge me. I'm a needy woman. And he looks like a man
in need." She chuckles, her eyes never turning away from
whomever she has in her sight.

Curious, I follow her gaze. That's when I see them—familiar
brown eyes, watching me from across the lobby. *What is he doing
here? How...*

My hearts freezes, unlike my feet. They keep going. It's at that
precise moment my foot catches on Ari's suitcase. I stumble—arms
and legs flailing in the most ungraceful fall ever.

"Kali." His voice barely registers through the chaos of me
falling to the ground.

A few curse words escape my lips on the way down, and my
hands smack the cold tiles, catching most of the fall. My left hip
makes contact next, and I roll into a ball of embarrassment. I sit up,
shaking out my hands. Everyone's eyes are on me.

"Ow, that freaking hurt." I half moan, half laugh, with my
cheeks burning.

"You just can't help falling head over heels for me, huh?" His
voice is rich with teasing as I stare up at him, shaking my head.
His cocky demeanor hasn't changed a bit. *God, I've missed this man.*

"Here, let me help you up," Paxton offers, extending his hand.

"Always the hero," I quip, accepting his help and dusting
myself off.

"Sorry, I thought you saw me stop," Ari says with a grimace

while fixing my errant hair. Her eyes widen as she subtly tilts her head toward Paxton. "You know him?" she mouths.

Yep. Know him, love him, and apparently become a damsel in distress when I'm around him.

Paxton's half-cocked grin finds this all amusing. And damn, he still looks mouthwatering. His dark-blue button-up shirt hugs his shoulders and chest, showcasing his muscular arms underneath.

I tilt my head, taking a moment to process his reaction upon seeing me. It's almost as if he was expecting me. "Did you know I was going to be here?" A rush of hopefulness surges inside me. "Did they find him?"

He takes two steps closer, standing right in front of me, and leans down. I catch his masculine scent, sending a familiar flutter through my stomach. He smells really good. I swallow.

"No, I'm sorry. I just needed to see you," he replies.

I lift a brow. *He came all this way to see me?*

"Have you had dinner yet?"

I hesitate and then shake my head. "I haven't."

"The people at the front desk told me about an amazing Italian restaurant down the street."

I'm very familiar with the place. It's one of our regular dinner spots when we're in St. Louis. "Can you give me half an hour to get my room and change?"

"I've waited months to see you again, half an hour is nothing."

His words catch me off guard. I probably look ridiculous standing there, staring up into his eyes, searching for answers.

"I'll apologize for this later," he mutters right before his hand wraps around my waist and he pulls me into his chest. His lips crash onto mine, taking me back in time. The kiss is heated, rushed, and intense. His lips demand every ounce of my attention.

No apologies needed.

Remembering we're in public and I'm still in uniform, I break the kiss but savor the lingering sensation. One kiss from the man and my legs turn to jelly. I blow out a shaky breath, sweeping a strand of hair behind my ear.

"I've missed you," he says, voice raw and unapologetic, his arm still tight around me. I melt into him.

I've missed us. There's a moment of silence, a pause, uncertainty about what happens next. "Should we skip dinner and go straight to dessert?" I murmur, half joking. The other half of me is on fire, desperate for more of his touch. His lips twitch into a smirk as he bites down on the bottom one, studying me. I wonder why he's hesitating. Judging by the bulge pushing into my hip, he wants me, too.

"You and your dessert," he finally says. "And who am I to argue with that suggestion?"

"I'll go check in." My cheeks warm as I hold up a finger. "Be right back."

"I'll be here."

Ari waits for me by the desk with a megawatt smile. When I get in line, she rolls her bag over and stands beside me. "What was that?"

"What?" I reply, feigning innocence.

She huffs. "You suck. I need details. Who is Mr. December? And where have you been hiding him?"

December? To me, he's totally Mr. July. If she saw him without his shirt, she'd agree.

We shuffle forward a few steps, and I glance over my shoulder at him. He's leaning against a column in the lobby looking at his phone.

"He's my ex."

She scoffs. "Is he aware of that? That he's an ex? Because I'd never kiss my ex like that. In fact, I'd punch him in the nuts if he tried to kiss me."

I'm new to the relationship thing, but considering we haven't talked in six months, we bypassed complicated and went straight to ex status. I know asking him to come away with me was selfish, but there was no other option. And he made it very clear if I walked away we were finished. *But his kiss....*

"*I've missed you.*" His words echo in my head.

I can see why she's confused. *I'm confused.*

And now he's agreed to *dessert.*

I've missed him so much. But am I making our situation worse by hopping in bed with him? Should I just go to dinner and see what he has to say first? *But his kiss,* my inner minx who's been neglected for months reminds me. I sigh, not knowing what to do.

"He lives in Austin, and I'll never live in Texas again. Ever."

"What did Texas do to you?" she jokes.

It only tried to murder me.

I walk up to Paxton, holding my room key. "Ready?"

His eyes lift from his phone, locking onto mine. My heart skips a beat. "I almost didn't recognize you earlier. Kalico, you look great. I mean, you've always been beautiful. Besides the obvious." He tugs at the ends of my short, dark hair. "There's just...something in your eyes that's different."

Hearing my nickname tugs at something deep inside—a pang of guilt mixed with longing. But I won't apologize for finding me. I'm in a good place right now. "I'm living," I murmur, fiddling with my purse strap, trying to keep my voice steady.

"I've learned," he says, a slight edge in his voice. "When I found out you were a flight attendant, I was shocked, to say the least."

I narrow my eyes, standing taller at his slight dig. "Did you come to make me feel bad for moving on? You haven't caught him, Paxton. What was I supposed to do? I wasn't going back there with him still on the loose. That's a hard pass for me and you—"

He grabs my hand, cutting off my rant. "Hey, hey, hey," he interrupts, exhaling heavily. "I'm fucking this up. I tried to tell myself not to be selfish, but as you can see, I'm a selfish bastard that wishes it was me who put that sparkle in your eyes."

Thinking back to the person who lived in Blackburn, they're worlds apart from who I am today. I'm truly happy. There are moments of loneliness that creep in, especially when I see couples enjoying each other's company or during the holidays, but I push those feelings back. Because having someone to love is not the backbone of being, loving myself is.

Don't get me wrong, Paxton standing in front of me, looking edible and edgy, stirs up a storm of emotions. Especially in certain...ahem...regions. Out of the corner of my eye, I spot Ari and Mac staring at me, whispering as they walk through the lobby. A grin pulls at my lips when Ari flashes me a thumbs-up.

"They going to be okay without you?"

"I hope so. I'm the sensible one of the three."

He chuckles as if he's not surprised. "You're walking on the wild side tonight. Dessert before dinner?"

I step into his space, closing the gap between us. "I usually skip dessert," I murmur. "But I wanted to make sure dinner didn't fill me up."

A deep-seated groan comes from the back of his throat. He leans down and whispers, "That's a great idea because you're about to be filled with something."

Yes, please.

Lucky for me, I'm only on the second floor. The moment the room door clicks shut, he's unzipping my dress as I unbutton his shirt, and we peel off the rest of our clothes in a mad rush to the bed. He pushes me onto my back, the white comforter swallowing me, and lifts one of my legs in the air. The dimmed lights by the bedside offer just enough light to showcase his perfect physique. Slowly, he drags his fingers along my black pantyhose until they hit the lacy top of my thigh highs.

"These are sexy," he says, kissing my bare inner thigh. I hum as he moves higher. "I think we'll keep them on." He inches higher and higher until he hits my panties. "These, on the other hand, need to come off." He drags them down my legs and tosses them aside. He goes to lean down, and I put my foot on his chest, shaking my head.

"Those need to come off too." I slide my foot down and outline the bulge in his slacks with my toe.

He grins as he undoes his buckle, slides his zipper down, and lets his pants fall to the ground. I bite my lip, staring up at him when his cock springs out of his underwear, and he strokes it twice.

"Is this what you want?" He takes his other hand, plunging two fingers inside me, stroking both my insides and his cock at the same time. I cry out. "Tell me you haven't fucked anyone since me."

"I haven't," I breathe. It's the truth. I haven't even been able to look at another man. I want to ask him, but I'm afraid to know the answer. I left him, so do I really have that right?

He curses and drops to his knees on the floor, grabbing me under my legs and yanking me to his mouth. He sucks, licks, and thrums across my sensitive clit. And then repeats, adding his fingers to the mix until I can't take it anymore. I buck against his hot mouth, screaming his name, fisting the comforter below me, as I ride out my orgasm. The delicious heat of ecstasy spreads from my core to my entire body.

His tongue darts out to his wet lips, and he hums. "I've missed tasting you."

And I've missed his tongue. No toy could ever come close to the way his tongue moves. I've tried.

He kisses my belly button, pushing off his knees so he can drag his lips up my stomach. He takes my boob into his mouth, the other one into his hand, and a guttural groan vibrates from the back of his throat. "I've missed your delicious tits. Perfection," he mumbles as he continues his ascent, nipping along my collarbone up to my neck. I tilt my head to give him better access as I fist his hair and softly mewl.

"I've missed you," I admit out loud. Everything about him. His touch, his hair, his scent, his cockiness—everything. It's the first time in six months I've allowed myself to let go on a sensual level. It's only because it's him.

Even if this is a mistake, there are zero regrets.

As long as he doesn't expect something in return.

He presses a kiss to my lips, and I taste myself, an aphrodisiac in itself. Our tongues tangle in an instant mess of moans, desperate to drown in each other's touch. His hand snakes down between us and guides his thick shaft inside me, filling me to the hilt. I wrap my legs around his narrow hips and meet his thrusts, needing more. He can't get deep enough. He growls against my lips and thrusts his hips in and out at a punishing pace. And then he stops, staring down at me, searching my eyes. My breath catches at the depth of his gaze.

He lowers his forehead against mine, hovers over me, and continues a slow, rhythmic pace. I tremble, and my back arches each time he pushes into me. The sensations ripple through me, taking me closer to the edge again, and I moan out loud.

"That's it, baby," he murmurs.

Picking up speed again, our moans grow louder as our bodies let loose, thighs slapping, chests heaving—almost animalistic. Heat explodes once again at my center, and I pulse, milking his thickness. He drops his face into my hair, groans and curses, letting go of his release. His hips jerk against me as if there were aftershocks from an earthquake.

Is that what we are now? Two fault lines colliding?

When he pulls out of me, a hollow feeling aches in my heart. As if it knows the only time we can be together is when he's inside me.

The next earthquake.

. . .

"WE MIGHT NEED two helpings of desert tonight," he says, returning to the room from the bathroom after cleaning us.

I agree. The bed dips, and I feel the warmth from his kisses trailing up my spine, sending shivers down my arms.

"I didn't think you could get more beautiful, but damn, woman, this new you is gorgeous."

I turn over and he hovers over me, my fingers threading through the thick, dark hair I've missed so much. He groans, lowering his mouth over my right breast, gently sucking and twirling his tongue around my nipple. I gasp, my back arching into his touch, my fingers tightening around his hair.

When he drops beside me, a bite of cold air hits my wet nipple, making me shiver. He pulls up the white down comforter over us, nestling his face into the crook of my neck.

"Are you still hungry?" he asks, his lips brushing against my shoulder. I shake my head, afraid if I move, he'll disappear. He still hasn't told me why he's here. One thing is for certain—our sexual chemistry hasn't faded.

"It's too cold outside." My blood still bleeds Texas—thin and easily freezes.

I feel his smile. "That's my southern girl."

His girl.

His possessiveness shouldn't be this attractive. But damn, I like it.

"Oh. I have some news that you'll find interesting." He leans over and grabs his phone. He messes with it for a moment before handing it to me.

I gasp reading the title of the article. *Small town Texas mayor gets arrested for child pornography possession. Resigns after he's arrested.* "No freaking way," I mutter to myself while reading it.

"Thanks to you, that asshole is going away for a long time."

"Wow," I say stunned, handing his phone back to him. "And y'all are sure he didn't have anything to do with what happened to me?"

He sighs. "I can promise you, we've tried to find a link. It would make sense if he was afraid of you causing problems for him. They found a lot of sick stuff, just not anything linking to your case."

We lay quietly as I take in what I just read. I shouldn't be surprised to find out he was a wolf in a sheep's skin. I knew it. It might be because of me that he was caught but was it me that started this sick aversion. Did witnessing me having sex with another kid make him want more? Or was he always wired wrong? I swallow the sour taste in the back of my throat, forcing myself to not focus on him. He's not stealing this time I have with Paxton. He's where he belongs and that's the end of that.

I smile at Paxton. "Let's talk about something else."

"Hmm," he says, thinking. "Is being a flight attendant everything you ever dreamed of?"

I stare up to the ceiling and nod, finding it hard to concentrate with his thumb tracing small circles on my stomach. I grab his hand and link our fingers, then roll to my side to face him. "It is. Well...minus the guy going into cardiac arrest or the unruly passengers, people who decide getting drunk on a plane sounds like a good idea. But the places I've seen already makes it all worth it."

He props himself on an elbow, resting his head in his hand. "You have enough money that you can visit all those places without having to deal with all that bullshit, right?"

His words linger in the air, a mix of concern and a desire to protect me. It's sweet, but ironic, coming from a police officer. They deal with more bullshit than a cow farmer, and he still does it—because he loves it. "I've been working since I was fourteen. I don't know how to not work. The month I stayed at the house in Arizona, doing nothing, drove me insane. I became this peeping tom, a borderline stalker. For the entire neighborhood. I need to do something with my time. That money will be there when I need it. It's more of a safety blanket for me, a promise that I'll never live like I was in Blackburn—working only to live another day."

He nods in understanding. "Tell me about some of the places you've been."

I light up, thrilled to share with him. "Oh my gosh. I've only been flying for a month, but Ari and I are taking full advantage of the flight benefits. I've seen Alcatraz in California and the Statue of Liberty in New York. I went to a Packers football game and wore a cheesehead." I laugh, recalling the memory when one coach on our flight overheard me say I'd never been to an NFL game and secretly handed me two tickets to the game.

Paxton grows still next to mine. When I look over at him, his expression shifts to an unsettling ease. I sit up, clutching the sheet up around my chest with me. "What's wrong?"

"Nothing."

It's something.

There's an awkward moment of silence.

"Don't lie," I press, cutting into it.

He inhales and then blows it out. "I'm trying not to be an ass." He shakes his head and then rolls over, pushing off the bed. He finds his underwear and pulls them up. I go over in my head what I said to set him off. Finally, he says, "Nope. There's no way around it." He leans against the dresser, crossing his arms over his chest. "I've spent six months going over every inch of your case, hoping I could find something we missed. Hoping I could help catch the bastard so you could come home. I guess...I convinced myself you were hiding away, scared to live. Clearly, I was wrong."

I sit stunned, taking in his confession. The room turns colder. Or maybe it's just the space he put in between us. I didn't expect him to pour his heart and soul into my case and put his life on hold. Now I feel like an asshole. *I'm the selfish one here.* That's what I've had to do my entire life. Selfishness was a means to survive, one that I had to adapt to. But seeing the man I love stare at me through disappointed eyes, it stings. I never expected him to pause his life for me.

"Did you even miss me?" he asks and then drops his head, cursing under his breath about being a pussy.

"Every day." He looks up. "I can't see a dog or a cop or *pie* without thinking about you. You're the only person I've ever loved, and distance didn't change that. It might have healed my scars, but it hasn't let me forget about you. It could never." I chew on my inner cheek, wondering if there is anything I could say to fix this. Even though I don't know what this is, we can't leave it like this. Sorry doesn't erase the hurt I seemed to have caused him. "Why did you wait for me?"

His expression softens. "Is it that hard for you to accept that someone is on your side?"

"Yes," I say without having to even think about it. "Paxton, leaving you was the hardest thing I've ever done. And I would never have intentionally done anything to make you this upset with me. I..." I pause, blinking back tears. "I thought you would've been happy that you didn't have to worry about me anymore."

He pushes off the dresser and sits back down on the bed, his voice losing its edge. "You couldn't be more wrong."

"I can't go back," I whisper, wishing things could be different for us. He nods with a defeated expression. "I want you to stop looking for him." It's time for him to move on with his life. He opens his mouth to say something, but I stop him. "If you love me, you'll let me go."

He lets out a bitter laugh. "I'm trying. For fuck's sake, I came here for closure."

I tilt my head, surprised. That was not the vibe I got when he pulled me in for a passionate kiss. "Hmm. We probably should've skipped dessert, then."

He points between us. "I did not plan this. But then you walked into the lobby with this air of confidence, wearing a hot flight attendant uniform. Look at you." He throws his hands up, and I snicker. My uniform isn't that attractive. "I couldn't stop myself."

I didn't stop him either.

"If you couldn't tell from earlier, I'm very happy to see you," I say, scooting closer to him, letting the sheet fall to my knees. He reaches for my hand and guides me until I'm straddling him. "Let's have tonight. Tomorrow we'll say goodbye," I say, cupping his neck.

His hands slide up my back, one of them slinking through my hair. He grips it tight, and I moan at the delicious tug. "I hate that I can't have you forever." He nips my chin with his teeth, dragging them along my jawbone. "You're supposed to be mine."

I swallow, the heat from his words igniting a frenzy of desire again.

I am his.

I just can't be his in Texas.

My hand slides between us, dipping under his briefs and pulling out his hard cock. He groans as I wrap my fingers around the shaft and pump it once. His eyes darken with need. I position myself over him and slide down, letting him fill me. We fit perfectly. Unlike earlier, where the sex was fast and furious, this one is slow, passionate, controlled. Our bodies move in a perfect harmony of thrusts, moans, delicate kisses, and a slow burn.

We both realize what this is, and neither of us wants it to end.

But we're at an impasse.

A dead end.

Closure.

Early the next morning, I feel his movement as he rolls out of bed and gets dressed. There's enough light coming from the sliver in the curtains to see him. I stretch my arm to his still warm spot, swallowing back the regret. I want to say I'll come back to Austin. That I'll do it for him, but something stops me—the thought that I'll wake the sleeping bear.

Instead, I keep quiet and watch him.

He stops in the small hallway and looks over his shoulder. "Maybe I'll show up at another stop."

"I hope you do."

He pauses and then says, "I love you, Kalico."

I inhale his words—the warmth and the loss—all at once. "I love you too, Pax."

I'm pretty sure I just lost one of my lives.

CHAPTER 38

Kali

A year later...

"WE'RE SORRY, folks, we're going to reroute to Austin because the storm doesn't seem to want to move. We'll get you home as soon as possible."

Ari and I both groan simultaneously. We hate when this happens.

Well, I promised I would go back one day. I just didn't think it would be like this. A year and a half and a whole new life later, I've moved on from this hell. The only thing that couldn't move on was my heart. I miss Paxton, especially after our night together in St. Louis a year ago. I often wondered when walking into a new hotel if I would find him waiting for me, but he was never there.

Eventually, I stopped looking.

"Get ready to deal with bitchy people," she leans over and whispers. People can get downright mean when plans deviate. Gone is any understanding, and the knives come out. The long fight from Hawaii just turned into hours more. It just messed up our connection, too, and I'm certain we're stuck here for the night. The first flight attendant call button goes off.

She sighs, seeing it's a person in her group. "You want to flip for it?"

"No, I'll go. But if 5A goes off, she's all yours." I made the mistake of telling her I loved her necklace. It turned into a three-minute explanation of where she got it. Three minutes doesn't seem like a long time, but we were in the middle of boarding, and she was blocking people. Later, when I offered her a drink, she launched into a ramble about her favorite drink from the past that they no longer offer.

"Deal."

As I pass rows of disgruntled passengers, I avoid all their glares, but their anger is swirling in the air. People, I don't want to go to Austin, either. But humans need to place blame on someone, and we're ripe for the taking. Another flight attendant light dings ahead, but I focus on the first one.

Reaching underneath to turn off the light, I ask, "What can I help you with?"

Dull brown eyes lock onto mine, and an eerie sensation courses through me. The man's weathered face remains devoid of any expression, and his hardened stare makes me uncomfortable, so I stand up straighter.

"Is there something you need?"

His eyes sweep down my body and then back up. I'm about to ask again what the hell he needs because I'm not about to stand here another moment for him to size me up, but he finally asks, "If my final destination was Austin, do I have to return to Dallas?" His monotone voice matches the humdrum of his appearance.

I swallow. He won't like my answer. He already looks to be on the verge of destroying something with his hands clenched in his lap. Or someone.

"That's a question for customer service. I'm positive they'll have agents able to assist you as soon as you exit the plane."

"Are you new? Why don't you know the answer?"

No asshole. I know the answer, but you're not going to like it.

I plaster on a fake smile. "Things change by the minute in these circumstances. So, rather than tell you one thing that might not be true, it's best to find out from the people who know for certain." With that, I spin around and put as much distance in this small tube from him as possible. Ari can take care of her own section from now on.

I quiver with a chill when I sit back down.

"What?" Ari asks.

"That guy was creepy. Did you see him?"

"Hmm. I don't think so. But now I want to go check him out." She gets up and is gone before I can stop her. Within a couple minutes, she's back. "Um. Yeah. He could totally be Lurch from the Addams Family." We both laugh.

As expected, all the flights into Dallas-Fort Worth are suspended for the night. We're stuck too. Thankfully, I'm working the galley, so I don't have to see everyone and their sour faces.

"Hey, Kali, can you grab me a water?" Jay asks from the cockpit.

I lean over to grab a can and hand it over.

Knock. Knock. Knock.

My hand freezes mid-air. The pilot tilts his head as I stop short, and he has to reach a little farther to grab the can. "Thanks?"

Ignoring his questioning gaze, I spin around, my heart seizing in my chest as I search for the source of the noise. It can't be him. Right? People continue to deplane one by one. Nobody stands to the side, waiting to see my reaction. But did he ever? Wait? No, he did it knowing he would get my attention.

"Did you hear that knocking?" I ask Ari, hoping it was my imagination, or her making the noise.

"Yeah." She rolls her eyes. "Either a pissed-off passenger or a superstitious one." She laughs. "I didn't see who did it, though. Are you okay? You look pale."

I'm being ridiculous. It can't be him. He's not the only one in this world to do things in threes. She's right. It's probably just someone taking their frustrations out on the plane.

I nod, taking in a few deep breaths, leaning against the station, giving air a chance to move to my brain so I don't pass out. Waving her off, I say, "I just think the humidity is getting to me already."

Her impeccably shaped brows arch upward. "Aren't you from Texas? Speaking of, let's make the most of it and go out tonight. Find me one of these Texas cowboys."

I emit a strangled laugh. "As much as I'd love to see you on a mechanical bull, I'm hanging out in the room tonight. I'm exhausted." I've only been in Austin for fifteen minutes, and a sense of panic is already settling in. Even after two years, just the mere thought of being here does something to my psyche. It's a bad vibe. The faster I can leave this place, the better.

She wrinkles her nose at me, confused. The last year and a half, we have been on a million adventures together, exploring new cities, the nightlife, the people, the food—that's why I took this job. Despite me not looking for hookups for myself, I make a great wingman for her.

But not here.

The air is suffocating me already.

"Fine. Mac and I will have a great time without you." Her attempt to make me feel left out is nothing but a relief.

"Just be careful."

"Always."

THE SHRILL of the alarm blares, tearing through the early morning darkness. I fumble around until I find my phone, somewhere between the comforter and the sheet down at my feet. How the hell did it get down there? Still pitch-black outside, I groan as I roll out of bed. Not hearing Ari's alarm, I knock on our connecting door before opening it. We always get connecting rooms and keep it unlocked in case either of us needs something.

Her room is quiet and dark. "Hey, party girl, it's time to get up. Just remember, this is your fault," I taunt, dragging my feet across the floor to flick on the bedside lamp. In an instant, I'm jolted awake, staring at the perfectly made king bed. Ari's overnight bag lies open, its contents scattered across the bed, while her uniform hangs untouched on the outside of the closet. It remains in the exact spot it was when we talked about the places to hit on Sixth Street before she left.

I rush back to my room and grab my phone, pressing Ari's number. It goes to voice mail, so I call Mac. She answers in a perky voice, wide awake. "I was just about to call to make sure you both were awake."

"Ari isn't in her room. She didn't sleep here last night," I reply, attempting to keep my panic under control. "Were you together when you came back last night?"

"No," she replies. "Her and Jay were hanging out." The captain. I release a sigh of relief. I mean, pilots and flight attendants...it happens. She must've slept in his bed.

"I tried to call her, but I'll try again," I tell Mac, then hang up and call Ari's phone again. Voice mail again. I mutter a few curse words. Why isn't she answering her phone? And why don't I have Jay's number? Not bothering to curl my hair as planned, I throw it up in a bun, and I'm down in the lobby in record time. Waiting. I asked the lobby if they could call Jay's room, but he didn't answer either. Mac comes down first.

She chuckles when she sees me by myself. "Ari had too much fun last night, running late?"

"I still haven't talked to her." An unsettled feeling takes root in the pit of my stomach.

"Guess her and Jay hit it off?" She wags her brows. I hope that's it. "Oh look." She tilts her head toward the fully dressed pilot, stepping off the elevator with his hat under his arm. "Trying the old you go before me so it doesn't look suspicious." She laughs, rolling her eyes.

I don't wait for him to join us, and instead, I take long strides, meeting him halfway. "Where's Ari?" I demand as his mouth opens to greet me.

His eyes move to the side for a beat, and with a flick of his hand, he offers a dismissive gesture. "How would I know?"

"Jay, you were with her last night. And she wasn't in her room this morning."

"Kali. She wasn't with me last night. I mean, we hung out on Sixth Street, and she was talking with a guy."

He left her alone? Our hotel is only a block off Sixth Street, and it's not like I haven't left her at a bar with a guy before, but it wasn't in Austin where my psycho is still on the loose.

He shrugs at my annoyance. "She's an adult, Kali. She said she was going to grab one more drink to help her sleep."

Fuck. Fuck. Fuck.

Austin. The weird man on the plane. The knocking. Ari disappearing. The unsettling rock in my stomach morphs into a level of panic I haven't experienced since I heard about Shanna disappearing.

"Kali, I'm sure she's fine. We both know Ari. She likes to have her fun." He rubs my shoulder, but his reassurance does nothing to calm my nerves. She's never spent the night in one of her one-night stand's beds. There's a first for everything, but even if she did, she would've set her alarm. "Let's talk to the front desk and see if they remember seeing her come in during the night."

We walk over. "Excuse me," I say to the front desk staff member. "Another flight attendant that was with us didn't come back to her room last night. I was wondering if you saw her at all last night? Her name is Arabella Lancaster."

He winces. "Sorry, I only came on at five, but I can check with a night staff member for you," he answers.

"Please," I say. *Stay calm, Kali.*

When he appears from the back, he shakes his head. "Sorry, none of the night staff can confirm seeing her."

This can't be happening. I pull out my phone and press the one number I was hoping never to call again.

CHAPTER 39

Kali

"KALI, we don't know if this has anything to do with you," Martinez says, his eyes following my anxious pacing around his office at the Texas Rangers headquarters.

A sense of déjà vu looms overhead. I've felt this icy fear in my heart before, and then a woman was found dead. Martinez called the police department to start a missing person's report when she didn't show up for work. They questioned everyone and let Mac, Jay, and the other pilot leave.

They said I could leave. No way. Not this time. This time, he's made it personal.

"He was on the plane," I insist. "He knocked for god's sake to let me know, too. Then he followed me to our crew hotel, which isn't a secret. How does this have nothing to do with me?" I clip, my voice trembling as tears threaten to fall.

"We're getting the plane's roster right now. If—and that is a big if—he was on the flight, our suspect list just went from millions to less than a hundred."

A glimmer of hope swirls around my spine as I freeze, struck by a realization. "No, it's less than that. There were only a handful on the flight continuing on to Austin."

Martinez points at me, nods, and then picks up his phone. "Get me the names of people flying on to Austin that were on that flight." What are the odds he was on my flight? Was it a coincidence, or did he find me knowing I worked that flight? *Paxton figured out where I was going to be.* Maybe it's easier than I thought. He hangs up, and I stop walking. "Still not on board that we're dealing with your guy. Last time, he made it clear it was him, and so far, nothing. I had the local cops go out to the place Paxton found you, assuming he'd send a message if it was him, but..." He shakes his head.

"I understand. As much as I feel it deep in my bones that he has something to do with this, I need the focus to be on finding Ari. She might be hurt somewhere."

Or worse, buried alive.

A text ding goes off on his phone, and he glances down at it. "Got it," he says, reaching for his mouse. I walk around his desk, not caring if I'm breaking some sort of privacy law. He says nothing, so I lean over and read the list over his shoulder. The first list is the plane roster from Hawaii.

"Look at seat 55B. There was just something off about this guy." He scrolls down, and the seat is unoccupied.

"No one was sitting in the entire row."

This is the reason we hate when people move around. The row was empty, and he probably wanted more room, so he changed seats. Martinez opens the next file. Thirty names are on the list who were continuing to Austin. He scrolls as we read the names. None look familiar.

Until my eyes stop at one that grabs my attention.

Oh my gosh. She was on my flight, and I never even saw her.

"We'll start working on researching the guys on the list," Martinez says as I grab my purse.

I didn't tell him I saw a friend's name on the list. She's not who they're looking for, and their focus should be one hundred percent on researching the men on the plane. His dark eyes narrow at the purse in my hands, and he tilts his head. "If he is back, I'd rather you not go anywhere by yourself."

"I'm not worried about me. Focus on Ari."

He sighs. "This is a long shot, and it could lead nowhere, but just in case there is something with the guy in 55B, the police are wondering if you'd be willing to work with a sketch artist? Since he's fresh in your head."

"Of course. Anything that might help."

"I'm going to have one of our guys walk you over to the police station." Of course he is. "One question before you leave...did Paxton know you were coming to town?"

This again? What is with his blatant disapproval of Paxton? I can't help the snarky tone when I reply, "No. We haven't talked in a year. And I wasn't even supposed to be here."

It stings to think about us growing apart. We were perfect for each other. But Paxton's world is rooted here, and I can't have that life. I needed to find my own path, and he needed to stay on his. It's a truth that still hurts after all this time.

But I've accepted it.

He raises his palms in a defensive gesture. "I wouldn't be doing my job if I didn't ask."

I bite my tongue, wanting to argue that they cleared him. So why keep poking at a dead end?

As we walk out the front doors of the building, I blow out a long-winded breath. The scorching August sun beats down on me, its heat clinging to my skin. It's been a long time since I needed to shower from just walking outside.

When we pass a homeless man, sitting against a building, he's not moving, and I wonder if he died from heat exhaustion. But then he coughs once and opens his eyes. His weary eyes lift when he grins at me, showing off his toothless smile. I smile back and then dig into my purse, pulling out a hundred-dollar bill. I fold it up and hold it out for him. He holds his calloused and weathered hand up. I imagine those hands have lived a couple of lifetimes.

He glances at the Ranger and then back to me. "God bless you," he says as he unfolds the single bill and notices it's a hundred.

"Keep that safe," I whisper, glancing around to double-check no one is watching us.

His grin grows devilish as he nods and sticks the money down his pants.

"Don't you worry, nobody will try to get it now." He laughs at my wrinkled nose. I guess if that's what works. But, gross.

"You really shouldn't be doing that if you're carrying around large bills," the Ranger warns. "There's people always looking for their next target."

I nod, realizing he's right. I just felt sorry for the guy in this heat. The distant hum of cicadas fills the air, blending in with the city sounds—occasional honking and the construction happening across the street. I've found it interesting that each city has its own sounds. Something I never would've thought about before all the travel I've done during the past year and a half.

I blow the hair out of my face when I make it to the building and push through the front doors to the busy lobby, the scent of coffee from the street vendor following me in. It feels weird being back here, and memories creep in. A couple late-night dinners I brought Paxton when he was busy with a case. Just so I could see him that day.

"Ma'am?" the Ranger prompts, shifting my attention back to him. "We need to go through the security line."

Once through, the Ranger tells the lady at the front desk who I'm here to see.

She gestures to the bench. "They'll be right out."

An hour later, I'm being walked out by the sketch artist. It was almost impossible not to think of Lurch as I was describing the guy. At times, I wondered if I was mixing them up. Describing someone in enough detail to create a perfect picture is challenging. I didn't remember anything distinctive about him, so the picture looks like any other guy. In the end, the only thing I was certain of were his hollow eyes.

"Thanks for coming in," he says, holding his hand to shake mine.

When I reach for his hand, a bark stops me. Lots of barks follow. The guy looks past me to see where it's coming from. I close my eyes for a beat, and my lips twitch.

"He must've found something," he says.

Yeah. He found me.

I spin around to find Riggs leading a confused Paxton right toward me. When he sees me, I see the confusion play out in his handsome features. Riggs trots over and sits perfectly still next to me as if telling his handler, *look here.* I laugh, bending down and wrapping my arms around Riggs.

He doesn't hate me for leaving.

"Kali." Hearing him say my name kickstarts the beat of my heart. I stand back up, and his eyes bounce between me and the sketch artist. He's dressed in a blue suit, his badge on his hip, and damn does he look good. "Wha…what are you doing here?"

"Ms. Stevens, it was nice to meet you," the guy says. He gives Paxton a quick nod and then turns to leave.

He points to the guy. "And why were you meeting with Dante?"

The question stabs me in the heart, reminding me why I'm here. My vision blurs with tears. "My best friend's missing. And I think *he* took her."

His entire body hardens. The uncertainty of my visit, *of us*, vanishes, and he morphs into Officer Turner.

"What? She's missing from Austin? When did you get back in town? Have you filed a police report?" He takes a breath, slightly irritated. "I need you to start from the beginning."

I exhale sharply and blink back my tears. I need to keep it together for Ari.

"Our flight was diverted to Austin. Ari never came back to the hotel after going out. There was a creepy guy on the plane, someone knocked three times, and now she's missing. I know it's him." The words fall out quickly, and I can see he's trying to keep up. "I just left Martinez, and he called the cops. Her name is Arabella Lancaster."

He quirks his head to the side. *What part is confusing?* "We had a meeting this morning about her before I had to go to court. They never said this was linked to you."

"Martinez said they're treating it like a typical missing person because he hasn't left his signature anywhere. But I know it's him."

He bobbles his head left and right. "I kind of agree with Martinez. Most perps don't stray from their MO, especially if this is your guy. He'd want you to know he still has the upper hand."

Why can't everyone see that he's made himself known? *Three knocks. Ari.* He couldn't be any more obvious. I think about the name on the list. Maybe she saw him. Maybe she got a better look at him and can help with the sketch. "I have to go. I'll catch up with you later?"

"Where are you going?"

"I have to go to Blackburn."

His eyes roam past me, scanning the precinct. "You're by yourself?"

I nod, and his mouth turns down and his jaw tics.

"How do you plan on getting there?"

"I was going to call a rental car company."

He shakes his head. "You can tell me in detail everything while I drive you there." I open my mouth to object. "That wasn't a question," he states, taking a step closer to me. *Bossy Paxton is in the building.* "Let me get my keys and tell my boss." His eyes flicker up and down, and he shakes his head as if still in shock that I'm standing in front of him. "It's good to see you."

My heart falters when there's not an ounce of heat in his words.

They're words you tell a friend that you haven't seen in a while. Not a woman you love. He's moved on. He's no longer mine.

But I answer him honestly, as I'm not sure I'll ever stop loving this man. "I wish it wasn't under these circumstances."

He nods with a tight smile. "Riggs, stay with Kali."

Riggs moves from a lying position to a sit, and he hands me his leash. I narrow my eyes at Paxton. Dirty move. He did that on purpose, so I wouldn't leave without him.

"I'll be right back."

THE FIRST HALF of the drive went by in a blur as I spilled the details of everything that happened up to that point. Now, silence hangs between us, and everything is sharply defined, every passing mile stretching the quiet tension that lingers in the air.

"I like your new truck," I say, breaking the silence. The lifted black Ford F150, blacked out in every detail, fit him and his dark, rugged style perfectly. He smirks, glancing at me before returning his focus to the road.

The soft leather seats embrace me, and I draw in a whiff of the new leather scent. The afternoon sun casts warm hues on the dashboard. Despite the seriousness of everything, there's an unspoken comfort in being around him.

"I got it a couple months ago," he replies. "How have you been? Fly to any new places?"

"Too many to remember. Ari and I started doing international flights eight months ago." I start to tear up again. Will we ever get to experience another city together? I try to talk through my emotions. "The cherry blossoms in Japan were the most magnificent thing we'd ever seen." I start to ugly cry. "I can't do this. What if we can't find her? What if I never see her again? She's my best friend."

He reaches over and grabs my hand and squeezes it once. "I

remember Ari, and she's pretty feisty. I imagine she's a fighter. Just hold on to that." That she is.

I sniff, remembering the times I felt uncomfortable when we were on dark streets in foreign cities and how she would always show off her wannabe jiu-jitsu moves, saying she would protect me. It's not that it made us any safer, but our laughter would always settle my fear.

We pass a sign that says we're ten miles away. Paxton turns to me, his eyes curious. "What's in Blackburn?" I can't believe it took him this long to ask.

"Remember when I talked about Pearl?"

He nods. She's the only person I ever talked about.

"Well, her name was on the passenger list. I didn't see her, which isn't uncommon because I was working the galley during boarding and deplaning. But maybe she saw the guy. He was hard to miss. It's a long shot, but I need to do something."

"Do you remember any of the guys' names?"

I try to recall any of them, but I scanned them too quickly to memorize any. Once I saw Pearl's name, I somewhat expected Chip's name to be there. But it wasn't. I shake my head. "I didn't recognize any. Only Pearl's name."

"I'll ask Martinez to send me the list."

"Thank you for helping. I can't imagine helping your ex was on your to-do list today."

"That it wasn't," he says, staring straight ahead. And then adds, "But I'm glad you came to me."

As we roll into town, Main Street comes into view. The diner appears unchanged, except for the new specials sprawled across the window in bright red and baby blue letters. Whoever handles the display has much better handwriting than I ever did.

Paxton parks and unbuckles his seat belt. I stare at him, debating if he should come in.

"What?" he asks, confused why I'm not moving. "Why aren't we going in?"

I shift in my seat. "It might be better if you stay out here. If Pearl catches sight of me with a guy, she'll think we're together and bombard us with a million questions. I don't want to be here for very long. Plus, you wanted to text Martinez anyway, right?"

His expression says that wasn't his immediate plan.

"Don't take long, or I'm coming in."

I swing open the truck door, hopping out with a quick, "Be right back," tossed over my shoulder.

Riggs barks once, and just before I shut the door, I hear Paxton mutter, "I don't like it either."

A surge of curiosity has me looking down the sidewalk, wondering if I'll run into someone. The realization hits me—this is how Ann felt coming back to this place. Shaking out of my thoughts, I refocus on my purpose for being here because I'm not here to prove I successfully moved on. I don't care what any of these people think of me. Then or now.

As I reach for the door, I wonder if Pearl still works here. Are she and Chip together? Or did she meet a wealthy man passing through and chased him around the world? It could explain the expensive trip to Hawaii.

It's different, yet the same, as I pull open the door. It's an unsettling sense that I'm home, which makes me think I haven't found one outside Blackburn. And that irritates me even more.

"Well, poke me done and turn me over. Look who's here," Pearl squeals, darting toward me and throwing her arms around my neck. I inhale a whiff of her familiar scent. It doesn't seem like two years have passed. She pulls back, holding me at arm's length, her eyes moving up and down. "You're looking like a hot summer night." She whistles, making me blush. "You've finally glowed up."

"Stop." I laugh, appreciating her attempt at using teen lingo. "Look at you, looking all tan and sexy." Her hair is swept up in her typical bun and lips painted bright red to match her hair. I can't recall ever seeing her with a tan; she's ghostly white or sunburned white.

She waves off the compliment. "I had a staycation at the house. Blew up a swimming pool and made me some of those fruity drinks with the little umbrellas. It was perfect."

That's bullshit. My smile slips. Why is she lying?

"Are you sure it's not a Waikiki tan?"

Her eyes narrow with a questioning glance around before she grabs me by the arm. "Shhh," she says, dragging me outside the front doors to the sidewalk. She releases me. "How in the world did you know that?"

"I was on the same plane. I'm a flight attendant." Fear flickers in her eyes for a second before her lips break into a wide smile. I tilt my head. "Why the big secret?"

She crosses her arms, scanning both directions down the strip. "So soon you forget. If those nosey people in there"—she points to inside the restaurant—"find out, they'll all be questioning how I can afford to go to Hawaii. They'll all tip less." Her lips purse as she rolls her eyes. It's a valid reason. Hawaii isn't a cheap vacation. "I met a man there, so I'd like to keep this between us. I can't believe I didn't notice you. The plane ain't that big."

"I was working first class the whole time." Except for the one time I ventured out to help someone. "But that's why I'm here. Did you by chance see a guy sitting by himself, dark hair and dark brown eyes, but his eyes were..." I take a moment to think of the perfect word. "Hollow. Like there was no life behind them." A chill runs up my spine with the recollection.

A car door opens in the parking lot, diverting both of our attention in that direction. Paxton steps out, his intense eyes bouncing between the two of us, and his mouth in a hard line of pissed off. Pearl gasps beside me. Now, my eyes are darting from him to Pearl and back to him, waiting for someone to say something. Why is Paxton mad, and why is Pearl surprised?

"Mom. What the hell are you doing?"

Mom? Wait, what?

That is not what I was waiting for.

CHAPTER 40

Paxton

My entire life, I wondered if my parents had adopted me. While I bear a small resemblance to my dad, there's nothing of my mom in me. Her wild, red hair is about as crazy as she is. Free-spirited, she would call it.

Kali froze, eyes wide, as she struggled to comprehend while pointing at my mom.

Yeah, my exact thoughts when I found you talking to her. That's not Pearl; that's not her name. It's Elizabeth. And who knows what her last name is now?

"Get in the car, Kali," I demand, my pulse ramping up to a thundering stampede.

"Paxxy."

That damn nickname! I cringe, slamming my door shut to keep Riggs inside.

She rushes toward me before I can stop her, wrapping her arms around my chest. I roll my eyes, keeping mine flat against my sides. She's putting on a show. She wasn't this excited almost two years ago. When she was supposed to be moving to California.

This isn't California.

Peeling myself out of her hold, I take a step next to Kali. She's confused, as she should be, because so am I. Finally, she finds her voice.

"That's your mom?"

Not by choice.

I nod and grab her hand. "Let's go. Now." She might think she knows this woman, but she has no clue.

Kali stops behind me, and our hands break free. I whirl around when I hear her say, "You never told me you had a son." No shock there. She probably threw a party the day I left.

She hikes a shoulder. "It's not like he ever visited me. It felt like I didn't." Classic victim-playing. I refuse to engage in a debate over parental responsibilities at the moment. "How do you two know each other?"

"That is none of your business," I say before Kali can answer. I open the car door, nudge her inside, and shut the door myself, fearing she might jump out if I don't. As I round the car, I skewer my mom with a frosty stare. "If I find out you had anything to do with Kali's kidnapping, I'll arrest you myself."

I ignore Kali's confused expression as I slam the car in reverse. The tires squeal in protest when I hit the gas. My hands tremble from rage, and my focus is laser-sharp on the road ahead.

From the second I saw Kali, it's been impossible to think straight. Keeping my feelings in check is a constant battle. I have to remind myself that she's not here to see me. We're done. I'm helping her because she's important to me. *Even if I can't tell her how much.*

And now this?

"Do you…do you think she had something to do with…" Kali's voice trails off.

I swerve to pull off the road, slamming the truck in park, and release a painful sigh with a death grip on the steering wheel.

Fuck, yeah, I do. *Somehow.*

I turn in my seat, finding sparks of shock in her eyes. "Everybody's been looking for a connection. I think I just found it."

"Pearl wouldn't…" she starts.

"There is evil inside that woman, Kali. She put me through hell after my dad died."

Realizing the potential connection, she whips her head around so fast, I heard it crack. "We need to go back, Paxton. Right now!"

My principles escape me for a moment. I hear Kali, and she's right. But it's *her*. I'm not sure I can control myself if I find out she's the reason for all of this.

"My best friend is missing. If she knows anything…" Kali squeezes my bicep. Hard. "Paxton, we need to find her." Her jaw sets, and her eyes burn with a fierce intensity. I'm afraid to tell her no.

Fuuuuck! Confronting my mom again sends a ripple of dread through my veins, but what choice do I have? I need to put aside my personal demons. We could call Martinez, but he's an hour away. Despite my stand-down with this case, I'm still a cop, and time is crucial. Riggs senses the shift in atmosphere, his ears perking up as he whines from the back seat.

"Hold on," I say, shifting the vehicle into drive and making a harsh U-turn.

Kali glances at the back seat, checking on Riggs. He's fine. He's used to this. So there's no question I'm hiding anything, I give Martinez a quick call and tell him what happened. There's not much to say, but I want him to be aware of my mom. *Of the connection.*

We only have a link. But one link hooks to another and another until you find your anchor. The answer.

Who buried Kali alive?

The fear of discovering the answer and facing the possibility that the woman who birthed me is capable of such a heinous crime gnaws at me.

Kali's quicker than I am, already swinging open the door before I put the truck in park when we reach the diner. She bolts into the restaurant. I let the engine idle for Riggs's sake and chase after her.

By the time I make it to the door, she's already rushing back toward me.

"She's not here. Roberto said she just left because she wasn't feeling well." Her voice is mixed with frustration and haste. She grabs my hand, pulling me back to the truck. "C'mon, we can catch her at her home."

Not likely.

What have you gotten mixed up with, Mom?

The drive starts off quiet. God knows what Kali's thinking. Me, I'm wondering if I'm about to come face-to-face with the man I almost killed ten years ago. Maybe that's who Kali saw on the plane. He fits the description. Considering he locked a teenage boy in an underground storm shelter for days at a time, without food or water for punishment, it's not too far-fetched he buried someone alive. If he did it, I'll kill him myself. Nobody will stop me this time. I glance at my phone to check if Martinez has sent me the names yet, but he hasn't responded.

"She's a nurse. Why the hell was she a waitress?" I'm still confused. She's lived here all this time?

"Pearl's a nurse?" she blurts out.

I nod. At least that's what she was in Oklahoma. "Is she married?" I ask.

"She wasn't. At least the entire time I knew her. She told me she had been married four times before, though." She turns in her seat, questioning, "How long has it been since you saw her?"

I take a moment to remember when it was. "She popped up at work. Not long after you found the note on your car." Thinking back to the timing, I should've questioned it more. "I hadn't seen her in a decade, and there she was. She told me about moving to California and wanted to say bye before she left."

"You never told me that." She sounds hurt.

The white SUV in front of me blurs, my focus clouded by regret. "I just...there wasn't a point in bringing it up." Kali remains quiet. She doesn't agree. "She was leaving the state, and truthfully"—I look over at her, wishing I could make her understand—"I was hoping to never see her again."

She nods, dropping her head. "I guess I never knew her," she murmurs, shaking her head. "There." She points to a small, weathered house.

Despite the old siding needing a new paint job and the shutter hanging by a screw on one window, it's the vibrant red flowers in pots that stand out. My mom always loved her flowers.

Probably more than she loved me.

The truck comes to a stop, and this time I'm prepared for Kali's quickness. I catch her by the elbow before she can get out. "Stay in the car," I assert with a firm voice. She parts her lips to argue, but I cut her off. "You're safer in here with Riggs. I'll check to see if anyone's home."

Securing my gun at my side, I open the door, fixing her with a stern look until she signals that she's staying put. She holds her hands up in surrender. "Okay, fine." It's confirmation enough for me. She doesn't have to be happy about it.

Dirt and rocks crunch underfoot as I walk up the gravel driveway. There isn't a car anywhere on the property. Off in the distance, the mooing of cows carries in the wind. My knocks on the weather-beaten front door echo unanswered. Waiting a few seconds before knocking again. It's pointless. She's not here. I cast a brief look back at Kali, shaking my head, before turning to do a perimeter check. I glance through each window until I hit the back door. Taking a chance, I try to open it, but it's locked.

"I have a key."

Kali's voice startles me from behind, jolting me into a defensive stance. My hand instinctively flies to my gun until my eyes land on her, holding up a gold key. "Didn't we agree that you'd stay in the car?" My voice is a low rumble of frustration.

"I recall you saying you were going to check if she was here first. You checked, and she's not. So, I thought since I have a spare key, we should use it."

"Are you trying to get me in trouble? I don't have a warrant."

For a moment, she just looks at me, her expression faltering. "But you tried the door."

"That wasn't meant for you to see."

"Well, I did."

With a determined stride, she moves past me, sliding the key into the hole. I should stop her, but if my mom gave her a key, she gave her access. With a cautious glance around, I relent and follow her inside. Kali calls out her name, but we're met with silence. I check the small two-bedroom house before returning to where Kali is in the living room.

"What do you expect to find?" I inquire, scanning a cluttered desk with bills and magazines. Using a pen from my pocket, I nudge a magazine aside, revealing Pearl's last name. I'm happy to see it's not still Houston, but why did she change her first name? There's a bill with a huge past-due stamp across it. It's for an MRI.

"I'm not sure," Kali replies, pulling my attention away from the bill. She stands in the middle of the living room, spinning in place. "You're the cop. What would you be looking for?"

"If I had a warrant, we'd be looking through everything. Every single square inch. But we don't." Riggs barks from my truck, and my spine straightens. Shit. This was a bad idea. The drawn shades obscure the view outside. Without wasting any more time, I take two swift steps toward Kali and guide her to the back door. If we can exit before someone spots us, it'll be a lot easier to offer an excuse.

"Freeze. Hands in the air." A burly cop, gun drawn, beats us to the back door. He fixates on my firearm holstered at my hip. I throw my hands up, and Kali does too, stepping out from the shadow cast by me. The minute he notices her, he drops his weapon. "Kali? What the hell?"

"Chip!" she replies, her chest rising and falling from fear. We both lower our hands. "Thank God it's you. Have you seen Pearl? She left work not feeling good, and I had just seen her, and she seemed fine. I was worried something had happened." Words tumble out of her mouth like a torrent, rapid and urgent.

He keeps his defensive stance and his hand on his holstered gun. Ignoring her question, he keeps his focus on me. *Chip? What the fuck? I know this guy.* But I know him as Charles. Of course, he wouldn't remember me, but it's the man my mom grew up with. I can't remember the exact year he moved, but it'd have to be at least fifteen years ago, back when I was a pimple-faced, stick-thin kid. A lot has changed since then.

But why are my mom and Charles, *or Chip,* living in the town that took my brother?

"I'm a friend of Kali's, and I'm also a police officer. I can show you my badge." I wait for him to nod before pulling my wallet from my back pocket and flashing him my badge. If he doesn't recognize me, he will now. He glances too quick at it. There's no way he looked long enough to catch my name.

Maybe he does remember me.

"If you're a cop, then you're aware that you're trespassing."

"Trespassing?" Kali clips, holding up the key as evidence. "Chip, I have a key. I told you, I was worried about Pearl."

"She's the one who called it in. She thought someone was breaking into her house."

That's a lie.

She's running. And this is nothing but a distraction. The idea that my mom had something to do with Kali fires up an anger that I'd long buried in her absence. I just don't understand. What is her involvement in this? How did my mother and Chip end up here? Is he involved? Was Kali always her target? Is she so evil that she would have someone buried alive?

Who am I kidding? There is something wrong with her. She didn't seem to mind when my stepfather threw me down into the storm shelter in the middle of the night. Always waiting on the other side, releasing me like she saved me. At first, I thought she was, but after a few times, it was obvious she was doing it on purpose. She was not the hero; she was the orchestrator.

"Well, c'mon." Chip steps outside, holding the door open. "You guys can't be in here. Only because it's you, Kali, I won't arrest you. She didn't know you were the one at her house."

We follow him out, and Kali locks the door behind her.

"Can you call her and tell her it was me? I have to talk to her, but she's not answering her phone." He nods, and I keep my eyes on him, scrutinizing his every move, searching for signs of nervousness or fidgeting. He appears calm. "She might not recognize my number."

He holds out his pad and a pen. "Give me your number, and I'll tell her."

As she writes her number down, she says, "This is urgent. Can you call her now?"

He pulls out his phone and puts it to his ear. After a few seconds, he shrugs. I make a mental note of the time so Martinez can verify if he called her. "She didn't answer. But I'll tell her you need to talk to her as soon as possible. Are you guys staying in town?"

"No," I spit. Kali might be in danger here. There's something going on, and we don't need to be stuck in this small town. Martinez is putting out a statewide lookout for my mom. She'll be on the radar of every cop in the state of Texas.

"You might want to check your messages," I suggest to Chip, my hand gripping the door handle as I settle into my truck. "There's going to be a BOLO for Pearl any minute."

His eyes widen, and a furrow creases his forehead. "What? What'd she do?"

"She's wanted for questioning in connection with the girl that went missing last night."

A droplet of sweat beads on his forehead. His calm demeanor shifts. "This is ridiculous. She hasn't left Blackburn. What does she have to do with anything?"

"That's for the Austin PD and Texas Rangers to find out." His face is beet red by the time I back out. I glance through the rearview mirror, and he's on the phone yelling at someone. Chip's involvement is still up in the air for me. But he knows something. The pieces of the puzzle don't fit together neatly, and I'm left with more questions than answers.

Leaving town, Kali stares out the front window. Every couple seconds, she's shaking her head, engaged in an internal conversation. I give her a moment to take everything in. She finally says, "She was like a mom to me. She couldn't have had anything to do with what happened to me." I sense her questioning eyes on me, but she won't like my answer.

"She's not the person you think she is. I told you that after my brother died, something broke. She didn't care who she was with or what they did to me. She'd let my stepdad beat the shit out of me with a switch for not eating one carrot on my plate and then tell me I deserved it. And that was one of many. He was a hothead who had a thing for hurting people."

Her gasps reverberate in the truck. Holding her hand over her mouth, she utters, "Oh my god. Was this revenge for what my dad did?"

"I wish I could tell you how that brain of hers works, but I don't speak crazy." Gave up trying to figure her out after she married Carl. I hold off telling her about Chip because she's already freaking out. I'll tell Martinez as soon as I get back to the precinct because I'm not sure if he's involved, but that connection is definitely worth looking into.

There's a heavy silence, and I want to reach for her, reassure her that her friend had nothing to do with this, but I can't. "You never saw her at the diner? We work the same shifts."

Her question surprises me at first, then grates on my nerves because I think I'd know if I saw my mom. "She wasn't there when I went in for pie."

Another gasp escapes Kali's lips. "She knew you were there.

That day...she was fine one minute and the next, she hurried out of there saying she was sick. I was so confused because she never calls in sick. Now it all makes sense. Well, clearly, not all of it," she adds. That's why they were short-staffed and everything was backed up. She must've seen me come in.

Guilt tightens its grip around me, and a bitter taste of responsibility that I set the entire plan in motion sours my stomach. *She hid herself from me. Why? Why didn't she want me to know she was there?* Had I left well enough alone, Kali would've never been taken.

Buried alive.

Fuck.

Kali was right moving away from me. No other women have been taken—that we know of—since she left. *This was personal. My mom. Revenge. Hatred.* But where does Shanna Clark fit into this picture?

I might not have put her in that grave, but this *is* all my fault.

CHAPTER 41

Kali

A DOOR SWINGS OPEN, and my gaze locks on Martinez walking toward me. The Texas Rangers found Pearl two counties over from Blackburn, headed north, and brought her in just a little while ago. He's only been in there with Pearl for five minutes. While he allowed Paxton to watch the interview, I had to wait out in the hallway.

"What's wrong?" I ask as he approaches.

He shakes his head. "She won't talk until she talks to you first."

I bite my lip. A part of me needs to hear what she has to say while the other part is being shredded at the mere thought that the woman I looked at like a mother had something to do with my nightmare.

Yet, she might tell me where Ari is.

I stand, taking a deep breath. "Okay."

"She knows everything she says is being recorded," he says as we make our way through the doors.

With a nod, he opens the door for me. The room is bright, with a table in the middle and three chairs. Pearl watches me as I scoot a chair back. The chair's screech against the cement floor bounces off the walls, making me wince as I sit down. She waits for me to get settled. She's aged at least ten years in the past twenty-four hours. Of course, it could be the unforgiving glare of the fluorescent lighting.

"I'm so sorry, Kali." She extends her hands across the table, but I jerk back, hiding my hands in my lap.

"Don't touch me."

She frowns, as if I just offended her. "You have to know my heart was in the right place."

Is she trying to justify burying me alive?

I force myself to swallow the knot of bile in my throat as I stare at her in utter shock. No apology can make this right.

"The light of a hero shines brighter from the darkest of moments." What the hell did she just say? Why is she speaking like that? I replay her words in my mind, hoping I misheard them. "You and my son were meant to be together."

Nope. I heard them correctly. Paxton was right, this lady is nuts. She doesn't even sound like the Pearl I know.

My mouth gapes open, but there are no words. Anger digs in and takes root, and I have to take a couple calming breaths so I don't fly over the table and slam her head into it a few times.

"Let me get this straight…you had me buried alive so I could meet your son?"

"So he could save you," she says with pep and a smile, as if that changes everything.

So he could save me? Who thinks that way? Who believes drugging someone, locking them in a box, and tormenting them—*thump, thump, thump*—would be a recipe for romance? Why not let nature run its course? He sent me a pie and then came back to the diner. Wasn't that enough?

She's delusional. Her heart is in the wrong place. Wired wrong. *Something.*

She doesn't care about her son. She only cares about herself. She left him. She chose someone over him. So, why now? Why does she want to offer me up on a silver platter to him?

Was it the money?

Was she going to wait until we got married and then kill us both so she would end up with the money? *Shit. This is a rabbit hole I don't want to go down.*

I see why Paxton hates her.

Don't kill her, everyone is watching.

"This is not a fucking fairy tale!" I slam my palms on the table, causing her to flinch. "Thanks to you, I have mental and emotional scars I live with every day. Fears! I was stuck in a box, thinking my last breath would be any minute. I couldn't move. I felt spiders on me. I peed myself!" Not able to keep still, I jump up and start pacing. I stop and turn toward her. "What if he hadn't come?"

"He would," she insists. "I knew he would find you." Grinding my teeth, I spin away from her and stare at the mirror where Paxton and Martinez are watching. Do they find this as absurd as I do? "And you got help. You were better, and you were so happy with my Pax." Nails dig into my palms as I fist my hands. "But that idiot, Carl, had to mess everything up. He was like a cat who had his first taste of blood. He acquired the taste for tormenting women."

The tension knots between my shoulders, spiraling up to the base of my neck. A small voice in my head screams at me to leave. Walk out of here because I've had enough. But there's more she needs to say, more they need to hear, and she might not tell them. So, I take hold of the power she's given me and spin around, determined to get more answers.

"Who's Carl?"

"My crazy ex-husband. Pax's stepfather." Did she just call someone else crazy? Hello pot, meet kettle. "I should've never had him help me."

My eyes close, and I ask between gritted teeth, "Where's Ari?"

"I swear, Kali, I don't know. I don't know anything about that other girl, either. Carl's gone off the deep end," she says, her accent heavy with emotion.

"So, Carl is the one who kidnapped me?" I ask, my voice strained.

She nods. "But I didn't tell him to do all the other stuff. I swear."

I've had to deal with a lot in my life. Mentally, physically, and emotionally, but I've survived each time. And there's no doubt I'll survive this. But right now, the pain from her deceit hits right in the center of my scarred heart.

She was my friend.

"Was this revenge for what my dad did? For killing your son?"

Her stare hardens as I hit a nerve, no doubt. "I know you had nothing to do with that."

"Then what brought you to Blackburn?"

"In a weird way, I kinda felt closer to my Jack. And then I met you soon after I got to town, and we formed a special bond. I knew I was meant to be there."

My fingers grip the back of the metal chair, and I lean on it, trying to understand. But no matter how I look at it, there's nothing to understand. What burns me the most is meeting the one person I loved in this world was orchestrated by this vile woman.

Anger and humiliation churn inside my chest. "Why the name change?"

She leans forward on the table. "I tried to get away from that bastard. I figured the last place he'd look for me was the town that took my baby. It took him a few years, but he found me, begging for me to take him back. So, I told him if he did this small thing for me, I'd consider it."

Small thing?

"I can't. I can't do this anymore." I glance over my shoulder at the mirror. "I'm done."

"I'm dying, Kali," she calls out to my back. Her words hang in the air for a beat. *No, she didn't.* Does she think I'm going to fall for that? Show her some sympathy? Erase the torment she caused me?

I don't think so.

"Well, I know where there's a hole. It's ready for you."

The door opens, and I storm past Martinez. I can't hold the tears back anymore. As I head for the quickest exit, I catch concerned glances from a few officers as I wipe my cheeks. Paxton catches up, grabbing my arm to halt my escape.

"Kali. Wait."

With a deep breath, I turn, shaking my head. "She manipulated us." I swipe another tear. "I feel like a fool. Like nothing is real."

"Don't." Paxton moves close, maintaining a firm grip on my arm. "Don't let her discount our feelings. They are one hundred percent real."

"Are they?" I clip. He jerks back in offense.

"I fell in love with you the second I saw you in the diner."

"I just don't know what to think. I can't trust my own feelings and thoughts right now," I say out of frustration, disregarding his sweet sentiment all together. Everything she did was in vain because look at us. We're not even together. "You lied to me, and then I had someone who I trusted throw me in the trenches of her convoluted game."

His grip loosens, and he drops his hands, shoving them into his jeans, and I can't help the sob that escapes my throat.

"I'm sorry," he murmurs. Regret knocks the wind out of my anger at the resolve in his voice. "I didn't know she was connected to our story. I really didn't. And now...now I'm just as lost as you are. Mostly, I'm sorry I brought her into your life."

I squeeze the bridge of my nose. "I...I can't do this right now. What we had isn't important anymore."

Because there isn't a we.

"I fucking beg to differ."

"Paxton, I have to keep my focus on Ari." My voice shakes. "I have to go."

I spin around before he can say anything and storm out of the police station. The humid air hits my already heated face, and I scowl at the beautiful sunset, feeling a disconnect between Mother

Nature's tranquility and the turmoil inside me. I look up at the sky. *"Why can't you be on the same page as me?"*

BACK AT THE HOTEL, I can't seem to sit still. My room feels suffocatingly small, almost claustrophobic. There is barely enough space to pace around the bed. My mind jumps from Pearl's excuse to what Ari is going through to Paxton's words—*I beg to differ.* The way he said it. As if there's something there.

There's enough energy running through my system, I could run a marathon. And we know how much I love running. My muscles tighten, and my scalp tingles when I hear a knock at the door. *It has to be Martinez.* He's the only one who knows which room I'm in.

I glance through the peephole, and intense brown eyes meet mine. I rest my forehead on the door. Am I ready to see him again? Rehash the past? Because that went well earlier.

"Kali, I saw you look through the hole. Please open up." I open the door and stare at him. "Can I come in?" He's angry. Well, I am too. I open the door wider and then shut it after he passes.

I follow him into the brightly lit room. He peeks through the connecting door that's wide open into the other room. I paid for Ari's room, just in case she was able to get back to it.

"That's Ari's stuff."

He nods and walks to the window, staring out, and sighs. I can't believe it's been a year since we saw each other. In some ways, it feels like yesterday, but in others, it feels like a lifetime ago. "I wasn't done earlier."

I lean against the dresser, crossing my arms. "What's left to say?"

He whips around. "I thought I could get over you. *Hell,* I thought I was over you. But the moment I saw you standing in the police station, right then and there, I knew that wasn't possible. Do you know how hard it's been not to touch you? Not to pull you into my arms? You could be married for all I know. And I don't know how to ask."

"I'm not," I whisper and then the next word slips out before I can stop it. "You?" He shakes his head.

"I know this is the wrong time to be doing this. But you being here and me acting like you were just someone I knew *back in the day* is killing me inside. I had to tell you." I stare at him, stunned by his admission. Between Ari and now Pearl—*his mom*—words aren't coming easy. "That's it. That's all I had to get off my chest. I just needed to tell you that I'm here for you."

"That means a lot to me," I finally say, finding my voice. "And hey, what I said earlier about it not being important, I didn't mean that. You will always be important to me."

He sighs, nodding. "I have a shift tonight, but if you need me, I'll find a way to be here. You still have my number?"

I chuckle once at his sarcastic, raised brow. He's wondering if I erased him entirely from my life. I could never. "Yes."

As he walks past me, he grabs my hand and squeezes. In that fractured moment, the simple two second touch, where every raw nerve sparks, proves that I, too, will never be over Paxton Turner.

He stops at the door and glances over his shoulder. "Will you have lunch with me tomorrow?"

Can I? Should I? A layer of guilt engulfs me as I think about Ari. I can't go on a date when my best friend is missing. There's too much going on in my head. I can't.

"Paxton," I start.

He holds his hand out. "First lunch. And then we'll go door to door, looking for anyone who might have seen Ari last night."

I chew on my inner cheek. It's a good idea, and at least I'll be doing something rather than waiting around. "Okay."

"Meet me at the precinct around noon?"

I nod, and he lets himself out.

Ari, don't give up, girl. We'll find you.

AN HOUR HAS PASSED since he left when my phone rings. It surprises me when I see who's calling. He's probably heard by now what happened.

"Hey, Chip." I sigh into the phone.

"Hey, kiddo. How are you doing?" I crack a smile at the once-familiar voice.

"I've had better days."

"Yeah. We got the BOLO for Carl Houston, and I saw the arrest report for Pearl." He pauses, his breaths heavy on the other end of the line. "But Pearl? I'm having a hard time accepting that she had anything to do with what happened to you. And the other girls? What the hell is wrong with people?"

It's a question I've been asking myself since I was eight.

Silence hangs for a moment. "Kali, there's no way you could have known. There's a special place in hell for people like her and Carl." I think hell is too luxurious for them. "I have to come to Austin to give a statement mid-morning. Are you going to be around? We can grab a coffee beforehand?"

My mind races with conflicting thoughts. I want nothing to do with anyone in Blackburn anymore, but this is Chip. Once I head back to Phoenix, I'm not sure if there will ever be a reason for me to come back. *Except Paxton.* And I don't even know what the heck is going on there yet.

"If it's too much, no worries, kid. You have a lot to process."

"No. I'd love to see you." This might be the last time I ever see him. "How about ten? I know how much you need your coffee before you can function," I say, surprising myself with a bit of humor.

"You know me too well. Text me the address where we can meet, and I'll be there."

Instead of searching for a nearby coffee shop, I text him the address of the hotel. They have a little café on the first floor, and with Carl still on the loose, I shouldn't be wandering around.

"Wow. I don't think I've ever seen you in regular clothes." Chip chuckles as he walks up to the table wearing khaki shorts and a striped polo. He puts his coffee down, and I stand to give him a hug.

"It's my day off. They told me I could come in street clothes. Lucky me," he says. His eyes scan the busy café, studying each person. "You here by yourself? Why didn't they assign someone to you?"

I shrug. "They offered. I'd rather them use their manpower finding Carl. And Ari." He twists his lips, disappointed. "I don't have any plans except to have lunch with Paxton."

"That's the guy you were with yesterday, right?" I nod, taking a drink of my coffee. "Are you guys together?"

After his confession in my hotel room, I don't even know.

I shake my head. "I don't even live in Texas anymore."

"Really? Where'd you move? What've you been doing?"

I give him a quick snapshot of my life, not really feeling like diving into my life. I thought I'd feel better being with someone that I've known forever, but it's just a reminder of Pearl. And how close I was to her. But Chip is close to her too. This has to have thrown him for a loop.

"I can't believe what Pearl did to me."

His lips form a hard line, and he shakes his head. "It's incomprehensible. I've seen a lot of shit in my days, but I've never..." His words trail off in a heated growl. "I'm so sorry I couldn't protect you."

Story of my life.

"Yeah. And now my best friend is missing. Did you ever see

Pearl with her ex, Carl? She says he found her, but I never saw a strange guy hanging around."

He looks at me over the rim of his coffee mug. He swallows. "Not that I was ever at her house, but I never saw him around town. Did you know he's a retired cop? From up in Oklahoma. Makes it worse that one of my brothers was able to do this. It's a shame."

"He was a cop?"

Chip nods and checks his watch. I glance at my phone to see the time. "How are you getting to the station?"

"I'll call a ride share."

"The heck you are. I can take you. It's almost eleven already, so you shouldn't have to wait long. I'd much rather you be sitting up at the station than having a stranger take you places."

"All right, Dad," I joke, finishing off my coffee. "I'm ready when you are."

He holds the door open, and I step outside, sliding my sunglasses down from the top of my head to shield my eyes from the never-ending sun.

"I'm parked down the street," he says, pointing to the left.

I nod and gesture for him to lead the way. As we walk, he glances down at me with a sad half-smile, and I wonder what thoughts are running through his head. We just had a great conversation.

"If I'm ever in town, I'd love to meet for coffee again," I say, linking my arm through his.

He pats my arm. "I'd like that." I'm surprised when I hear him sniff. I glance up to see the big guy wipe his eyes and then cover them with sunglasses. Is he crying? He clears his throat and says, "I'm right there."

A Blackburn cruiser is parked on the road. "Don't you have a normal car?" I joke.

"Nope," he replies, opening the back seat door for me.

"Well, this is one experience I never expected to have. You going to cuff me too?"

He chuckles. "Sorry. It's protocol. Considering we're going to the station, it's best I don't break it."

I settle onto the hot black faux leather seat, grateful for the sun hitting the other side. Playfully, I grab onto the grill separating the front and back seats. "But officer, I swear I didn't mean to run down the street naked. It was so hot." Glancing at the seat, I think about all the people who've sat here and wonder if I'm occupying the exact spot that a murderer once did. How surreal. "Ouch!" I yelp, holding my hand to my neck where it stings, receiving a familiar pinch. "What the hell was that?" The door slams shut. Chip jumps into the front seat, starting the car and pulling out. "Chip!" I scream. He ignores me. I search for the handle, but there isn't one. My purse is gone too. He must've snatched it before shutting the door.

"Calm down, Kali. You're going to be okay."

Each second that passes, I fight, feeling myself being pulled under. Why is he doing this? Suddenly, clarity, like a beam of light piercing through a foggy patch, brightens my mind. I'm not in a seat where a murderer sat, I'm in a car with a murderer.

CHAPTER 42

Paxton

"I THOUGHT you were headed out to lunch," Cates says when I walk into his office.

I thought so too.

Flicking my wrist, I check the time again even though I checked it seconds ago. I'm pretty sure I said noon. It's one o'clock. Riggs nudges my side. "Yeah, I agree. We've waited long enough." Zero texts from her either. I look up at Cates, staring at me as I try to call her again. My gut twists with unease. "Something's wrong. Kali said she'd meet me here, and now she won't answer her texts or calls. Calls go straight to voicemail."

"Martinez put someone on her?"

I shake my head. "She refused."

"Call Martinez and head over to her hotel. I'll keep a lookout for her here."

My fingers tighten around the steering wheel as I race toward her hotel. My mind floods with unsettling possibilities as I search left and right, scanning the streets, hoping I'll see her.

There's no way she flew back home. After learning the truth from my mom, I wouldn't blame her, though. The thought keeps popping up, explaining the silent phone. But that makes little sense. She wouldn't leave knowing her friend was still missing. Martinez is working on checking with the airline, just in case.

I pull up in front of the hotel and let Riggs out. If anyone can find her, it'll be him. It takes a few minutes to hunt down the manager and get her to agree to open her hotel room door. As soon as I walk into her room, I know she didn't leave. Her bags are open and rummaged through. Just like yesterday.

Dread coils my insides, squeezing like a vise. I'd rather she left me than face the possibilities of what happened to her, especially with Carl out there. I jab my finger at the elevator button five times, frustration mounting with each passing second. Once the doors open to the lobby, I release Riggs.

"Find Kali."

Without hesitation, he darts off. He knows her scent, her sound. I follow him closely as he dashes to a small restaurant next to the lobby. His nose guides him to a table where two people sit. The pair startle at the sudden intrusion of a dog sniffing around the table and then sitting. She was here this morning. I pull up Kali's picture, flagging down a passing server.

"Did you see this woman this morning?"

Studying the photo, she says, "I think so. Her hair is different, but I'm pretty certain it was her. She was with a guy."

My mind bounces with who the hell it could be. "Did she look like she was distressed? Can you describe the guy?"

"Not at all. They were here for about an hour. Laughing. He has a really deep laugh. I remember glancing their way a couple times because it was so loud." Who the hell was she with? "He was a big guy. Older than her. I'd guess in his late forties. They just had coffee."

"Anything else you can tell me about him?"

The server furrows her brows, tapping her chin, deep in thought. "Hmm. Brown hair. Had a striped polo on with khaki shorts. Seemed like a friendly guy." She winces and then shrugs. "I'm sorry. There's not anything else I remember about him. I know they left together. I overheard him say he'd give her a ride when I was picking up the check."

What the fuck? A ride where?

"Find your manager and tell him the Texas Rangers are going to show up any minute. They'll need any video you have from this morning."

Her eyes widen. "Okay," she says, hurrying off.

I call Martinez on the way out the door and tell him what I just learned.

"I'll send some guys over, but are you sure she just didn't meet up with a friend?"

No, I'm not sure. She's been gone for over a year. I don't know who her friends are anymore. Ted comes to mind. He fits the description, so I hang up with Martinez and call him.

"Hey, Ted, it's Paxton Turner."

"Hey, Paxton, how's it going?"

"Not good. You don't happen to be in town, are you?"

There's a pause. "No. Why?" His voice gets deeper, sensing something is wrong.

I tell him the quick version about Kali being here and Ari going missing. And then I shudder internally, knowing what's coming next. "We also found out who buried Kali alive."

"Who?" he barks.

Ted's a big guy. And I have a feeling his bite is bigger than his bark. I take a deep breath and blow it out. "Remember Kali talking about Pearl? It was her and her ex-husband." I hear Amy's gasp in the background. "And that's not it."

"What aren't you telling us?"

"Pearl is my mom."

"It was your mom?" he roars into the phone. The guilt is already eating me alive, so his words can't make it worse. I hear Amy in the background asking something, but he hushes her. "And now she's missing?"

"Everyone is out looking for her. I promise we'll find her."

"You better," he warns.

"Leave that poor boy alone," Amy says in the background.

"Keep us updated," he says, and then hangs up without letting me reply.

The distant hum of traffic surrounds me as I sit in my car trying to figure out who else it might be. I can't imagine she'd leave with anyone knowing how much danger she's in. A chill runs down my spine, afraid she didn't leave on her own. Martinez's text pulls me back to reality, demanding I get to the station, stat—they found who she left with.

CHAPTER 43

Kali

"KALI, WAKE UP."

I take a minute between the time I hear my name to open my eyes. My hands are bound behind me, and I'm sitting in a chair. In front of me, at the far end of a lengthy table, sits Chip. A gun rests right in front of him, a silent, implicit threat. His eyes are red and swollen as if this were causing him pain.

"It was you," I hiss, the accusation escaping my lips.

He bows his head and nods.

"Why?" I scream, tugging against my restraint. "Why are you doing this to me?"

Tears shimmer in his eyes. *No! He doesn't get to cry.* "Please calm down, Kali. I promise I won't hurt you."

I seize up, a deer-caught-in-the-headlights response. How much more condescending can he be? How on earth am I supposed to calm down? With a level voice, I respond, "Besides the fact that you've already hurt me, I'm tied to a chair after being drugged! Again!" Okay, so my voice didn't stay level. I'm screaming by the end. "Why would I believe you?"

My attention flickers to the gun and back to him. He catches the shift in my focus and sighs. Panic surges through me when he stands up, taking the gun with him. I jerk to the left, away from him, as if the inches of space between us will somehow stop a bullet. He places the gun in front of me and returns to his seat. I pinch my brows together. I'm not complaining. It's not within his arm's reach anymore. But it's not of any use to me either.

"Where's Ari?" My voice trembles as I demand an answer.

"The other girl and your friend, that was Carl."

None of this makes sense.

"You want to know why, so I'm going to tell you. Then I'll let you go."

Let me go? I can almost taste the skepticism hitting the back of my throat. There is no way he's going to spill his guts and then allow me to walk out of here like I just left a friend's house.

I keep quiet, my heartbeat echoing in my ears.

He licks his lips, and a heavy sigh escapes him before he begins. "Beth was my high school sweetheart. Or Pearl, as you call her." My eyes fly open wide. What the actual hell? They've known each other this entire time? "I always knew I couldn't keep her. She was this wildfire, and I was the chubby kid in school who played oboe. Man, I loved her. I could feel it in my bones. But as I expected, she broke up with me when we graduated but kept me at arm's length, just enough to leave me with hope. Until she met Paxton's dad. He was able to tame her wildfire."

It's hard to accept he's talking about Pearl. I replay the count-less times we have all been in the same room, and I never sensed any history between them. "After Paxton's dad died, she reached out to me. I had lost weight, became a cop, and was confident in myself. It was going to be our time. There was hope again."

I glare at him like the pathetic man he is, recognizing the predictable narrative of a man driven by love…blah, blah, blah. Anticipating the next part of the story—she marries the man Paxton despised—I tune him out, scanning the room we're in. Pictures of a family adorn the walls and various decorations catch my eye. Whose house is this? And where are they?

As he mentions Paxton's name, my attention snaps back to him. "He was an asshole to that kid. A real jerk. And while his dad tamed Beth's wildfire, Carl pissed on it. I couldn't stay and watch him destroy that family. That's when I moved to Blackburn."

Why didn't Paxton tell me about Chip? Did he recognize him when we were at Pearl's house? Paxton would've been a teenager when Chip left town. He should've known who he was.

The entire sob story isn't evoking any sympathy from me. Quite the opposite. He's a loser consumed by an unhealthy obsession with his high school girlfriend. She took advantage of him, probably by making empty promises that led us here.

"How?" I ask. I didn't question this when I was with Pearl, but now, knowing that Paxton grew up with Chip and said nothing, I don't know who or what to believe. "Paxton said he hadn't talked to his mom in years until she popped up at his work—after everything happened. But how was Pearl so positive that he'd find me?"

He twists his fingers in front of him on the table. "I had seen an article with him and his dog and showed Beth. She was excited to learn he was close, but she figured he'd want nothing to do with her. She wanted to see what he was up to, so she had me put a tracker on his Jeep. That was so long ago, she forgot we had even done that until he showed up in the diner. She had me pull the last year of info to see if he had been to the diner before. We found out that he spent most of his weekends at the ranch."

Isn't that illegal? He's a cop, for God's sake. She gets crazier by the minute. And he gets more pathetic.

"So, did you at least get the girl in the end?" I ask with a snide tone, lifting a brow, remembering their flirting. "Was it worth ruining your life?" A swift shadow of anger sweeps across his face. His jaw twitches and his eyes darken.

There's the guy who buried me alive.

"I did until Carl showed up," he says between clenched teeth.

"Boo-fucking-hoo. You still buried me alive!" I scream, letting my anger roll off me in waves. "You started this horror by putting me in a box and listened to me scream and plead not to do it. How can you sit there and be okay with your life?"

He shoots up, and the chair falls over from the force. "I'm not! Your screams haunt my dreams every night. They will haunt me until the day I die." His admission hangs heavy in the air, and there's a tiny glimmer of satisfaction inside me. I hope he lives a long life. "You weren't supposed to wake up. Beth said you'd still be sleeping and wouldn't be down there for long by the time Paxton found you."

I squeeze my eyes shut, attempting to shake off the unbelievable ridiculousness of his words. "I can't believe you went along with this plan. You're a cop! You took an oath to protect people, not bury them!" I swallow the knot in my throat. "There is no way you would've known for sure that he would find me."

"We had a plan for that. We would've tipped the police off to your whereabouts if he hadn't found you by late afternoon."

The thought process they put into this ruse is beyond comprehensible. "If I wasn't supposed to be awake yet, why torment me? Three shovels at a time! Why?" My voice scratches from screaming so loud.

He picks up the chair and drops back down into it, scrubbing his face. "It wasn't meant to torment you. It was a way for me to focus on something else. Almost a mechanical movement. It was the moments in between that I regretted every second. But I was in too deep, so I forced myself to continue. It wasn't intentional."

"I don't believe you. For something not intentional, how did it become a thing?" The anger radiates off me. "You or Carl tormented me with that three times bullshit over and over."

He rubs his temple and sighs. "The college stunt? That was Beth's idea. She figured it was a trigger for you. That was me. You were pulling away from Paxton, and Beth was worried. She believed that a small push would bring you back to him. They manipulated me over and over, using my fear to fulfill her dream."

She's a narcissistic psychopath.

And he's her minion.

"Where does Carl fit into all of this? Why did Pearl say he did this to me?"

"She was trying to protect me."

I roll my eyes. How noble of her.

"Carl must've bugged Beth's place, because he knew about what we did to you when he showed up one day. He wanted Beth back. So, he blackmailed both of us. Her into going back to him, and me into telling him everything that happened. Every detail. We made sure not to tell him you had won the lottery, though."

I blink twice. "Thanks?" Give them the friend of the year award.

His finger pokes at the table, getting defensive. "If he would've known, he would've found a way to get that money out of you."

"Why did he take Shanna Clark? Why did he have to kill her?"

"Beth tried to run away. She went and saw Paxton that day to say goodbye. Carl got wind of it. It was his way of punishing Beth. He kept reminding her that it was her fault, she made him do it. It was his way of controlling her. As long as she stayed with him, he'd not do it again."

"Pearl was with him a couple days ago, flying back from Hawaii. She was *still* with him. So, why did he take Ari?"

He shakes his head. "I'm not sure. She told me she saw you on the flight when he pulled that stupid stunt, knocking three times. They got into a huge argument afterward. She told him to get out, that she never wanted to see him again. He got physical with her, so she locked herself in the bathroom and called me. By the time I arrived, he was gone, and that's the last time she saw him."

They're all sick.

The room falls silent. It seems his energy has drained as well. What's his next play? If he truly is sorry, then why am I here, tied to a chair? Why would he go through the trouble of kidnapping, drugging, and tying me up just to apologize?

"How could you act like nothing happened when I saw you after?"

His mouth forms a hard line as he shakes his head, shrugs, and then shakes his head again, telling me there's no reasonable answer. He finally says, "I had to tell myself that you were doing great, that you were getting the life you always wanted."

I let out a bitter laugh. "A life with nightmares, thanks to you. I could've had that life without the added PTSD."

"If I could go back and make different choices, I would."

"But it's too late for that. You know what happens next." He's going to jail right next to Pearl. I look around the room and then back at him. "They probably know by now who took me."

"I told you I wasn't going to hurt you."

He pushes his chair back, walks toward me, then unties the knots. As soon as the rope loosens and my hands are free, I lunge forward and grab the gun. Putting the table between us, I slide around and keep the gun pointed at his chest.

"Don't get any closer to me," I warn.

The gun is heavy in my hands, so I keep both wrapped around the handle, steadying it. He casually walks back to his chair and sits down, leaning on one elbow with his hands folded in his lap.

"I'm going to walk out of here," I threaten, "and I will shoot you if you come after me."

After a simple nod from him, I run out the front door, glancing over my shoulder once to see him staying seated. It's not until I'm outside that I see that we're in the middle of nowhere. Heavy wooded trees surround the house, and the long winding road disappears in between them. I run to the police cruiser, searching the front seats for my purse. I spot it on the floorboard on the passenger side. Again, with a quick glance, checking that he's not coming, I run around the car, open the door, and grab my purse. My fingers tremble as I power on my phone. The seconds feel like eternity. My heart pounds against my ribs. When the apple finally disappears and the phone lights up, I call Paxton.

"Where are you?" he snaps.

"I...I don't know. He took me to a secluded wooded area."

"Chip?"

"Yes. It was him. He's the one who kidnapped me. Well, not Ari or the other girl, just me. He's taken me to some ranch."

Someone says something in the background, but I can't make out what they said.

"Martinez says that he found your location. We're on our way. Are you hurt? Where is Chip now?"

Bang!

I jump and jerk my gaze up to the house where a single gunshot rang out. The air around me gets eerily quiet, as if nature itself is holding its breath. Noooo! I shake my head violently. My head screams at me to run toward the house, but my feet stay rooted, freezing me in place. I squeeze my eyes shut. This is why he wasn't worried about what would happen next. There was no next for him.

"What was that?"

"Kali!"

"Answer me!"

It takes a moment for me to regain my senses and hear Paxton yelling through the phone. "I'm here. I'm okay."

"Was that a gunshot?"

Tears roll down my cheeks as emotions get clogged in my throat. "I think..." I hiccup. "I think it came from in the house," I mutter, staring at the open front door.

"Was Chip in the house?" he murmurs, understanding the heaviness.

"Yes."

CHAPTER 44

Kali

WITH MY BACK to the cruiser, I sit in the shaded part on the driver's side and wait. The keys to the car were nowhere to be seen, and I wasn't about to go inside and see if they were in Chip's pocket. I stare at the open front door and mourn the man that I would memorize a dad joke for every morning to make him smile. To the man, that would bring me yellow roses for my birthday every year.

Say goodbye to the man who buried me alive.

Still, a half hour later, I'm praying he'll walk out. But he's not and never will. My hatred for Pearl grows tenfold. Her game has spiraled out of control, now leaving two people dead and another one missing, if not dead already, and a madman on the loose.

I muffle my sobs with my hand, not sure why. There isn't anyone around. Maybe it's because I'm mad at myself for feeling sympathy for Chip. He doesn't deserve it. He didn't deserve to be driven to death, either.

He was desperate.

Desperate for Pearl's love.

At the sound of tires on gravel, I stand, dusting off my jeans, relieved that Paxton found me. I stare at an old beat-up blue Chevy pulling up the long driveway. Not Paxton. Or the police. Shit.

The truck comes to a stop, and I have to squint my eyes to see who it is, the sun bright overhead. I stare at the older man as he slinks out of his truck. There's a moment of vague familiarity before I'm thrown back to the plane. To seat 55B. The haunted eyes bore into me, his expression still as flat as a deflated balloon.

It's him.

Carl.

I grab the gun in the front seat and point it at him. He laughs, a bitter sound that echoes around the trees as he shakes his head and opens the back door. *Come on, Paxton, where are you? I don't want to shoot someone.* My heart sinks when he yanks Ari from the back seat, holding a gun to her hip. Duct tape covers her mouth, and her red eyes widen when they see me. Her hands are taped together in front of her. Thank God she's alive.

"Let her go!" I scream, keeping the gun pointed at him.

"Put your gun down, Kali," he says, almost put out. I shake my head. Ari's muffled cries get louder when he puts the gun to her head. "I'll kill her before you ever pull the trigger."

Countless scenarios run through my head like a quick film reel. She dies. I die. We both die. The cops get here. He dies. Paxton dies. My hands tremble, and my mind races with fear and desperation.

What am I supposed to do?

Ari's eyes plead with mine, begging me to find a solution. I'm trying! Carl smirks, the twisted satisfaction clear in his eyes, knowing he has us trapped and I don't have any options. I jerk my head around to the house, the front door at least twenty feet away.

"You can run. But your friend here dies if you do."

"Chip is inside," I say, trying to deter him.

He leans to the left, looking at the wide-open door past me, and then glances at the windows. "You sure? Is he alive?" His eyes drop to the gun in my hand.

"I didn't kill him," I scream in defense, but then bite my tongue. That was dumb. I might have scared him if he knew I could use this thing.

"But he's dead." He tilts his head when I don't reply. "That doesn't surprise me. He's always let his feelings get under his skin. He couldn't handle the guilt." Unlike the madman in front of me. Carl has zero remorse for killing that woman.

Just like he won't for us.

I lower the gun in painful realization; I'm no match for him. I'm not going to choose to live so Ari can die. Time would never erase that pain. "I have money. Lots of it. If you let us go, you'll be set for life." He contemplates it for a moment, but then narrows his eyes.

"If you had money, you wouldn't be working. Especially as a glorified airline waitress. Put the gun on the ground." It'd be pointless to explain everything. He won't believe it.

What would Zander do? *Evaluate the threat. Can you use anything for self-defense? Memorize your surroundings. Is there a place to hide?*

I squat down, placing the gun on the ground. In my other hand, I grab a fist full of dirt and gravel. I could throw it in his eyes when I get close.

When I stand, Carl gives me a knowing glare, as if looking at a petulant child. "Drop the dirt, Kali." I groan, releasing my fist. "That's it. Now, walk over here."

I do as he says but keep my steps as slow as possible. I'm not sure what his plans are, but the longer I can keep him here, the better our odds are. Paxton and the police are on their way. They have to be close.

"Faster, you little bitch." The rushed emotion in his voice surprises me, but when he looks over his shoulder toward the street, I wonder if he already knows that the cavalry is on their way.

When I make it to them, I rush to wrap my arms around Ari. "It'll be okay," I whisper into her ear. Her body shakes against me.

"Enough," he barks, pulling us apart. "Grab the shovels in the back." He pushes me forward with the head of the gun shoved in between my shoulder blades.

For a moment, I close my eyes, horrified at what he plans on doing. He hasn't said yet, but I can guess we're digging our own graves. I round the back of the truck and lower the tailgate. Tears prickle the inside of my eyes, and I blink them back, needing to stay strong. I am not going to dig my hole and lay in it, giving up.

I'm going to fight. Save both of us.

I grab the shovels and wait for his next instruction. It's no surprise when he tells me to walk into the heavy lined trees surrounding the property. Maybe he doesn't know that the police are on their way. Maybe he doesn't care.

I'm ahead of Ari and Carl, my eyes constantly scanning the area, looking for anything that might help us. I glance back to make sure Ari is okay, but Carl motions with his gun to keep going. The sound of sticks breaking and crunching dead leaves is the only sound around as we navigate through the trees. I swat away patches of gnats and spiderwebs as I try to memorize the path we're taking while listening for sirens or cars. At first, I was dragging the shovels to leave a trail, but Carl's not a stupid man and caught on quick and shot his gun once in the air. My knees buckled, and I tripped on a rock as I looked back to make sure he hadn't shot Ari. I yelp as my left palm catches the corner of a sharp stick.

"Get up!" he yells. "And pick up those damn shovels." Tears run down Ari's face, but she nods to tell me she's okay. "Next time, your friend here will have a hole inside her."

I shake out the pain and stand back up, making sure that the shovels don't touch the ground as we continue our trek into the woods.

The crunching behind me stops, and I turn around. Carl has stopped and is staring at the trail we came from. He turns in a slow circle, staring through the trees. Did he hear something? Is this the moment I've been waiting for? It's time to fight. My grip tightens around the shovel in my right hand as I drop the other one. With every ounce of adrenaline I can muster, I swing the shovel like a bat, hitting Carl square in the head.

He moans and falls to the ground, and I hit him one more time in the head. Zander's words echo in my mind: "*Immobilize the threat and run like hell.*" I grab the gun he dropped, and Ari and I take off running. I didn't account for the fact that through the panic, we didn't care which way we were going. Away was most important. I pull her behind a large oak tree and pull off the tape over her mouth. She draws in a bunch of shallow breaths as I fumble with the tape around her wrists.

"Do you think he's dead?" she whispers.

Both our faces jerk up when we hear footsteps rustle over the brush off in the distance. I put my finger over my mouth and hold the gun out, ready to shoot.

"You're a lot tougher than I gave you credit for." Carl's voice grates out in anger. He's not close, but close enough that if we run, he'll hear us and catch us. I pull Ari down so we're squatting. "But you can't hide from me. I've hunted animals my entire life, and when I catch you, I'm not going to bury you. I'm going to make you suffer, stuff you, and stick you on my mantle as my most prized possession."

I grip the gun tighter. His voice grows closer, and the crunch of leaves becomes more defining. He can throw out disgusting threats all he wants, but I have the gun, asshole. My heart pounds against my ribcage as I focus on his steps, each one getting closer. Ari squeezes my arm, and I nod. I know. I'm going to shoot him.

"Gotcha!"

We both scream in surprise as Carl jumps out from behind a tree in front of us. I gather my wits, point the gun, and squeeze the trigger.

Click.

I tighten my finger around the trigger again.

Click.

Nothing happens. No. No. No! This can't be happening.

Carl's laughter bounces off the trees surrounding us as he pulls out another gun from under his shirt. He waves his gun back and forth in the air, taunting me.

"Just in case I underestimated you."

"Please, let her go," I plead as the fight drains from me. "Please. You can do whatever you want with me."

"What? No. I'm not leaving you," Ari mutters.

He laughs again, flashing his yellow teeth.

"See. She wants to die too." He walks toward us, and I stand in front of Ari. She needs a chance to run. This is all my fault. She would've never been in this position if I had died in that box.

Out of nowhere, a brown streak of fur darts past us, tackling Carl to the ground. Growls and screams fill the air.

Ari and I both gasp at the horrible sounds. She screams, "Run!" grabbing my hand. We both take off as fast as our legs will go, hurdling fallen trees and trying to keep our footing so we don't fall. My legs burn as the sounds of Carl's yells get further and further away from us.

Bang.

The sound of a dog's loud whimper stops me in my tracks. "Nooo!" I scream, bending over, not able to catch my breath.

"We have to keep running," Ari begs, trying to pull me, but I shake my head, my legs paralyzed, my heart breaking in half.

Paxton appears with a half-dozen other officers, all with their guns out, through the clearing ahead. "Get them out of here." He barks out the order, still running full speed ahead. I watch him until he's disappeared into the trees.

Another shot rings out, and my stomach twists in fear.

Two officers run over. "Are you okay to keep going?" an officer asks.

Ari nods. Me, I'm not okay. I glance back to the thick brush, not seeing or hearing anything before they usher us back to the house.

This is not how it ends.

My hero can't die.

CHAPTER 45

Kali

THE FRANTIC SCENE continues to unfold as I stand, rooted in one spot, staring into the woods. Waiting and praying. They've already tried to check me out at an ambulance, but I brushed them off. I'm fine. Physically, I'm not damaged, emotionally is another story. A group of EMTs ran into the woods minutes ago, carrying a stretcher.

Nobody will tell me anything.

All I want to know is if Riggs and Paxton are okay.

Where are they?

My heart stops, and I hold my breath when I notice movement between the trees. A cluster of officers and EMTs gather around a stretcher. I strain to catch sight of the figure within. Denim-covered legs come into focus. I rush over, hoping to find Carl dead. Bile rises in my throat when I catch a glimpse of Carl's face. Or what used to be his face. I have to turn away. But it's too late. The haunting image sears into my brain.

An officer rushes over as I double over. "You all right?"

I nod, covering my mouth with my hand. "Please tell me if Riggs is okay? And where is Paxton?"

He juts his chin forward, and his gaze moves over my shoulder.

I spin around, finding Paxton and Riggs walking side by side. I run over and fall to my knees in front of Riggs, lifting my hand to touch him but not knowing if I should. He sits, and his dark eyes stare at me, his tongue falling out the side of his mouth as he takes quick breaths.

"You're bleeding. Where was he hit?" I ask, looking up to Paxton and back down to a blood-covered Riggs. I wouldn't even know where to begin. There's blood everywhere.

"He wasn't hit."

"But I heard him yelp."

"It could've been from the sound of the gun. But I searched him from head to toe. Carl missed. He's good."

I tilt my head back and blow out the breath I'd been holding since I heard him yelp. The relief is immeasurable. I feel an ugly cry coming on.

Paxton helps me up and lets me get it out, holding me tight to his chest. He murmurs into my ear, "It's over, Kalico. You're free."

Chip died from a single gunshot to the head.

Carl died in the ambulance. I'd never wished anyone dead until I saw him pull Ari out of the truck. Ari and I share tearful glances, our emotions mingling in the confined space. It's a strange mixture of sorrow and relief.

"Why didn't you ever tell me about what happened to you?" Ari asks, wiping tears off her cheek with the back of her hand.

We're in the back of Martinez's black SUV, headed to the police station. Before we left the house, she told me that Carl was too busy trying to track me down that he hadn't harmed her. Yet. She didn't know what he planned on doing, but I can guess it was to bury both of us. He tracked Chip's car, saw him go to Austin and a rural residence, and took a chance I was there. Martinez grumbles in the front about how small towns don't always put trackers on their cruisers or they would've found me sooner.

Why is it so easy to track someone? There will be a weekly care check in my future.

"It's a chapter in my life I never wanted to revisit." She nods in understanding. "I never thought it would catch up to me, let alone put someone close to me in danger. I'm so, so sorry."

Her arms wrap around me in a reassuring embrace. "This is not your fault," she murmurs, the weight of guilt still lingering despite her words. "Even if you would've told me what happened, that was two years ago. I wouldn't have done anything different." I rest my head against her shoulder.

"Yesterday, when I woke up and saw you hadn't come in…" The sinking feeling in my stomach hasn't yet subsided. "I knew something was wrong. What happened that night?"

"After Jay left me, I continued talking with a guy. I think his name was Garrin. Or Darrin. Something like that. He works at some tech company here. He was cool at first, but the more he drank…" She cringes. "The more he became a dick. So, I left him at the bar and started walking back to the hotel. It was only a block or two away. But that's the last thing I remember. I don't think I was out long because when I woke up, it was still dark outside. I was tied up in an old shack. I thought I was going to die." She squeezes my hand harder. *I know that feeling.*

"I wonder if Carl was watching you and slipped something into your drink."

She shrugs. "When I left, I was a little more buzzed than I thought I should be. I just chalked it up to strong drinks. You know I always try to keep my drink close to me. We were sitting at the bar the entire time, talking. And it was really packed in there, so I don't know…" Her voice trails off, and I leave her to her thoughts.

Mine are a jumbled mess. There's a lot to unfold from the last forty-eight hours.

Mainly, Pearl.

A ruse. A *deadly* ruse.

All to get me and her son together.

The worst part is that she didn't regret it. In her eyes, her plan worked. I just don't understand that level of evil.

"Thank you for saving me," Ari whispers.

I sniffle and let out a sarcastic chuckle. "I didn't do much. In fact, I made things worse."

She pulls away, pinning me with a sincerity that cuts through the shadows of doubt. "He was ready to give up looking for you. He was getting more agitated, throwing things and screaming. This morning, he told me he was done waiting." The weight of her words sends shivers down my spine. He planned to kill her, with or without me. Martinez's eyes meet mine in the rearview mirror, his expression softening. "There is no way I could've fought him myself. I tried. I tried, but he was too big. But you fought for us."

Tears fall down my cheek. I don't feel like the hero. I feel like I caused this. That is where the fight came in—deep inside the guilt. I owed it to her. Dr. Betty would disagree. I can already hear her soft words. *"Responsibility lies solely with the person who chose to hurt you."*

She's right. Pearl is to blame.

Chip is to blame.

Carl is to blame.

I am the survivor.

The rest of the ride is driven in a solemn hush, embraced in each other's arms. When we arrive at the station, a swarm of news reporters gathers at the doors. A protective barrier of officers ushers us through the glass doors. The second we step into the lobby, Ari's parents and twin sister scream her name and rush over to her, encasing her in a tight circle.

I flash her a bittersweet smile as I keep walking. A pang of longing resurfaces, reminding me of all the times I had to stand on the sidelines during school events where moms, dads, and grand-parents came for the day. As an adult, it doesn't hurt any less.

Martinez joins me and wraps his arm around my shoulder. "You did great out there. Glad you're okay." I lean my head against his arm, welcoming the sentiment regardless of if he's doing it because he feels sorry for me. It's all I've got at the moment, and I'll take it. He stops walking and turns toward me. "I was also wrong about Paxton." His words catch me off guard. I don't imagine he's the type of man to eat his words often.

"Well, in a way, you were right about it being linked to him."

"Eh." He bobs his head a little. "I still had my doubts. But he proved me wrong. He's a great cop and a good man." He's still wrong. He's the *best* man. *Even though I haven't figured out if he'll ever be my man again.*

"Kali!"

The call of my name snaps my attention upward. Amy barrels down the long hallway, Ted hot on her heels. Her arms open wide, and then she engulfs me in the warmest, tightest hug ever. If my heart could burst open, it would.

Someone cares about me.

Ted joins in, cocooning the both of us with his large embrace. "Thank you," I cry. "Thank you for being here."

"Sweetheart, when we found out, there's no other place we could be. We've been here all afternoon, worried sick about you." She pulls back, scanning me for any signs of distress. "Are you okay?"

I manage a nod. "I still can't believe it was Chip. But he's..." *Gone.* The word gets caught in my throat, refusing to come out.

Amy nods, her eyes fill with empathy as she wipes away my tears. "We know." I sniff a couple times. Ted walks over to the front desk, grabs the box of tissues, and hands it to me. I take one with a grateful yet sad smile.

"I was so scared," I confess, my voice trembling. "But Zander's words kept me fighting, kept me searching for ways to escape. If it wasn't for my time with you guys, I don't know if I would've found the strength to fight him."

She huffs, shaking her head. "That's hogwash. Your entire base is built on strength and determination since you were a child. Every time life knocked you off, you came back stronger. Zander might have taught you how to physically fight, but mentally? You're the strongest person I've ever known." Her voice cracks with emotion, and I can see the fierce love and pride in her eyes.

"Oh my gosh," I cry, falling into her arms again. "Thank you. Thank you for believing in me. Being here for me. It means more to me than you'll ever know."

"We know, kid. We know," Ted says, joining in.

I will feel this hug for the rest of my life.

Amy pulls back and snatches a tissue, blotting her eyes. Ted smiles and does the same thing. Then Amy blows out a shaky breath. "We know you have a lot going on, but we'd like to have dinner with you before you leave town," she says.

I grab her hand, still needing her touch.

"Of course. I'd love that."

Ted bends down, planting a kiss on top of my head. "I'm proud of you."

Overwhelmed with gratitude for this unexpected support system, there's no way I can stop the tears. "You guys," I cry, pulling them into another hug. "I love y'all."

"We love you, too," Amy cries with me.

After our emotional moment, they say goodbye with a promise to meet again before I leave. As far as when that will be, I haven't thought about what happens tomorrow. Then Martinez grabs me to make a formal statement of everything that transpired.

Walking out of the conference room, there's a sense of freedom buzzing throughout my veins. The finality of the previous two years is liberating, the weight of fear being released. But what's next? I glance back into the police station.

Martinez walks up to me. "He's waiting for you back in Detective Cates's office," he says.

My eyes drop to the dirt and blood covered Rolling Stones T-shirt and ripped shorts that must've caught on something at some point when we were running. The only thing remotely clean on me is my hand where the paramedics bandaged a shallow cut. I look like a hot mess right now. Maybe it'll be better if I get cleaned up first.

He nudges me, reading my hesitation. "He won't care."

I nod, taking a deep breath before turning to walk toward the office, my heart pounding in my chest. My pace is slow and steady as I try to figure out what I'm going to say. What do I even want? Despite the distance and time, my heart still quickens whenever I'm around Paxton. But it's not up to me now.

I had that choice a year ago, and I didn't choose him.

I spot Paxton talking with Liam in the doorway to the office. Liam acknowledges me with a smile and a quick thumbs-up before walking away and disappearing into another office across the hallway.

"Hey," Paxton says in his sexy, deep voice, leaning on the door-frame. He's freshly showered in street clothes, his curls still wet. He smells like soap, and it makes me wonder if I smell like sweat and dirt. I chuckle to myself. You can take the girl out of the ground, but you can't take the ground out of the girl. "What's so funny?"

I match his posture on the opposite doorframe. The tips of our toes brush against each other. "Nothing. Just wishing I had taken a shower."

"You look beautiful."

I blush, biting the inside of my cheek as the air charges with unspoken tension. I shift on my feet and glance around the floor. I jerk my head back to him. "Where's Riggs?"

"The vet took him. They called and confirmed that he's in perfect health and they're cleaning him up." I let out a sigh of relief. I couldn't help but wonder if Paxton had missed something. Riggs has so much damn hair. I was still worried. "How's Ari?"

"Considering everything, she's doing all right. She left with her parents. She's going to take some time off."

"How about you? When are you leaving?"

His penetrating gaze makes me fidget. "I'm going to stay for a little while. I have some unfinished business." I swallow hard. "I think."

He lifts a brow. "You think?"

The heat from my cheeks spread. "I hope?"

My heart sinks when he drops his head. I'm too late. We said goodbye. Why should I expect him to drop everything for me because I'm here now?

"It's okay," I whisper, blinking back tears that are trying to form.

"It's not what you're thinking." He reaches for my hands. "I just—"

"Just kiss the girl!" Liam yells, interrupting him from across the hall, and Paxton can't help but chuckle.

Thankfully he listens to Liam.

The kiss is urgent and deep as he pushes me against the doorframe. I wrap my arms around his neck with the same urgency, letting go of any doubts. His hand presses into the curve of my back, as if not able to get close enough.

"All right, all right. That's enough. You are at work," Liam jokes.

Paxton chuckles against my swollen lips and pulls back, resting his forehead against mine as we catch our breath, the warmth of his skin creating an intimate connection in the unlikely setting. I make a mental note to give Liam a fantastic birthday present next year.

Paxton stands taller, cradling my face with his hands, and his brown eyes search mine for an answer.

"Will you ever be able to get over how we got together? Will you always question the validity of our relationship? Because I need to know now."

I thought about this. A lot. Last night in my hotel room, in the night's quiet where sleep eluded me, thoughts of the lengths Pearl went through to get me with her son played over and over. *Is that really why we're together?* Because of her? I've been introduced to people in the past, and just because there was an introduction, it didn't mean there was instant chemistry. She did not force my heart to fall in love. It did it of its own accord.

"I didn't fall in love with you because of what your mom did," I say, our eyes locked, my expression serious, but then a smile plays on my lips. "I fell in love with you because of your dog."

Epilogue

PAXTON

"YOU DO NOT GET the middle seat," I say, snapping at Riggs to keep moving. Kali's laugh echoes behind me. I never imagined I'd be competing for my girlfriend's attention with my own dog. If he could talk, I'm sure he'd be cursing under his breath, plotting his revenge as he settles by the window. "You're lucky I didn't stick you in a crate."

"Aww. Be nice to him," Kali says, giving me a playful poke in the back. Of course, she's always on his side. *I know my place in this relationship.* He's become our spoiled rotten kid.

I lift her carry-on and stow it above us as she slides into the middle seat. She rubs Riggs's ears, and I swear he throws a spiteful glance my way. I throw it right back when the second I sit down, her hand slides into mine.

"Are you sure your grams and pops are okay with me coming for Christmas?"

More than sure.

We've been officially dating for six months now, and Grams has been bugging me five of those months to meet her.

Kali took a couple of weeks off work. If you ask her where she lives, she still says Phoenix, but she's in my bed every night that she's not flying. She's mentioned to people that she's moving back to Austin. I'm not pushing because she needs to do this on her own timeline, and as long as she's with me doing it, I can be patient.

Despite my mom, everything has worked out. I don't even care if she thinks we're together because of her while she rots away in prison. She wasn't lying when she said she was sick. But fortunately, the tumor was benign, and she'll live a long life behind bars. Where she belongs.

But it's time Kali meets the family. The part that I love dearly.

"Oh shit," I snap. "I knew I had forgotten something," I mutter. She tilts her head, confused.

"I forgot to tell them you were coming."

She gasps. "What? They don't know?" I can't help but laugh at her panic. It's cute. I've already reassured her they're excited to meet her. Someday she'll realize that she's worthy of love and she's not alone in this world. She slaps me on the chest. "You're a horrible boyfriend. I'm so nervous. What if they hate me?" Her fears run deep.

"They will love you. Just like I do."

We land in Grand Rapids but still have an hour drive ahead of us. Snow blankets the fields on either side of the highway, glistening under the sunlight and turning the landscape into a winter wonderland. The cold air seeps into the car whenever the heater isn't blasting, and I can almost taste the sharp crispness of winter.

"I hope I brought enough clothes. This type of cold calls for layers."

"I saw what you packed," I say, recalling the two heavy suitcases in the trunk, both for her. The ones that tipped the scale at fifty pounds each. Plus her carry-on. "You're good. For a month."

Without even looking at her, I know she's narrowing her eyes at me. I chuckle, glancing over to see her pouting.

"Winter clothes and boots take up a lot of room," she says defensively. "And I was going to give you your Christmas present early."

"Kalico. *Right now?* While we're driving. *Riggs is in the car,*" I tease, giving her thigh a playful squeeze. She laughs and slaps my hand away.

"Do you always have sex on your mind?"

With one hand on the wheel, I tap my thumb to the rhythm of the song playing on the radio and shake my head. "Don't get me wrong, it's at the top of the list." I avoid looking at her because while I wasn't thinking about it before, now I am. It's too easy to get lost in the way she looks at me. The way those blue eyes have an undeniable magnetism that has a direct pull to my heart and my dick.

She twists in her seat. "Lucky you, I'm too excited to hold off any longer."

I glance over and see her radiant smile. There are times she catches me off guard. She's a force to be reckoned with. Two and a half years, and everything has changed about her. Except her will to fight. She'll never lose that. She's found her footing in this crazy world, and she charges through it head-on.

"You're staring again." She blushes and drops her head.

"It's hard to look away from a shooting star."

She rolls her eyes with a half laugh. "Well, I'm about to make your wish come true."

I lift a brow. "Oh yeah? What's that?"

"I broke my lease in Phoenix."

My gaze flicks between her and the road, uncertainty and anticipation tightening my chest. "You did?" She bites her bottom lip softly, a hesitant nod confirming what I hoped. She's right. She made my wish come true. "Are you going to live…" I trail off, not wanting to pressure her.

"If you'll have me?"

"Are you kidding?" My voice breaks higher than I intend, but fuck, this is the best present ever. Makes my present for her even better. I reach for her hand and bring it to my lips. "Have you? I want every part of you. Forever."

For the next few minutes, we talk about how we're going to get her stuff from Phoenix. I'm more than happy to make the trip myself.

As the car's navigation system announces we're ten minutes away, I notice Kali fidgeting. She pulls the visor down and checks her hair. When I flick on the blinker to exit the highway, she snaps the visor back up and stares out the window. Her jittery nerves are contagious. I feel them in my own chest. I've never brought a woman home. Grams will love her, but everything about this weekend is important.

We turn down the long drive on the three-acre property, and Kali gasps. "Wow. It's picture perfect here."

It is. A true winter wonderland when it snows, and a laid-back country retreat in the summer. It's one of my favorite places to visit. My grandparents have lived on this land since the seventies. Of course, back then, it was just a trailer. Now, there's a main house and a guest house.

"Why are there so many cars?" she asks as we pull up to the front of the house.

I'm not surprised by the line of cars along both sides of the driveway. I might have left out the part where it's not just Grams and Pops she's meeting. I didn't want to scare her off. She's been stressing enough as it is.

I put the car in park and twist in my seat to face her. "Okay. So, here's the deal. My dad has six sisters, and they all have at least three kids. And then some of them already have kids."

Her eyes widen. "They're all here?" I slowly nod, bracing for her to freak out. But to my surprise, her smile grows, and her eyes fill with wonder. Not quite the response I expected, but damn, I'll take it. "You have a huge family?"

"I do."

"And they're all here for Christmas?" she repeats.

"I'm sorry I didn't tell—"

"This is the best Christmas ever!" she squeals, barely able to contain her excitement. I've never seen her this excited. Not sure if I should be offended or relieved.

"Well...you haven't met them yet." I chuckle. "They can be nosy, say the most inappropriate things, and flat out are assholes, sometimes."

"They already sound amazing. Let's go!" She pushes the door open, already out of the car before I gather all my stuff from the center console.

If I had any doubts that she was the one for me, this solidifies it. These people, while they can be annoying at times, mean so much to me. But I already had zero doubts. This just makes it that much sweeter.

Riggs barks from the back seat. "Don't worry, buddy. We won't forget you."

"Hide the weed, the cops are here." I'm pretty sure that fucker isn't kidding. I watch Brody jog down the pathway. I meet him at the front of the car, and we do a quick hug. "About time you got here. Justin's asking every five minutes when his favorite uncle is getting here." Justin's the youngest of the second cousins, and nobody has ever corrected him that I'm not actually his uncle.

"Brody, this is Kali. Kali, Brody—the guy with all the jokes. Cousin number one."

"More like number *one* cousin." He laughs, shaking her hand.

"It's nice to meet you." She glances between the two of us, noticing the resemblance. Yeah, yeah. We look alike, though Brody could benefit from hitting the gym a few times a week. He's what I'd look like if I were a limp noodle. He rubs his thin arms. "Fuck it's cold. Let's get you guys inside."

Warmth and a sweet, familiar smell greet us as we step inside the house. Kali chuckles at the two rows deep of boots and mountain of coats in the mudroom. We add ours to the piles.

"Grams, where are they staying?" Brody yells.

"No need to yell, I'm right here," Grams jokes, rounding the corner. She immediately pulls me in for a hug, but not before I notice she's limping.

"What happened?" I ask, pulling back, my eyes on the black brace up to her knee.

"Don't worry about me." She shakes her head. "Just getting old. Slipped on some ice out back a couple weeks ago. Not as nimble on my feet as I used to be."

I stare down into the warm blue eyes that mean the world to me and sigh. It's hard to accept that she's getting older. "You need to be careful."

She tsks and turns toward Kali. "Pax, stop being rude and introduce me to your lovely lady."

I shake off the worry, excitement taking its place. The two most important women in my life are face-to-face.

I introduce them, and Kali sticks out her hand. "It's so great to finally meet you," she says.

Grams, instead, pulls her in for a warm hug. "Welcome to our home," she says. "We're so happy that you're here." All the nervousness in Kali's face melts away as she embraces her. Grams has that effect on everyone.

"Woman. Thanks for telling me they got here," Pops says, appearing in the doorway.

Grams releases Kali and slaps him on the belly. "I did. But, as usual, you didn't listen."

Kali's wide eyes lift to stare at the man most of the cousins call Big Poppa. The six-foot-five grizzly bear of a man smiles wide beneath his bushy gray beard.

"Hey, Pops." After a quick, manly hug, I introduce him to Kali. She stands a little more awkward, unsure of what to expect. Sensing her apprehension, he shakes her hand. He's a hugger too, but from the outside, he's a guy you don't fuck with.

"Brody, they're staying out in the guest house," Grams says. "Can you take their bags out there?"

"On it," he says, heading for the door.

Kali slips her hand into mine as we head into the house. I feel a twinge of guilt for what's about to happen. The sheer number of people she's about to meet would overwhelm anyone.

Grams and Pops built a great room that would hold everyone. They wanted a place where everyone could relax and be together, and the house was built around it. So, when we walk into the room, Kali pauses for a beat, taking it all in.

"That tree is gorgeous," she whispers, staring at the twelve-foot Christmas tree in the room's corner. All eyes turn toward us.

"Uncle Pax! You're here." Justin tosses his toy truck aside and rushes over to me. I throw him up in the air, immediately regretting it. He's grown since I saw him last.

"Kylan, what are you feeding this kid?"

"I eat lots of goldfish," he says proudly.

"I can tell," I joke, poking his pudgy stomach. He giggles in my arms. Everyone else stares at us. *Time for roll call.* "Ready for this?" Kali nods with uncertainty in her eyes. "Everyone, this is Kali. Kali, this is"—I point around the room—"Sadie, Matt, Kylan, Saige, Colt, Vance, Mabel, Brody, Emma, Riley, Carson, Oakley…" I continue all the way around the room and blow out a breath after the last name. They give me a round of applause. Damn, I'm good.

Kali stares at me like I'm crazy. She probably only picked up the first and last person's names.

"Can we wear name tags?" she asks, scanning the room. "Wait. I'll get this." She rolls her shoulders and shakes out her hands. If there's anyone up for a challenge, it's Kali. She starts at the beginning again. "Sadie, Matt, Kylan…starts with an S?" She winces.

"Saige," my cousin chimes in.

"Saige. Yes! I love that name." She stumbles through more names, but she's determined. Out of thirty-some names, she got about thirteen correct. But she makes a valiant effort to memorize each name as she goes. As she concentrates on that, Grams and I share a glance. She smiles and gives a subtle nod.

The tiniest motion is what I was waiting for. Her stamp of approval.

After the introductions, the women whisk her away to decorate cookies. I keep an eye on her, half expecting her to hesitate or give me a sign that says she needs saving. But my woman happily joins them.

Grams slinks her arm through mine and rests her head on my arm. "It's good to see you, Pax. And so happy in love."

Laughter echoes from the kitchen. This is turning out better than I imagined. Kali fitting in was never a concern. I just didn't think it'd be this easy. "I told you, Grams. I was going to marry her someday."

A COUPLE HOURS LATER, with a full belly of decorated cookies, I call out, "It's time to go ice skating."

"Ice skating?" Kali says, glancing back outside to the small lake. "Is it frozen enough?"

"It's frozen solid," I assure her.

"But I don't have skates."

"I got you covered," Oakley says, heading to the mudroom. "Pax told me your size before you guys got here." She appears with a pair of white skates, holding them up.

Kali stares at them, then looks at me with wide eyes. I thought she'd be more excited. "Do you ice skate?"

"Paxton!" Oakley scolds, giving me that same disapproving gaze she always has when I do something dumb. "You didn't tell her?"

I shrug. It never came up. "Tell me what?" Kali asks, glancing between us.

"He kills it on the ice," Oakley says.

Kali's smile widens. "Like a figure skater? Can you do things like turns and jumps?"

My mouth falls open as Oakley throws her head back in laughter. "Do I look like a figure skater to you?"

"Well, she said you killed it on the ice."

"As a hockey player," I blurt out.

Oakley's still laughing, doubled over now.

"Oh my gosh," Oakley says between gasps. "You guys!" she screams out, and I roll my eyes.

Really? It was an honest mistake. She walks away, and I hear her tell everyone what happened. The room erupts.

Kali winces. "Sorry."

I pull her close and kiss her on the forehead. "Don't be. You just made their day. I'll just have to take it out on them on the ice. They won't be laughing long."

She hums. "Any other skills you're keeping from me?"

"I've shown you the important ones," I reply with a wink, and then lean down and kiss her.

"I hope he kisses better than he skates," eleven-year-old Carson says, interrupting us. I chuckle against Kali's lips. This kid.

I playfully push him away. "You can't even put your own skates on without your mommy's help."

"Shut up. I do too," he retorts, puffing out his chest.

Everyone, still making twinkle-toe jokes, joins us in the kitchen, gearing up to go outside. "Have you ever ice skated before?" Emma asks.

"I've only ever been once. My dad took me when I was six…" Her voice trails off, and her body stiffens beside me. I glance around the room to see if anyone's reaction triggered this. There's not one ounce of judgment in their faces. But a mind's guilt is heavier than reality sometimes. "I'm sorry for mentioning him," she whispers, walking out of the kitchen.

I rush after her. "Kalico. Stop."

She falls against a wall, crossing her arms with one hand

covering her face. "I knew this would happen. How can I look all of them in the face and talk about my dad?"

I wish I could make her see. No one here blames her. Grams rounds the corner, giving me a knowing, soft nod.

"Walk with me?" Grams warmly asks Kali. Grams will know what to say, so I smile and give her a chaste kiss on the lips.

"You're in good hands," I say.

Grams waves me off. "You guys go out skating. We'll be out there in a few minutes."

KALI

Grams makes me nervous. Paxton loves her so much, and her opinion will carry a lot of weight with him. Ugh. Why did I bring up my dad?

What was I thinking?

Grams wraps her thin arm through mine, and we walk, stopping at the front door. "The other side of that door," she says, pointing and looking at me, "that's where we leave all our guilt. There is no place inside this home for that."

I let her words sink in and inhale. I nod, feeling the warmth of Grams's touch as she gently squeezes my arm. Tears well up in my eyes.

"C'mon," she continues, leading me down the hallway to a closed door.

When she opens the door, I'm taken aback. Floor to ceiling pictures in sleek black frames adorn three of the four walls and half the other wall, with memories captured in time. A teal velvet couch sits in the center of the room. Grams walks us to the couch and sits down, patting the cushion beside her. I follow her lead, sinking into the softness of the velvet. My eyes wander from picture to picture, each telling a story through vibrant colors and frozen moments in time.

"This room is my memory room. See that picture?" I take a

moment to find the one she's pointing at. *There are so many.* It's obvious once I see it. It's Paxton and his brother. There's no denying that they are brothers. "That's Jake. We have eighteen wonderful years of memories with him." A pang of guilt hits my belly despite her earlier words about leaving it at the door. Showing me this is doing the exact opposite. "And you have eight years of wonderful memories of your mother and father. We want to celebrate *all* those memories. They are what keep them alive in our hearts." She turns toward me, taking my hand in hers. Her hands are soft and cool, her eyes tender and warm. "We'd never want to take that from you, Kali. Never regret remembering them. Especially around us."

I blink back tears, her words wrapping around me like a warm blanket, soothing the chill in my bones. "Thank you," I manage to say through the feelings lodged in my throat.

Grams looks over her shoulder. "And see that wall right there? It's waiting for new pictures. New memories. Hopefully, with some of you and Paxton and maybe some more grand babies." She winks at me when my cheeks blush. She's not wasting any time. "He loves you, dear. And we love you because of that. *All of you.*" Her words fill me with a sense of belonging I haven't felt in a long time.

"You're making me cry," I murmur, wiping my eyes at the same time I'm wearing a smile.

"Ok, enough of that." She pats my hand and then glances toward the door as if expecting someone to be there. I look over my shoulder, but no one is there. When she smiles, there's a mischievous glint in her eyes. "Before we head back out, I have to ask, what'd you think of the pie?" I squeeze my brows together. We haven't eaten pie yet. She leans in and whispers, "You know, *the cherry pie.*"

"Oh, that pie." Still not sure which one, because Paxton bought me two cherry pies.

"When he told me he had met you and what happened at the

diner, I gave him a little nudge on what to do next." *That was her idea?* I think back and remember the pie delivered the next day. Paxton called his Grams right after? How adorable is that? "And then hearing what happened next—about what that vile woman had done—I was worried about Pax. It didn't look good. I told him to tell you right away."

"Sometimes he's too stubborn."

"That he is. But his heart more than makes up for it." She gazes at a picture on the wall with a wistful sigh. "I was worried when his mom married that god-awful man that he'd grow up with so much hatred in his heart he would have a hard time finding his way back. But he has his dad's heart." She looks at me and lets out a bitter laugh. "Praise God because that woman's heart is defective."

No objection there.

She wraps her arms around me and gives my shoulders a squeeze. "Ready to go back out? I'm sure Paxton is waiting right outside the door. That boy never listens."

I nod, but I'm making Paxton bring me back to this room later. The memories in here are rich and full of life.

Sure enough, Paxton's perched on the hallway bench, engrossed in his phone. He springs up as soon as we walk out. Grams pats his arm as she passes him.

"You okay?" he asks.

"I am. I love your family. It's all I've ever wanted. I'm so afraid I'm going to mess it up."

"Kalico," he says, pulling me into his chest and kissing me on the forehead. "Just be yourself, and they'll all love you like I do."

Be myself. That I can do. I've never tried to be anyone else, and I shouldn't try now. It might take time for me to feel comfortable talking about my parents, just as it did with Paxton, but I trust it'll happen. The tension I was holding in my shoulders releases.

"Do you want to just relax at the guest house for a while? I won't mind," Paxton suggests.

"Heck no! I want to see you on skates."

PAXTON ON SKATES with a stick and a puck is my new favorite fantasy come alive. *Hot. Damn.* Sex on ice. Yes, please.

I, on the other hand, was a hot mess. Not sexy at all. But I survived without breaking anything, so it was a success in my book. While helping dry dishes, the cousin's voices fade away as my mind wanders back to watching Paxton on ice. He's so good, I wonder why he doesn't play in a league in Austin.

"Kali, did you hear me?"

I shake out of the daydream and turn my head to Emma. "Sorry, I was just in my own little world."

She chuckles and leans in close to me. "If Paxton wasn't my cousin…" She blushes and turns away, picking up a plate to dry. My mouth falls open in amusement. "Shh… you never heard me say that." I mean, I don't blame her.

We both start laughing. "Hey, I want to hear the joke," Oakley says, walking up.

"Nope. You missed it," Emma quickly blurts out, finishing up with the last dish. She puts them away and turns to me. "You ready to head out to the barn?"

Her eyes jump to Oakley, and they both exchange wide, almost mischievous, grins. My eyes dart between the two of them confused.

Oakley steps closer to me, glancing around conspiratorially before saying, "It's where Santa does all his last-minute preparations."

Ah, now it makes sense. It's where they keep all the toys from little prying eyes. That explains where all the guys are. We pass by the grand room where the kids are sprawled out, under blankets, engrossed with "*Scrooge.*" The twinkling lights from the Christmas tree illuminate their cute little faces.

Someday, ours will be there.

After donning my snow boots and coat, we step out into the still night, the snow crunching beneath our steps. "We have to stop by the guest house to grab a gift," Oakley says. "We hid most of the gifts out there, but Brody just texted and told me they forgot one."

The guest house is set up similarly to the main house, but on a smaller scale. With just two bedrooms compared to the main house's six, it's cozy and intimate. The living room boasts a wall of windows overlooking the lake. Earlier, when we arrived to get ready for dinner, I couldn't stop looking out the windows. While the main house is stunning, if I had to choose, I'd pick this one to live in.

"Can you run in and grab it? Brody said they left it on the couch. That way, we don't all have to track snow in," Emma asks.

"Of course. I'll be right back," I reply. Like the main house, there's a mudroom where I slip off my boots. Soft music drifts through the air as I make my way to the living room. I don't recall music playing earlier. As I step into the living room, I gasp, my hand covering my pounding heart.

The lights are off, but the room is aglow with the soft flicker of candles scattered everywhere. Their warm light dances against the walls. A crackling fire adds to the ambiance, casting a gentle glow across the room. In the middle of the windows, a furry blanket is spread out on the floor, with a dozen plush pillows arranged around it. Paxton stands in the middle, a faint smile playing on his lips.

"What is all this?" I say, shrugging off my coat and carefully draping it over a chair, avoiding any candles. "I thought I was getting a gift."

"You are. Yours." He walks over to me and guides me back to the blanket. The flickering candlelight reflects on the large windows, creating a magical backdrop. He stops abruptly, first looking to the ground, then letting his gaze drift up to find mine. A smile dances on his lips. "You're stunning," he murmurs. "Every part of you fits perfectly into my world. I wanted to do this tomorrow, on Christmas Day. But I decided…" His words hang in the air, causing my heart to skip a beat.

He drops to one knee, his eyes never leaving mine. Tears gather at the corners of my eyes as he pulls out a small blue Tiffany box from his pocket. Just like the one my bat necklace was in.

He opens the box to reveal a beautiful solitaire diamond ring that sparkles in the soft candlelight. My breath catches as he holds it out to me. "I want to wake up on Christmas morning with you as my fiancée. Will you, Kali Stevens, marry me?"

A tear falls on my cheek, and I hiccup through my overwhelming emotions, nodding fiercely. "Yes. Yes, I'll marry you." He takes my trembling hand and slides the ring over my finger. I have no idea why I'm shaking. I've never been so sure about anything in my entire life. I hold up my hand, admiring the brilliant single diamond, still in awe of its beauty.

Paxton's face lights up with a radiant smile. He jumps to his feet, pulling me into his arms, lifting me and spinning us around in a whirl of happiness.

"Kalico, it's you and me forever."

Epilogue 2

Nine months later...

KALI

I STARE OUT THE WINDOW, the view a blur through my nervous excitement. The rows of chairs are filled with people—a sea of familiar and new faces. "That's a lot of people," I murmur, feeling a flutter of anxiety in my stomach. Rusty's tethered to a post to the right of the chairs. Amy suggested that I ride in on him, but that was a little *too* extra for me.

When we started wedding planning, I envisioned a small wedding, *maybe twenty people*, at Paxton's ranch house—*or ours*, as he keeps reminding me. But between Paxton's large family and what seems like the entire police force, the guest list outgrew the ranch. Amy insisted we have it here. When I saw how excited she was, I couldn't say no.

Ari's hand slips into mine, her touch warm and reassuring. "I know you have a hard time admitting it, but you are loved by many." I'm starting to believe it. I've built a home of my own with love. *Home.* I've finally made it home. "It's time," she says. "Ready?"

"I'm getting married!" I squeal, still in a state of wonder. It's hard not to admit that the journey to this moment was worth it. I can't go back and change our path, so I've accepted it. And an amazing thing came out of evil—the love of my life.

I check myself in the mirror one last time, soothing out invisible wrinkles and adjusting my veil.

"Well, you're not getting married if we don't leave this room. We're already late." She grabs my hand and my bouquet, practically dragging me out the door. The soft strains of music playing outside filter in, mingling with the distant murmurs of our guests. "So," Ari says, biting her lip and glancing at me sideways. "There are a lot of *hot cops* out there. Don't shame me for enjoying my night."

"I'd think something was wrong with you if you didn't."

After what happened to us, I thought she'd never want to see me again. I tried calling her the week after, left message after message, but her mom finally answered and said she needed some time to process what had happened. I understood, but it broke my heart. It was her way of telling me goodbye. But then she called me a couple of weeks later, wanting to meet for dinner. I'm thankful every day that she's still a part of my life.

"Liam is pretty hot," Oakley purrs, joining us with a playful grin. Since the Michigan trip, we've kept in touch. The quick flight to Dallas has made it easy for us to hang out, and she and Ari are my bridesmaids.

"Yes. Yes, he is," Ari agrees.

I playfully gasp and poke Oakley. "Lady, you are married."

"I'm not blind." She laughs.

"This is what it's like being with a bunch of girls, huh? Always talking about the 'hot guys,'" Ted jokes with air quotes, striding over.

My eyes jump to Ted, and a burst of warmth fills my heart.

Looking sharp in a black tux and a white cowboy hat, his smile alone makes me blink back my tears. I blow out a quick breath and fan my face.

"No crying yet," Oakley says, jumping in front of me and swabbing the corners of my eyes with a tissue.

"I know. But Ted, I can't thank you enough for walking me down the aisle."

He pulls me in for a hug, the scent of his woodsy cologne filling my senses. "I'm the one honored you asked me." There wasn't anyone else I wanted. I blink through the tears.

"It's time ladies," Amy announces, walking through the back doors with Riggs. Her smile widens when she sees me and Ted hugging. Ari and Oakley slip outside the doors. Riggs trots over to my side, his little tuxedo making him the most dapper dog ever.

Everything is perfect.

I couldn't have dreamed of a better day.

Amy cups my face, her eyes filled with adoration. "You look beautiful, sweetie. This is your day, so take moments throughout it and just breathe it in. There's so much love here, and you deserve every last drop of it." I nod, trying to hold it in. "Okay, okay, I'm done. I won't make you cry anymore. Love you, sweet girl. See you at the end," she says, giving me a quick kiss on the cheek and then hurries off. She slips outside, leaving me with a smile and a heart full of warmth.

I draw in a deep breath and let it out slowly. "You ready, Riggs?"

He barks once.

With him at one side and Ted on the other, our elbows linked, we wait at the door for our cue. "Don't lock your knees up there," Ted warns.

I chuckle through the nerves.

"Don't be like Amy and pass out in the middle of saying her vows."

I burst out laughing. "She didn't?"

"She did. But don't tell her I told you. I'd like to live a little longer."

The doors open, and we step out into the humid air. A slight breeze whips my side tendrils of hair around. I stare at the clouds overhead, and for a moment I regret not having the wedding inside. But then my eyes meet Paxton's, and all my worries fade away.

"Wow," he mouths, shaking his head. He looks up and blinks and then whispers something to Liam. Liam responds with a reassuring squeeze on Paxton's shoulder.

The scene is magical. Fairy lights twinkle in the trees and overhead. Fresh flowers and the soft hum of music fill the air. My heart races as I take it all in. *Breathe it in.*

Paxton's eyes never leave mine as the wedding march starts.

With each step, I draw closer and closer to him, but the aisle feels like it stretches for miles.

When we reach the end, Ari steps forward to fan out my train. Paxton rubs his hands down his suit, then grabs my hands, a nervous chuckle escaping my lips. At least I'm not the only one who's nervous. Riggs stands next to Liam.

I draw in a deep breath and release it slowly, trying to steady my heart.

The clouds above darken, and I stare at Paxton, trying not to panic. *It's not supposed to rain. So much for a five percent chance of rain. Please don't rain yet.* Not now. At least our vows aren't long.

He squeezes my hands and winks at me, whispering, "We've got this."

The pastor starts the ceremony, but his words are a blur. My attention is completely on the man in front of me, so I hardly hear a word he says. The warmth of Paxton's hands, the scent of his cologne, the unwavering love in his eyes—it's all consuming.

Paxton begins with his vows.

"Sweet Kalico," he says. I bite down on my quivering smile as

I'm transported back to the song on the roller coaster. "How do I say in words how much I love you? Because I don't think they exist. Forever isn't long enough. The ocean isn't deep enough, and the universe isn't big enough."

I stand as still as a board, letting the rawness of his words wash over me, feeling them like a tender caress on my skin.

"So, let me show you every day for the rest of our lives. You often say that I'm your hero. But you, my love, are the hero of our story. Your strength alone has built the solid foundation that we stand on. You inspire me every day to be a better version of myself, to grow and prove that I'm worthy of you. I promise to make you laugh, hold you when you cry, and never make you ride a roller coaster again."

I will hold him to that promise.

"I will protect you. I will cherish you. I will love you till death do us part."

God, I love this man. With every fiber of my being.

"Kali," the pastor prompts.

Oh. It's my turn.

"Paxton...*my* hero," I say, lifting a brow in playful defiance. He will never change my mind about that. "But you are so much more than that. You have shown me that love can heal the deepest of wounds. And I was able to be loved." I pause to clear the emotions clogging my throat.

He squeezes my hands, his eyes glistening with unshed tears.

"I was alone in this world, and now my heart is overflowing. You have stood by me through every trial and triumph. And we made it." My voice cracks as it hits a higher octave. I stare down at our joined hands and focus on breathing. Sniffles come from the crowd. *Finish, Kali.* I lift my gaze, and his concerned expression asks if I'm okay. I nod. "You...you gave me a fam—" The word gets caught in my throat.

"And we all love you," Grams says and the cousins whoop and

holler. If Paxton wasn't holding me, I'd melt into the ground in a sobbing mess. I turn and glance at her in the front row and hold my hand to my heart.

"I love y'all," I whisper.

She blows me a kiss, and I turn back to Paxton.

"They aren't helping me get through this," I say through a sobbing chuckle.

He chuckles once and brings my hand to his lips.

"Thank goodness I went second." I blow out the nerves. "I love you, Paxton. You are my hero, my love, my forever partner in every sense of the word. I promise to love you with everything that I am, today, always, and forever."

The pastor looks at Paxton. "Do you have the rings?"

Paxton snaps a quick command, and Riggs trots over, sitting obediently next to him. Paxton pulls the rings from the little pouch around his collar. I give him a rub on the head. Best ring bearer ever.

We each repeat our lines, slip the rings on, and then hear the pastor say, "You may now kiss the bride."

Paxton wraps his arm around my waist and pulls me in. He kisses me with a promise—a silent vow that we'll finish this moment later.

"Wife," he mutters against my lips, his breath warm and intoxicating.

"Husband," I whisper back.

"I'd like to present to you for the first time, Mr. and Mrs. Turner."

The crowd stands, claps and hollers as we rush down the center aisle, sensing the skies are about to open. I can smell the rain coming. We couldn't have timed it any better. The moment everyone is safe under the tent, the raindrops fall in sheets. The air is alive with the sound of raindrops and the gentle rustle of leaves. The perfect romantic backdrop for our perfect day.

We move from table to table, talking, laughing, and dancing. My heart is so full, I think it's going to burst wide open. Dancing under the tent, the rain drumming overhead, Paxton pulls me in close, his lips brushing my ear. "This is our forever," he whispers.

And then one of the kids says, "It's hailing."

A memory surfaces, sharp and clear.

What? Where?

I rush to the edge of the tent, watching tiny pellets of ice bounce on the ground. "Oh my god." I hiccup, tears rushing down my cheeks, my hand on my exploding heart.

"Babe, it's okay. They aren't big enough to damage anything." Paxton pulls me into his side.

I shake my head, patting my cheeks dry. But the tears keep coming. "It's not that," I choke out. "It's just...they're here."

"Who?"

I stare up at the sky, then close my eyes, letting the sound of the pitter-patter wash over me. She was really with me in that box.

I miss you.

I miss you so much.

I wish you were here to meet Paxton.

I pull in a ragged breath, letting the thick, damp air fill my lungs.

Thank you.

Paxton leans into me, whispering, "Kalico, what's going on, babe?"

The hail stops as quick as it started, and I dig my face into Paxton's chest, crying. "My parents. They were here."

He doesn't say anything, probably thinking I'm crazy. But I'm not. How else do you explain a day that wasn't supposed to rain, let alone hail?

My mom told me. And she made sure I knew they were watching.

Golf balls from heaven.

Thank you for reading Deadly Ruse!
Turn the page for an excerpt from Blinding Echo!

Blinding Echo

PROLOGUE

EVERLY

LOVE STORIES typically begin with boy meets girl. *Ours did.* Yet, our story is anything but typical.

I had always thought the heart led us to 'the one.' But, I've learned the heart doesn't have a memory. Its beat is steady until our brain triggers an emotion, making the beat so unmistakable it takes your breath away. It's blinding, life-altering and sometimes earth-shattering. The feeling of true love. We grow up with the grand illusion there is only one person made for us—our soul-mate. But what if your memories are stripped from you? Your soul-mate forgotten. The unmistakable heartbeat gone. The love that completely filled your heart, now an empty space.

That was my heart. Vacant.

He was a stranger, determined to make me fall in love with him. He made it easy. Even though I didn't know him, he felt familiar. The scars that riddled my body, illustrating my past, he made them feel invisible. Made me feel like I deserved to be cherished and loved.

He was also lying.

Doctors told me my memories were locked in my brain. Eighteen years of my life was under lock and key inside my head somewhere. It was Pandora's box.

I wish I had never found the key.

Our love story began with boy meets girl. Now...

I love two men.

He loves two women.

CONTINUE READING HERE: Blinding Echo

More books by Tina

TWIST OF FATE Trilogy

Aiden and Addison

Fate Hates

Fate Heals

Fate Loves

Twisted Wings

Max and Sydney

Blinding Echo

Kase and Ellie

Wild Distortion

Ryker and Aspen

Wedded Chaos

(Coming soon)

Brooks and Gracyn

Join my reader group to get to know me and get early access to what I'm working on! Saxon's Sirens on Facebook

FOLLOW ME!

Tik Tok

Facebook

Instagram

Website

Made in the USA
Middletown, DE
09 September 2024

60052062R00194